THE LONG WAY TO GET TO ME

MARC LINDON

Matador
9 Priory Business Park,
Wistow Road, Kibworth Beauchamp,
Leicestershire. LE8 0RX
Tel: 0116 279 2299
Email: books@troubador.co.uk
Web: www.troubador.co.uk/matador
Twitter: @matadorbooks

ISBN 978 1838591 96 0

British Library Cataloguing in Publication Data.
A catalogue record for this book is available from the British Library.

Printed and bound in Great Britain by 4edge Limited
Typeset in 12pt Baskerville by Troubador Publishing Ltd, Leicester, UK

Matador is an imprint of Troubador Publishing Ltd

For J³R

What a strange thing man is;
And what a stranger thing woman.

Lord Byron

PROLOGUE

VICTIMS?

It's the same every morning. There is a moment upon first awakening, the very briefest of moments, when she feels nothing. Or more to the point, she just doesn't feel.

And in that vacuum, there is a sense of ease that she longs to retain, but which, as soon as she becomes conscious of it, is swept from her by a wave of profound emotion that leaves her floundering. And she's back in the place she left the night before, when sleep rescued her. A place of loss. Regret. Of stifling loneliness.

She has but one weapon at her disposal and with perverse satisfaction she shifts her limbs to ignite jolts of pain that rack her body. Where once she had bemoaned this early morning blight, she now sees it as the lesser of two evils. It's a battle she can at least compete in.

Welcoming the distraction, she tentatively shifts and stretches until the aches start to back off. She has to grab this moment before she's enveloped once more, so she heaves herself into a seated position and reaches over to turn on the radio. The voices are welcome guests, and with company she can turn more easily to the day ahead.

Her senses now free to wander, she notices two things. It is late, almost ten o'clock – Ernest would never have permitted such wantonness – and unseasonably warm; a welcome forerunner of the spring to come that had warranted leaving the bedroom window open last night. But there's something else layered on top. A stale and sickly-sweet aroma that she can't quite place.

Deciding it must be coming from outside, she lowers her feet to the floor, painfully stands, shuffles over to the window and pulls the curtains apart.

Oh dear God. The lawn. His lawn. His pride and joy. And that smell…

*

Her face puckers as she contemplates the depressing juxtaposition of the cushioned comfort of last night's stalls seats at the Palais Garnier and the disconcertingly stained fabric of the taxi's upholstery, on which she now shifts distastefully; while up front Lionel is performing; that intensely irritating 'social chameleon' thing – his words, never hers – he takes such idiotic pride in, waffling moronically about cricket and football with the ghastly little driver. The marks of the man those tasteless, tasselled cushions on the parcel shelf, the wooden-beaded seat cover and whatever that *ethnic* thing is hanging from the rear-view mirror. Is there a white taxi driver left in High Wycombe?

As they near home, the sight of scaffolding at The Birches further sours her mood; an unwelcome reminder of a rare battle lost. But a builder's van outside Ravencroft brings a renewed sense of purpose. She'll need to keep an eye on that one.

The reassuring crunch and crackle of the gravel heralds their arrival and she gratefully escapes the car's clammy clutches, leaving Lionel to say goodbye to his new best friend.

As she enters the hall, she knows immediately that there's something not quite right. The light is all wrong.

She walks through to the drawing room.

"Lionel?" she calls out.

"Yes, darling?"

"The conservatory."

"Yes, darling?"

"It's gorn."

*

There's no good time to see your mother with an erect penis clasped in her hand.

Once seen, it's never forgotten.

And that is the sight before the eyes of seven-year-old Laura, who has taken up her usual evening vantage point at the top of the stairs behind the laundry basket, affording the much-prized view between the banister posts of half the sitting room below. Normally this encompasses the TV screen and, occasionally, the lower half of a pair of outstretched legs, but tonight there's a strange sight indeed, one that's beyond a young mind to fully comprehend, though it tries nonetheless…

Mr Chivers, who Mummy says lets us stay in this house, has the zip on his trousers undone and his thingy is sticking out, which is naughty, and it is pointing up at the ceiling. Mummy is standing right behind him and is giving him a hug. But her hand is by mistake actually touching his thingy, which is naughty and a bit yucky and Mr Chivers is mumbling 'no' over and over again. That means he wants to get away and he's much stronger than Mummy so he could do so easy. But I don't think he does really want to get away because he's squeezing Mummy's bottom lots and has got a smile on his face. I can't see Mrs Chivers. Maybe she's on the sofa or making tea or something. She could maybe help. Now they're moving around the room and Mummy still won't let go. It's like they're stuck together. Mr Chivers has stopped saying 'no' but Mummy must be doing something else because he's moaning a lot. Now he's saying 'yes' and 'oh dear' and Mummy's being really rough with his thingy. And Mr Chivers says they should go to the sofa and I can't see them anymore. But I can hear him and he's saying naughty words and he still sounds like he's in pain and then he shouts out and then he starts whimpering. And then it all goes quiet and I creep off to the bedroom. I hope this doesn't mean Mr Chivers will say we can't live here anymore.

*

There's a warm sensation spreading in his crotch, then a trickle running down his leg. Muscles too numbed by fear to contract. But he's in a place far beyond embarrassment. The pain from whatever it was that struck him is a fading sideshow to this paralysis. He just wants to be home. Wants his mum – *how was your day love?… meal almost ready… wash your hands* – the comfort of the sofa; something rubbish on telly; arguments with his little sister over the remote control; Mum shouting at them to cut it out or she'll turn it off and tell Dad.

Wants anything but this.

Home is only a hundred yards or so in distance, a half-minute sprint at most. But it might as well be miles. The first contact, a thud on his back, had brought him to a halt. The second, a glance to the side of his head, had sent him to the ground in a heap, the sound of something bouncing along the pavement duetting with the ringing in his ears. Instinctively he'd struggled up and tried to walk on, head bowed, as though by ignoring it, this couldn't be happening. But then they'd appeared and surrounded him. Four of them, all with woolly hats over their heads. Holes cut out for eyes and mouths. He'd taken a few more steps, as if they weren't there, and when they'd made it clear there was no way past, he'd resorted to wittering polite talk, desperately trying to script a more palatable reality; even tried to laugh it off. But then they'd started talking about hurting him and now the situation, like his body, is out of his control and they're scaring the hell out of him.

"It's really very simple," continues a muffled voice. "You say sorry, you promise never to do it again, you take your medicine and if you or your little gang of pals ever step out of line again, we'll be back. And next time we won't be so pleasant about it. So, let's start with that apology, shall we?"

"Lad's pissed himself."

A sob wrenches itself clear of his heaving chest.

"I'm sorry," he splutters. "I promise."

"Good boy. Now pick a finger."

*

Same route. Same time; just after midnight. Same thrill. Same release. Five nights a week.

He takes the corner at thirty and twists the throttle. There's a lag as it's countered by the sudden incline, but soon he feels the pull; a delicious surge of speed kicks in and he sweeps, glides and rolls through the corners as the unlit lane curls and rises into the darkness. Never below forty; nudging fifty.

He breasts the summit and guns it along the straight stretch. Off the accelerator as he takes the bend. Then the bike disappears from under him and he's sliding, skimming across a lake of pitch black… waiting for the inevitable impact.

*

"Mummy."

"Go downstairs, Kevin."

"Mummy."

"Please love. No."

"What's the matter, Mummy?"

"Oh love. You shouldn't have to see this. You really shouldn't."

*

Gloucestershire Royal Hospital.

Casualty department.

Late morning on Tuesday, July 6th, 1993.

One receptionist.

Three patients-in-waiting, seated as far apart from each other as the room's logistics permit.

A man enters. Casually leans on the reception counter. Dr James Newing in all his bleary-eyed glory, nearing the end of a twenty-four-hour stint on call.

"Good morning, Deborah," he says, forcing a smile from which she recoils an inch. "I see you've drummed up some custom for us idle doctors. Tell me do, what have we here?"

"Bit of a mystery, this one," she whispers conspiratorially, regaining that inch.

"Three ambulances called out to the same school this morning. There's NHS efficiency for you. Local press will have a field day if they find out."

"A fight, by the look of it."

"The matron at the school didn't think so. And none of them had much to say in the ambulance. Two of them claimed they walked into a door."

"The same one?"

"Who knows."

"Curiouser and curiouser," attempts Dr Newing, with only partial success.

"But something must have happened. The medics reckon we could be looking at two broken noses, a fractured eye socket, cracked ribs and a few missing teeth. And a lot of blood spilled judging by their clothes. They haven't said a word to each other since they got here."

"Let's take a look then. Better kick off with the boy, I suppose."

"I'd rather you started with the one in the far corner. He hasn't stopped blubbing and he's getting right on my nerves."

APRIL 2007

MONDAY

Kevin sets out on the walk to work with a spring in his step and a dull pain in his groin, its source a particularly athletic session the night before with the girl from the local newsagent; one so gratifying that it warranted a repeat, though altogether more laid-back, performance that morning. She'd said he was going to make her late for work, but it hadn't been a rejection, merely a statement of fact.

*

The journey from front door to glorified cubby hole takes David up one flight of stairs, oddly down two flights, round twenty-seven corners and through eight sets of doors, two of which require codes. His pristine shoes squeak on the polished floors every time he changes direction. He is the recipient of a "Hercule", a "Morse", the ever popular "Sherlock" and, coming from left field, a "Cadfael." One WPC has the courtesy to greet him with his actual name, though her mannered amiability reeks of pity.

With customary relief he reaches his office, enters and closes the door behind him; inner sanctum attained.

*

Kevin flashes her a knowing smile as she takes his money. A bit spottier and younger in real life, but a furtive up-and-down glance reassures him that there's still mileage to be had here, albeit in need of some selective mental photoshopping.

*

A knock. Something mumbled. Laura opens her bedroom door to find a letter at her feet. No sight of Mrs Jacobs, just the sound of her shuffling retreat downstairs. She knows what it is before she even picks it up. Less than a fortnight since she moved in and already he's found her; she has to admire his ingenuity, if nothing else. The handwriting confirms it. A year or so earlier it would have been typed, its contents also; great pains taken to achieve an anonymity immediately betrayed by its sentiments. But they're past that now.

She opens it carefully and pulls out the single sheet of paper.

One word.

'PLEASE.'

Over the months the threats and bile have gradually softened, and now all he has left is this pathetic pleading.

She sighs with a shake of her head, opens a drawer, takes out a large book and from between the pages retrieves an envelope, into which she places the letter; with all the others.

*

Maggie's waiting outside the shop; eager to please as ever and all the more irritating for it. Kevin struggles to stomach so much treacle; enough to have him longing for a spot of opposition, not this unceasing acquiescence.

Of course, she might just be genuinely nice.

"I'll stick the kettle on," she gushes as he lets her in.

"No, Maggie. That's about all I feel capable of first thing on a Monday. You get going on the papers."

"Anything you say boss had a tiring weekend have we?"

"Something like that," he says.

*

Where the hell is she? The club is in Watford. The underground station is called 'Watford'. So where is Watford?

The bus journey to the interview had been a sorry tale of changeovers and stuttering traffic. The tube had to be an improvement; only two stops and she'd be there. So much for that logic, as *there* appears to be nowhere in particular; some sitcom-suburban hell. A clear case of misrepresentation.

Taxi it is then.

*

First dickhead of the day. And if every other day is anything to go by, he'll be the first of many. He makes his dishevelled way to the usual corner stool. Rummaging in the inside pocket of an incongruous tweed jacket (always that jacket, those stained brown trousers and the never-ever-in-fashion trainers) he produces a ball of paper which he stares at like some third-rate magician midway through a trick.

On contact with the counter it dissipates into a number of scrunched-up betting slips. He takes each in turn and examines it through moist, red eyes. He makes his choice, slides off the stool and approaches Maggie's till. She's lost in tabloid tittle-tattle and doesn't notice him immediately.

"Maggie," Kevin prompts her. "The gentleman?"

"Oh sorry Kevin morning luv you're in early what can I do for you got a winner have we?" Champion of the unpunctuated sentence.

The old bloke hesitates, frowns, and reverentially places the slip on the counter. He prods it towards Maggie with a fat, nicotine-stained finger, as if to instil in it a value in excess of its non-existent intrinsic worth.

"Can ya check that one dear, can ya? I think there mebbe a bit to come back on it."

"Let's have a look shall we luv," she says breezily, commencing an inevitably fruitless search through the pile of 'returns'. That horizontal learning curve ensures she's genuinely giving the slip every chance of coming good right to the end. "Sorry luv don't look like it I'm afraid."

He looks temporarily crestfallen, before a glimmer returns to his puddled eyes.

"Will ya get your guvnor there to check it pliz dear?"

"Course luv here's hoping eh."

She defies belief at times. This tiresome pantomime is a near-daily performance, yet every time she summons up the same unfeasible, giddy enthusiasm.

Kevin takes the slip from her with a pained expression she fails to fathom. As always. Same old mug bet: a Lucky 63. The kind of bet to give any self-respecting bookie a hard-on; the 'lucky' ironic; the '63' the number of ways to say "I've lost" courtesy of your six selections. Although this particular mug has found a way to increase that number with this charmless deceit.

Kevin peruses the slip wearily and warily. The 'writing' comprises near-random flicks of a pen, the horses only identifiable by the occasional legible letter and the course and race time Kevin had insisted on after yet another heated argument over disputed identity. Add to that an apparent predilection for horses with names similar to others running on the same day, and you've got a punter looking to cover a dozen or so horses with six selections.

But professional courtesy demands this charade. Kevin knows it's a loser; as does the con-man at the counter. He's given himself away early on in their acquaintance when he'd correctly queried a pay-out rounded down by a penny. He knows all right.

"Nope, all losers I'm afraid."

"Are yer sure now? Tha' Green Orbit won, yer know."

"Correct. Pity you were on Green Olive."

"I were on tha' Green Orbit. Says so on bettin' slip."

Here we go again…

*

"You've done this before, ain't ya?"

"No Eamon, honest," Laura replies drippily, allowing herself to be patronised; even throwing in a girly giggle for extra effect. Wouldn't do to upset her immediate superior less than an hour into the job, even if he is calculatedly clumsy, taking every opportunity to brush against her; and clearly of the opinion she has an intellect to rival the pints he's teaching her to pull. She can sense his wandering gaze pawing at her.

Eamon's interest is growing with each smile, each blush, each dip to the lower shelves, each stretch to the higher ones. Very nice, and most definitely up for it. He knows when they're interested. Bit feisty maybe, and the disappointing flat-heeled shoes mean the standard white blouse and black skirt outfit doesn't quite possess the inherent momentum he'd have liked. But time and a touch of the old charm should see him home.

A bloke orders a couple of Pineapple 55s – bit gay – and it's time for another eyeful as she stoops to retrieve one, bending from the waist a real Brucie bonus; the pose held for a pleasingly long time as she struggles to locate it. Very nice. And she knows it, which only adds to the buzz.

He watches her take a fiver from an equally impressed punter – "keep the change love" – and then she's his once more.

Competition?

"Your fella don't mind you working behind a bar then?"

"What?"

"You know… fella… boyfriend… does he mind? Working in a place like this. Being ogled at all day by a load of blokes like that last loser."

"I really don't think that'll be a problem."

"Trust me, Laura. I know what these blokes are like. Only one thing on their dirty little minds."

"Whatever you say, Eamon."

She's proving a challenge; one he hopes to rise to.

Time to accelerate proceedings with a spot of humour.

"Word of advice, Laura," he begins with premeditated spontaneity. "There's a lot more to this job than people give it credit for. It ain't just about pulling pints. You gotta know your punters. Take that bunch over by the fruit machine… no… please… do."

He can't prevent a smug chuckle at this slice of comedy gold.

"What about them?" she replies, deadpan.

He feels his face flush.

With lunchtime approaching, she's dispatched on her first solo glass-retrieval mission.

The door to the downstairs hall belches open and she's engulfed in a near-darkness heavily laden with regurgitated tobacco and alcohol; oxygen coming a poor third. Immediately the pungent air grabs at her, bringing a sheen of sweat to her skin. Her eyelids instinctively close to the second-hand cigarette smoke and the tacky carpet sucks at the soles of her shoes.

Ahead of her lie two puddles of multi-coloured light populated by anonymous midriffs. These take it in turn to lean forward, intent faces thrust over cues. The only sounds are the clacks of ball on ball and the occasional thud and rustle as a ball disappears from view.

She sets off on a circumnavigation, collecting on her way seven glasses – most with fag ends lurking in the dregs – four pairs of eyes openly frisking her, a wolf whistle and a dose of smutty innuendo.

"Things are looking up, boys. Lunchtime menu's certainly improving. I'm feeling a bit peckish," leers a voice, its sentiment echoing in murmurs of complicity.

"Think I might try and pot myself a pink," says another.

She walks on and escapes into the relative purity of the bar.

*

"Oh go on Kevin don't be such an old stick-in-the-mud it'll be good I promise."

"I'm really not sure, Maggie. Racing's due off shortly."

"We've got over an hour yet and the punters will love it where's your sense of adventure you waste this board you really do there's never much on it and I've seen other shops where they've experimented a bit and it looks really cool honest."

"Go on then," he sighs. "But it better be good. I'm off to get a sandwich while it's quiet."

"Oh you're a gem Kev you won't regret it promise."

"Yeah well, we'll see about that. Don't forget Ron will be in soon."

*

"Two pints of Fosters, gorgeous." These are the last words he directs at her. "Just what this place needed, eh Eamon. Something a bit tasty behind the bar. Better than your ugly mug any days."

"Up yours Tony, leave her alone," replies Eamon for the benefit of Laura's ears and shamelessly out of character. If anyone's going to objectify her, it most certainly won't be this gobshite.

Something pours on in silence.

*

Luigis is as busy as ever. Kevin has seen a succession of hard-working, customer-valuing sandwich bars come and go over the years, yet throughout, very much in the land of the commercial living, has remained Luigi and his seemingly never-ending stream of ever more distracted and cheesily merry Darwin-denying extended family members. And a gullible public can't seem to get enough of their tasteless fare of faux-Italian corn, grease and sexism down their throats. Nor does anyone appear to share Kevin's grammatical outrage at that missing apostrophe.

The place is unjustly heaving. Blinking through the oily haze, Kevin begins his assault on an infuriatingly unordered queuing system. Squeezing his way through the chaotic throng hemmed between counter and tables, all of them bathing in the smouldering gazes of the assorted unshaven Italian footballers mounted proudly on the walls, he stands behind a woman who is smiling awkwardly at the floor, chancing only an occasional glance up at the cocky teenager preparing her lunch. He's desperately trying to strike a relaxed and easy balance between Elvis and a young De Niro, but looking more like he's suffering a minor stroke. All the while he's showering her with a tried and trusted patter no doubt passed down from one obsequious generation to the next. Age and looks don't actually matter. She's female and has a pulse; more than enough. No point in narrowing his odds prematurely. And he really does believe she's flattered by his attention.

Kevin's in time for the climax of the show.

"Mayo, my darlin'?"

"Yes, thanks."

"Very good." Eyes fixed on her to ensure undivided attention, he grabs a yellow plastic bottle and spins it nonchalantly into the air. Its spiralling downward trajectory evades his hand and a recovery swipe takes out a knife and the ketchup, sending them clattering across the surface. There's the merest glimmer of panic before the leer refixes itself. He fishes the bottle out of the sandwich and attempts to return the fare to something approximating its pre-impact glory, ignoring a gleeful snort from Kevin.

"Theres you go, gorgeous. Specially for you, eh," he says with a wink, any embarrassment already forgotten. She pays and makes hurriedly for the door.

Kevin steps forward, but is made to wait as the dickhead raises himself on tiptoes and cranes forward, better to view her departure.

"Lovely lady, eh sir?" he smirks, forcing a half-hearted murmur of assent from Kevin.

He orders a cheese and tomato roll, then turns to pudding. "And a banana sandwich on white, *no butter*." But lulled into a false sense of security, Kevin's slow to follow the sly, sideways glance. He realises his fatal oversight all too late. "Hang on a sec. I'll just get you one," he blurts, turning in the direction of the glowingly healthy-looking bunch in a hanging basket mocking him from the far end of the counter, where they float like some mirage above the heads of the other customers.

For a split second, logistics cloud Kevin's mind and he hesitates.

And all is lost.

"Issokay sir, I already got one here," says his tormentor, gingerly holding up a decidedly sick piece of fruit hanging on desperately to the last vestiges of bananahood, before lowering it from Kevin's view.

Kevin takes a step back in order to gain a line of sight through the smeared glass and assorted foodstuffs, and witnesses the 'banana' imploding on impact with the chopping board. Somehow managing to separate the mottled, near-black skin from its dubious contents, he makes a ludicrous show of slicing the decomposed flesh before scooping and smearing the brown puree onto the bread.

On his way out, ashamed at his timidity in not demanding a remake, Kevin glances at the bunch that might have been. Another few weeks and it'll be their turn.

Yellow for show, brown for dough.

*

She places the second pint on the drip tray and accepts the money.

"Cheers darlin'. Lovely looking pair… the pints I mean."

Much chortling ensues.

*

"What the fuck is that?"

"Language Kevin."

"Sorry. Actually, I'm not sorry. What the hell is it meant to be?"

Under the glare of her inane grin, like a child waiting for parental approval, he vainly searches for artistic merit in what looks like the aftermath of cuddly-toy-meets-grenade.

"Don't you like it then?"

"Maggie. What is it?"

"A horse of course dummy what else."

"Where? What on earth are those?"

"They're its big fluffy ears silly cute isn't he?"

"Maggie. Horses don't have *big, fluffy ears.*"

"I know that I'm not completely stupid I just wanted him to look friendly and after all you can take a few liberties with a cartoon can't you?"

"You've certainly done that," he sighs wearily. "What kind of a body is that?"

"It's not his body silly that's the fence."

He senses the pride ebbing from her and summons up a smidgeon of compassion.

"Obviously. Well I have to admit he's friendly looking. That's a great big smile he's got there. Only thing is… there's something missing. What about the jockey?"

"Oops silly me I forgot don't worry I'll do that now."

"Don't forget to make him look happy, Maggie."

"You do like it then."

Words fail him, as they clearly do Ron, whom Kevin turns to find looking over his shoulder, having sloped in unnoticed, a puzzled look contorting his angular features.

Ron is old-school. Touch of the Leonard Rossiter, although anyone dismissing him as some lecherous Rigsby, exasperated Reggie Perrin, or the bumbling oaf from the Cinzano ads would be well wide of the mark. For behind the public face lies a calculating commercial brain.

When faced with change, the easy option can be to go with the flow. If other betting shops are getting in banks of TV screens, beaming in every race they can, ensuring non-stop verbal and visual activity, automating the settling of bets and populating redundant space with fruit machines and the like, the overwhelming pressure on the small is to ape the big and hope to grab enough of the action to get by. It takes a brave bookie to buck that trend and aspire to be different. Niche marketing isn't new of course, but it's easier to talk about than to take the plunge and put it into action.

Ron took that plunge, although a love of the limelight was as much a factor as a thirst for profit, and he enjoys the maverick kudos that goes with being different.

Whilst the vast majority of shops now offer a seemingly unlimited number of ways to lose your money, and can effectively be run by anyone with an IQ greater than their shoe size, Brigstaff Racing puts on an altogether different show; retro racing for those with a fondness for those good old days.

One large TV screen is the only apparent concession to the last ten years, though it's for showing races only, not for imported betting shows or results. Instead, along one wall, there's a huge white wipe-board, half of which is set up for the race results to be entered by hand; the other half left clear for the sheets of runners on which the ever-changing odds are scribbled. Beneath it runs a raised wooden platform a few feet wide. This is Ron's stage, and for three hours a day he dances up and down its length, coloured marker pens flitting between pockets, teeth and hands.

But best of all, Ron takes a view. If he doesn't fancy a horse, you can get a point or two added to any odds your computer-governed bookmaker would offer. Then there's betting in-running. Folklore has it that no one reads a race like Ron. And there are plenty of punters willing to put it to the test. He'll offer all manner of ad hoc markets during a race to pit his wits against the assembled clientele and respond to requests for odds on pretty much any eventuality; and tell you to fuck off if he can't make a call. The punters love it and that breeds loyalty; there's never been an in-running bet struck verbally that hasn't been faithfully honoured once the race is over.

But this takes more than form studying, quick thinking, manual dexterity and an eye for a race. It needs a keen mathematical brain to keep track of the book, stay alert to imbalances that need rectifying, not to mention settle a wad of betting slips by hand as you go.

Cue Kevin: 'A' grade maths prodigy with curtailed career aspirations.

Many years on, the team has got it off pat. Reliable Maggie patrols the counter, gently teasing the punters and taking their bets with the personal touch they enjoy. All slips straight back to Kevin who maintains an approximate book, mainly in his head but occasionally with the help of a few written notes when it comes to the bigger handicaps. Nothing definitive, but accurate enough to determine which runners they need to accommodate and which they don't. If the book gets too unbalanced – no fixed rules, Ron trusts him – he activates a microphone and passes on the news to Ron via a tiny earpiece.

They're flying on their wits basically. Ron loves every minute of it. And Kevin enjoys the mental acrobatics.

As the runners at Ludlow pass the stands for the first time, Ron determines to spice up a flaccid market.

"I'll give hundred to thirty the winner's number is divisible by three."

Kevin inwardly groans at this random interjection and a near-perfectly-balanced book is knocked off kilter.

*

"Yes?"

"Hello, Mrs Warburton. I'm here about the recent instance of vandalism to your garden." David hands her his card.

"Took your time. Police?"

"I do represent the police, madam, yes."

"What does that mean? *Represent?*"

"I work with the police and have been sent to talk with you about the crime."

"That was weeks ago. I assumed you'd given up on me. And you're not a policeman, are you?"

"Strictly speaking, no. I'd be lying if I said I was."

"In which case, you can go away."

"Mrs Warburton," he says forcibly, then makes a conscious effort to soften and lower his voice. "I am not a policeman. I would have liked to be one, but for reasons I won't bore you with, that is not possible. I do however work with them and, indeed, from their premises. You may not think much of me, Mrs Warburton, but much as I concur that this world would

24

be a better place if a team of crack detectives and forensic scientists had parachuted into your garden the moment you discovered the vandalism, that is not going to happen. To put it bluntly, and there are valid reasons of course, the police don't give a damn. However great and justifiable your personal outrage and upset may be, they have bigger fish to fry. I, however, have all the time in the world and am very interested to hear what you have to say. I can't guarantee you anything, but I can assure you that I will listen and do my utmost to assist. That may not strike you as much, but I'm afraid that is all there is on offer. It is me, or nothing."

"Then you'd better come in. Shoes off, please."

*

No mistake. He pinched her bum. Well, more a stroke with a nip, delivered in passing as she was handing a pint over the counter.

Perfect. Couldn't have done it better. Nothing obvious. Open to whichever interpretation she fancies. And she hadn't flinched. She's up for it all right. *Come on, my son.*

*

It's quiet, even for a Monday, and despite Ron doing his best to enliven proceedings. Kevin juggles some bet settling with *that* banana sandwich and a half-hearted appraisal of Maggie's backside, on the basis that none of them warrant his undivided attention.

No matter how hard he tries, no matter how many liberties and detours his imagination takes, he can't find a remotely attractive physical angle to Maggie; something to hang even the flimsiest of fantasies on. She may yet prove to be one of his greatest challenges, right up there with Anneka Rice and Gail off *Coronation Street.*

Further contemplation is arrested by an alien taste permeating his buds. He warily peels apart the sandwich and winces at the sight of a well-camouflaged, but unmistakeable, lump of rogue tuna. He reaches for a drink to drown the protests.

*

"Do you mind if I ask you why you can't be a policeman?" she asks, placing a second pot of tea on the coffee table between them.

"Not at all. It's because I suffer from epilepsy," replies David.

"I'm sorry to hear that."

"Don't be. I gave up feeling sorry for myself a long time ago. It's just part of who I am." Feels compelled by her silence to carry on. "There were some complications at birth. Some of the repercussions were physical, but mainly it was the epilepsy. Most of my childhood felt like one seizure after another. It dominated all our lives. The drugs have it pretty much under control these days. I can't drive of course, and you won't find me operating any heavy machinery, but I haven't had a seizure for a while now. Let's just say it's limited my options."

"You've made something of yourself though."

"That's a matter of opinion. There are plenty who think I'm little more than the product of pity, guilt and nepotism."

"Well I think you're a rather marvellous young man."

Which catches him unawares.

She sees the discomfort she has engendered, then the panic as he scrabbles for an appropriate response, so steps in to save him.

"I'm also sorry about…" Then she too struggles for the right words.

"What for?"

"For taking all my anger and frustration out on you, when I answered the door."

"That's no problem at all, Mrs Warburton."

"You must get a lot of that. The real, I'm sorry, the uniformed policemen doing such a poor job, and then you turn up to try and help, and all you get is people ranting and raving."

"I'd be lying if I said it didn't happen, but I don't blame them. It's a perfectly reasonable response. Please don't worry about it. I've become very thick-skinned over the years."

"There were two of them who came out," she says, staring down at her knees. "You could tell they thought it all highly amusing. Couldn't keep a straight face. One of them – Bowing or Bowen, I think his name was; I'm sure I have it written down somewhere – kept cracking jokes to his little sidekick. Probably thought I couldn't hear, but it's my joints that have gone, not my ears or my mind, and in any case, I doubt they cared. Knew from the outset they wouldn't do a thing. Saying that this was what happened if you don't look after your garden, you end up with a crap lawn. And how maybe they could take all the… *things* away and get them analysed in the lab; find out who had done all the dirty deeds. Whether they could dump the case on someone else. What *poo-er* behaviour this was. Then putting on a Scottish accent like that Taggart on television and saying 'merd-er' over and again. Okay, I'll grant you that one was quite clever," she says in response to the glimmer of a smile that plays on David's lips. "I remember showing them the card that was stuck in one…"

"*Card*? What kind of card?" Hears the eagerness in his own voice.

"A playing card," she says, slightly taken aback at the abruptness of his delivery. "I don't remember which one precisely, but I asked them if it might be a clue and they just said no, it had probably just been left there by some joker and that set them off all over again."

"I don't suppose you kept the card, did you?"

"I'm not sure. I may have. Why? Do you think it might have been important?"

"I doubt it. It just struck me as unusual, that's all. Sorry if I made it sound more significant than it was. I just have an ear and an eye for detail that can see me over-reacting at times. Why don't you tell me some more about Ernest?"

"Haven't you got other cases to work on?"

"Nothing that can't wait," he replies, selecting a Bakewell tart, twisting off the glacé cherry and popping it in his mouth with relish.

*

It never rains…

"Right then darlin', three pints of lager and a pint of lager and black for me poncey mate here, if you'd be so kind. None of that blackcurrant bollocks for me. I always prefer it *straight up*, don't you?"

Hardly the best of innuendos. In fact, it probably doesn't even qualify as one. But a grin in the vague direction of his little *gang*, in all their moronic glory, ensures a group guffaw. He's encouraged to press on.

"When we've finished our next frame, I'll remember to hand you my balls."

"Whatever you say," Laura replies, with undisguised weariness.

"What's the matter, love? First day getting you down a bit, is it?"

"Something like that."

"You know what you need, don't you?"

As he struggles with a doubtless feeble follow-up, she weighs up the alternatives: she can nip it in the bud with an embarrassed giggle, cut him short and leave it at that, or engage in a spot of aggravated verbal assault. Check her self-respect in at the door or prejudice her employment security. Some choice.

"You wanna relax, that's what. And I'd be very happy to help out." The words are shrouded in fetid, lager-tinged tobacco, rendering them all the more unpalatable. "Keep the change," he says as he hands over the money, making it sound contractual.

She makes a point of handing over the correct change with the last pint. "There you go." He really should take it and walk, but there's a groin-induced inertia driving him on. After all, she is dealing with that most precious of commodities here: the male ego. He doesn't really expect to get anywhere; a spot of titillation and an entry in that album of shared experience that will be dragged out for mirthful reminiscence whenever the pint-count nudges double figures. Just a bit of harmless fun. Or not. She tired of this time-honoured gender power play long ago.

"I said to keep it, so I guess you must be making a deposit for services to be rendered, eh?" he says, placing his forearms on the counter and leaning forward provocatively, the tip of his tongue protruding wetly between his lips.

Mirroring his movements, she places her face no more than six inches from his. "I'll tell you what," she sighs, and her smiling lips move towards his left ear. The words she whispers are delivered with maximum clarity and intent. She pulls her head back in time to catch his face contorting as he steps back. He pauses for a moment, during which his expression flits from surprise to indignation to fury.

"Fuck you, bitch." The words jettisoned in a salivary spray.

Now it's her turn to be momentarily taken aback, and she's relieved to find Eamon at her side.

"Oi. That's enough, Sean," he says.

"She can't talk to me like that."

"If you can't stand the heat…" She can't resist the interjection, even if it's bound to fan the flames. But she's miscalculated here. Messed up by not leaving him a dignified exit option in front of his mates.

"What the *fuck* is she on about now?" he enquires of the ceiling before lowering his inflamed eyes and levelling them at her. "You're one screwed-up c——"

"I *said* that's enough, Sean," comes in Eamon with admirable steel, his left hand resting lightly in the dip of her lower back.

"But…"

"*Enough*. Let's just leave it, shall we?"

The man hovers in uncomfortable limbo between cowardly retreat and violence. Eamon helps him out with an escape route that saves face.

"Look, Sean. Have your money back. Drinks on the house. Session as well. Both tables. Let's just call it an unfortunate misunderstanding. Eh?"

The offer is reluctantly accepted and Sean slopes off with what he's fast convincing himself are victory spoils.

"You all right, Laura?" Eamon asks, mightily relieved to have bluffed his way through that exchange with uncharacteristic bravado. The resultant shakiness brings a tender quality to his voice that he hopes will come across as empathy. To emphasise this new-found depth, he throws in a comforting squeeze of her left buttock for good measure, copping a rather pleasant feel of arse and elastic. She turns in towards him and he's just bringing the other hand into play when, with a clench of her jaw and a flex of a limb, the trickle of pleasure he's been enjoying is swamped by a torrent of nauseating, debilitating pain.

Hearing the escalation at the bar, Steve had walked to the door of his office, then hung back for a ring-side view of the negotiated entente discordiale, Eamon's wandering digits and Laura's knee-jerk reaction. He could and arguably, as a responsible manager, should have stepped in earlier, but there's always something so very compellingly car crash when Eamon ineptly closes in on another newbie-conquest. But this one's gone way too far and it's time to assert some order on this chaos.

"You two. My office… *now*," he hisses through clenched teeth. "And Eamon, get up will you. It's unprofessional."

"Sack in half a day. Not bad going, you bitch," gasps Eamon, battling against a severely curtailed oxygen supply as he struggles up on to all fours.

Steve wearily shakes his head and beckons them to follow.

"Right then, you two, what the hell was that all about?" he commences, spinning around with intended aplomb, but resultant debacle, as his hip sends a desk lamp flying. "Shit. Where the *hell* is Eamon?" he shouts at a volume that owes more to embarrassment at his own clumsiness than any anger.

"I think he's having a little trouble walking," Laura offers needlessly, making scant effort to hide her amusement.

"Not bloody surprised, after what you did to him."

"He deserved it."

"Maybe, but that doesn't…"

"*Shit.*"

"Come on in, Eamon. Pull yourself together."

"You *what*? Steve, I'm in bloody agony here. Did you see what that psycho did to me?"

"Stop whingeing. That's what we're here to sort out. Now just sit down, will you."

Eamon reaches for the back of a chair with an over-dependence defying the basic laws of physics and which sends him tumbling to the floor in close conjunction with the aforesaid article of furniture, an angle of which embeds itself in an already much-harassed groin.

"Ahhhhhhhhhh…" he begins, holds it for a good five seconds and then concludes "…hhhhrrrrrrrrr."

"Are you all right there?" Laura asks, with mock concern.

"Ahhhhr *shit.*"

"Have you finished now, Eamon?" asks Steve with growing exasperation.

"Right in my fuckin' nuts again."

"Oh *dear.*"

"Leave it, Laura. I think you've done enough damage already, don't you?"

"I was only…"

"I know exactly what you were doing, and I said *leave it.*"

"Sorry," she trills.

"Now Eamon mate, I know it hurts, but try and get yourself up on this chair." He's starting to feel a little sorry for the bloke.

"Okay, I'll try." With much difficulty and grunting he props himself up on an elbow, pauses for reflection, then collapses back down. "No. Maybe not. If it's all right with you, Steve, I might stay – ahhrr – where I am for a while."

Steve surveys the workforce carnage before him.

"What a fucking mess," he concludes, hypocritically clinging to the moral high ground in spite of the nagging thought that *there by the grace of God…*

*

"Kevin."

"Yes, Ron?"

"That monstrosity." He replies to Kevin's quizzical expression with a nod towards the back wall.

"Ah, yes. Quite something. Maggie's noble contribution to the world of impressionistic equestrian art. The jury's out."

"The verdict's pretty fucking obvious, I'd say."

"You like it, then?"

"It looks like she ate all my marker pens, bent over and shat them on the wall."

"Harsh, but undeniably fair."

"Get rid of the abomination. It's putting me right off my stride. I keep catching it out the corner of my eye, grinning at me."

"It is indeed a very happy horse. Leave it to me. I'm humouring her for an afternoon in the interests of maintaining staff morale."

"That's an afternoon too long. Make——"

"Fancy a cuppa Ron luv?"

"Er, Maggie, hi. We were just discussing your… er… artistic effort."

"What do you think then a little bit rushed I know but I think I got it in the end don't you?"

"You certainly did."

She emits a chuckle that has no obvious genesis.

*

Unbelievable.

One knee raised in anger and total respect is hers. The last bloke she served actually apologised for bothering her.

Awkward feeling though; no one even looking at her.

Less than a mile away, after a consolidating and consoling couple of pints in The Estcourt Tavern, Eamon hobbles painfully down his road; a hundred or so yards ahead in which to finalise a remotely persuasive cover story. Wouldn't want to bring on the baby too soon.

*

The final race of the day and a classic get-out stakes. A Trojan horse of a race to tempt, tease and trap this captive audience, most of whom are chasing their losses. A last chance saloon for a bunch of addicts eager for their final fix. And *the* dickhead of the day – of any day – is in the house.

The guy's a regular and always a compulsive watch. Mid-forties, eighties hairstyle, casual golf-wear; bullshit on legs.

He's expected. Nestling in the pay-out box is a rarity: a winning slip with this moron's fingerprints on it. And boy, is he pleased with himself; even has a little sidekick in tow to witness the triumphant pick-up.

Let the performance begin.

"Hello mate, how's things?" he smarms to a complete stranger, then commences what he doubtless considers to be a masterly swagger across the room, lapdog in tow. In his mind's eye, he's a sauntering 'king punter' collecting yet another monster pay-out; an impartial observer might suspect a dislocated hip.

He tosses the slip down in front of Maggie and, while

she searches for its carbon twin, turns to face the room, elbows resting on the counter behind him, soaking up a communal admiration only he could interpret from the marked indifference of the assorted clientele.

"Nice win Jeff."

"Luvly jubbly. Cheers, Mags. Gotta keep you lot on your toes, eh?" He strolls back nonchalantly counting the notes from one hand to the other, bathing in the near-tangible admiration of his acolyte.

"So, you do all right at this game then, Jeff?"

"I have my days."

"Not bad. You got a system or something?"

"Naaaah. Fuck off. Systems are for mugs. No, what you need is what I call the four golden rules."

"Four?"

"Yep. Done pretty good for me, they 'ave."

"Well? What are they?"

"Shush will you. Don't want everyone to know, or we've lost our edge."

"Right. *Edge.* I see," he says, lying.

"Look," whispers Jeff, with a conspiratorial glance around the room. "How I see it is, you need patience, a solid working knowledge of the form and…" Pause for effect.

"What?" Hook, line and sinker.

"Oh nothing. Prob'ly sound stupid to you."

"*What?*" The poor bloke's almost beside himself with the suspense.

"Well, it's a sort of seventh sense; the ability to *see* a race."

"How do you mean? Like on the TV there?"

"Blimey, do I have to spell it out for you. Not 'see' like you're meaning, but '*see*'." He surfs the confusion etched on his mate's face and glides on regardless. "It's like this. While your average punter is busy watching the horses at the front, your shrewdie is more interested in what's going on behind. Your winner's form is there for all to see and that means he's at no sort of price next time he runs. It's often the horse running on nicely back in sixth or seventh you wanna look out for. That'll be your value, and value… well that's what it's all about mate." He pauses, before going in again. "*Value*, Stu, *value*. Right, time to play up these winnings. You on for the ride?"

"You bet."

"Yeah, nice one, Stu." But the pun had been unintentional. Stu's open-eyed inanity is all-encompassing and leaves no room for a wordplay that would probably have eluded him even in his most lucent of moments. "Time to listen and learn." He scans the paper on the wall and locates the impending race, all the while rapping his knuckles on the counter, lips tightening into an exaggerated pout. "Here we go. Looks bloody impossible dunnit, but you gotta be able to see the trees for the wood. The ones with the obvious form are pushing up the odds of the rest of 'em. And most of them are donkeys. Throw in a couple of talking horses and…"

"What?"

"Oh sorry, Stu. Getting a bit technical there. A talking horse is one that's well thought of but has yet to do the biz on the course. See?"

"Yeah." No, not really.

"Anyways. This is most definitely my kind of race, and when you've been at it as long as I have, it's a relatively simple task to narrow a big field like this down to the one to be on."

"And?" Stu may be about to spontaneously combust.

"Well." Another furtive glance, but Kevin's the only other person listening, and he's more than happy to take this idiot on. "That's our baby, there." He places a finger against a name near the bottom of the list of runners. "I've had my eye on this light-weighted animal for a month or so now. Couple of running-on efforts over too short a distance, followed by a disappointing show that can be excused because it was a muddling sort of race run on sticky going that prob'ly didn't suit it. Stable's hinting at a return to form and he's got a decent young apprentice on him that's great value for his seven-pound claim. That'll do for me." Throughout his little speech he's careful to keep his finger on the page, thereby ensuring that his wrist obscures from Stu the 'expert' summary printed beneath the runners that he's been paraphrasing. To complete the deception he swings round, dragging Stu's attention with him, and proclaims, "Now for the price. Where are we now? There you go. Twenty to one; or double carpet to those of us in the know," he says, extravagantly tugging twice at his ear lobe. "And on a horse that should be eights max. Time to lump on, Stuey-boy."

It is indeed a massive price for his selection. Just a pity that in his preoccupation with disguising his plagiarism, he'd read out the passage for the wrong horse: the gambled-on third favourite. The paragraph on his pick includes such phrases as 'past his prime', 'prone to errors' and 'lengthy lay-off'; the poor animal's form figures even spell a word: PUFF21-. The only reasons he's not a rank outsider are that second and a win in his last two races. But the second was by a distance in a two-horse race, while the win was over a year ago on totally different ground, and he finished alone. Just the type of horse you can go short on.

"How much you betting?" gawps a Stu still stalled at the *talking horse* stage from a comprehension perspective, not helped by the insertion of a carpet, but deeply impressed by his mate's obvious expertise. He's always seen it as a fool's game, but the way Jeff's talking it's more like a science. He's got twenty quid clutched in a sweaty palm and he wants a slice of the pie Jeff is cooking up.

"It's gotta be the big *one-errrr* for me," announces Jeff, not getting quite the awed response he'd hoped for. "Better make that two," he adds, eliciting a satisfying gasp from Stu, who rapidly hands over two damp tenners.

"Are we doing it just to win? There's a lot of runners."

"Win or bust, buddy. Each-way's for poofs. And losing poofs at that. If you don't reckon your horse is gonna win, you shouldn't back it… er… you shouldn't back it to get a place when you don't need to, like." Having lost his way, he reverts to more familiar ground. "Remember it's value we're after. I can't say it often enough." It appears he can. "We're getting a massive price on this *equine machine*," he says, impressively getting the two words to rhyme, before scribbling out the betting slip and sashaying over to Maggie.

"I'll take the price please, Mags. You can look after our money for a couple of minutes. Usual rate of interest, mind." He finds himself very funny, glances over and mistakes Kevin's amusement for shared mirth.

"All right, Kev?"

"Yeah. You?"

"All the better for a nice touch on Saturday."

"I saw. Very nice. You going to take it easy on us today?"

"Keep 'em on the ropes. That's my motto."

"Well, let us up for air sometime, will you?" Kevin adds, daring to mix metaphors with a master of the art form, and happy to push this idiot to an even greater height from which inevitably to fall. He drops a few hundred into their laps every week and that's the first decent take-out he's had for ages.

"What was the fourth?" asks Stu.

"Fourth what?"

"Golden rule. You said there were four. You only said three."

"Fuck off, Stu," comes the response, accompanied by a loud clap of the hands and much rubbing of palms. "Don't waste time on semitics when we've got a winner to cheer in. *Come on, my son.*"

*

An estate agent would want to call it a dining room and try to convince potential buyers of their need for that downstairs equivalent of the spare room or garage. But to the regulars, for whom these Monday night sessions are a cornerstone of all their diaries, it's the poker room.

In broad daylight, and stripped of its nocturnal charms, that same estate agent would wince imperceptibly before tactfully suggesting that a degree of sprucing up, maybe a more conventional design scheme, might well be advisable in order to achieve a higher asking price.

The room's centrepiece is the circular poker table: obligatory green baize, padded 'leather' surround – no built-in cup holders or chip racks; strictly for gimmicky amateur gift sets only – and a wobbly leg thanks to a makeshift replacement for a missing screw; all for a hundred quid on eBay.

Nothing overly impressive in itself, but what transforms the table and the ring of seats is the light. The hundred-watt bulb may be dwarfed by the fifteen-inch diameter round metal shade that can be pulled down or pushed up, but at just the right height, with the heavy curtains drawn, it deposits a puddle of golden glow on the table that infuses the green of the baize with the most beautiful of hues. And whatever else may be going on in their respective lives fades into the periphery for those few hours.

The rest of the room is all about ambience. A couple of movie posters – *Cincinnati Kid*, despite its ludicrous technical content, and *Rounders* – compete for wall space with signed photos of the poker gods, courtesy of Andrew's annual World Series pilgrimages to Vegas. A stack system stands on the floor in a corner and sends out the evening's soundtrack – choice circulating, one session at a time, anything permitted – through four small speakers set on brackets high in each corner.

The only misstep is the grotesque presence of The Joker in disconcerting triplicate, staring down maniacally from each of the three *Batman* comic front covers framed and presented to Andrew by Tommy with such ceremony and gravitas that Andrew hadn't the heart not to grant them pride of place; the playing cards splayed in The Joker's talons the most tenuous of links.

Otherwise there are no more distractions in the room, although a 'den' along the corridor past the kitchen boasts a pool table, darts board and TV; a wind-down space for the early losers, though there's never anyone who wouldn't readily swop its creature comforts for a seat back in the game.

A cliché-fest maybe, but Andrew's got it down pat, and early tries of different venues led to a unanimous conclusion that there wasn't one of them who would rather be anywhere else than here for their weekly investigation into whether No-Limit Hold'em poker is a game of luck or skill. The vote's usually six to one on that score, the one being somewhat richer.

Kevin loves that pre-revelatory moment when he first grips the two cards dealt to him. They could be anything: 7-2 unsuited, the worst hand of all, though easy to play; Q-7 unsuited, the average 'computer' hand, also easy to play; maybe, just maybe, a premium hand, one that plays itself while you struggle to look ambivalent; or the kind of hand, above average and full of teasing promise, that tempts you to the edge and leaves you teetering there as the trash talk flows, the chips dance and the cards fall.

This is the moment to savour; when everything remains possible. He looks at his cards the same way every time: brings them together face down, peels up the near end to view the bottom card and, holding them tight, eases out the other, millimetre by millimetre. No emotion. No second glance, for now at least. Nothing given away. Cards placed back on the table face down. Poker face. Ready for action.

Two red sevens.

There's five of them playing in what is an appetiser before the main course; a more common occurrence since the starting time of the latter was put back to eight thirty on the dot – be late and the blinds inexorably nibble at your stack in your absence – to cater for the increasing number of late arrivals courtesy of traffic, jobs, other halves and the like. Tonight is a rarity; Pete has turned up early. He never normally arrives until just before the off – a source of amused consternation, given he has by far the fewest calls on his time – and when he does, he strides wordlessly from front door to table with the focus of a psyched-up boxer approaching the ring. But the rest lack his discipline, are inevitably lured here much earlier, and finding themselves with an hour or so to pass, they're never going to be able to resist a little aperitif. So they've got into the habit of playing a quick-fire knockout, blinds rising fast, fiver each in the pot, winner takes all bar money back for the runner-up; the latter a concession for Sinéad, Andrew's ten-year-old daughter, who gets to tag along for this one now and then. Tonight is one such instance. A treat for her before bedtime, apparently. A pain in the arse for Kevin, and not just because of the emo dirge bombarding his eardrums, courtesy of *her* selected soundtrack.

Two passes and it's Kevin's turn to bet. He has a favourite way to play pairs. Creep in and hope for as many callers as possible but no raises. Get to see the flop and hit your trips. Impossible for anyone to put you on and you can take down a huge pot. And if you miss your card, you can back off with minimal loss and the knowledge that you gave it every chance and it didn't come off. Plays itself. The big blind is two hundred, so he pushes in two black and white chips.

The dealer passes and Sinéad on the small blind puts in one chip to call. That's the thing with kids. They have to be in every hand. Can't stand not to be involved. The big blind taps the table and it's time for the flop.

Andrew's dealing. He burns off one card and deals the flop in his patented style: two cards dealt face down, third card flips them over; he spreads them apart and places the third card between them.

Two of spades, jack of hearts and... the beautiful, beautiful seven of spades.

Poker face.

Sinéad checks. Tommy checks. Can't overplay this monster. Need to keep them in the pot. He checks.

Poker face.

Andrew flips over the ace of diamonds.

Perfect. He needs someone to make a play and walk into his trap. Sinéad, bless her, puts in a small bet. Your average fish pairs an ace and thinks they've got the nuts. Can't resist playing it, like a lamb to the slaughter. Serves her right for this crap he's having to listen to. He doesn't want to scare her off, so he just calls, making out it's a no brainer for such a small amount, like he's desperate to fold his trash. A master puppeteer at work.

The last card is the five of spades. Perfect. Little Sinéad bets her ace. It's clumsy, but you can't blame her. Fallen for her pair and lost perspective. Believes she's struck gold and not thinking about what he might have.

He's tempted by a small raise, but that smacks of strength and she's got all those lovely chips with his name on them. Best to look desperate. He plays with his chips a while, like they do on the telly, pretending to look strong in a way that you'd have to be stupid not to read as weak, before theatrically pushing them forwards with transparently false bravado.

"All in." A tremor in his voice for good measure. A master at work. Watch and learn, little girl. Bed time for you and a life lesson learned.

Eight thirty, and with Sinéad off to bed and all consenting adults now present, the main event can commence with Andrew's usual spiel. "Good evening, gentlemen. The main event will now begin. The game is No-Limit Texas Hold'em. The buy-in is thirty pounds for a thousand in chips. Unlimited buy-ins available until ten forty-five when one last top-up will be permitted before we adjourn for a short break to eat, drink, micturate, defecate and listen to Pete moan about his bad beats, while the rest of us wonder how the fuck anyone can play so few hands without falling asleep and still have so few chips. We then move into freeze-out and play to a conclusion. Sixty/thirty/ten split of the pot to the first three. First out on kitchen duty for the rest of the evening. Second out deals. Blinds start at twenty-five/fifty and go up every fifteen minutes. Good luck to one and all. Deal 'em up."

*

Dad would never have let her play if he'd known she had homework to do. But now the game's under way, he won't notice her light on. Of the four essay choices given that day, one had stood out, and she gives the end product one last read-through.

YOU CAN'T PUT A VALUE ON GOOD ADVICE

Texas Holdum poker is a very simple game. The aim is to make the best 5 card hand from 7 cards, which are the 2 you have been dealt and which no one else sees and 5 comunity cards that you all share and which are dealt face up in 3 goes 3 then 1 then 1. You bet between each but its only chips.

My dad says people think it is bad for children to play poker because its like betting and you can lose lots, but in America kids play it all the time as its just a game and you can only lose what is in front of you and that's usually just chips so what harm is there in that. He lets me play with his friends every now and then. Everyone puts in 5 pounds and gets 1000 in chips back, all of different colours. Daddy gives me my money in secret before so I'm not really gambling or anything like that. The last one left in gets almost all the money which is an awful lot, for me anyways.

There were 5 other players tonite. My dad, his friend Tommy who is sometimes also called Paddy I don't know why and who has known dad for years and does stuff for him but I don't know what and he is a bit serious and scary maybe because he is also bald, Kevin who wears very bright coloured shirts that don't suit him and is quiet and a bit sad and Steve who looks after dads snooker club and always seems tired and Pete who always gets annoyed when things don't happen like he thinks they should with maths and stuff. Carl was late which is a pity because he always teases Kevin and Pete, as they have nown each other for ages, and it is very funny to watch them get angry while he just smiles. I just listen to them talk as they forget I'm there or think I'm too young to understand. I like that.

In poker, you need to play the player not your cards. You have to think about what cards the other players have and also what cards they think you have. It sounds complickated but it is not really. This is GOOD ADVICE my dad has given me. He also told me that Pete only thinks about his own cards, thinks everyone else has the best cards possible and will not take a risk unless he is sure he is winning. Dad calls him a rock, which makes the others laugh but Pete gets angry. Dad also told me that when Kevin gets dealt a pair he puts them slightly apart on the table and if he likes the flop he looks away quickly and tries to look like he doesn't care. In fact dad says Kevin is an open book which I like as a saying. This is all GOOD ADVICE. He has given me more but this is the advice that was good tonite.

Pete sat on my left which is my favorite. Every time it was my turn to bet and no one had raised yet I just raised even if my cards were no good. Pete folded most of the time but if he raised me I knew he had a good hand and I just folded. Except once when he stared at me hard like he was a bit evil or something so I raised him back and he folded. I ended up with more chips than him so when we did both have good cards I can take a chance and still be in even if I lose. This was how I knocked him out to win and although he had the better Q-Q to start with and I only had J-10, I then got two more jacks. He got all angry, but then he had to smile because I'm only 10 and my dad was there. But I could tell he was still annoyed.

Before that I had knocked out Kevin as well. I saw he had put his cards a bit apart and I knew he had a pair. When he did not bet I decided he had a pair of 9s or lower. I do not know what he has at that time but I like to guess and it helps me play the hand. I had the queen and 4 of spades which is rubbish normally but it only cost a little bit to see the flop which is the name for the first 3 cards you all share. I got 2 spades but I knew Kevin had got 3 of a kind because he started looking at the posters on the wall. I needed one more spade for a flush to beat him unless the board paired when I might lose to a full house (my dad tells me to always look for that which is more GOOD ADVICE), but if he bet I had to fold. I didn't bet after the flop because that would show I wanted a spade and he would bet and I would have to fold. So I did not bet and he checked as well because he didn't want to scare me away and I don't think he even noticed the spades. The turn was an ace (not a spade) so I still needed a spade and only had one more chance. I wanted to see the last card so I made a very small bet so he would think I had an ace and had just gotten a pair. This worked as he just called me. I got a nice spade on the river which means I had a flush which is higher than his trips and because he thought I just had A-A, I was able to bet and he put all his chips in for me to take which I did, saying thank you of course. I didn't laugh but everyone else seemed to think this was very funny, except Kevin of course who went very red.

This is how I used the GOOD ADVICE my dad gave me. I think you can deffinately put a value on good advice and that value is 25 pounds.

*

The re-buy period comes to a close, the pizzas arrive on cue – standing order in place; they even have a rewards card – and they grab plates and cans and make their way to the den.

Before they resume Andrew turns to business, while something approaching unity prevails.

"Any developments then, you lot?"

No takers. Just a deal of residual chomping and slurping.

"Okay, then I'll kick things off. You know that bus stop just down from the club; the one they keep having to replace the glass on?"

"Probably just some kids messing around," offers Kevin.

"Maybe, but rumour has it there may have been some more serious repercussions."

Andrew proceeds to put some meat to the bare bones. Fleshes it out until he's grabbed their attention. It's put to the vote, unanimity prevails and Andrew has a project to work on.

"Carl, how about that fly-tipping?" he asks.

"I've altered the dog walk route to take in the allotment and got talking to the old geezers whenever possible. Few more redundant white goods decorating the place and they're pretty certain they know who it is. Some family from the small estate down the road."

"Didn't think you had that kind of estate round your way?"

"It's quite a long way down the road. More a drive than a walk. Anyway, I went past their place the other day. Garden's littered with crap; cars and bikes being done up by a succession of teenage knuckle-draggers, oil everywhere, damaged fridges and cookers. Only trouble is, I'm struggling to see what we can do that'll make a difference. Doubt they'd even notice."

"Fair point. Plus, of course, you're no longer two steps removed, are you?"

"Suppose not. Guess it's a non-runner then."

"Anyone else? Steve, you with us?"

"Sorry Andrew," says Steve. "I'm not in the right frame of mind."

"Nice one," offers Kevin.

"What?"

"*Frame...* of mind.'

"What happened?" asks Andrew, rescuing Kevin.

"Eamon grabbed the arse of the new starter."

"Anything I need to get involved in?"

"All dealt with."

"What happened?"

"She kneed him in the balls."

General crossing of legs.

"Fair play to her," says Kevin.

"She sounds like a challenge," adds Carl.

"You're welcome to try," says Steve. "But I would recommend a hands-off approach. Eamon was rolling round on the floor of my office for ten minutes. It's the first time I've ever given someone the sack while they're lying on the ground at my feet. I didn't really have any choice."

"No problem. Your call. That's what you're there for. Anyway, Eamon's a walking lawsuit, and a thieving one at that. He's had enough warnings. We're best shot of him. How did he take it?"

"Mmm. Not great. Several chairs went flying. A glass of liquid was thrown. Laura, that's the girl he sexually assaulted, was a 'bitch', amongst many other less polite offerings, and I, apparently, am a *marked man*. I tell you, there are times – yes, Andrew, I know what we've all agreed – but there are times when I would really love to make it personal."

"If we do, I've got a tosser in mind," offers Kevin and fills them on that afternoon's four grand betting coup and his failure – Ron's word, though entirely justified – to initiate evasive action.

"Well boys," interjects Andrew. "You all know the rules. This has only ever worked because of them. It has to be *right* and we have to be protected. Nothing relaxes the rules, even if we run out of ideas. They'll come, but there can be no connection. Twice removed at least is essential. The moment it gets personal, we're exposed. That's the beauty of it all."

The others nod. They get the logic. Most have loved where it's taken them. It's just that when they see what can be achieved – what they have achieved – it's only human nature for thoughts to turn to targets closer to home; to imagine the pains of nearest and dearest contra'd out; to see perceived wrongs righted.

Andrew senses the need in their reflective silence and offers them a conspiratorial smile and the chance to dream a while longer. "However, that doesn't mean you can't amuse me with your more venomous flights of fancy as and when you wish. In complete confidence of course. Get it off your chest. Let me release some of that pressure. I'm all ears for a good gripe against someone who deserves it. And who knows?"

Andrew leaves the offer hanging in the air for a few moments before curtailing bittersweet reveries with a theatrical waft of notes before their faces and the announcement of the prize fund and split.

SUNDAY

Kevin may not share Pete's masochistic passion for physically punishing himself, but he doesn't need asking twice; the gym is a rich seam of inspiration that he never tires of mining.

He collects the exercise card that affords him legitimacy and eases into his session with a series of half-hearted stretches against the rear wall of the large open-plan gymnasium; the perfect location for the reconnoitre that will dictate the hour to follow. His casual survey suggests promise, so he abandons a hamstring stretch that only seems to make his calf hurt and moves forward to the back row of machines and sets a cross-trainer in sedate motion.

Faking a yawn-stretch he casts a look over to the right. A woman with long blonde hair and a tight-fitting lycra leotard and leggings, face as-yet-unseen, is standing on a mat, feet planted shoulder width apart, arms hanging loosely by her side, a weight in each hand. She bends her knees so her thighs are at forty-five degrees to her calves, then straightens her legs. And repeat. Up and down.

He closes his eyes and he's lying on his back between her legs; he loses her clothes, and those weights, leaving her hands free to play with her... *that's the only way she'll be getting any satisfaction.* She's loving it. *She's shagging fresh air. At her lowest point she's still almost two feet off the ground, and we both know you're not up to bridging that gap.* It's my fantasy. *And it's a logistically insurmountable one. There's a pun in there somewhere.* Enough. *So how does it work?* Doesn't need to work. Since when was that the point? *Of course it does.* I'm doing a bridge. Like I used to do at school. *Arms will be getting tired.* I'm strong enough. *And your face will be twisted back. You won't be able to see a thing. You'll miss all the good bits.* Fair point. Got it. I'm lying on an exercise ball. *Too wide for her. She'd have to be seriously bow-legged.* Okay, I'm on one of the weight benches. Ha, yes, that's it. *Not bad. Then what? Too late. She's finished. Here she comes. Oh dear, I don't like yours much. Mid-forties?* Shit. *If you're not doubling dick length, you're halving ages.*

Undaunted, he strolls over to a favourite machine, where a verifiably age-appropriate woman sits, pushing weights outwards with her knees. Splay. Together. Splay. Together. He grabs a couple of the lightest weights from the racks by the wall to authenticate his loitering presence and turns to find the splayer now lying on her front on a bench, the weighted arm of the machine resting on the back of her heels. As she pushes up the weight her cheeks tighten, and as she lowers it there's a delicious little rise of the buttocks, the material stretched taut, every crevice invaded. This is truly excellent. No need to redirect this scene or introduce himself. It's more than enough just to observe, which he does standing in no man's land with a couple of weights clasped in front of a slightly tented groin, before the onset of self-awareness sees him heading for the machine offering the best view, albeit one he's never used before, where he takes a ringside seat.

This really is great. *What's that stain?* What? *That stain.* It's just the shading of the material. *You know it's a stain.* Okay, it's a stain. *Is it sweat?* What? *Yep, that's what it is.* Go away. *Just saying.* Sweat's fine. Sweat is sexy and we've been at it for ages. *It's a sweaty crack. Fancy that?*

The sudden realisation that he's aimlessly twiddling something that should probably be being pulled precedes only marginally the awareness of the man who is standing a few feet away watching his every movement with barely disguised impatience.

"There you go," Kevin says, throwing in the kind of sigh only the toughest of workouts can justify. "All yours now, mate." Nice touch, throwing in that 'mate'. He exhales audibly, sounding like a young child trying to blow out birthday cake candles, and shakes his arms as he moves away with accentuated casualness. And almost walks into a couple of blokes; one on his back on a bench straining to push up a bar laden with cartoon-like weights, while the other stands above him, his hands cupped under the bar but not touching it. 'Spotting' him, isn't that the expression? His supine pal completes his set, re-cradles the bar, sits up and studies the veins on his bulging biceps; while the spotter takes a loving look at his own well-defined musculature and adjusts his clothing ready for his upcoming performance. Kevin is momentarily disarmed by the incongruity of it all; the tenderness. Here are two *geezers*, alpha males of the gym, ticking every box on the inventory of machismo clichés. Envied by men. Certainly envied by him. Surely fancied by women. Putting on this public performance with the gravitas of actors in a Shakespearean tragedy. And yet it's all so fundamentally homoerotic; couldn't be more so if they were licking golden syrup off each other's upper thighs while murmuring "mmmm". He smiles to himself, taking brief refuge from his own insecurity.

"Can we help you, mate?" asks one of them.

"Er, no, er…" He glances around in mounting panic. "Weights. I'm just deciding on what weight to… er… lift. Yep liftimundo." *Lifti-fucking-mundo? What the…?* They look as puzzled as he feels, so he turns to face the bank of weights and takes stock: the two blokes behind him are thinking Christ knows what, the previous bloke obviously didn't buy his little act, the girl is now walking off, her backside no longer holding the same charms under the pull of gravity, and to cap it all he's just tried three different weights and not been able to lift a single one of them clear of their rack. He must look like some kind of fetishist weight-fondler. All in all, this area of the gym is proving a touch problematic today, so, sweating more now than at any other time, he heads for the tranquil anonymity of the upright exercise bikes and sets off his usual programme.

A figure glides before him under the TV screens and heads for the mat area off to his right. She wants him to see her. There were other ways she could have gone. *Longer ones.* The rear view sways pleasingly, and the front view is… come on, turn. She leans side on against the wall to stretch her calves, and reveals a pert frontage. Pert is very good. And she is most definitely pert. And pretty too. There's a knowing look as she sticks out her bottom lip and blows her fringe away from her eyes. Bingo.

He closes his eyes and they're in one of the small rooms off the main studio. It's late. She's wandered in and found him doing Pilates, or some shit like that. Something that reveals his feminine side, setting him apart from all those sweating, grunting posers. She seems interested and coyly asks him what he's doing. She's very impressed when he says it's Pilates. He offers to show her. *She says no thanks gay boy, I want a proper man.* She says yes please. He talks her through some exercises, his fingers brushing her firm curves as he guides her, his eyes drinking in her body as it strains against the lycra. She pauses. Eye contact. Faces close in on each other, her hand moving to his... who the fuck's he? *Boyfriend alert.* I can ignore him. *Yeah, right. Good-looking guy.* Kevin leaves them to it.

A glance at the clock reveals he's only done about forty minutes. Pete is mid speed-row and won't notice, so he slopes over to the mats, lies down and engages in some random convulsing. There's a woman, probably in her early forties, but still in really good shape and she's doing some ballet thing with her foot on the hand bar, leg straightened with no apparent discomfort. She flashes him a smile. *Grimace. She's stretching.* It was definitely a smile.

Ten minutes later finds him in a shower cubicle fingering a half-hearted erection fuelled on the agile ballet dancer fantasy he's been nurturing since he ran out of body parts to stretch. But it's just not happening. He thrusts his groin into the hot stream of water, hoping for a titillation top-up. It stirs a little, but not above a lolling state that's good for nothing. She's just so... two dimensional. Cue a montage of tried and tested images that soon do the trick and he climaxes against the wall. He watches the viscous emission slide slowly down, scoops handfuls of water over it and switches the temperature gauge to cold to return everything to normal size and colour as quickly as possible before getting dressed.

Kevin likes wanking. A lot. Not for him the occasional filler, substitute or compensator that suffices for most, beyond the incessant and fervent prepuce-pummelling of the teenage years. For Kevin it's all about the wank.

It's his hobby.

He'd read an article once that said that if you wanted sex, then wanking came a poor second; but that if all you wanted was a wank, then there was nothing better. He'd had sex, a few times; struggled to recall a single redeeming feature of those experiences and saw little reason to expose himself again.

What masturbation gave him was control. When, where, how and who were up to you; without ever needing to ask why. *She* was who you wanted. *She* looked exactly how you wanted her to. *She* was always in the mood, or you knew that no meant yes. *She* was always wearing what you wanted, however impractical. *She* smelt great, having bathed recently. *She* never protested as you removed her clothing. *She* exclaimed "ooo" as you removed yours. *She* even gasped if you tugged or ripped clothes off her. Naked, *her* skin was always smooth and silky and blemish-free. *She* longed for you. *She* moaned at your touch. *She* moved at your speed, never protesting if you fast-forwarded through the preliminaries or rewound the good bits. *She* said what you wanted to hear. *She* loved whatever you did. *She* didn't need you to bother with contraception. *She* came when you wanted her to. *She* didn't care when you came. *She* didn't care where you came. *She* didn't care if you came. *She* loved it all, yet love was irrelevant. And *she* didn't require a moment's thought after ejaculation. No awkward silence; no apologies; no post-mortem; no lies.

A win-win option every time.

Unless, that is, the voice pipes up.

The logic-enforcer. The nagging reality check. The rebuffer of all things improbable; like some fussy over-zealous editor redacting out chunks of his carefully-scripted fantasies with a black marker pen.

The erection spoiler.

It's the voice that incessantly critiques whatever arbitrary scenario has facilitated the imminent coupling, swamping flights of fantasy with the most mundane of logistical concerns. It's the voice that wonders when she last washed. Asks when you last washed. It's the voice that wonders at what aromas lurk under each item of clothing, waiting to be released. It's the voice that asks what you've both eaten earlier. Whether you've brushed your teeth since. It's the voice that whispers "*period?*" It's the voice that points out pimples and hints at acne; seeks out inevitable cellulite. It's the voice that spots the bored look in her eyes; the disappointment. It's the voice that queries the constant shuffling of timelines to suit the endgame, demanding the deflating distraction of a logical narrative.

That voice… an occupational hazard for the serial wanker, and one Kevin has to overcome time and time again in his pursuit of uncomplicated, uncluttered, inconsequential pleasure.

It doesn't always make itself heard and it isn't the only impediment he faces, but it's a permanent resident in the dim recesses of his imagination; inching forwards; sniggering.

His own private golem.

They're passing through the turnstile in reception when a voice halts him.

"Excuse me sir."

He glances over his shoulder to find that the words are addressed to him.

"Me?"

"Yes, you sir. Can I have a word in *private* please?"

"Er, fine. Okay. Hey, Pete, I'll catch you in the café. Can you get me an orange juice and a packet of salted nuts?"

"Sure you want salted?"

"Absolutely certain."

THURSDAY

It transpires that reports of the exploits and pompous glory of the A team – of which there have been many in her first few days – have not been exaggerated.

Laura gets it. They have every reason to be piqued, forced as they were a few years back when the club first opened to start in the bottom league and work their way upwards. If ever there was a rule to be broken by the league committee, this had been it. And if a succession of five-nil romps wasn't enough to ram the message home, they've also won the all-league District Cup competition in two of the three years of their existence. But the committee wouldn't budge and their stickler-like tendencies have created a monster; a juggernaut of cockiness and dismissive arrogance that has routinely run over, ritually humiliated and alienated every team in the lower three leagues and is currently steamrollering League Two with complete disregard for anyone else's feelings. No one likes losing five-nil, but to be beaten by a right-hander playing left-handed, a pirate or Father Christmas tends to be an ignominy too far for the average lower league player, for whom positional play is an advanced sexual technique and a twenty break enough to warrant rounds of applause, drinks and an anecdote to dine out on for months to come. That they've avoided physical harm along the way is a testament to gift of the gab and some astute and speedy tactical withdrawals.

Laura experiences tonight's graceless performance second-hand via the frequent visits of players and hangers-on to the bar for refills and clumsy flirting.

"Priceless. Fucking priceless. I almost pissed myself," says Dean, arms clinging to sides, presumably to prevent their splitting.

"Really? What's happened now?" asks Laura, hating herself for asking.

"Gizz had to win by exactly sixty-nine…" He actually pauses for comedic effect at this hilarious number, raising a hand to his mouth to suppress a titter. "… points. Eh? Anyway, he keeps missing colours and the muppet he's playing has only gone and fluked a thirty break. Left Gizz only twenty-seven points ahead with just eighteen on the table. He spends twenty minutes getting five snookers and then has to bribe the bloke a fiver not to give up until he's sunk the black. Fucking funny, I'm telling you."

The humour is lost on Laura, feeling pity for the opponent. "Bet the other side loved that," she says.

"They were laughing along as well. Thought it was brilliant."

She doubts it, and the tale doesn't get any funnier when Gizz himself appears to regale her with an embellished first-hand account.

It's after ten thirty when the opponents wander wearily past the bar. There isn't much bonhomie in evidence as they head off in search of good company and fresh air.

As the seven squad members – six rotating the five places; Dean more sycophantic mascot, his playing appearances either token or unavoidable – settle down for the customary and entirely appropriate post-match game of brag and Laura starts the clear-up, she finds herself bristling at the smug air of mutual appreciation that wafts over from their recollections of the night's bravura performance. Unable to distance herself, she feels guilty by association.

"Hey Laura," calls Wayne. "Leave all that, darling. Come over and join us for a drink."

Like it's some kind of treat for her. An honour even. She's sorely tempted to tell him where he can shove his invite, but a mischievous whim wins the day.

Playtime.

"Some of us have a job to do, I'll have you know," she says, sauntering over with calculated coyness, hands clasped loosely behind her back; a look that has always served her well. "But how could I possibly refuse an offer to hang out with the esteemed, all-conquering *A Team*."

She has their attention and can see the saliva pooling in Gizz's slack lower jaw. His eyes haven't left her breasts since she started her approach.

"If I'm ever on *Desert Island Discs* and they ask me what my luxury would be, I'll be sure to choose a snooker table and you lot to watch wielding your cues to such devastating effect."

"One," blurts Gizz, messily. "You can only have one."

Confusion reigns.

"Luxury. You can only have the one," he expands. "One of us, I mean," his words dribbling away as he recognises he might have sounded a touch over-enthusiastic.

"What Gizz wants to know," purrs Wayne, already anticipating the cream, "is which one of us you'd choose to take as your luxury item if you were to be washed up on a desert island on your bikini-clad lonesome. That right, Gizz?"

Gizz nods, a little too vigorously, before closing his mouth at long last and taking a much-needed swallow.

"Gosh. What a decision. Any one of you would be a real catch."

"Yeah, but which one?" asks Gizz, a man with little comprehension of sarcasm and for whom her words have been tantamount to a caress of his privates.

He's not alone.

"Got it," exclaims Gizz, with Archimedean excitement. "Brilliant," he shouts, the as-yet-undisclosed idea sufficiently stunning to propel him from his seat and send a fist punching into the air. "Fucking brilliant."

He has the floor by now.

"I have to warn you, Gizz," says Wayne, "that if this is not an outstanding idea, and I mean truly outstanding, I will be compelled to kick your sorry arse all the way back to Italy. Comprendo?"

But Gizz isn't listening. He's on a road heading for his own personal Damascus and the light is blinding.

"You go out with each of us, one at a time, not together like, and we take you somewhere that we would normally go. Do what we'd normally do, you know. And at the end you decide who's the best, I mean the most enjoyable… who you fancy, no, not fancy… whose company you enjoyed the most."

His words are chewed into intelligible order by the others and contemplated, all eyes momentarily sightless as individual fantasies are constructed; none of them witness to the look of mild horror rippling across Laura's face. She feels over-extended and desperately scrambles for an appropriate spoiler, but isn't quick enough.

"We could do it over the next few weeks. Be a nice

way to introduce her to a new area. Give her something to do on her nights off. Show her the sights."

"Of Watford?" asks Kevin, reasonably.

"Depends on what you come up with. I know mine already. She'll fuckin love it."

"Hello?"

"Yes, love?" says Gizz.

"I'm still here."

"Right," says Gizz, as if talking to a simpleton.

"Shouldn't you ask me first before you debate the suggestion?"

"We haven't debated anything yet. We're only talking about it."

Carl snorts. Kevin looks at the ceiling. Wayne kicks Gizz. Gizz is confused. Dean looks worried.

"All right by me," exhales Wayne, allowing his raised knee to drop away outwards with a sigh that grabs her attention. He flicks his gaze down and instinctively her eyes follow, alighting on the unmistakable outline of his penis, momentarily reminding her of something out of *Tremors* and holding her attention fleetingly longer than she might wish. Then it flinches and jolts her into the ocular clutches of its owner, the gloating look on his face telling her that he knows what she's thinking and that he's in control. He doesn't, and he isn't; but that lesson can wait for another day. She can feel the heat rising in her cheeks and knows it's only fuelling his imagination as he plots the course of the impending seduction with the practised assurance of the experienced predator.

Fortunately, pandemonium has broken out by now, so she sits back and observes. It's true; she has nothing better to do. Her four nights off a week are usually spent on the sofa, channel surfing, waiting for the microwave to ping and rationing out comfort foods. Surely this lot can improve on that between them? Set the expectation bar low, accept the free meals and should all else fail, maybe she'll appreciate her poky little flat a bit more. But ultimately, it's simple curiosity that carries the day.

"Okay," she says, to no effect. "*Okay*," she shouts, and the teeming cesspool gradually stills. "You've got me any Friday, Sunday or Wednesday night. Monday nights are mine. You lot arrange it amongst yourselves. Just let me know where and when. You can wine and dine me, take me train-spotting, do whatever it is you do in your spare time. Only ground rules are incidental contact only…" Too many puzzled looks. "That's no physical intimacy." Frowns still in evidence. "Hands off. That clear?" Gizz is staring at what he's thinking of touching. Wayne is contemplating his own crotch. Carl is smiling. The others are nodding seriously. "Give me an insight into the real you and I'll let you know whose company I enjoyed the most. For what that's worth. Agreed?"

Motion carried unanimously.

"What does the winner get?" leers Wayne, with the air of a man holding the winning ticket, giving his prize the slow once-over; pausing at points of interest en route.

"Not what you're thinking of."

He shrugs, clearly not believing her.

"Tell you what," she says. "I'll take out whoever I pick for my idea of a dream evening."

Whatever the hell that is.

SUNDAY

DATE 1: CARL

On paper at least, this should be the clear stand-out date: a trip to an awards ceremony held at some swanky hotel in London. It has certainly pushed her wardrobe to breaking point, though to little avail it would appear, as she observes the stream of shiny baubles passing by their overly-adorned alcohol-strewn table, wafting air kisses and insincerities at each other, the truth alighting on their faces only as they turn away.

The evening's remit is proving somewhat evasive to grasp. The compere, who she can dimly recall from some sit-com a few years back, delivers an in-joke-laden preamble, from which she gleans that they are gathered to acknowledge and celebrate contributions to that peripheral sector of the journalistic world known informally as lads' mags. A world created by and for voyeuristic men who need to ridicule or be revolted by people they can feel superior to; or who just want to look at and read about young women who are desperate to do *it*, or have *it* done to them, and are willing to remove most of their clothes, bend over and contort their faces into pouts and pained grimaces to prove it. Legitimised, guilt-free pseudo-porn basically, for those who can't face the prospect of being caught by someone they know casting a hungry eye over the more blatant top-shelf offerings.

Their fellow diners have already informed her that Carl is "talented" and "a hoot" and that he is nominated for an award, something Carl neglected to mention on the journey in, presumably to appear endearingly modest and disinterested. When his hoot-inducing talent fails to reap the trophy – a vaguely Oscar-like golden effigy sporting double D breasts and, presumably to stop her falling over, voluminous buttocks – his fixed grin and hearty applause for the victor are evidence enough that it had mattered to him greatly. His feigning abilities are further tested as three trophies are cheered, collected and wedged into the Manhattan of bottles and glasses on their table. Just after eleven the effort finally takes its toll, his eyes dull and the yawning attacks start.

They have a couple of half-hearted dances, welcome breaks for her from a features editor called Guy who seems to believe that seniority and gender entitle him to place his hands wherever he wants, her left knee apparently top of his wish list; misogyny camouflaged as flattery, and all delivered with a banal line in patter that washes across her face in a warm current of whisky-infused garlic.

She gives Carl the out he's been looking for and tells him she feels exhausted. He does his best to look disappointed, before they both get what they want, rising to a disingenuous chorus, doubtless to be forgotten long before they have even collected their coats.

MONDAY

Kevin constructs two tall towers. The table jolts sharply and they topple over.

"Oops. Sorry. Slipped," says Carl.

Kevin calmly recommences construction, but another jolt sees them collapse again.

"Have you learned nothing from 9-11?" says Carl, to much merriment. Kevin can't think of anything funny or clever to come back with, so he opts for blocks of flats instead and forces out a smile, because that's what a relaxed, super-aggressive player who's been at it all night would do; and that's the very much atypical image he's been cultivating for the past few hours. And to ensure no one forgets, he raises the next three pots, winning one and backing down to re-raises on the other two, each time with the embarrassed shrug of a man who's been caught at it. All he needs now is the big hand to profit from this new image.

A couple of hands later and he's on the big blind staring at a red queen. He slowly squeezes out the second card. Another queen. Bingo. Payday. Such is his apparent disinterest in the hand that he has to be reminded it's his turn to bet.

The hand progresses and he's staring down at the Jack of hearts, five of spades, four of hearts, and the eight of clubs; all in a neat line beside a pile of chips to which he has contributed roughly half of his property portfolio. Just him and Carl left. Kevin knows he's ahead.

The river delivers the ace of diamonds.

Not what he wanted, but there's no way Carl would have called all those raises sitting there with ace high. Kevin is convinced he is still winning this hand, so he fixes Carl with his most inscrutable stare.

"Blue Steel?" enquires Carl.

Kevin rides the sniggers and gives Carl the Bruce Lee come-on; starting to enjoy himself. Carl responds with a wink and shoves all his remaining chips into the middle.

"All in," he adds, superfluously.

Kevin has Carl beat.

Doesn't he?

Into his mind float the hands that would beat him: an ace, king-king, six-seven, a pair of jacks… in truth there aren't many, and he knows the maths has him a long odds-on shot, but those hands are suddenly all he can see. Then come the self-justifying mantras of the rock's handbook, flooding to the fore. The recollections of those monster hands all the great players have put down at one time or another. It's what makes them great; what makes them legends.

He folds.

Carl shrugs, lifts his cards extravagantly into the air and brings them down with a flourish, face up. 10-2 of clubs.

"Now *that's* how you play poker," he announces loudly and milks the spontaneous round of exclamations.

Kevin's face burns. He breaks into a sweat. There's a pressure building in his temples and he can feel his bowels loosen.

"You had me beat all along," he tries half-heartedly, but he's fooling no one. Only earns himself more abuse.

He takes stock. He's still got an average stack. And this is where his strength comes into play: the ability to ride the downs and keep to his A-game. Tilting is not an option.

Kevin blinks against the fluorescent glare of the kitchen light, fills the kettle, turns it on and leans over until his forehead rests against a cupboard door, which he gently head-butts. Then again, slightly harder. And again. Until the heat of the steam becomes unbearable and forces him to withdraw.

He fetches down the mugs, throws tea bags in two and spoons coffee in the others, then pours on the boiling water. He separates Carl's mug from the others. He coughs up a mouthful of phlegm and kneads it with his tongue until, like a cook separating a yolk from the egg white, he has a jellied, sickly-sweet globule between tongue tip and lips. A moral debate ensues. The motion is carried and easing his lips apart, he ejects the mucopurulent pellet and lets it drop into the mug, giving it a vigorous stir.

Having added milk and sugar he fetches the tray and loads up, noting the very obvious foreign object floating in Carl's mug. He lifts it out with a spoon and feels a little more at ease with himself.

When Pete's pair of fives get out-drawn by Carl's A-Q, it's down to two and time for the customary pre-dénouement break; some kind of homage to the TV format that consumes so much of their leisure time viewing, only minus the procession of showgirls bearing suitcases of banknotes, a tacky bracelet and an advert break.

Andrew leaves the room and returns with a cardboard box that he drops with a loud clank on the floor beside his chair. He reaches in and takes out a batch of envelopes.

"Right then. I call this meeting of the HBVC, blah, blah, blah. Only matter on the agenda is next Saturday night."

"Don't you mean this Saturday?" Pete offers.

"What?"

"Do you mean this Saturday or the one after, which… er… would be…" he fizzles out under the weight of Andrew's stare.

"The *fuck* are you on about? Next Saturday is the next fucking Saturday. What can possibly not be clear about that?"

"Well… er… nothing. Sorry."

Andrew smiles, releasing Pete from his momentary disorientation, then continues, brandishing the envelopes. "As I was saying before I was rudely interrupted by this pedantic knob, I've got one of these for each of you. Inside you'll find everything you need, including an address, a map of the immediate vicinity and a specific time. One of you for each target. Don't bother looking now. Let me know over the next few days if you've got any questions. Up to you whether you have a look at the location beforehand. But if you do, just be subtle about it. Time of first incursion is 4 am, the others staggered to give the appearance of a lone assailant, so apologies for buggering up your beauty sleep. And it goes without saying that at that time, whilst it'll still be dark of course, any sighting will be more memorable and easier to link to whatever's just gone down. Any questions?"

None.

"If there are, just give me a bell. Now for your weapons of choice." He pauses for effect, reaches down into the box and straightens back up with a grey and red block in his hand. He places it on the baize and sits back proudly. It's a red metal double-decker London bus, about six inches long and half as high, though it's seen better days. It looks like it's just been dug up from a sandpit.

"Pick it up," says Andrew, his hands now clasped behind his head. Carl reaches forward and picks it up.

"Shit that's heavy. It's like a brick."

"That's pretty much what it is. Bit of a brainwave really. The bus was obvious, but pumping it full of liquid cement was a stroke of genius."

"Looks like a Turner Prize entry," says Kevin, and meets with confused silence.

"Anyway," continues Andrew. "Not quite as polished as we'd have liked. Apparently, it's a bugger trying to keep it all inside and pretty much impossible to scrape the stuff off. But it makes the point and it's functional."

"What's that on the top?" asks Kevin.

"R.I.P.E.N.T.," reads Carl, repeating the letters crudely etched into the red paint of the roof to reveal the metal beneath. "This on all of them?" Andrew nods and smoothes the furrowed brows with an explanation, one that generates smiles of approval.

A cunning plan is indeed afoot.

WEDNESDAY

Carl is beginning to regret accepting the offer of sharing a car on the big night. The logic was irrefutable given that their targets are a few hundred yards apart, but he hadn't bargained for his Wednesday evening being hijacked by a surprise visit from Kevin; a cardboard wallet clutched to his chest and a glint in his eye.

He makes the mistake of asking what's in the file, and out comes an Ordnance Survey map, a clutch of Polaroids and some hand-drawn diagrams that are soon smeared all over his coffee table. From bachelor pad to Churchill's Map Room in under a minute.

Once he's unpeeled his gaze from the ceiling, and no matter how hard he resists, Carl is soon hooked, though he does baulk at Kevin's repeated use of the phrase 'strike zone'. But he bites his lip and lets Kevin take centre stage. He's done his homework all right, including two drive-bys, one on the way back from poker two nights before.

The road is little more than a lane and runs for a couple of miles beside some woods, the houses on one side only, all detached to the point of not being readily visible from their neighbours.

"These people must be seriously loaded. Sort of makes this all seem more… poetic somehow, don't you think?" asks Kevin.

"I don't bother rationalising it that much. Little gits getting what they deserve is how I see it. Are we just going to pull up outside, pop out and do the dirty deed?"

"Too risky. See this track running into the woods from the other side? There's a small car park right in the middle. Picnic tables and stuff. We can park up without anyone seeing and there are paths leading to the lane. If we take torches then we can easily leg it back under cover and we'll be out the other side and away before they've worked out what's hit them."

Carl senses Kevin has made a joke, but by the time his conscience prompts a laugh, it's too late. So he opts to reverse Kevin's visible deflation with a point at the table.

"What else you got here, then?"

SUNDAY (VERY EARLY)

"Have you got a handle to go with the new look?"

"A what?" replies Kevin.

"You know. A nickname. Something like Shadow or Spectre or Man in Black. Or is it just Johnny Cash tribute night?"

"Funny guy."

"Not bad, but I prefer mine."

"Have you not heard of camouflage?"

"It's not *Raid on Entebbe* for fuck's sake. It's a quick walk, a lob and a jog back. That's all. But this is like being stuck in a Chris Ryan novel."

"Who?"

"Never mind, but if it was, it would be called *Operation Total Sodding Overkill*. I just think it's a bit excessive, that's all. I mean the only thing missing is you blacking up with boot polish or donning a balaclava."

Kevin hesitates, purses his lips, reaches down into the door compartment, grabs the balaclava, pulls it down over his head and tugs at the material until holes approximate to sensory organs. He suppresses a smile as he turns to face Carl, but he needn't have bothered as Carl's head is already buried in his hands. And he's wearing a poorly-aligned balaclava.

"Fuck me," groans Carl through his fingers.

"I'm merely taking appropriate precautions."

"Kevin, what time is it now?"

Kevin looks down at his watch but can't locate it. He manipulates an eye hole until it appears.

"Three hundred hours and about fift—"

"In English, shithead."

"Quarter past three."

"And our *targets* are where, exactly?"

"Through the trees that way a hundred or so yards. I've got a compass in here if—"

"*No.* You get a compass out and I swear I'll ram it down your throat." Deep breath. "Tell me, what is our estimated time to delivery, or whatever bullshit terminology wannabe-pseudo-military twats like you go for?"

"Forty-five minutes. Actually, forty-four now."

"And the journey here took how long?"

"I dunno. Ten, fifteen minutes?"

"And how long was the journey?

"Seven point three miles."

"And how long have we been here now?"

"Not too—"

"Thirty minutes Kevin. *Thirty... fucking... minutes.*"

"I didn't want to take any chances."

"*Chances.* It's a seven-mile journey in the middle of the night. What the hell was on your list of things that could possibly go wrong to justify leaving that early? Natural disasters? One mile per hour speed limits? We could have walked here and been early."

"Okay, point made. I was overly cautious. But surely it's better to be safe than sorry. And I hate being late, you know that."

"I do now. And here I am stuck in a car in a wood at four o-fucking-clock in the morning with bloody Al Jolson. Whoopee-fucking-do. I want my mammy," he adds after a pause and waves his hands in the air.

"Sorry if I've sold you down the Swanee River," counters Kevin, surprising both himself and Carl. But after a promising beginning their shared knowledge is exhausted, the routine falters and they drift into silence; the only sounds the occasional hoot, the squelch of backsides shifting on leather and Kevin scratching at his itchy scalp.

Carl catches a flash of light in his wing mirror. "Shit. A car's coming."

"What do we do?"

"Christ knows. What kind of person comes down here at this time?"

"Should we just drive off?"

"Too late. Hide the buses, make sure the key's in the ignition, just in case, and lock all the doors," says Carl, turning to face Kevin. "And take that stupid bloody thing off your head."

A vehicle eases into the small car park and drives slowly round their car. It's more of a van than a car, its single visible occupant a man maybe a little older than them who glances across as he passes each of them in his circumnavigation. They remain rigidly staring forwards, eyeballs straining to assess what they can of the interloper. The van comes to a halt behind them with a gentle scrunch of gravel, the engine left running.

And there they all sit for a few minutes.

"Shit, he's getting out," whispers Kevin, chest

tightening, insides churning wildly, heartbeat drumming in his ears.

"Act natural," replies Carl, the stupidity of the comment and situation forcing out a nervous and incongruous laugh.

There's a knock on Carl's window. Their heads jerk towards it as if invisible assassins are simultaneously breaking their necks. The man has a friendly enough face, though maybe that's just because he's smiling. He gives a hand signal and Carl lets the window down an inch or two. The pungent scent of a cologne wafts in and light from the beam of the headlights glints off the pendant hanging from his neck.

"Hi guys," he says, leaning against the car, his bicep flexing. He's wearing a tight-fitting T-shirt, despite the chill in the air that's turning his breath to mist.

"Hi," says Carl, his voice slightly strangled.

"You boys been having some fun?" the man asks, glancing down at Kevin's thighs, on one of which the balaclava has been neatly laid out. "Nice touch, guys," he adds, with a complicit smirk, his tongue probing disconcertingly at the inside of his cheek. "Role playing can be soooo much fun, don't you think?"

Kevin and Carl frantically search for the right combination of words, and fail.

"Fancy some company?" asks the intruder.

"Badgers," blurts Kevin.

"*What?*" chorus the others.

"Badgers. Yes. We're on a badger watch," persists Kevin.

"Sorry mate. You got me there," says the man.

"There's a... er... colony."

"Sett," interjects Carl. "It's a sett. A colony is... um... the name given to the surrounding... er... environs. The place where they live is called a sett. But you know that, of course."

"Yeah. Of course," nods Kevin. "A sett. Anyway, we belong to the local nature club and there are some badgers living in the woods. We're here to observe and… catalogue them."

"There's a national consensus going on."

The man frowns, with every justification, then slowly shakes his head.

"Pity. Thought we might have had some fun there. Better leave you to it. You're sure now?"

Heads nod vigorously. The man pushes himself off the car and gives them a wave and a regretful smile. He turns to go, but checks himself.

"One question," he asks with thinly-disguised mischief. "Seeing how you're nature experts and all. I've always wanted to know. What's the collective noun for badgers?"

"A platoon," says Kevin with unhesitating authority.

"Platoon. *Right*. Now I know. You two have a good night then."

They hear the crunch of footsteps and a door clunk shut. Headlight beams sweep the trees that surround the clearing and the light behind them turns from white to two red eyes, which shrink and dwindle to nothing.

"What the…"

"Was that what I think it was?"

"Yes."

"Fuck."

They stare into the darkness.

"Do you think he bought it?" asks Kevin.

"Well provided he has a single figure IQ and Gullible as his middle name, I think we may just have pulled it off."

"So no, then."

"What do *you* think? Two blokes sitting in a car in the middle of the night, one with a mask – nice touch, by the way, laying it out like that for him to see – and both of us breathing heavily and acting suspiciously as if we've been caught in *flagrante delicto*. And then we feed him a load of old bollocks about counting badgers from the front seats of our car. Oh yeah, we nailed it all right."

"It was the best I could come up with. You weren't exactly brimming with good ideas."

"I know that, but *badgers*? And what the fuck is a *platoon* of badgers?"

"At least I didn't say *consensus*."

"Fair comment. Anyway, the more ridiculous we were, and I think we may have scored rather highly on that score, the more clear the subtext was, and that's what made him go away."

"Subtext?"

"That we're a couple of nice boys who go into woods at night and bum each other senseless but aren't into threesomes. The headgear makes you my gimp, so I guess I'm the dominant one."

"Shit. What if he reports us?"

"I doubt it. 'Yes officer, I was out cruising for gay sex when I saw two blokes sitting in a car counting badgers in the dark.' More likely to end up in a cell himself. He's probably back home with the wife and kids by now."

"You don't think he'll come back?"

"Have you got an alternative location as a back-up?"

"No."

"Then I guess we stay here and hope he doesn't. Not quite the logistic mastermind, are you? Choosing the gay pick-up hot spot of Hertfordshire takes some doing."

"Yeah, well they don't mark that on the map."

They endure an uncomfortable and interminable half hour or so, punctuated with further recriminations and nervous glances in mirrors.

"Come on, we'd better go," says Carl at long last. "Let's get this over with."

They grab their torches, Kevin stuffs the balaclava into a pocket and they traipse along a path as quietly as the arboreal detritus will allow.

It takes Kevin a short while to get his bearings once they reach the lane. He points Carl towards his quarry.

"Synchronise watches?" whispers Kevin.

"You bloody love this, don't you?"

"Trust me, I don't. What time have you got?"

"Almost ten to."

"Be precise."

"Er, eleven minutes to?"

"Right."

"Don't you mean check?"

"What?"

"Nothing. Come on, off you go."

"See you back at the car and... good luck," says Kevin, taking a small step towards Carl. Some form of embrace feels appropriate, but he pulls back and sticks a hand out instead. Carl shrugs, laughs and shakes it.

"Go on, you daft sod. And try not to miss."

*

Kevin enters his haven, pulls the door shut behind him and leans back on it, breathing out lengthily and closing his eyes. But two inches of wood doesn't feel enough to protect him from the clutches of the outside world. The humiliation it visits on him. The tricks it plays. The threat it poses to his cobbled-together defences. He feels exposed, so pushes himself off, triggering flashes of pain across his body, the worst of them doubling him up momentarily with a groan. Catching his breath, he takes his bruised and battered body through to the bathroom, turns on the hot water tap and tilts the bubble bath container, momentarily losing himself in the hypnotically glacial progress of the viscous pink liquid.

He reclines, shifting the back of his head and neck against the edge of the bath until a comfortable enough fit is established, then closes his eyes and lets the heat do its work.

He washes as best able, the dull ache in his shoulder limiting the range of his right hand, the use of the left curtailed by the scuff to the knuckles. As the bubbles expire, they leave port holes of visibility that reveal the reds and purples that now adorn his body. Yanking the plug out, he leans back again, legs raised at an angle, feet flanking the taps at the other end, and once more closes his eyes.

The first sensations from the water's withdrawal come on his chest, the backs of his shoulders and calves. The lightest prickling on his skin. Then the tops of his thighs. Like the patter of tiny caterpillar feet. Working their way slowly towards, then under, his knees before starting down the back of his thighs. At the same time, he feels the first pulling at his chest. Tiny hooks tugging at his skin. As it approaches his crotch, it splits and heads down either side of his stomach. His abdominal muscles tighten at the downturn in temperature. The tingling waves ebb along and round his ribs before joining and moving down his spine. The touch of a feather on his lower back. A tickling commotion in his pubes. Then a lingering caress of his testicles and buttocks before, with a final pinch and gurgle, he's left high and drying.

Unpeeled.

*

His eyes open to a hazy, faintly peachy glow; what's left of the morning sunshine after it has permeated his duvet.

Buried.

Something he normally wouldn't be able to stand, sending him scrabbling to the surface in a mild panic. But right now, Kevin can't think of anywhere he'd rather be. Another layer between him and... everything else.

At first there are no specifics, just the awareness of an approaching dread. He tries to ward it off with a stretch and the conjuring-up of the sideshow of an erection. He's naked. He usually hates that as well, though he has to admit he's enjoying the sensation of cotton on skin and the cool areas of the bed he can unravel into. But each movement brings a new ache or spasm and the first stirring of his groin generates a painful testicular throbbing. The impending tumescence bids a hasty retreat as specifics ambush him and he lets out a long groan, pulling the duvet down tighter over his head and curling into a tight ball.

No matter what he tries, the events of earlier that morning keep replaying in all their slapstick ludicrousness in his mind's eye, his attempts to suppress them no more successful than a cartoon character trying to push in a bump on his head. As a diversion, he searches for compensatory plus points elsewhere, but in doing so only succeeds in dredging up the suppressed memory of that little tête-á-tête at the gym a week earlier. His subconscious mischievously presses *play* and he hasn't the energy to reach for the off switch.

*

"This way please, sir," says the man proclaimed by a shiny badge to be *Grant – Assistant Manager.* He offers Kevin a professional smile, wafting his hand in the direction of a door leading off from behind the reception desk, this simplest of movements enough to cause several muscle groups to press at the cotton of his pristine white shirt. Kevin dislikes him immediately.

"Certainly," says Kevin, with the calm air of someone for whom this is as logical as his next breath, only the hint of a tremor in his voice.

What could there possibly be to worry about?

Nothing at all.

Then why does he feel so hot all of a sudden, as though his self-assurance is leaking away through the pores of his skin?

He follows *Grant – Assistant Manager* through a doorway into an office-cum-storeroom. A girl reluctantly drags her bored gaze from her fingernails and takes the hint, standing up from her desk and heading for the door. Kevin instinctively observes her departing rear, admires the sway and books her in for a guest slot later that day. A cough jolts him back into focus to find *Grant – Assistant Manager* proffering a friendly smile and a hand.

See, nothing to worry about.

Emboldened, Kevin senses an opportunity to assert early in the exchange and goes in for a crusher.

"Ow," he gasps, his hand instinctively retreating to the sanctuary of a damp armpit.

"Sorry about that. I forget my own strength at times."

Like fuck, thinks Kevin, trying to resurrect his mangled digits whilst drawing his elbows in tight to conceal the outward spread of saturated cotton. Game on. Time for a cheap shot.

"I recognise you now. You were just a personal trainer until recently, weren't you?"

"Yes." The assured finality of the response throws Kevin and an intended belittling follow-up catches in his throat. Too late. "Anyway, as I was saying, I thought it best we talk in private and I didn't want to embarrass you in front of your friend."

"Embarrass?" asks Kevin, with thinly-disguised much-disguised disinterest.

"It's a personal matter. Hardly something for public consumption." Kevin forces a smile in vain contradiction of the worrying direction the conversation appears to be heading. "We've had a complaint, sir. A serious complaint we are duty bound to investigate, I'm sure you'll appreciate." Kevin's smile of denial widens yet further. "From another gentleman who was in the shower adjoining yours a little earlier." Kevin's cheeks are hurting by now and he realises his teeth are bared. *Grant – Assistant Manager* appears momentarily disconcerted, but recovers. "Well, actually his son was." *I'm fucked.* But maybe not. Because *Grant – Assistant Manager* and his toned, fucking perfect body is starting to falter. "It's er…" A pause. *He's going to bottle it.* "Um…" *He's looking down at his own feet. Hah, he's weakening.* "He has voiced his suspicion that… er… that you may have been indulging in… um…" Sensing that the very formulation of the words may prove a hurdle too high for *Grant – Assistant Manager* to negotiate, Kevin sniffs an opening and permits himself an internal sneer. He circles, hones in and swoops down for the kill.

"Look, Grant. Do you mind if I call you Grant? Or would you prefer Assistant Manager? Can we please stop all this beating around the bush? We've both got better things to do than pursuing the idle insinuations and misinterpretations of some bloke in the showers. So, unless you have something clear to say, can we please save ourselves some time and——"

"The gentleman is adamant that you were having a wank in the cubicle next to where his five-year-old son was taking a shower. Is that plain enough for you?"

And there he stands, rumbled; wishing he'd never strayed from Planet Innuendo. He dredges up the energy for one final salvo.

"And you believe him? Just like that? His word against mine? That's all you've got?" Voice rising with each feeble syllable, the last word shrill and desperate.

"I had hoped not to have to go into detail."

"Maybe that's because you don't have any, eh?" he retorts.

"He says he clearly heard you say 'oh yes' and there was audible heavy breathing. For Christ's sake, he says you shot your load over the bloody smoked glass screen between the cubicles and then pushed your erection against the glass and let out a moan."

"A moan?" Concentrate on the lesser of many evils.

"A moan."

"A moan." Any chance of the word slipping unnoticed into the wings now long gone.

"Yes."

"Well I deny it."

"The moan?"

"No … yes … but mainly the other … stuff. All of it."

"I found him very persuasive."

"He can prove nothing." He tries a hands-on-hips pose but feels more camp than reinforced. He snaps his hands away, clamps the left on his thigh and waves the right round in the air, before it comes to rest pointing accusatorially at *Grant – Assistant Manager*. All he needs now is an accusation.

Grant – Assistant Manager raises an eyebrow. Kevin now wags the finger. *Grant – Assistant Manager* frowns. Kevin jabs the finger forwards for added emphasis of something he's hoping to think of any second now. *Grant – Assistant Manager* raises both eyebrows. Kevin stumbles over an idea.

"I'm not happy." And starts the search for a better one.

"Look, sir. This is getting us nowhere."

"Maybe there's nowhere to get."

"Maybe, but I think you're not being entirely honest."

"Prove it."

"I had hoped to avoid this, but if that's your approach you leave me no choice but to report the matter to the police and let them have the shower water sample that health and safety regulations demand we routinely retain. Then their CSI forensic department can test it against a sample of your DNA. You'll have to wait for them to arrive and they may have some questions, so we had better let your friend know."

Kevin inputs the stream of data, cranks his befuddled brain into motion, wills it to process what he's just heard and waits for the read-out.

"Fuck it," is the considered conclusion, though possibly it should have remained unspoken.

*

From the snug confines of his togged cocoon he winces at the memory of that moment of surrender when all hope had dribbled down the drain like carelessly discarded semen. His mood is not improved by the niggling suspicion that the CSI line that ultimately snared him was quite possibly total baloney; and the nagging near-certainty that his claimed penile circulatory problem, necessitating thrice-daily painful discharges in warm soapy water under doctor's orders, had been rumbled as early as "circulatory", a word that had expanded to eight syllables by the time he'd given up fumbling with it and started on a rambling and ever-more ridiculous list of symptoms plucked from hazy recollections of every hospital-based TV drama he'd ever watched. Although his excruciating embarrassment had arguably been a price worth paying, propelling *Grant – Assistant Manager* as it did to a place of such desperation that letting Kevin off with a warning, a two-week membership suspension and a promise not to repeat-offend had been a more than workable compromise if it saw the back of this pathological, hypochondriacal nutter with a penis obsession.

So here he lies, oscillating between two taunting traumas, welcoming the distraction of the shots of pain each movement generates.

MONDAY

Andrew takes a back seat during the typically feisty early exchanges and finds Kevin's performance far from convincing. Carl has already filled him in on the events of the previous day. Andrew had listened with a mixture of concern and guilty amusement, before urging Carl to keep quiet and allow Kevin to set his own agenda; which has been to offer nothing, deflecting enquiries about the black eye, plasters and limp with vague references to a child, a bicycle and a collision. The others are too intent on chip accumulation and mental warfare to be bothered to challenge his explanation to any great extent; nor do they appear to notice his forced levity and feigned interest in the hands being played.

But Andrew does.

After two hours of distracted and transparent poker, Kevin ignores a show of strength to his right, calls a raise he should fold to, chases three outs and misses. He disguises his relief with histrionics and a loud bemoaning of the ensuing tea duties, before limping off to the kitchen.

Andrew plays another couple of hands before announcing he's sitting out a while as he has a call to make. He pauses at the door of the kitchen and observes Kevin, eyes closed and deep in reflection, leaning against the counter like a half-filled inflatable struggling to stay vertical.

"How's it going?" There's a tell-tale hesitation before Kevin's eyes open and his head snaps up. "Bad luck with the hand."

"Really?"

"Well no. It was a shite play, as you know full well."

Kevin shrugs and smiles feebly.

"What's up?"

"Nothing. Just tired, that's all."

"Cut the crap. Tell me about Sunday morning, and make it the truth. You look like you're close to breaking and I think it might help to share it with someone."

He is, so he does.

"I had it all so well planned. I'd covered everything, so nothing could go wrong."

"Dressed in black? Balaclava? What the fuck was that all about?" And seeing the puzzled look, he adds, "Carl had a word. He was concerned. Don't worry. It was just him and me. It goes no further."

"I get scared, Andrew. I really do. It might be a bit of a laugh for the rest of you, but some of what we do is pushing it. I mean one wrong step and we could get in serious trouble. I know it sounds pathetic, but that's just the way I feel. It was full-on vandalism. I kept imagining what could happen. Maybe some kids would be having a sleep-over or there might be a dog in the room. And then I got worried about what could go wrong afterwards; who I might run into and so on. I put all that gear on and I felt sort of protected." He pauses and shakes his head.

"Then what?" says Andrew softly, tentatively spinning the metaphorical plate before it crashes to the floor.

"It bounced."

"What did?"

"The bus, brick thing. I threw it and it bounced back off the window. Maybe all that worrying meant I held back a bit, but it should never have bounced. I just stood there for a second and then had to find the bloody thing. I was scrabbling about on the patio, scared stiff a light would go on. Then finally I found it, took a run up and threw it as hard as I could. Fortunately it smashed this time, but there was this odd noise from inside that made me pause. I moved forward a few steps to have a closer look, this security light came on and there I was, lit up and standing there like a lemon. I just legged it... and fell off the patio into a bush. I lay there to see if anything hurt and then scrambled out and got to my feet. But that sodding balaclava had got twisted round and I couldn't see a fucking thing. I'm trying to find the eyeholes and I hear this voice coming from inside the house, so I just turned and ran. I knew it was lawn, so I thought it would be all right, but there was this bloody concrete ornament or something in the middle, no more than three feet tall, and I just ran straight into it. More like onto it actually. One minute I'm running and the next it's like someone's kneed me in the balls and I'm bent over the fucking thing. Then we topple over and I'm lying on the ground in excruciating pain gasping for breath. I've had it before, but nothing like this. You know what it's like. You want to vomit. You feel faint. Well this was worse. I just wanted to curl up and die, but a woman shouted something, then a bloke, so I pulled myself up and hobbled off as fast as I could. I decided the shortest route would be through the hedge along the front of the house as I'd noticed on one of my recces – why are you smiling? Anyway, I'd noticed it was pretty thin, but what I hadn't seen was the low wooden fence running through it, so that didn't go well either. By now I'd taken the balaclava off and I just ran into the woods, completely lost my bearings and ended up running about like a prat until I finally got lucky and found where we'd left the car. It's *not funny*, Andrew."

Andrew and Carl find themselves going heads up a few hours later, with the matter of over four hundred quid to resolve. Pete pockets his third-place prize with absurdly misplaced triumphalism, makes his excuses and leaves. As do the others as they get tired of feigning good grace and interest in a game that no longer involves them, disappearing into the early hours to nurture their grievances.

All bar Kevin, who wordlessly offers to deal.

If either Carl or Andrew find this out-of-character selfless gesture strange, neither of them say so. But they do agree to split the pot after a dozen or so silent hands, and Carl heads off.

Kevin half-heartedly collects together the chips, then stalls.

Remembering that look on Andrew's face in the kitchen.

Feeling the need to provide some context.

Background; by way of explanation.

Which he does – all the way back to Nethercott.

NETHERCOTT

(1989-1993)

Derek Arthur Clarke was a weak man. And lest he ever forget it, his wife Angie was on hand to remind him at every opportunity.

It hadn't always been that way. Once she had loved him, and loved him for who he was, not who he might become. And nor had she despised him for what he had never been. That came later. Who he was when they met was a salesman. Who he might have become was a regional, maybe one day national, sales manager. What he became, or rather remained, was a salesman.

But there was a time when she did love him. Only later would she realise that what she had most loved about him was what he was not.

Her father had been a man of dreams and he had pursued those dreams with scant regard for the financial or emotional wellbeing of his family. At the outset, the dreams were of business deals struck, of angles seen and exploited, of goods acquired cheap and sold for huge profits. And when the margins failed to materialise, he turned instead to fantasies of horses and greyhounds winning races and the investments became more and more speculative. Angie spent her childhood watching her mother struggling to make do with what scraps came her way, trying desperately to provide some solidity and certainty for her children amidst the shifting sands of her husband's whims and fancies.

Angie's memories of her father were of long periods of absence punctuated very occasionally by fleeting and intense contact defined by his wildly fluctuating moods. There were good times, no more so than when he'd whisk her up in his arms and swing her around, legs flailing in the air behind her, his beaming face the only reference point in a world gone blurry. In that dizzying moment she'd be sure everything had changed and would now be fine. And then his smile would fade, his mind could be seen to drift, and with it would go her hopes… until the next, tantalising time.

As she grew older, she grew wiser to his ways, but he never lost that ability to build up her hopes and then crush them with his self-obsession. Even on his deathbed, he'd still held the balance of power as she waffled on about a family he'd so abjectly failed in the hope that some spark would dissipate the rheumy pools of his eyes and a moment of reconciliation might be achieved; that he'd recognise his errors and somehow make everything *right*. But when his eyes did clear and his mottled, frail hands jerked into life, it was only to push the merits of the latest get-rich-quick scheme. To the very end, he succeeded only in failing them.

Angie and Derek had started courting by that time. She never understood exactly what it was he sold, who he sold it to, or how he did it. What mattered was that he had a salaried position, a commission plan, a Ford Cortina, a defined career trajectory and a pile of shirts to be ironed each Sunday evening. Stability personified. The very antithesis of her recently-deceased father. An anchor; not the storm.

She got pregnant – "an accident" she lied to everyone, Derek included – and he asked her to marry him because he was decent and that was what decent men did. She said yes and the photographer outside the registry office was very understanding, extending the legs on his tripod and cutting all the photos off above the unmentionable bump. Wouldn't do to tarnish the memories.

Belinda was born – a name from a book Angie had liked as a child – and her mother babysat for them as they headed off one Saturday evening in December. For Derek's job brought perks, and none better than the annual Christmas Dinner Dance cum awards do. His third. Their first. The firm's fortieth. Which meant somewhere special. Not the upstairs room at the local Italian like the previous year, where a lack of space had meant no invites to partners. No, somewhere very special: The Savoy. She had indeed married a man of substance; a man whose employer thought highly enough of him and his fellow employees to hire out a huge, grandiose room in the poshest building she had ever been to.

A revolving door, no less, like a portal between two worlds: their reality and this potential. Coats exchanged with a polite young lady for a numbered ticket. Pause for a photograph. A "good evening" from someone obviously important. A floor plan. Their table, at the back, but where better from which to view the magnificent room. Twelve to the table. Nice people. The men joking, discussing wine – where did Derek learn about wine? – drinking it, asking for more, drinking it; moving on to spirits; removing jackets, foreheads glistening with sweat; cigars offered from expensive-looking wooden boxes and lit by waiters – where did Derek learn how to smoke cigars? Much enthusiastic clapping and cheering as awards are dished out to people she doesn't know, but Derek seems to; *her* Derek, an integral component in this sparkling machine. The wives and girlfriends smile when observed and compare when not, nervously fiddling with earrings and bracelets; wary when it comes to selecting cutlery or deciding when to start eating; not getting the in-jokes but laughing anyway; relieved the attention is not on them. They all lean forward over the table as the photographer tells them to "say cheeeeese". Laughter and smiles. Derek's arm draped across her shoulders. A happy day. The happiest of days. This is where she belongs. The past escaped. It holds no sway over their future.

The photographs arrived in the New Year. The two of them before the meal and one of the whole table. She didn't much like the way her dress clung to a body that had never recovered fully from the pregnancy and birth, but she bought bright orange and lime green frames and they took pride of place on the sideboard. Wonderful memories. Celebrations of what they had achieved together. Of where they were heading.

The following December saw them back at the Savoy, such a success that it's now a fixture.

Another outfit. More photos. Some of the same faces as last year on their table. Connections remade. The other women tell her she looks "marvellous". She very much doubts it, considering she gave birth only weeks before, to Rachel; Derek had wanted Raquel, necessitating a hasty compromise. She doesn't feel marvellous. She feels abused. Exhausted. Emptied. But this is Derek's night, so she fixes a smile and plays her part. Knows there will not be a third. Can't be. That's her lot.

Years pass. Themes change. Outfits change. The faces at their table change. But it's always The Savoy and that must prove something. An annual yardstick to reinforce the distance travelled.

So here she sits at yet another table. Pregnant. Unwittingly, carelessly, hopelessly pregnant. The baby she doesn't need. The baby she doesn't want. The baby that has her wearing some god-awful smock thing. No flattery coming her way this year. And Derek drinking;

laughing; oblivious. That drunken roll-on-roll-off encounter he's long-forgotten; the start and end of it all. Him invasive. Her invaded. The act done to her, not with her. Him spent and snoring. She knew right then. His seed infecting her, a ticking time bomb echoing in her mind. And the start of her nightmare – not his, hers – that leaves her fat and tearful and tired and unattractive and lonely.

And in this state, the veil lifts. She searches the room for familiar faces from previous years and locates them one by one, all nearer the stage than her peripheral vantage point. Eyes meet and are at once averted. What is that? Embarrassment? Pity? One woman does hold her gaze and smiles, but the smile is empty. And in this way the strata are revealed; a rock face teeming with climbers fighting their way to the top. But Derek is not among them. He's looking after the equipment at the bottom. She looks back at her table. All much younger than Derek, his hairline receding already. Trying to keep up with the other men – more like boys – as they fill and empty glasses, accosting polite but weary waiters for more. The gentle goading and casual dismissal of Derek's overly eager attempts to hijack conversations he doesn't understand comes not from fondness or kinship. He is clearly not their superior; he is their equal, rendered inferior and faintly ridiculous by having taken so many more years to get to where they are. They have no respect for this old man; the father of this baby that is eating away at her and sucking her dry. A rope tethering the hot air balloon of her hopes and ambitions to the ground. She feels no protectiveness towards Derek, no indignation. Just a growing realisation that here is another man who will ultimately fall short and disappoint her.

Because of course it's all been an illusion. She wanted stable. She got static. She rejected risk and chose instead to stash her cash under the mattress, but inflation has seen the value of her investment deteriorate.

From somewhere deep inside she summoned up the compassion not to judge, the perspective to see a bright side and the patience to play a long game; but they were superficial emotions, beneath which stronger and more painful feelings swirled and eddied. She knew that. But to give them precedence would only have dragged her below the surface and what good would that have done anyone. She had to remain strong.

*

A son is born.

Derek surprises her, and himself, by being present. He says nice things. He absorbs her tightening fingers, her swearing and the unreasonable requests for miraculous pain abatement. He takes the snivelling, bloodied, towelled bundle in his arms and his face lights up. And in that moment, he is a good man again. And she will not let him down. He is faulted. But he is hers. She says he can choose the name and they have a Kevin, named, she hears him tell a doctor, after a footballer. Boys will be boys, it seems. Thank heaven for her girls.

And her reward, years later?

She fears the worst the moment he arrives home from work one Tuesday evening – before seven o'clock is unheard of – with alcohol on his breath, sweat dotting his forehead and steely intent furrowing his brow; a determination to get *this* over as quickly and painlessly as possible, at least for him.

They've not been happy for ages, he tells her. They should both be happy. The kids come first. It can't be good for them to see their parents so unhappy. They're both still young enough to have a chance to rebuild their lives. To be happy. For the kids. And when she shakes her head and reddens and pours scorn on this stream of bland, self-serving platitudes, he loses his temper at a plan foiled – at her deviation from his script – and hits her with the cruel stuff; hits her hard. He doesn't love her anymore. He doesn't fancy her anymore. She's let herself go. Not looked after herself. Not made an effort. She's cold in bed. He's only human. He's a man with needs and she just doesn't seem interested anymore. Sandra – *who the hell is Sandra?* – makes him happy. She understands him. She wants him. She makes him feel young again.

Seeing he's inflicting too much damage, he backs off into the comfort zone of practicalities. He'll not be walking out on his responsibilities. He'll provide as best he can. Wants to do his best with the kids. Have them weekends, maybe. Well, when he's not busy that is. Whatever suits her best. Important their father remains a big part of their lives. The kids come first. They're all that matter. And anyway, Sandra loves children.

"Fuck you." She can't recall ever using that ugly word before.

"Look, love…"

"Don't you bloody *love* me. And don't you bloody bring that slut's name into this house."

"There's no need for that. You don't know her. You'd like—"

"Don't you dare tell me what I'd like."

"I'm just saying…"

"Well don't. I'll tell you what you're going to be saying," she shouts. "Kids. Come and say goodbye to your dad. He's leaving us. Going off with some tart. Isn't *that* great."

"I'll be in touch," he throws back unconvincingly over his shoulder. A door slams and he's gone.

"What's happened, Mum?" asks Belinda, emerging from a darkened doorway, trailing a blinking Kevin in her wake. A car engine starts, revs and then disappears into the distance.

"Where's Daddy?" asks Kevin, his lower lip trembling.

*

The deceit hadn't started with Sandra, but a year or so earlier when Derek was sacked from his job.

Ask his line manager, and he'd never been a salesman in anything other than job title. Whatever talents he might have possessed, getting businesses to bulk order plastic products via him was most definitely not one of them; his apathy for the product pervading every limp attempt to convince potential customers. His chief redeeming quality was a low-maintenance familiarity; more an integral constituent of the fabric of the company, than a functioning part. It proved sufficient to skirt the swing of the axe and see him alight in the customer-free zone of the accounts department, where he was transmogrified into an assistant bought ledger clerk – as with university degree courses, the longer the title, the lesser the worth – a role for which he proved remarkably suited; his listless passivity and deficiency of acuity the perfect tools in the frustration and delaying of suppliers chasing payment, and the antithesis of the credit controllers across the room, with their remorseless hectoring and badgering of customers.

On the downside, his transfer came with a salary cut and the loss of a commission plan that, whilst he'd rarely troubled it beyond the slightest of sporadic increments to his wage packet, had at least alluded to the kind of package that could hold its head above water at a dinner party. Now he plotted a near-horizontal career progression trajectory, but the biggest bugbear was the week's notice to return the company car, that most visible of status symbols.

People react to setbacks in some very strange ways, and Derek's failure to come clean with Angie that very first night was stranger than most. Cowardice and pride had a lot to do with it, only abetted on arriving home to hear Angie on the phone to her mother yet again proclaiming – less glowing pride these days, more clinging by the fingertips – the merits of her husband's vocation, painting a picture of slow-burning ascendancy even after so many years of inertia. He hadn't the heart to disappoint; nor the guts to confess. So he took the easy option; as he always did.

With each day it got easier to deceive and harder to envisage coming clean. He took a staff loan and bought himself a third-hand car that he hoped would maintain the illusion of constancy. The five o'clock end to his working day was a logistical problem, but he grew to enjoy the early evening naps in lay-bys and car parks; in any case Angie was so much better at that whole early evening feeding and bedtime chaos and he'd only mess up her tried and tested routine if he interposed himself.

The immediate curtailment of the nationwide travel and frequent overnight trips that had characterised his time as a salesman were a further challenge. So once every fortnight he would take a room in a small B&B on the other side of town for one or two mid-week nights.

His occasional landlady was called Sandra. With Derek usually being the only guest, and them both feeling lonely – him within and her without a relationship – they talked. He compounded the magnitude of his omission in not telling Angie the truth with his easy readiness to reveal all to Sandra. Over the months he came to view the B&B as his haven and home as the deceit. Sandra enjoyed the company and he enjoyed what he hypocritically saw as the honesty of their relationship. She played the slow game and a year or so later snared her man as the hinting and innuendo was finally acted upon. Once again, Derek had proven himself to be slow on the uptake.

It took him another two years to pluck up the courage to walk out on his family and the arid, featureless desert of his marriage.

Although he had been promoted to bought ledger manager by the time he walked, Derek's was now a world of invariable relative impoverishment and his solicitor had little trouble keeping the maintenance payments down to a manageable level. Angie argued for Sandra's income to be taken into account, but the B&B made little official profit and her true *worth* was more potential than actual, hidden as it was in the properties, bank accounts and share portfolios of various antecedents who, emotionally maimed by their own childhood experiences, had taken the collective decision not to breed, Sandra the sole anomaly.

A few years after the decree absolute had been signed, Aunt Agnes, whom Sandra hadn't met in over a decade, shuffled off her mortal coil and the day after a funeral that she'd manufactured an excuse not to attend, Sandra was informed by a solicitor that she was the principal beneficiary. There was a spot of bother with a dog sanctuary that claimed they had been assured of a sizeable legacy, and the rambling Dorset mansion took a while to sell, but the end result was financial security.

Derek wasn't so much consumed by guilt at the overall turn of events, as lightly licked, and managed to assuage what little guilt did permeate the inheritance-induced haze by dedicating a sizeable chunk of the money to the ongoing benefit of the family he had, after all, abandoned. That he chose to spend it for them on the education of his only son worked for him on so many levels.

YEAR 1

Nethercott Hall nestles in over a hundred acres of Gloucestershire countryside and for at least three times as many years has done its well-remunerated best to hand-select the more financially-privileged and able thirteen-year-olds in the land in order to *assist them in the navigation of the choppy seas of puberty and through to the calmer waters of adulthood, bestowing upon them during the course of their five-year stay the many gifts of knowledge and experience that will stand them in good stead as they embark upon the voyage of adulthood.*

Having flogged the naval metaphor to death, the prospectus refuses to let up, gushing forth in prose as glossy as the paper it adorns: *a fine and much envied academic tradition specialising in the arts and delivered by a staff of leading exponents at the vanguard of their profession, an unrivalled heritage in the core sports of football, rugby and cricket and an array of extramural activities ranging from bridge and chess through the entire physical gamut to real tennis, fives and the much vaunted CCF corps.*

At the helm of this educational galleon for some thirty-three years has stood its headmaster, Sir Reginald

Shawcross; the title given for suitably vague *services to education* courtesy of a junior Conservative cabinet minister and Old Nethercotian – the soft t's having defeated the hard tt's in the famous pronunciation vote of 1934 – who had made the mistake, at the tender age of fifteen, not of indulging in homosexual fumblings, but of being caught engaging in said fumblings by an ambitious young Latin teacher who knew when it was prudent to lay down a secret and let it mature for another day.

Sir Reginald's tenure was further secured by a purported bloodline – witness the elegantly-scripted family tree in the sealed glass display case in the vaulted entrance hall – tracing back to the Earl of Nethercott himself, in whose former residence the school luxuriates. A D-lister at best, the Earl of Nethercott had more than made up for what he lacked in fame or notable achievement with inherited wealth and ceaseless self-publication. The walls of the communal areas of the school were crowded with paintings celebrating the life and passions of an unprepossessing, pug-nosed man in all manner of '*Boys Own*' poses.

Upon first entering the school, visitors are treated to a twenty-foot by twelve-foot portrait of the Earl seated on what appears to be a throne and bestowing a withering glare of constipated disdain on all who pass beneath him. As you shrink away, there he is again above the fireplace, this time in scarlet military uniform with his legs planted wide apart, their angle bisected by a huge sword he would doubtless have struggled to lift, let alone wield to any practical effect.

On his first day, a month after his fourteenth birthday and a week into the summer term, Kevin arrived with his father during the becalmed quiet of lesson two, the incumbent pupils secreted away in their classrooms. This facilitated an unrealistically serene and peaceful sweep up the grandiose mile-long drive curving its way between the fifteenth and sixteenth holes, past the 1st XI cricket pitch awakening from its nine-month hibernation, before emerging from a rhododendron-swamped bend to deposit them in the huge gravelled area stretched out before the ornate splendour of Nethercott Hall.

The eerie near-silence was unsettling for a nerve-wracked Kevin, their crunching footsteps sounding obscenely loud as they approached a revolving front door that spat them out into the cool, varnish-smelling, echoing vastness of the entrance hall.

Kevin's bottom squeaked as he slid onto one of the twin leather sofas which — save for a prospectus-laden coffee table, a display unit that looked like it belonged in a museum, a couple of large potted ferns and an incomprehensible sculpture titled "Plunge Forth" — were the only items in a room of cathedral proportions. A clock tocked ponderously somewhere out of sight. He attempted polite conversation with his father, his faltering voice betraying his studied mask of casual indifference.

The introductory meeting with the Head was a one-sided affair. Sir Reginald mustered up a front of enthusiasm he didn't feel, but frequently lost his way as he meandered half-heartedly through an oft-delivered spiel of directionless waffle designed to strike a mixture of awe and respect into the snivelling new pupil before him. Phrases such as "seat of learning", "moulding minds" and "maximising the student's potential" made dramatic entrances, inducing frantic nods from Kevin and his father. Finally, apathy won over professional duty and the Headmaster's weary rhetoric faltered. He gratefully pressed an intercom button and summoned a Mr Flanders.

An effeminate man looking exactly how a Mr Flanders should look flounced in, trailing in his wake a timid little creature whose hands fluttered together nervously in front of his chest, an excited smile playing on his thin lips.

Mr Flanders was introduced as Kevin's form master and his young companion as Morris, a fellow classmate and resident of C Dormitory who would be showing Kevin the ropes on his first morning, and chaperoning him through what remained of the summer term. Morris peered out from behind his teacher's gesticulating frilly cuff to give a little wave and flash a smile, the sheer unabashed exuberance of which dispelled the apprehension and fears that had laid cramping siege to Kevin's stomach for the past few days.

Seizing the moment, and after a brief and awkward farewell, his father abandoned his son to the vagaries of a purchased and largely recourse-less education. But not before heaving out of the back of his estate and half-lifting, half-dragging across the gravel the vast standard issue packing case (compulsory; just the one vendor, a close friend of the Head; high mark-up, small kick-back to the 'school'; no discernible design progression, the addition of wheels having been dismissed as at odds with *ye olde* feel of the place, not to mention cutting into the margin). The thirty-yard journey brought swear words to his lips and sweat to every crease on his body, and it was with immense relief that he deposited the ridiculous object at the foot of the concrete steps, as instructed, for ongoing transit, presumably by the entire 1st XV pack. As he followed the smear in the gravel back to his car, easing out the tightness in his shoulders and lower back, he couldn't help but nurture a relish at the very public school-ness of it all. Already getting value for money.

As he swung the car round, taking in the magnificent frontage one last time, and made for his escape, he honourably did his best to conduct a balanced debate as to whether this whole exercise was about doing the best for his son, winding up his ex-wife or assuaging his own guilt. Whilst his powers of self-deceit concentrated on guaranteeing the *right* outcome, delicious sensations of personal space, distance and yes, revenge – though for what he'd have been hard pressed to say – permeated his defences and brought a smirk to his face.

Meanwhile Kevin, henceforth required by school rules – on pain of detention – to be known solely as Clarke within school boundaries, was being taken on a guided tour of the establishment by Morris. They wandered through the warren of corridors and communal rooms, up and down flights of polished wooden stairs, snatching glimpses of class after class of pupil hunched over desks through small latticed windows in doors. Other windowless doors hinted at all manner of hidden worlds. It was dizzying, daunting yet exciting, not in the least because of the infectious enthusiasm of his companion. Never before had he come across someone so overtly friendly. Morris was happy here, and so would he be. It really did seem that simple.

The tour ended with a stroll across to the dormitory blocks: four identical, modern, rectangular eyesores that accommodated the first and second years; set apart from the main buildings in architectural disgrace, sent to a distant corner of the site where they sulked incongruously.

"We're in Pitt," said Morris redundantly as they passed under a sign bearing an elegantly scripted *Pitt,* through a door into a dark room lined with named pigeon holes, squeaked along a corridor, squeaked round a corner and turned left with a squeak into a long room whose otherwise immaculate symmetrical order was blotted by what could only be his case lurking at the foot of the bed nearest the door.

"You're next to me," said Morris. "New boys usually get the beds by the door. I actually don't mind being this end. Some of the lads up the other end can be real crazy jokers at times and they can get up to more high jinks away from the door. I can play the fool too, of course, if I want – have them all laughing – but I'm not as nuts as some of them. Anyway, we can have just as much fun, you wait and see. We'll show them."

Clarke's bed was the only one unmade; a striped mattress adorned with a small pile of stiff-looking linen and a naked stained pillow. A breathless and wordy lesson in the art of bed-making followed, a brief intermission in the running commentary on life at Nethercott, which then recommenced apace.

"Pretty much everything is done in houses here. Not houses like buildings," he giggles, "houses like... er, you know... houses." More giggling. "We're all Coleridge in here and so's everyone in 'D' next door. We all have yellow stripes on our ties. The two dorms on the other side are Spenser. They've got red stripes. Milton and Clive are blue and green. They're in Gladstone, the next building." And on he went. Too much detail delivered too quickly, but Clarke lapped it up.

A percussion of footfall in the distance reminded Morris that lesson three was about to start. Clarke quickly transferred the contents of his case to the wardrobe and drawers and pushed the now empty case under his bed, there to stay untouched on threat of corporal punishment until the last day of term. The two boys left the dorm block and wandered towards the main building, twittering excitedly, Kevin's nerves and homesickness dissipating fast.

*

Morris proved to be his inside track on every rule, tradition and nuance of Nethercott Hall, and the remainder of the term flew past. Without the prep school booster assumed of all students, Latin and Greek proved as incomprehensible to Clarke as the rules of cricket and he struggled with the rudiments of all three, with negligible success. The two of them drifted happily through the weeks.

Clarke's favourite place was the refectory, where he curiously came closest to elite sporting activity. With the exception of a large portrait of the good Earl – a rare informal scene finding him on one knee, outstretched hand resting on the head of a dog, the look on his face a disconcerting cocktail of love, authority and intent; that on the dog's one of uneasy apprehension – the ubiquitous wood panelling was plastered with a myriad of coloured shields each displaying a year, the name of a 1st XI or XV and the players in that team. Rugby, football, hockey and cricket all featured, each with their own colour. Like so many other pupils before him, Clarke would spend meal after meal scanning the shields, looking for names appearing in more than one sport or year; knowing his would never feature amongst these faceless legends.

Morris appeared to have taken upon himself the role of dorm jester, always playing the fool, talking in silly voices and allowing himself to be the butt of jokes, all of which he took in good, pink-faced humour.

It was Morris who incorporated a burp in the customary "here, Sir" at roll call. Morris who substituted salt for sugar on the staff table in the refectory. Morris who always farted the longest and loudest after lights-out. Morris who followed through one night with a betraying squelch and, faced with a night lying in his own faeces, owned up, shuffled off to the toilets and entered folklore. Morris who in Physics plugged his poorly-wired practice plug into a live socket and shorted out the entire science block. Morris who sang in all manner of silly voices at assembly. Morris who ensured his "amen" outlasted everyone else's by a few seconds. Morris who tiptoed lightly about the dorm blocks turning on lights in the middle of the night.

And on those occasions when he was caught, it was Morris who shrugged his shoulders, reddened, smiled resignedly and trudged along to the headmaster's office to hear of his punishment.

It was also Morris whose trousers flew at the top of the flagpole on Speech Day. Morris whose clothes regularly disappeared from the changing rooms during games; on one occasion, in Clarke's absence, sending him scurrying naked across the lawns back to the dormitory, one hand cupped over his genitals, the other covering as much of his backside as its desperate span could manage. Morris who was regularly sent flying by outstretched legs. Morris whose shrill voice was remorselessly mocked in class. Morris who unzipped his pencil case a minute into the end of year biology exam to find his pencils leadless, his biros inkless and his ruler snapped in six. Morris who Clarke, on returning from a night-time wee and before an audience of fourteen craning necks and twenty-seven sparkling eyes – Smith had a lazy one – released from the cramped confines of the case tucked under his bed; the escapee emerging blinking back tears, shakily exclaiming "That was a good one, you guys. Up to your old tricks, eh Marsh?"

Not all physical exercise was off-limits. Clarke's principal achievement in his first term was to gain widespread acknowledgement as the fastest wanker on C dorm; no mean feat for someone who had arrived so late in the year, a masturbatory virgin. Not once did he lose a biscuit race and face the salty snack of shame. At the Year 1 Wank-Olympdicks, he shot to glory in the blue riband '100 metre spurt' and came away with a silver and bronze in the 'high jerk' and 'long jerk' respectively. "A whitewash of medals within your grasp," as one wag put it.

A love affair with public school had begun. A place where boys were boys, teachers were men and the only women were menial task-performing cooks, lunch ladies and cleaners of no discernible physical appeal; apart that is from the buxom, pouting, ever-willing sirens adorning the well-thumbed, tacky pages of the never-ending supply of pornographic magazines that circulated the dorms.

In the belief that parents had paid for the right not to be over-burdened with time-consuming and excessive detail, the annual school report was an exercise in begrudged minimalism and the abrogation of responsibility, culminating in three brief statements.

Head of PE: a paucity of effort; no discernible talent.

Form teacher: Clarke only joined us at the commencement of the Summer term but has settled in well enough.

Headmaster: a satisfactory, if unspectacular, start by a boy who has clearly been ill-served by state education.

*

Returning home was a shock, and not just for him. The interjection, after almost three months, of a male presence into a female world that had yet further strengthened their collective metaphorical hymen against the proddings and probings of the opposite sex proved difficult for all.

At first, they listened with feigned enthusiasm as Kevin prattled on enthusiastically about all things Nethercott. But after the measured politeness of that first day, the same old veil descended upon the house.

Of indifference.

Of difference.

Salvation for all came a few weeks later with an invite from Morris to spend ten days with him and his parents at their holiday cottage on the Cornwall coast.

Those ten days were the highlight of the summer break and a wondrous insight into what family life could be like. Mr and Mrs Morris insisted on being Trevor and Nancy. He and Morris metamorphosed into Kevin and Charlie. And time passed in a joyous Blytonesque blur of long winding walks down to and up from beaches, sandcastles, building dams, picnics, sailing trips, cream teas and laughter. Lots of laughter.

The evenings were spent on the enclosed veranda playing games, Kevin relishing each slurp of his shandy; the only sounds the scratching of pencils on paper, the click and clack of playing pieces, gentle banter and the occasional thud of a moth against the windows.

He was introduced to bridge, Trevor and Nancy hardly able to hide their glee at Charlie having a partner-in-making. With great patience they taught Kevin the rudiments of the game and by the end of the holiday, he and Charlie were 'talking' basic Acol to each other.

There was something very special about the small green baize-covered table bathed in light, the shininess and crispness of the cards, the strict protocol, the covert communication and the quiet; save for the bidding, post-mortems and occasional "double," "redouble" or "thank you partner". It all seemed so very adult. Rubbers. Talking as equals. Pots of Earl Grey or Darjeeling. Plates of biscuits. Staying up well past midnight.

On the last morning, as they loaded up the car, Nancy gave Kevin a hug and announced herself overjoyed that Charlie had found such a wonderful friend, before turning away to deal with something caught in her eye; affording Kevin a welcome opportunity to disguise a confusing erection.

*

The rest of the holidays were spent in more subdued circumstances with his father and Sandra; a well-intentioned, choreographed traipse through cinemas, London tourist attractions and the west coast of Ireland that left him desperate for a return to Nethercott Hall.

YEAR 2

Overjoyed to find themselves again in the same form and dorm, Clarke and Morris started the new school year as they'd finished the last, primarily in contemplating or enthusiastically engaging in the act of self-relief at the merest provocation or opportunity.

With masturbation a given year-round pastime, what differentiated the winter term from any other was football, the point of which escaped Morris and Clarke entirely. Hands invariably in pockets, they ambled aimlessly about a muddy pitch twice a week in what amounted to the remedial group; although even as politically tactless and beyond censure an institution as Nethercott Hall would have shied from calling it as much, opting instead for the ludicrously optimistic appellation of 'Development Group.' Its protagonists took on the appearance of convalescing, shell-shocked war veterans being allowed a supervised wander on the sanatorium lawn, the ball a largely stationary inconvenience more likely to trip than inspire, goals occurring less often than full moons, and even then, only through some freak and unintentional convergence of limbs, laces and leather.

January brought rugby, the school's flagship sport and that Marmite of all disciplines. You either got it, willingly throwing yourself about and rejoicing in intimacy with friends and foe alike, or you didn't. And Clarke and Morris most definitely didn't. Whereas in football they had occasionally altered course towards the ball and even achieved fleeting contact with it, rugby demanded the use of hands that were often cold and came with the implied imperative of bodily contact with other boys. Consequently, those lower echelons on the school-wide physical and coordination scale treated the egg-shaped ball like a live grenade. It came with unwanted attention and the threat of imminent assault, and the merest movement in an individual's general direction, even a flail of arms at a distance or a slightly threatening noise, was normally enough to see them relinquish the ball with an "uhhrr." Occasionally a ball-carrier might inadvertently succeed in sending the ball backwards, but more often than not it would either go straight up in the air or be pushed forward towards the perceived threat like a hastily arranged peace offering.

Incidences of actual physical contact, let alone tackling, were extremely rare, and seldom intentional. Bodies would attain the horizontal, often for minutes at a time, and usually as a result of tripping over their own feet in frantic retreat from the ball, or simply a tiring of the inconvenience of verticality. Highlights of the first few weeks included Pattison falling asleep and Morris being handed the ball, breaking into a run, falling over the halfway line and proclaiming excitedly that he'd scored a "try-thingy."

If football had been exercise time at the sanatorium, those early rugby sessions were more *Dawn of the Living Dead*.

However, by the end of the term, and despite Morris's protestations, Clarke found himself starting to enjoy the feel of the ball in his hands and of bouncing through a bagatelle of scared faces, half-heartedly out-flung arms and retreating bodies. So much so that he was drafted in for the final match of the house round robin competition. With the Coleridge contingent of year two numbering thirty-two, his selection raised the probability of Clarke being above the fiftieth percentile in a sporting activity other than masturbation.

With the summer term came a further spell in the sporting wilderness, until recognition of Clarke's promise in the field of mathematics saw him drafted in as scorer for the U15A cricket team. So pleased was the manager to escape his usual burden of scoring on a clipboard whilst umpiring or standing at square leg, that he acceded readily to Clarke's request that Morris be permitted to accompany him as his assistant.

Their ascent from rank incompetence to calm assurance was rapid, the sport's manifold intricacies proving manna from heaven for two borderline nerds with keen mathematical minds. The scorebook was a treasure trove of opportunity to measure, grade and analyse. In came the times and overs in which batsmen arrived and departed, as did their dot balls and consequently the number of balls faced. And as the level of detail increased, so did the interest from their own players, fuelled by the many rivalries that dominate a team sport for individuals and the constant search by each player for that statistic – there's always one – that favours them the most over their teammates. Even Cooper-Williams, a number eleven batsman who very occasionally bowled the variety of spin that didn't and was a liability in the field, could boast a Houdini-like sequence of sixty-three consecutive dot balls.

However, their eyes were truly opened to the glory that could be theirs by Uppingham's scorer, and his coloured pens.

Granted supervised access to the school stationery room, they came away with two packets of ten extra fine tip marker pens in a kaleidoscope of colours. A flash of them on the minibus brought immediate interest, followed by pandemonium once they announced that each bowler was to be allotted a different colour to record every ball they bowled. As the players fought for their preferences, they were at once a part of the team, welcomed to the inner sanctum.

The pens brought them influence and power. The next match's scorebook was a kaleidoscopic triumph and spawned another slew of ultimately meaningless trends, statistics, boasts and rivalries. Freshly-routed batsmen headed straight for them for whatever praise or solace the scorebook might offer. Uninvolved batsmen made frequent visits to wallow or envy in the then incumbents' performances. And as the team traipsed off after fielding, it was to the scorers that the bowlers instinctively drifted.

*

Head of PE: lacks coordination. The school cricket team were well served with the scorebook in his hands.

Form teacher: it has been my second year with the form and Clarke has begun to prosper, albeit quietly. A fine mathematician and a popular form member.

Headmaster: a pleasing contribution to the year. Member of junior chess team and formed a promising bridge pair with Morris. Is clearly a mathematician of some promise.

*

The summer holiday started off badly with a call on the very first day from a tearful Morris, reluctantly withdrawing the invitation to a repeat Cornwall trip for reasons unspecified. And with that went Kevin's oasis; the only watering hole in the barren domestic wilderness stretching into the distance. And without the distractions of Christmas or revision that had made the last two holidays just about palatable, hostilities soon resumed. The gender gap widened into more of a chasm, and no one was that interested in trying to bridge it.

In just a year, as if to taunt them, Kevin had grown four inches taller, put on over a stone, sprouted hair in new places and now needed to shower every day. Oozing adolescent masculinity from every pore and orifice, the insertion of his lumpy, awkward frame into the feminine sanctuary that was term-time home life proved a shock to all; not helped each morning by the sight of him traipsing through the kitchen, arms loaded with sheets and the occasional sock, to load up the washing machine.

Faced with this very physical presence, a representative of the never-to-be-trusted-again male race, his mother and sisters had regrouped, their new battle strategy one of rejoicing and wallowing in their womanhood.

The functional furniture and bold colours had been replaced by all things pink, floral, fluffy and frilly. The bathroom overflowed with tampons, make-up, make-up remover and 'smellies'. Conversation majored on period pains, menstrual flow, men who were dishy, a man who was a bastard, men who could be trusted, a man who couldn't be, women they admired... the woman they despised.

Angie very much doubted, as she resignedly prodded at a saggy abdomen variegated with stretch marks, that the *lovely Sandra's* body cascaded southwards when *she* stood naked in front of the mirror. And that final kick in the teeth: she'd enriched him, and in doing so validated his decision to abandon them.

By now, she was struggling just to get by, taking a job in a library to supplement the meagre maintenance payments, the books a constant reminder of the educational achievements denied her by circumstance; the absence of her son for months at a time a constant reminder of the wealth denied her; her empty bed a constant reminder of her foolish naivety and misplaced trust.

Belinda worked behind a bar in town five nights a week, whilst completing her degree at a local college. Rachel had wanted to take a year off after A Levels, but that had been abandoned as she waited for her results, and her first choice of university had been replaced by one no more than a daily commute away.

"We're comfortable enough," Angie would say, attempting a saintly stance that rarely hid the resentment. "Just don't go expecting any luxuries."

Kevin's annual Nethercott school fees exceeded the total disposable income of the Clarkette household.

Ignorance of that fact was comparative bliss.

For his part, an emotionally undeveloped Kevin remained largely unaware of the impact he was having; more unknowing catalyst than wilful contaminant. Incapable of deciphering the prevailing mood, he bounced off it, their smouldering enmity only serving to hasten him into the arms and loins of the women his imagination readily summoned, and who granted him immediate and unconditional gratification.

YEAR 3

Two's company,
But three is a crowd.

Several weeks into their third year, October witnessed the rarest of occurrences: a new pupil in GCSE year. And in time-honoured tradition, it was Clarke, as the previous new boy, who was dispatched with his form master to stand outside the headmaster's office until summoned. Morris was permitted to accompany them, at Clarke's request.

With the injection of Evans, two became three. But although that initial inter-dependence forged during the obligatory tour would always keep them to an extent together and apart from the rest of the year, it would prove to be a much looser alliance.

The writing was on the wall when Evans walked straight into central midfield for the U16 1st XI and even played a couple of times for the school 2nd XI. He gained access to a group of pupils with whom Morris and Clarke had never exchanged more than a glance, and with it a sub-life of his own entirely independent of them. Morris was secretly ecstatic; Clarke a little disappointed; Evans oblivious.

For their part, Morris and Clarke played boards two and four in the chess team and represented the school at various U16 bridge tournaments. Evans didn't play bridge, and in any case three didn't go into two, particularly a two already being talked of as having the potential to be the youngest ever first team pairing. He came along to chess club a few times but played with an erratic disregard for convention and recognised lines, frequently launching into extravagant sacrifices and seemingly growing bored as soon as the consequent chaos resolved itself into clear advantage either way. He refused point blank to enter internal competitions, let alone represent the school. Morris exulted. Clarke was disappointed; it was more fun with Evans around.

For the first time, the Easter term didn't have to mean rugby, an escape route offered courtesy of the option of choosing another activity; which many gratefully did. Evans chose hockey and made the school team. Morris and Clarke chose fives – Rugby, not Eton; a deliberate slight by Sir Reginald to a perceived and despised competitor – because it sounded interesting and they had always wondered what the funny-shaped courts were for. After two sessions of "ow" and "that really hurts" on the few occasions they succeeded in putting glove on ball, the master readily agreed to a change of option.

Morris went for badminton, a sport Clarke found only marginally less boring to play than to watch. Clarke, now nudging six foot, found himself the object of overtures from a master who knew an embryonic flanker when he saw one. Morris's initial hilarity turned to nervousness as Clarke's half-hearted complaints failed to convince; then to distress when Clarke finally acquiesced. The master was soon proven right, and by half-term Clarke had made the U16 1st XV. Morris was horrified. Clarke, however, was finding rugby to be the perfect vent for the androgens besieging his mutating body; an outlet for the budding and thrilling sense of competitiveness beginning to blossom away from the feminine mulch of home life, and which chess and bridge had only gone so far in indulging.

It also made him feel closer to Evans.

Clarke and Morris watched Evans' hockey matches when they could, sharing the frustration of the players as the ball flew or bobbled past sticks, rarely under control. It never ceased to amaze them how, in a game of so much movement, expended energy, wild swinging and clashing of wood, so little of genuine excitement or interest actually happened. The players seemed to spend most of their time chasing and then trying to tame the ball, usually to little avail.

Evans and Morris watched Clarke playing for the school whenever they could. Evans envied much of what he saw, but found it a game ruined by the constant threat and inconvenience of contact that seemed to stifle, rather than encourage, individual skill. It both puzzled and amused him that so many self-proclaimed and acknowledged *lads* who rejoiced in overt masculinity, spent so much of their time voluntarily grappling each other to the ground, rolling around together and sticking their heads and hands between each other's legs; the ball, virtually incidental to the main action, an excuse for physical contact. As for Morris, he was as excited as he was appalled by it all.

Hardly anyone watched anyone else play badminton, and no one watched Morris play. Indeed, it was debatable whether he was even playing badminton. Until, that is, a flu virus rendered his presence at the final school match of the season a necessity. Harrow boasted three county players, one of whom was destined to play for England and, in a ghosted autobiography that sold under a hundred copies, only seven of them to bona fide third parties, would many years later recall that game against *"the funny little chap with the mass of blond curls who faced thirty serves and failed to connect with a single one, each time chiding himself self-deprecatingly before he would bend down, pick up the shuttlecock and bound round the net – to begin with he had repeatedly failed to throw or hit it back, achieving all manner of random trajectories – and hand it to me with a 'silly me', a 'dreadfully sorry, can't seem to hit the shuttle-thingy' or a 'here's your cockywhatsitsname.' It was pitiful yet endearing and I resented his coach with his red face buried in hands and the fellow pupils who laughed awkwardly. One big guy, from his own school, seemed to enjoy every second of his pain, openly laughing and ridiculing him. Despite my being the instrument of his public torture, I grew to respect his dogged, good-natured determination and ceaseless good humour. My most one-sided victory would illogically teach me the art of losing with grace and humility."*

With summer came cricket, punctuated by the inconvenience of GCSEs, and the three of them all made the school squad, though only Evans warranted a playing role; the other two stepping aside from competitive sport for a term to record the team's performance for posterity.

Evans waltzed into the U16 1st XI as number three batsman and first change bowler. His father would occasionally turn up to watch, something frowned upon but beyond the power of the Head to prevent. He would often sit with the scorers, chatting about anything and everything. But the moment his son was being handed the ball to bowl or striding out to the crease, he'd at once become distracted and take himself off to a solitary outpost, where he'd unconvincingly effect a casual indifference.

Evans proved himself a joker to rival Morris, and whether by luck or good judgment always seemed to emerge unscathed.

Never more so than with their French teacher, the incongruously-named Monsieur Jones, who was astonishingly accepted unquestioningly by one and all as being French despite a broad Welsh accent that brought more Celtic than Gallic to their lessons.

School rules determined that classroom doors be kept permanently open at all times during the day when a teacher was not present. This was achieved by means of a metal hook attached to the base of the door being placed in a bracket attached to the wall or, in the case of this classroom, the wooden shelving unit on which sat piles of textbooks and the various persuasive *objets d'art* that reinforced his French-ness, and which Monsieur Jones would claim to have picked up during his many travels *en France,* but which in reality had been picked up in a Rhyl gift shop one wet and windy summer afternoon: a brass Eiffel Tower, a string of plastic onions, an embalmed baguette, a gaudy yellow scale model of a Citroen 2CV and a beret.

Whilst most teachers bent down to release the hook or gently eased it up with the toe of their shoe, Monsieur Jones had a very individual method honed over many years. He would storm into the room, tie flying back over a shoulder, thinning hair floating above his shiny pate. Grasping the door handle with his left hand, he would pivot extravagantly round the door on the ball of his left foot and bring his right foot down with an accurate thrust that would evict the hook from its clasp. Leaving the door to travel its arc of closure he would sweep up to the desk, deposit his briefcase on the desk with scant regard for any contents, step to the side of the desk and, hands on hips and chest puffed out, boom "Burnjeurre" to his audience, just as the door clicked shut.

One day, Evans removed the screws in the door handle so it came off in his hand. Despite being thrown slightly off balance Monsieur Jones still landed enough of a kick to dislodge the hook. Disaster loomed but was acrobatically averted as he turned a backwards stagger into a swirl that deposited him perched on the corner of the desk. Surprise and then relief swamped the anger long enough for the applause to begin, whereupon pride kicked in and brought an involuntary smile to his reddened face. No culprit was ever sought and Evans was a hero.

Morris felt compelled to compete.

He waited a term before making his move, whereupon he superglued the hook to its clasp. Monsieur Jones followed up his first kick with a second, a third and a fourth, each progressively harder and noisier. Two more followed before he recognised their futility. And there he stood, in front of twenty-three boys having just repeatedly kicked an immovable object. Too late to laugh it off. Nowhere to go but retribution. Under threat of group punishment, Morris owned up and was given a month of after-school detentions.

When Evans forgot his swimming trunks, he conjured a look of such penitence that the teacher backed down, mumbling "Sit it out today, but don't let it happen again."

When Morris couldn't locate the trunks he knew he'd packed – and which would later be found wrapped around a board rubber, earning him another detention – the merest hint of weakness saw the same Mr Luxley dispatching him on ten naked solo lengths of backstroke in front of a largely uncomfortable group of boys.

The dinner ladies found the quizzical musings of Evans on some of their more exotic offerings – anything containing a remotely foreign-sounding word – welcome and endearing diversions.

Morris's well-intentioned and entirely justifiable suggestion regarding the consistency of their semolina proved offensive enough to warrant a week of lunchtime detentions.

Suffering a crisis of confidence, he stepped into the wings and left the stage clear for Evans.

*

Head of PE: lacks coordination, but a fine rugby player in the making.

Form teacher: Clarke has progressed well this year, has an excellent head for figures and should perform well in his GCSEs. I see a bright future ahead for him.

Headmaster: a pleasing contribution to the year. Fine all-round performance.

*

Home life that summer was akin to staying at a small hotel. Meals and board provided. Small portable TV in his room. The place was kept clean. Tea- and coffee-making facilities were provided, as were communal areas where the guests occasionally, if they hadn't heard each other coming, spent uncomfortable time together. Service was efficient and coolly friendly.

Differences were many, entrenched and irretrievable without intensive therapy. They all clung to the life-raft of polite indifference and tolerance and there were times when they were able to overlook the holed ship that lay many fathoms below and convince themselves that things were on the mend and better than they had been for ages.

And when his GCSE results dropped through the letterbox – ten As and a B – they displayed no small amount of happiness for him, even resting hands fleetingly on his shoulders, although their root emotion was one of relief that the Nethercott buffer remained intact, and with it their haven of sanctimonious indignation and wronged righteousness.

LOWER SIXTH YEAR

The course of true love never did run smooth.

So quick bright things come to confusion.

Lysander, *A Midsummer Night's Dream* (1.1.134–49)

Nethercott portrayed itself as a seat of theatrical excellence, but then it portrayed itself as many things, and rarely lived up to the billing. All productions in the first three years were half-hearted internal affairs that ran for just two nights: a dress rehearsal and then a performance in the Great Hall before the Lower School and their families, policed by eagle-eyed masters instructed to frown and tut at any conduct other than unadulterated pleasure amongst the watching pupils. The prospect of a third night of staggeringly monotonous am-dram, hammy voices echoing around a near-empty school hall, was too much for Sir Reginald to contemplate, not to mention the presence of parents justifiably questioning the concept of excellence. So much less stressful to limit exposure to the one 'public' performance and marshal it. And so much more beneficial to the school's reputation to hire a photographer for an afternoon a week before and permit him extravagant photo-poetic licence. The resultant two-page spread of unscripted poses bore minimal relation to the play itself, but would have graced a West End production programme, let alone the truism that was the *Nethercott Hall Annual Yearbook*.

The Upper School years saw some fundamental changes. The production was put on in collaboration with Marlswood School for Girls. Humour, singing and even dancing were tolerated, and the public run lasted a full three nights, with parents actively encouraged to attend. By staging it in Marlswood's purpose-built theatre, with its limited capacity, full houses were assured, the blame for any artistic failures would sit more with the hosts, and Sir Reginald's domain could avoid molestation.

The potential for missing lessons alone should have led to a stampede for roles, both performing and supporting. But the common acceptance was that those who did get involved were either queers, oddballs, or creeps… probably all three. And as for girls, they were for mentally manipulating and then wanking over; the prospect of them actually talking back was as scary as hell to most of the boys.

So when Evans proposed in October that the three of them attend the introductory meeting, the initial response from Clarke and Morris was one of united derision. Evans persisted, emphasising the proximity to girls and the myriad of opportunities that presented. As to what those opportunities might be, Clarke or Morris hadn't a clue, but some vivid elaboration from Evans brought on a deal-sealing erection for Clarke; and where

Clarke went, Morris generally followed. And against all the odds, they were still on board when it came to the evening of the first melding of the two schools.

Clarke disembarked the coach after the short journey and approached the theatre with a mixture of adrenalin and paralytic fear. Inside, whilst the other Lower Sixth boys recoiled as if encountering a highly contagious disease, Evans confidently accompanied the cockier members of the Upper Sixth, invading deep amongst the girls already seated in the room.

Then he actually talked to the strange creatures.

Which was all very disconcerting for Morris who, observing Evan's casual and well-received infiltration and Clarke's thinly-disguised interest, albeit from a safe distance, determined that to not be involved would mean isolation for large expanses of time, not to mention leaving the two of them unchaperoned and free to bond. Reluctantly he resigned himself to a life theatrical, at least for the time being. And *A Midsummer Night's Dream* would be their first venture.

Casting took place in November. Specialisations and preferences were sought at the outset: lighting, set design and manufacture, sound, music, and so on. A few shuffled off, but not recognising themselves in any of these categories, Morris and Clarke stayed seated in the large group that remained; shrinking violets in a field of sunflowers. Any comfort derived from sheer weight of numbers disappeared the moment they were informed that they would be taking turns to file into another room, where they would be required to read to the directors one of a number of passages printed on a laminated piece of card. Evans confidently got to his feet. Clarke embarked on a forlorn quest for a muse. Morris felt his bowels shift, asked the person next to him where the toilets were and blushed when he realised he'd spoken to a *girl*.

Twice-weekly rehearsals began in January. Each school had put forth a co-director. Miss Palmer was a career spinster with a predilection for tweed two-piece suits, hairpins and the plays and poems of Shakespeare, Shelley, Wordsworth et al, in which she found the romance that eluded her in real life; unsurprisingly, given an appearance and demeanour most flatteringly described as stern. For their part, Nethercott weighed in with the 'heavyweight' of bantamweights, Mr Quentin Badger. A man in name, if little else, who pushed the concept of his gender to the boundary it shared with womanhood, on which it then teetered precariously. A man who made Mr Flanders look like a Neanderthal.

Tradition, protocol and an absence of creativity dictated that the bard's words be dramatised as conservatively as possible. No Nethercott-Marlswood audience was ever going to be subjected to a radical interpretation.

Evans had secured the role of Demetrius. Clarke had delivered an audition of such one-dimensional woodenness that even he had to concur with the appropriateness of his prompt dispatch to *set design*, which in this instance was theatre-speak for the unenviable task of transforming some large pieces of shaped hardboard, piles of crêpe paper and rolls of green felt into an enchanted forest. The Design Department, as they determined to call themselves, comprised Clarke and three others: a thick-set, humourless boy called Grafton with a penchant for design and technology inherited from a father who was apparently a famous carpenter, though no one at the school had heard of him, much to Grafton's chagrin; an even thicker-set, sour-faced girl called Babb who was at least creative; and a shy, unassuming, bespectacled girl called Wolsey who, by default, was the more attractive and appealing of the feminine contingent. Any initial awkwardness amongst the four was only compounded by Marlswood also insisting upon surnames at all times.

But as they relaxed in each other's company, Clarke was surprised at how easy it was to talk to one of *them*. Wolsey belied his initial, highly-stereotypical appraisal with an acerbic wit, in particular when levelled at the self-absorbed *luvvies* hamming it up in rehearsals, and had a smile, when it did emerge blinking into the light, that never failed to brighten Clarke's mood. He even ventured a few *funnies* of his own, with mixed but faintly encouraging results. With Grafton regularly disappearing off to the design and technology lab or shuffling round large pieces of wood apparently for the sake of it, and Babb stoically vacillating between creativity and disinterest, Clarke and Wolsey were relatively free to chat as they crimped crêpe paper, smeared brown and green paint over wood and pondered the tricky question of leaves.

Every second Tuesday saw the lunchtime appearance of cheese and onion flan: Clarke's favourite by some considerable distance. And that particular Tuesday he'd cashed in enough favours to accumulate six portions of the aforementioned culinary fare, which he proceeded to devour with relish, facilitating their oesophageal passage with a steady flow of baked beans.

The consequent distension receded through the afternoon, only for a very different disquiet to build, approaching its zenith as the set design team beavered away at yet another tree. Feeling like an inflating blimp, Clarke awaited the point of imminent explosion before making his excuses and exiting quickly, congratulating himself on a plan well executed. Delicious though the flan had been, his feasting on its delights had brought the ancillary bonus of facilitating an attempt on a record

Morris had held since the last term. Clarke had tried locating him to witness the assault, but to no avail, and the time was nigh.

Emerging outside, he paused, gulped down several mouthfuls of air and, theatrically throwing his arms out wide like a tightrope walker fighting for balance, took a tentative step forwards, to be rewarded as his foot landed with an encouraging squeak. Reassured by the sensation of much more gas in the pipeline awaiting expulsion, he took three more steps in quick succession, each landing accompanied by an audible fart of varying length, audibility and tonal quality. Pausing briefly on one foot and leaning slowly forwards – forward momentum required at all times – he contented himself that all was well, then launched into another series of strides, curtailed only when the sound of the ninth ended with a worrying squelch. But needs must, and with time and supply on the wane, he set off again in a rapid sequence of shortening steps that generated ever briefer and more strained noises until, announcing out loud the number of the approaching record-equalling seventeenth gaseous eviction, he triumphantly took one more jump high into the air, landed on two feet with bent knees and pushed, for all he was worth, for immortality.

The resulting anal fibrillation sounded like a whoopee cushion forcibly let off in custard, possessing a wet resonance that wiped the smugness from Kevin's face and necessitated a period of rectal manipulation before he turned around and waddled slowly back, his gait much reduced, heading to the toilet for damage assessment and reparations.

Wolsey hadn't been fooled by that feeble excuse and knew a ruse to escape the monosyllabic company of Babb and Grafton when she heard one. Encouraged further by what she took to be a collusive glance thrown back over his shoulder, she followed Kevin out. She had been halfway through the outside door and about to call out when something in his body language caused her to hesitate. Closing the door quietly behind her she remained in the shadows and watched, her jaw and eyebrows slowly heading in opposite directions as the strange cabaret progressed.

A preoccupied Kevin was only a few feet away by the time he first noticed her.

"Oh, hi."

"Hello."

"Have you been… did you…?"

"Unfortunately, yes."

"Oh."

"Quite a performance."

"Thanks."

"No. I was being… never mind. Shall we head back?"

"Yes… er… actually I need to…"

"Oh, right. Marvellous. Off you go then."

Nonetheless Wolsey took something of a shine to Clarke, though she lacked the worldly wiles to convey her interest overtly enough to deter him from a growing obsession with the more conventional charms of the petitely curvy girl playing Helena, whose character was besotted with Demetrius, and whose total disregard for Clarke's existence only stoked the glowing embers in his groin.

But if Clarke was feeling confused, it was as nothing compared to Morris. For Mr Badger had found his Puck the moment Morris walked into the audition room back in December. He positively purred in anticipation even as Morris fiddled awkwardly with the card, started to perspire and stared down at his own feet. The fixed look on Mr Badger's face was soon to show signs of strain, for what followed was an extraordinarily poor rendition, even by Nethercott standards: mumbling, monotonic, devoid of inflection or insight; and riddled with errors, each of which generated either an "oops," an "oh dear me," a hand placed over an open mouth, a hand slapping his hip or a little stamp of a foot. On one occasion he did all five.

Miss Palmer was taken aback and assumed, from the squirming in his seat of her co-director throughout the debacle, that her negativity was reciprocated. As Morris sloped off, she had no idea that this most self-evident of decisions, to discard the funny little boy without a theatrical bone in his puny body to a backstage role, would turn into a heated debate. Her realism earthed the lightning bolt of Mr Badger's enthusiasm; but only to the point where Mr Badger tempered lofty ambition with the recognition that there was considerable work to be done before Morris would become the finished article. A greater sense of self-worth might have led her to prolong the discussion until a more realistic compromise was reached, but without it she was left feeling that Morris must possess nuances of talent and theatrical promise that had escaped her.

Mr Badger got his Puck.

And his Puck was Morris.

For a time, anyway.

It was early February before defeat was reluctantly admitted and the role of Puck given to a more able, if less visually compelling, pupil. The mannerisms from the audition had not only remained, but had become more accentuated with each rehearsal. Mr Badger's ego would not permit an error of judgment, so Miss Palmer was compelled to allow him dramatic licence to engineer an alternative role for Morris, one that played to his strengths: no speaking, no acting and an uncanny elfin look achieved with nothing more than the addition of some Spock-like plastic ears. The more the other actors got into their characters and *acted*, the more they looked like teenagers in ill-fitting costumes. Morris may have been theatrically incompetent, but it was undeniable that he was elf-ness personified.

Faced with a boy possessing no dramatic awareness and no concept of, or interest in, the play, Mr Badger did his utmost to embellish and inspire, to *direct*, but it was like Victor Frankenstein trying to teach his monster to cross-stitch: pointless, misguided and ultimately doomed to failure.

In the end, Mr Badger settled for a form of avant-garde in-direction.

"I want you to simply *be*. To float about the stage throughout. There's no need to say anything *per se*. Just *be* as a forest dweller, an elf if you will, would *be*. Your presence on the stage authenticates the drama unfolding around you. You are an ever-present constituent of the play's very fabric, a constant that serves to highlight the transience of the emotional flights and fancies of the protagonists. In effect you are the very essence of the production and your silence only enhances the spoken dialogue."

Rather pleased with this rhetoric he pulled a self-congratulatory expression that involved the lower half of his face compressing and widening like a concertina, confusing Morris even more than what he'd just heard. But if it meant no lines to learn or speak, he'd go with the flow, even tolerating the frequent one-on-one sessions demanded by Mr Badger to "enhance conceptualisation."

*

Elsewhere previously separate worlds were beginning to collide.

The previous term Evans had been the only Lower Sixth pupil to make the 1st XI, a team that remained unbeaten throughout the term, thanks largely to his seven goals from central midfield.

Early in the term, Clarke and Morris would often stroll around the pitch during the 1st and 2nd XI after-school training session watching the players doing, as Morris put it, *athletic stuff* with balls and cones and brightly-coloured bibs. On one such occasion, as the session came to an end, a playful gibe at a fluffed shot observed earlier led to a half-serious challenge, a half-serious acceptance and a few minutes later Clarke was in goal facing penalties from Evans, who recognised fledgling talent when he saw it. Morris feared the worst.

When an accident with a Bunsen burner left Wilkinson incapacitated for the remainder of the term, a word from Evans in the master's ear saw Clarke turn out in goal for the 2nd XI's final game. Prowling the box throughout the game like a caged tiger, he scared the opposition strikers witless, recklessly gave away a penalty, saved it, let in a goal through his legs, gave away another penalty, saved that one as well and made a succession of saves that helped secure a 2-1 victory.

If Clarke harboured any hopes of returning the favour and converting Evans to rugby in the spring term, he faced a significant obstacle in the form of Evans' aversion to pain and excessive physical contact not of his own initiating. He was happy enough to a watch rugby training whenever he could, Morris always in vague tow, and afterwards he'd kick balls up high for Clarke to catch, or not; something of a concern given his move at the master's insistence out of the 2nd XV pack and into the 1st XV as full-back – the previous incumbent, Hill, convalescing back home after an unfortunate incident in the showers – a position of last resort and no hiding place.

Strangely it was Marsh who had given Clarke his first leg up on his ascension from total indifference to the 1st XV. That second-year house game when he'd taken the ball ten yards out, cut between grabbing hands and headed for the line. The only obstacle in his path was the not inconsiderable form of Marsh; he of the delinquent tendencies so often displayed. He expected to be taken off his feet and thrown backwards as he tentatively pushed out a flat palm, but something flickered across Marsh's face and his challenge was feigned and half-hearted. It may have looked authentic, but Marsh had definitely ducked it. And in doing so he had started Clarke on the road to empowerment.

The realisation freed that section of his mind previously so occupied by self-preservation to see things in a different light, at which point it revealed itself as a game of angles, territory, diversion, weak spots and pressure. And for a chess-playing mathematician there was more in common with those specialisations than he'd ever realised.

Now a 6 foot 2 seventeen-year-old nudging fourteen stone, he also had a considerable physical presence and from full-back he got to survey the whole game, his tackling and running strengths employed to the full. And when Hill returned to school, somewhat more subdued than before the incident, he had little choice but to acknowledge that his place had been taken by a more able player.

The three friends would often stay after rugby training and Clarke and Evans would have a conversion shoot-out, Morris collecting the ball for them. As they prepared to kick, he'd loiter behind the posts and the moment ball left boot, he'd start prancing around trying to anticipate its point of landing, the aim being to avoid it whilst looking like he wanted to catch it. Sometimes he'd get in too close and have to leap back, shielding his face with an arm in case the bounce took it in his direction. Then he'd frantically follow the drunken path of the ball, until it came to a standstill, whereupon he picked it up as you would an unexploded bomb, held it out with rigid arms and started to run towards the others. Passing the posts, he'd give it a kick, with a less than fifty-fifty success rate of contact; and if he did succeed in translating the very limited potential energy in his fragile leg to kinetic energy in the ball, it was with minimal success, the ball seldom travelling far and rarely in the right direction. With a giggle and a self-reprimand, he'd chase it down again before repeating the whole process. The laws of probability dictated that there would eventually come a point when he was within throwing distance. The first few times, he'd attempted to join the party with a rugby-style pass, but had retained contact for too long and sent the ball off at a right angle behind him. Then he resorted to running up and placing the ball at their feet, like a dog returning a stick.

Competitive sport à la Morris.

As for the contests, Clarke would normally win, unsurprisingly given his elevation to back-up kicker and specialist option for anything nearing the halfway line. But Evans was undeniably talented, and a quick learner.

*

As with all school performances, objective viewpoints of *A Midsummer Night's Dream* were sparse on the ground, but no one could deny that the most eye-catching performance was that of Morris, and the perpetual motion of the big-eared, effete elfin figure strolling distractedly from one side of the stage to the other. Occasionally his random path would carry him between speaking actors and the audience, once even between two speaking actors, taking everyone's eyes with him and causing lines to be fluffed and plot turns to be missed. Every now and then he would throw in a grimace or a skip or a knee-bend or a forced smile, always random and never in discernible context. The nagging noise you can't ignore once you tune in. The tiny wires embedded in a heated windscreen you can never see until you remember they're there; and on which you then can't stop your eyes trying to focus.

Visual tinnitus.

And when the cast filed on to take the applause, there was a noticeable increase in volume as Morris came into view.

The customary disco after the final performance was one of the very few occasions when a blind eye was turned to 'high jinks', albeit because Sir Reginald was elsewhere entertaining the more endowed and renowned of the parents; while the staff who remained with the students were the arty types devoid of authority.

Wolsey brought over a paper plate laden with cheese and pineapple on sticks – she'd remembered him saying how much he liked them – and two plastic cups of 'Tropical Punch', the inverted commas wholly justified given ingredients comprising ginger beer, grape juice, cranberry juice and orange juice heated up with a large packet of sugar before the oh-so-very-exotic addition of tinned fruit and some cinnamon sticks. Her intention was that the two of them might sit back in a quiet corner, maintain a disrespectful distance from the general idiocy, and comfort themselves with some fond ridiculing of the more ludicrous aspects of the night's events. Morris's 'performance' was the obvious starting point, but as she broached a subject ripe for amused debate, her intended companion for the evening took offence at what he chose to see as an attack on his friend, leaving her floundering between apologising, making light of it or getting angry. She shifted awkwardly as she struggled for a response, tried a smile that was not returned and took refuge in her drink, half a tinned pear gently buffeting her philtrum. After a varied selection of conversational appetisers had received similar short shrift, she recognised a losing battle, stood up, shrugged and turned away, her face fused with blood and disappointment. As she walked away, she glanced back over her shoulder, but his gaze was lost in a far corner of the room.

Oblivious to all this, Clarke took his heart in his hands and made his play for the girl cast as Helena, who he had discovered was called Helen, a fine and witty gift horse of an opening gambit if ever he'd heard one. Okay, so they hadn't spoken to each other yet, but they had enjoyed a contented courtship since the previous term in his imagination. The consequent reality/fiction blur emboldened his feet sufficiently to bring the shaking, sweating, awkward bulk of his body to stand before her. Her face had angled downwards at his approach, but she couldn't deny his presence for long and an upwards glance gave the green light.

For comedy gold.

"Hi."

"Er, hi."

"Thought you were great."

"Er, thanks."

"As Helena."

Pause for effect.

"Or should I say… Helen."

Punchline delivered.

Smile pending?

Or not?

Not.

"Ha," he chortled encouragingly.

No takers.

"Er… right. Don't suppose I can get you a… er… cake or something, can I?"

"No."

In truth there hadn't been a welcome to outstay, but here was one last chance to cut his losses and flee with the tattered remnants of his dignity. But inexperienced in the subtleties of rejection, he hesitated a moment too long, the weight of hopelessness pinning him to the spot.

"Excellent," he proffered inconsequentially, and watched the syllables float away into the black hole opening between them.

Rocking from ball to heel and back again, he took refuge in his curious-tasting beverage. Having negotiated an incongruous glacé cherry, his defences slackened long enough to permit a long, slippery peach slice to glide unnoticed over the lip of the cup and head towards the back of his mouth, where it lodged momentarily and triggered his gag reflex. His teeth caught the slice before expulsion but this could not prevent a loud wretch and lunge forward. When the watery glaze cleared from his eyes, they noted that he was alone. He took a consolation swig of his drink and was rewarded with a slurry of congealed sugar.

It was less than fifteen minutes later that he bitterly observed his Ice Queen thawing rapidly in the arms of Evans, who appeared to be taking her temperature with his tongue. Wheeling away in dismay, he walked straight into Babb.

"You're a pathetic fool."

"What?" said Clarke, taken aback both by this attack from a girl who had hardly spoken a word to him all term, but also by the inadvertent contact his hands, raised instinctively in defence at the imminent collision, had made with her not inconsiderable breasts.

"Chasing after the pretty bird and ignoring the one in your hand."

This was far too obscure for Clarke, who suspected a proverb but couldn't quite pin it down. His creased brow said as much.

"Idiot. She's worth ten of that insipid creature. You're all the same you boys; so bloody predictable."

This should have been the cinematic cue for a montage of flashbacks: mirth at arboreal design mishaps; amused glances when performers had their little hissy fits; raised eyebrows as Grafton disappeared off yet again with the line "I'll be away for a few minutes; I'm just going to grab a tool"; the doffing of an invisible cap with a "yes ma'am" on the few occasions Babb spoke; the hours of contentedly shared nothingness.

But instead he sulked; mourning his loss, cursing his supposed friend Evans, and conjuring scenarios whereby Helen's participation in that repulsive tonsil-hockey was reluctant, un-enjoyed and unavoidable. Wolsey held no sway in this tidal wave of emotion.

At the end of the evening, as the final song was announced and the dreamy, dreary and entirely appropriate dirge that was "I'm Not in Love" wafted across the room, it was with confused emotions that he watched Demetrius and Helena entwined – it was proving easier to deal with if he placed them in character; how could he hope to compete with all that shared history? – and then Marsh making a beeline for Wolsey. She hesitated uncertainly, momentarily panicked. Her gaze flickered in Clarke's direction, only to receive back a dismissive sneer, whereupon her facial features hardened and she consented with defiant resignation. The two of them shuffled stiffly around the dance floor, Marsh clamping a large palm on one of Wolsey's buttocks as he recognised the approach of the song's final refrain.

As Clarke watched them walking arm-in-arm to the side of the room, a profoundly debilitating loneliness swept through his body, forcing tears to his eyes and sending him scurrying for the door.

He needed Morris. Where was he?

*

The summer term began with the healing, at Morris's insistence, of a rift Evans had no idea even existed. Clarke was all for continuing with the stand-off, but the fact that Evans had not, upon reluctant examination, done anything wrong left him with nothing to stand off from. He gave up, and life returned to normal. Evans batted number three and opened the bowling for the 1st XI. Clarke scored. Morris manned the scoreboard and flittered about. Mock A Levels popped up now and again but did little to interrupt a leisurely stroll towards the summer holiday.

With A Level subject choices set in stone and next to no chance of children being withdrawn prematurely, the school had no incentive to offer an end of year report. So it didn't. Life could be that simple in the public school system.

*

Kevin had been on a couple of Aspire holidays when he was younger, the first time when he was just ten.

"It's an adventure camp for children; you'll love it," his mum had said a few months before.

"Wait and see, you'll love it; it'll be an adventure," said his dad.

"A chance to make friends," said his mum.

"You can… make lots of great friends," echoed his dad, commendably sticking to the script and compensating for a lack of invention with a weird upwards intonation.

But as the tag team ploughed on repetitively and competitively, their son wasn't listening. Emerging from the profound bewilderment engendered at this first meeting of his parents since the separation – or abandonment; opinions varied – was the mocking, cruel hope that if they just kept talking, the adhesive power of their words might in some way bind their shattered family unit back together.

But it didn't happen and the fortnightly handovers resumed their customary format, Kevin shuffling to and fro like a hostage walking between distrusting enemies, never sure whether to look ahead or back.

When they did next reunite, it was in a windswept car park in West London in early April. No script this time, just fractured utterances as they manoeuvred awkwardly around their son like two matching magnetic poles, unable even to make eye contact with each other. While beside them Kevin hovered miserably between the known hell of domesticity and the terror of the unknown: the prospect of getting on a coach alone with a group of strangers and travelling hundreds of miles to a boarding school in North Wales for what the brochure promised would be *a holiday of a lifetime, crammed full of games, activities, adventures and new friends.* He so desperately wanted his parents to tell him it would be fine. That they loved each other. That they loved him. That he didn't need to go. That they would pick up his suitcase and go straight back home for a warm drink and a night cuddled on the sofa watching television. All of them. Together.

But they failed him just as they had failed each other, and like a dead man walking, he dragged his case over to the coach, deposited it with the wide-bellied, sweating driver loading up the luggage compartment, climbed aboard, looked into a sea of strange faces, ducked into the nearest seat and fought the tears with sniffles and a tissue.

He survived the holiday and recognised the need in his parents by embroidering his reminiscences sufficiently to alleviate any guilt they may have been feeling. So much so that he was sent on another in the summer of the following year. This time he surprised himself by enjoying it and apparently had his first girlfriend, though the relationship seemed to exist more in gossip and implication than in meaningful contact.

Her name was Fiona. She had long light brown hair, matted like a horse's mane. They sat together on the coach on the way home. Kevin set out to impress: counting to thirty in German (until he got lost at eleven and switched to French), reeling off the prime numbers up to three hundred in order (until she pointed out that seventy-five couldn't be one), quoting pi to thirty decimal places (started well, but got lost and guessed the remainder) and generally being a waffling cretin.

All she wanted was for him to put an arm round her to validate a holiday romance before their public, but he was too busy thinking of the next feat of mental dexterity he could screw up. Just south of Birmingham, she voted with her feet.

And so it was with mixed emotions that he received the news that his father had secured him a summer job as a kitchen assistant on an Aspire holiday for nine- to thirteen-year olds in Shropshire. That he'd be treated and paid like slave labour were details tactically left out of the publicity spiel. And he could take a companion. He made great public show of the difficulty of the choice, but in truth it was easier than he dared admit to himself, only for a clashing of dates with a county cricket tour to Somerset to make the choice for him: it would be Charlie accompanying him on his first foray into the world of employment.

*

Bramley Grange was a brooding presence in the middle of nowhere.

There were five kitchen assistants. Kevin and Charlie were joined by two girls roughly their age who also came in a pair: Tracy, a dour, angular, bird-like creature; and Diane, a far more full-figured girl with a bob of dark brown hair, a face of blurred freckles and a predilection for tight dark blue jeans that bulged pleasantly as they struggled to get the contours of her backside under control. An older boy called Mike brought long, lank, greasy ginger hair and vibrant acne to the team, not to mention a Clint Eastwood obsession. He assumed, and was ceded uncontested, the role of unofficial team leader by dint of his more advanced years; all one and a half of them.

Food preparation was kept well away from the kitchen assistants. They spent their time laying tables, taking out food and drink, standing at the edge of the room in case any of the children wanted anything, clearing tables of detritus, receiving negative feedback on the quality of the fare, loading industrial dishwashers or washing ill-fitting items by hand, taking out more food, replenishing jugs of squash and water, receiving more insults, collecting dirty kitchenware and uneaten food, loading dishwashers, clearing tables, wiping down tables, sweeping the dining room floor, unloading dishwashers and cleaning kitchen surfaces.

Three times a day. Every day; bar the middle Sunday.

Mornings were filled with ad hoc cleaning duties but they did get two hours off in the afternoon to relax and enjoy the facilities on offer, at least when they weren't populated by the 'guests'. The evenings saw them clear by about eight o'clock. Contact with the team leaders, all of whom were a good few years older, was limited, their time being monopolised by the needs and deeds of their charges. That left the five of them to their own devices in those areas of the building where the chances of contact with children were negligible. Mike had brought cassettes of various comedy series with him and they'd spend hours drinking tea, listening to *Not the Nine O'clock News* and *Monty Python*, anticipating lines, doing the voices and basking in the reflected comedy.

Kevin developed a preoccupation with the gentle sway of Diane's backside and the rise and fall of her breasts. Inexperienced in the interaction of boys and girls, other than in his magazine-inspired imagination, even Kevin had to admit that the signs were encouraging. The smiles, the in-jokes, the playful pushes and prods, the hand left on his arm for a second longer than necessary. A session in the kitchen was enough to leave him exhausted, juggling whatever size and direction of erection his underwear and jeans would permit whilst still allowing him to remain vertical and capable of work.

They kissed one evening, then kissed some more the next; then whenever and wherever no one else was watching.

A stolen few minutes one afternoon in one of the wings off bounds for the children saw their lips glued together and him unsure as to when and how the hands were meant to enter the fray. She read his mind, grabbed his hand from where it rested loosely on her thigh and placed it on her breast. His eyebrows made for the crown of his head. They kissed some more, his hand frozen.

She reached up, placed her hand on his and squeezed it gently a few times.

"Ohhhooo," he groaned.

They kissed on. Then she fumbled with the front of her jeans, unclamped his hand from her breast, where it had long ago run out of original variations of movement, and to his incredulity, pushed it down, through the now-open fly and under the elastic. *Oh God.* She squirmed slightly against his motionless fingers. Encouraged, they went for a little wander, scampering about on the downy carpet, occasionally kneading gently; all of it to a soundtrack of pained groaning; his pained groaning.

There they were, his lucky fingers, having the time of their lives, frolicking gaily like new-born lambs in an April meadow, when one of them fell into a hole; a warm, damp, welcoming hole. Whereupon Diane let out a brief moan. Which had to be good, Kevin hoped.

"Wurrulydupooiinmu," she murmured through gnashing teeth and clashing tongues.

"Pwerdurn," he slurred.

"Wurr…" she started again, before giving up and pulling her head back. She waited until his lips unpuckered and his eyelids lifted, his eyes vacuous pools.

"Would you like to put *it* in me?" she asked, pulling his head forward and mashing their faces together again.

The dam burst and he promptly ejaculated in his pants.

Quite what she thought about the raised eyebrows, his tongue shooting around erratically in her mouth, the short burst of snorting, and a muffled "uhhhhooourr," he couldn't know. As the shudders besieging his hips receded, he resisted the temptation to break off immediately and proceeded as if nothing had happened, to be saved by the sound from down the corridor of someone approaching.

"Tonight," she whispered, pushing herself clear of his tentacles.

"I'll see you later," he mumbled and set off down the corridor just as Tracy appeared around the corner. For once her customary granite-like countenance softened at his approach and she even flashed him a smile. *Blimey,* he thought, *now they're all after me,* and his stride became as jaunty as a crotch full of congealing penis-porridge would permit. Such was the overwhelming joie de vivre he felt that he abandoned immediate reparations and took the scenic route back to their bathroom up on the top floor. Life was good and he felt like sharing himself with all and sundry.

"Hi," he said to Mike, pityingly. Poor old Mike with his angry, raw, lunar landscape of a face.

"Hi," he said condescendingly to some kids loitering at the foot of the main staircase.

"Hi," he said flirtatiously to one of the middle-aged cleaners pulling a trolley along the landing.

"Hi," he said knowingly to David, one of the team leaders, as he took the next flight in his stride.

"Oh, fuck," he cried a few minutes later, standing in front of the mirror in the bathroom, contemplated the impending remedial works. No matter how much he squinted or turned his body, the large dark blue stain down the left-hand side of the front of his jeans was unmistakable, and his embarrassment debilitating.

Now he was Kevin the little boy. Kevin the sexual failure. Kevin the boy with spunk in his pants and a wet patch on his jeans; everyone laughing at him.

Having kept his own company until the evening kitchen stint demanded his presence, he traipsed wearily along corridors and down stairs that only an hour earlier he'd strutted along and bounded up.

He passed groups of children. *They knew.*

"Hiya," said Mike, as Kevin entered the kitchen. *He knew.* Laughter broke out on the other side of the room. *They knew.* Charlie smiled at him. *Even he might know.* The children who called him "mister" or "servant" and the food "crap" as he cleared the dirty plates away. *They knew, all of them knew.* Tracy still being unusually friendly. *She definitely knew.*

But Diane seemed no different. Those smiles. Those touches. Those snatched moments of intimacy. And it dawned on him that maybe no one knew, and even if they did, they weren't going to mention it and why should he care anyway. She was the only one whose opinion mattered and she wanted to *do it* with him that evening, a fact confirmed as she sauntered past him as he wiped down the last counter.

"Have you got a condom for later?"

"Yes," he lied, observing the sway of her departing derrière.

Desperate times called for desperate measures.

"Mike."

"Yo."

"I really need your help."

"Shoot," said Mike, a spent matchstick clasped between his teeth.

"It's me and, er, a young lady. She... er... wants... you know."

"Hearing you loud and clear, stud," Mike replied, then whistled what sounded like a two-note bird impression, moved his tongue round in his cheek and further confused Kevin with a curious gesture involving making a loose fist with one hand and prodding at it with the forefinger of the other. "We talking the old seximundo?"

"Er. I think so. Look, I need your car."

"Woah, hold your horses. This place is full of beds."

"No, no," stammered Kevin. "I need a lift, that's all. I need a… you know."

"What?"

"A, er, thingy."

"You've lost me, mate."

"A johnny," whispered Kevin, the word sounding ridiculous. "There must be a garage or something nearby. I need it in the next hour or so and I don't have one."

"Fear not, big man, "said Mike, sitting up, reaching into his back pocket and bringing out a wallet, from which he extracted a small foil packet. "This do the trick, lover-boy?" he said, handing it over, a smug look residing on a face Kevin could, just this once, have kissed.

"You sure?"

"Be my guest. I've got another three or four to tide me over. You never can tell when the opportunity might arise." Kevin suspected he might, but nodded enthusiastically and, he hoped, knowingly.

"You okay, Kev?"

"Fine. Sorry. Look thanks, Mike. That's brilliant. But you've given me two by mistake."

"No problemo. Who knows how the evening might go," he said, relishing an unintended rap. "One condition though. You gotta tell me who the lucky lady is, studlio?"

"Diane, of course," bristled Kevin.

"Woah. Glad I checked. Might have made a move myself. I'd be lying if I said I hadn't been tempted but fear not, I'll back off and leave the coast clear."

With his stock of goodwill fast diminishing, Kevin made his exit before it could get any worse.

"Give her one from me, eh?" came Mike's tender parting shot.

The assignation took place in an unused dormitory on a mattress they had hastily covered with a blanket Diane had thoughtfully brought along. In the time she took to 'make' the bed, walk over to the door, close it, turn the lights off, walk back and remove her jeans and pants in a single efficient downwards motion, Kevin had managed to shift his throbbing penis into a position that didn't threaten spontaneous eruption and was wobbling uncertainly in the resulting pose.

"Get your kegs off then," she said, lying back on the bed, her breasts lost in a chunky jumper. "Best keep our tops on. Never know who might come along," she added, thereby enabling him to translate 'kegs' through elimination and basic logic.

He gratefully eased the pressure, gasping out loud as his penis breathed in fresh air.

"Come on then, big boy," she giggled disquietingly.

Kevin lurched over to the bed and attempted to climb on board. "Ow, watch it," she exclaimed, as he knelt on her leg. Kevin apologised. "Don't forget the rubber." Kevin apologised again, walked self-consciously across the room, located his discarded trousers in the half-light, found the foil packet in a pocket, tore it open, pondered the contents, fiddled with it, wrinkled his nose at the smell, placed it over the tip of his aching penis, tried to pull it down, turned it over the other way and tenderly coaxed it down, a process that left him teetering on the point of premature release. With mounting trepidation, he turned to face the unknown: quiveringly erect, feeling foolish but protected. Desperately needing to prolong, he started to fold his trousers neatly. "What the hell you doing? Get over here." Following her command, he knelt on leg again. "Ow, you clot."

In the absence of any movement from Diane as he crouched between her legs, Kevin leant forward and tentatively lowered himself to lie on top of her, his backside raised sharply to avoid direct contact. Still no discernible movement. He needed signposts from her, but was getting nothing, leaving him to the paucity of his own devices. The mattress smelled damp, its plastic covering, now partially exposed, squeaking in protest as he struggled to get a hand under one of the buttocks his weight was pinning down, whilst the other was failing to determine the precise location of her breasts. Finding her lips closed, his tongue prised them open, releasing a wave of garlic. Her teeth resisted further ingress, so he licked enamel until she gave in. He probed her lifeless tongue, all the while tentatively thrusting his hips, repeatedly failing to hit the target.

Not so much assured seduction as sweaty monologue.

With ill-disguised irritation, she reached down and woman-handled him into position. "Go on, then," she said, with more resignation than anticipation. He lowered his hips forward and pushed home. She gasped, which might have been encouraging had it not been generated by his forgetting to take his own weight upon the realisation that his penis was now inside a girl's vagina. With time now very much of the essence, he abandoned finesse and thrust for all he was worth.

"Uhhhherrrrruuhhhhoooooaaaarrhhhohhhhooo," he concluded, depositing his face into the staleness of the exposed mattress beside her head. Sensing her stillness, he pondered briefly if she had ever moved. It was so hard to tell in that flurry of activity.

Then she squirmed, squeezing him out, and twisted her body from under him and into a seated position on the side of the bed. After a brief pause and a disconcerting sigh, she started feeling around on the floor for the clothes she had shed like a cast. By the time Kevin had himself sat up and was carefully sliding off the condom, light flooded into the room and she was briefly silhouetted in the doorway.

Carefully laying the condom down on the mattress, he couldn't resist a self-satisfied smirk. Virginity lost. Sex achieved. Sex survived. Sexually… active. Not only that, he had lasted ages, just like in the movies and the magazines, delivering no less than *twenty-three* thrusts.

In the balmy glow of self-congratulatory, self-deceiving post-orgasmic reflection, it mattered not that he had started coming with the first thrust and spent himself dry by the fifth.

Breakfast the next day proved a rather tense affair, Kevin and Diane exchanging stunted pleasantries; from young lovers to married couple in twelve hours, Kevin reflected, finding the course of young lust a very confusing path to navigate. His musings on the vagaries of post-copulatory relations were interrupted as news broke of an emergency staff meeting.

Nagging concern at increasingly amorous tendencies among the more physically advanced of their charges had escalated into a panic upon the discovery by a cleaner of a used condom in an unused dormitory. Kevin resisted the temptation to say "I did that" and high-five the room. Diane had her reputation to protect. And Clint Eastwood wouldn't rat on his amigos.

Not that they needed to worry. It was clear to all that only a naïve thirteen-year-old first-timer would have laid out a used condom like a trophy rather than disposing of it as a matter of course.

*

Just hearing the phrase *wide game*, that traditional feature of the penultimate day of every Aspire holiday, had been enough to bring memories flooding back for Kevin – running through woods looking for clues, time running out, sweets for the losers, lots more sweets for the winners – and tradition demanded that all the staff, kitchen assistants included, must participate. This time, he was to be part of the puzzle, not solving it.

Unfortunately for all concerned, The Great Condom Mystery had monopolised the previous night's supposed planning meeting, which had degenerated following the introduction of a box of red wine. Consequently, the narrative of the wide game had been denied the attention to detail it required to be even remotely compelling.

The obligatorily alliterative Baron of Bramley had, for no discernible reason, been cursed by a witch, who had cast a spell that would make Bramley Grange disappear unless the Baron could say the eight-letter magic word that would negate the spell by five o'clock that afternoon. Eschewing all rational recourse, the good Baron had deduced that of the myriad options at his disposal, by far the most viable was to rely on the pre-pubertal talents of a bunch of children; then undermine the collective effort by splitting them into their eight age and gender groups and insisting they compete against each other.

To further muddy the already opaque waters, the word could only be found by taking the first letter of each line of a poem and forming a word; *the* word. And each line of the poem was guarded by a local *character* – Kevin listened with dread to the requirement to dress up – who would, upon being touched, and once the group had solved or performed a " challenging and entertaining" task, produce their line thoughtfully printed earlier on laminated card.

Even the devisers were drained of all enthusiasm for their own 'creation' as they finished the team briefing, wearily giving the confused throng directions to the school's drama department wardrobe. When Kevin looked round, Mike and Charlie had already departed.

On arrival, Kevin commenced a half-hearted search through the racks of costumes and boxes of shoes, hats and miscellaneous accessories. He couldn't help but smile at Charlie who, after ten days of doleful lethargy, was now overflowing with excitement. His child-like enthusiasm proved infectious and Kevin emerged, allegedly, as a peasant farmer, complete with straw hat, 'smock' and pitchfork. Charlie pronounced himself a "Victorian fop" having unearthed a top hat, waistcoat, velvet smoking jacket and a fob watch. Mike, not averse to type-casting, had selected a poncho, a cowboy hat and a toy gun and holster; and confused everyone by insisting they refer to him henceforth as "the man with no name."

It would have taken a team of Oscar-winning scriptwriters to weave into a cohesive narrative the motley crew of kitchen and administrative staff that collected nervously on a side lawn shortly before two thirty: Oscar Wilde, Clint Eastwood, a Red Indian, a Dalmatian, a nurse – a rather *too* sexy nurse to Kevin's eyes; surely Diane could have found a longer skirt – a policeman, a tiger and a bloke in a hessian sack holding a wilting piece of cardboard.

The 'custodians of the lines' in all their confused, confusing glory.

Charlie had with him a plastic bag containing nine tin cans and a ball of string for his task. Mike had picked up a packet of the slimmest cigars he could find, but had no task formulated, on the basis that he didn't plan on getting caught. Kevin too had yet to decide on his task and had a splitting headache. It surely couldn't get any worse.

The game was won at four thirty-eight by the eleven/ twelve-year-old girls, who successfully delivered the word d-e-a-d-l-i-n-e to the Baron and the witch, the pair of them getting on famously well considering the threat one purportedly posed to the other's abode. The winning group had only had seven of the letters, but word had spread by then of a *rogue* element in the game, so with time running out and no one wanting the oldest boys to win, a concession was made.

The devil, however, was very much in the detail.

Diane had been asked a succession of loosely medical questions, including "Ooo matron, what's this lump in my pants?"; "Can I take your temperature with my thermometer?"; "Any chance of a quick medical, love?"; and the inspired coup-de-grâce, "Fancy a fuck, Nursie?" The fact that a nine-year-old girl had said she liked her uniform, while another asked if she was a real nurse, was scant consolation for several hours of smutty innuendo.

Tracy had a far easier time, on account of lodging herself a dozen feet up in a tree and dispensing her laminated line upon receiving the answers to riddles she read from a book unearthed in the library.

Kevin had kindly been enlightened early on in the game that he had "a crap costume," asked if his mate was "queer," and told that his task was "totally shite"; fair comment considering each group was being asked to perform a dance in a style of his choosing. By the time the eldest girls had said "Stop being a prat and just give us the line," he'd lost the will for confrontation, not to mention exhausted his repertoire of dance styles, and handed it over meekly.

He would, much later and after the victory presentation, discover Charlie crouched under a small, ornamental hump-backed bridge over the stream that snaked through the woods. His tear-stained cheeks said it all: a downfall only magnified by the height of the expectations that preceded it. Kevin sat down beside him and waited in a silence that was finally broken with a sniffle and a noisy nose wipe.

"To think I wanted to become a teacher," Charlie said, emitting an empty laugh. "Stupid bloody idea that was," he added, thumping the side of his head between each syllable. "Thought I had it sussed and all. Make them think outside the box. Literally." He forced out an empty laugh. "I really did think they'd like it. It's such a clever puzzle."

"They were animals. Doesn't mean anything," tried Kevin.

But Charlie wasn't easily consoled and opted instead to wallow. The antithesis of Tracy's damage limitation, he had carefully laid out his tins into three rows of three and eagerly awaited the first group. It had been the youngest girls and they had deliberated politely before the leader whispered it might be a little hard for them and Charlie had led them to a solution they hadn't really understood, but which they greeted with gratifying enthusiasm, upon which he handed over the laminated card. That was the high spot of his afternoon. As successive groups treated the puzzle with less and less interest and decorum, Charlie's patience shortened, the children's behaviour deteriorated and the writing was on the wall. As one group walked away, he'd heard someone mutter "That was rubbish" and with it went all his self-confidence. The eldest boys had then walked up, grabbed the cans and ransomed them for the card, before running off with them anyway. The eldest girls arrived to find him rummaging for stones and twigs. They noticed the remaining cards sticking out of a carrier bag and as he shouted, "So sorry about this, I won't be a moment," over his shoulder, they simply took them all and walked away. His relief at arriving back with a stock of similar-sized stones was replaced by confusion at their disappearance. The next group arrived and the task worked well enough, but then he couldn't find the cards, which didn't go down very well, particularly as he'd never bothered reading what was written on them. Charlie, lacking the inner strength to ride out the confrontation, wilted visibly. The leader flashed him a concerned look as she led her charges away, her pity enough to precipitate a crumble. He'd made it as far as the bridge before slumping to the ground.

"Come on then, let's get you back," said Kevin, giving Charlie's bony shoulder a squeeze as he rose to his feet. Charlie shrugged, sighed and followed. They set off back towards the school, Kevin encouraging, Charlie slowly recovering.

For his part, as the starting whistle went, Mike had taken a position on the far side of a small clearing, lit a Hamlet cigar – his first ever – narrowed his eyes as he watched, through a cloud of smoke, the youngest girls' group tentatively approach, pulled a gun on them and shouted, "Well punks, are you feeling lucky?" One girl screamed. A second started crying. Another ran away. The others, lacking a working knowledge of 1970s San Francisco maverick cop cinematic gold, were predictably just perplexed; even more so when the leader's enquiry – once she had fetched back the traumatised escapee – as to the task they were to face saw Mike raise an eyebrow, smirk, look down at the ground, say, "Well, do ya punks?" and then leg it, deflecting off a tree with a grunt of pain as he blundered into the undergrowth. The implied "chase me" was ignored, but that didn't stop him running half a mile, the cigar clamped between his teeth.

By the time he came to a halt, the exercise-induced huffing and puffing had speed-smoked the cigar to a near stub. Checking he hadn't been pursued, he bent over to catch his breath and vomited his lunch and what remained of the cigar over his trainers. Bent double for a good few minutes, he eventually felt able to stand straight. At which point he lurched forward and was sick again. The nausea didn't subside, so upon hearing the cries and clamour of another group of children approaching, he crawled under a laurel bush and lay in abject misery for the next twenty minutes. Then he fell asleep.

Awakening to silence and a rank taste in his mouth, he crept out from his cubbyhole and made his leisurely way back through the now deserted woods.

*

Ten o'clock on the final evening saw the kids in their beds, stocked up for midnight feasts and excitedly anticipating dorm raids. A paranoid 'holiday controller' – "to be honest I don't care what they get up to, just so long as they don't fuck each other" – and his assistant had taken on sentry duties, leaving the team leaders and other members of staff, kitchen workers included, to a distant corner of the school, a modest assortment of alcoholic beverages and a free rein.

For them the evening comprised a succession of games, many of which the children had themselves been playing during the holiday: wink murder; shooting rabbits; a game involving a circle of seated participants and a rolled-up tube of sellotaped newspaper; and one called 'shoeing the horse', where two people were blindfolded, seven shoes scattered about the room and the first to scrabble about and place shoes under each leg of their chair was the winner.

The latter saw Charlie's reluctant and self-conscious debut, though his mood turned to unabashed glee upon whisking off his blindfold to see his 'horse' fully shod and

Tracy's shoeless, its supposed blacksmith off in a distant corner of the room, laughing hysterically and pulling at a trainer still attached to a leg. Charlie's triumphalism drew uncomfortable glances given Tracy was clearly inebriated on her first-ever alcoholic intake and was soon to repair to the toilet, where she spent the rest of the evening in grim contemplation of her stomach contents. Flushed with success, Charlie played on, but when the games took a turn for the slightly risqué, he headed for a quiet corner, where he wrapped himself around a can of shandy, sipping from it very occasionally, the feel of it in his hand thrill enough.

For his part, Kevin was thoroughly enjoying himself. He hadn't had cider before, but readily warmed to its beguiling charms, magnanimously forgiving Diane her highly impractical and inappropriate choice of wide game costume and embracing unquestioningly the sight of two of the leaders forming a human train. Jeff was the engine with Gail the carriage behind, her hands on his hips, as they trotted round the room going "choo-choo." The looks on their faces were suggestive of a private joke worth getting and the room waited expectantly, if a little uncomfortably. "Room for one more," they shrilled and Gail stooped to take the hand of the nearest male, Brian, who was pulled to his feet, had his willing hands – *lucky sod*, thought Kevin – placed on her hips and was led from the room with a confused look on his face. A final "choo-choo" was delivered, then the door closed behind them.

A couple of minutes later it opened again to admit a new-look train, same order but in-the-know smiles one and all, the largest on the flushed face of the final carriage.

And so the process was repeated, alternating the genders, noise levels increasing with the length of the train, until Kevin had his hand grabbed by Vicky, one of the older team leaders, whose plain and unremarkable features had benefitted significantly from an alcoholic makeover in Kevin's eyes, as had the vacuum-packed backside now shifting mesmerisingly between his hands. He could feel the elastic of her pants underneath his palms. As they made their last circuit of the room Kevin was doing a passable interpretation of a Red Indian war dance as he juggled a swelling erection, his grin widening insanely.

Bringing up the rear, he had a few unwitnessed moments after pulling the door closed to indulge in a spot of much needed genital rearrangement with his free hand, before re-establishing hip contact as they trailed the others down a corridor, around a corner and along another narrow corridor, where they came to a halt.

Seeing the others release their couplings, Kevin reluctantly let his hands drop and his gaze rise; to find Jeff and Gail looking in his direction. A reflex "what" stalled in his throat as Gail turned to Jeff, put her arms around his neck and, after flashing Kevin a deliciously filthy look, launched into a full-on kiss, lips clearly opening prior to contact. Their faces squirmed together for what seemed like an eternity and to a backing track of suggestive moans. Breaking off, Gail turned around, caught Kevin's gaze momentarily and then started snogging Brian. *Christ, I'm in an orgy*, thought Kevin, the head of his now fully-erect penis escaping the flies of his boxers and nudging at the inside of his zip in a bid for escape. Once unsuckered from Gail, Brian turned and passed it all – lips, saliva, gropes, the lot – on to Tanya, who appeared to lap it all up with scarcely-contained enthusiasm. And so on, along the line towards Kevin.

Before her turn arrived, Vicky leant towards him, attempted an eyelash-flutter that came across as rapid eye movement and whispered, "I'm going to enjoy this, Kevin." His jaw muscles momentarily failed, then tightened to lift his chin and permit the ensuing gulp. He was experimenting with lip formations and degrees of parting as Vicky noisily wrenched her lips away from his predecessor and turned towards him with a look of predatory longing. He leant slightly forwards, arms stretching out to form a Vicky shape, puckered his lips and closed his eyes – only for the darkness and his cheek to explode in a blast of pain from a contact that whipped his head to the side and sent him staggering into the wall.

As the initial shock subsided, his cheek recovering a hint of pink as the rest of his face turned red, his first conscious recognition was of seven faces laughing at him and one with a concerned smile, as Vicky clasped and unclasped a still-stinging hand. A cocktail of emotions surged through him in that moment: disappointment, surprise, hurt, rejection, embarrassment; with a lingering hard-on thrown in for bad measure.

Then he got it. Saw the beauty of it. And through the cloud of self-pity and confusion, he forced up the corners of his lips and, throwing his hands in the air, said, "You got me," to cheers and back-slaps all round. Vicky even gave him a peck on his cheek.

The ground-rules confirmed, they returned to the others and it was with Vicky once again in his grasp and Diane's hands sitting disappointingly loosely on his waist that he returned to the distant corridor for the next denouement.

He glanced at Diane repeatedly as the chain reaction worked its way towards her, seeing the same emotions he'd just felt muddling on her face. He tried a comforting smile and she returned a curious look he couldn't quite define. Then his arm was tugged and as he turned, his face was engulfed by Vicky's. He made the right noises, but in truth he felt guilty putting Diane through the uneasiness and jealous confusion, so it was with a degree of dutiful relief that he finally broke away and turned towards her. Kevin's first instinct was just to kiss her, but he was reality checked by an expression on her face suggestive of an expectation of something unpleasant. Could she possibly know? The will draining away, he cut his losses and flashed his hand feebly across her cheek. Fortunately, his cupped palm generated a convincing enough noise to compensate for the lack of power. She gave him another fleeting unfathomable look before the communal laughter kicked in and the joke dawned on her.

Kevin tried not to look too interested in Diane's choice of carriage and was content for it to be Danny, a quiet team leader with a pigtail and a silly-looking sprout of hair on his chin. He returned gratefully to contemplations of the snog-fest ahead.

It was almost one when the party finally broke up. Kevin took the opportunity presented by a rare spell of penile flaccidity to pop to the loo. When he got back to the room, most of the others had departed. He couldn't see Diane, but Tracy rose from her slough of inebriation and, very much out of character, helpfully pointed out the stairs she'd just seen her heading up.

After helping with the tidying up, Kevin and his turgid, expectant genital appendage set off in search of his quarry, the second condom residing snugly in his back pocket. Thrilling to the imminent kill, he bounded up the stairs to a landing, only to encounter the sobering reality of three possible directions and no idea which to take.

A distant whimper drew him up another flight of stairs. Pausing at the top, he listened again and was about to head back down when what sounded like a faint, sniffly sob took him down a corridor. It sounded like a crying child hidden in one of the rooms. With cider-induced empathy, Kevin investigated. Diane would have to wait.

A slither of light traversing the floor ahead brought him to a slightly ajar door. He reached to push it but something checked him. He edged his hand forward again, only to pull it back at a pained exclamation. Benign intent was at once superseded by apprehension. Something was being done to someone. A strangled "uhh" only heightened his concern. Edging closer, he moved an eye to the crack in the door and encountered skin. It took a bit of working out but he soon deciphered a bare bottom, clenched and pinned by two heels. It moved down and forward with a masculine "errrrr" echoed by a feminine "uhhhh", then up and back, then down and forward; each thrust generating noises ever louder and more urgent.

As the assignation reached its climax, Kevin took his leave and tiptoed back up the corridor, then hurried down, along, up, along and into the toilets. Tears in his eyes. Indignity in his soul. *Those* images on his mind. Straining erection in his trousers. In his hand. Pumping furiously; feeding on *those* images. Ejaculating. The high.

Then the low.

And with the come-down arrived the disorientating and miserable realisation that he appeared to have derived more enjoyment and satisfaction from watching Diane have sex with Danny than he had derived from having sex with her himself.

UPPER SIXTH YEAR

Clarke's final year at Nethercott would see him take three A Levels – maths, further maths and, having exhausted the mathematical variants, physics, being the nearest thing to maths – be party to two fights, commit three assaults, attempt an impossible challenge and take a second clumsy stab at sexual intercourse.

Most of the Upper Sixth pupils sported new ties. There were four design options: head boy, monitor, house prefect or the same as previous years.

Every pupil by default became a house prefect as they entered the year. Out of their ranks were selected seven monitors, each sporting a bright blue tie with the school's crest in its centre. They were the elite few, the crème de la crème; the best the school could offer at Speech Day, recruitment events or dignitary visits. A small room next door to the staff room was made available to them, complete with colour television and, more in hope than expectation, daily broadsheets. From their ranks came the head boy, chosen by the staff. Evans received the most votes, but Sir Reginald insisted no boy who had only been at the school for two years deserved the honour of being head boy.

Clarke was a house prefect, as was Morris, though he longed not to be. But the die was cast once term had started. Only the prescient few, usually those with older brothers at the school, had applied for exemption the previous term. Morris had not. Those who had, formed a clique that congregated in a corner of the tuck room during breaks, unshackled and free. The initial looks of condescension thrown their way soon turned to knowing respect for a choice well made.

There were privileges for the house prefects, most notably not having to queue for meals and access to the common room: a dog-legged ground floor room boasting a CD player, three kettles, a fridge, a black and white television, a video recorder, a selection of largely-ignored board games; the bulk of the floor space littered with tattered and sagging armchairs, stained bean bags, wobbling benches and graffiti-ridden tables. But those dubious privileges came at a cost, because house prefects were to all intents and purposes unpaid reservists called upon to do whatever duties the staff couldn't be bothered with. And the common room was little more than a teasing come-on, envied by all before their final year and relished for a short while, before the novelty wore off like the pattern on its carpet and they were left with lists and rosters to adhere to.

Worst of these was refectory queue duty.

Access to the refectory for meals was through a doorway at the end of a long, thin corridor. Excitable and hungry pupils would funnel down the corridor, to be confronted by a house prefect standing by the entrance, tasked with permitting no more than fifteen pupils through at a time, thereby saving the dinner ladies from a deluge they were not deemed able to handle. Scores of

Nethercott's finest would descend on the prefect, some happy to wait, some like greyhounds in the traps, others taking advantage of the anonymity of the crowd to hurl insults and innuendos and generally heckle.

A few prefects recognised an opportunity for legitimised violence. Marsh sported an expression that screamed 'bring it on' and drew an imaginary, and uncommunicated, line across the floor a good few feet back from the usual holding place. Any pupil stepping across that line without permission was promptly pushed, barged or thumped back with relish. He favoured subtle gestures that might easily be missed by the inattentive, thereby warranting a belligerent, "Well come on then," at startled faces; or the dummied beckoning that fooled boys to step over the line too early. And when he did permit access, Marsh insisted on counting them through, a process involving a slap to the back of the head as each number was called out.

At the other end of the spectrum cowered Morris, for whom responsibility highlighted a total absence of effective authority. He knew it, and after about five minutes, so did the boys. His voice had grown louder and shriller. The crowd had mimicked him cruelly. Small ripples of impatient discontent had become waves and then a surge that drowned a desperate Morris and swept the entire queue into the refectory. He was later found – by those masters not deployed dissipating the resulting scrimmage by the counters, clearing up smashed plates or comforting dinner ladies – a humiliated wreck quaking in a corner of the changing rooms.

By far the biggest change came on the accommodation front. Three years in the modern detached dormitory blocks had been followed by a year in smaller dormitories adjoining the main school building. Now their last year saw entry into the hallowed labyrinthine warren of study/bedrooms that littered the top floor of the main school building. Over forty wood-panelled rooms, all of them wilfully and randomly differing in shape – not a square or rectangle in sight – and each housing two or three pupils and as many beds, desks, upright plastic chairs, 'easy' chairs and fitted wardrobes, plus a mirror and a washbasin. Such were the layouts that one bed was rarely visible from another. A floor plan, not that anyone had been foolish enough to attempt one, would have looked like the most elaborate of parquet floors; or one of those wooden puzzles with various different shapes fitted deceptively neatly into a base, before you tipped them all out, never to be returned, and wished you hadn't.

For most, the move was a source of great excitement; a taste of independence and relative privacy previously denied them in the public performance that was dormitory life.

For a few it brought huge anxiety.

Spurning the concept of student choice, pupil couplings were ostensibly in alphabetical order, although *the school reserves absolute discretion to arrive at pupil groupings that take into account subject choices and such other criteria as the school might deem relevant and persuasive.* Decisions were final. Clarke and Evans were overjoyed to find themselves circumventing Cummings, Denman, Draper and Easeby to share a room. They were too busy celebrating and high-fiving to remember Morris, standing pale and shaking by the wall, coming to terms with the Marsh-Morris combo he'd feared so much. He'd even asked his parents to send a letter requesting he be allowed to share a room with Clarke; a letter full of persuasive logic, but doomed to failure given a recipient deeply resentful of parental interference.

As his only friends disappeared off to feather their nest, Morris felt a tap on his shoulder.

"You go up first and get ready," leered Marsh for the benefit of his usual henchmen. "And I'll be up shortly, darling."

Morris was confused. What was he on about? Should he laugh? Instead he did as he'd been told and was relieved as distance, the sound of his own footsteps and the clunking of his case on the stairs drowned out the ongoing mirth behind him.

It took him a few minutes to fully explore the nooks, angles and crannies of room twenty-two. He had selected what he saw as the least desirable bed and was unpacking his clothes when Marsh blundered in.

"What you doing with my bed, runt? Fuck off over there."

*

A few weeks into the autumn term, it was a surprised Clarke who leapfrogged Marsh in the logical pecking order and took over as goalkeeper for the 1st XI, the views of Evans weighing heavily in his favour. Clarke's performances brought a predictable unpredictability and much athletic lunacy to Nethercott's penalty area. But on balance, the gaffes were deemed outnumbered by the saves, many of them inspired and unlikely, so all bar Marsh permitted him his idiosyncrasies.

*

A blustery Sunday afternoon in November found the three of them cocooned in the snug warmth of room seven; Evans and Clarke lying on their respective beds, hands clasped behind heads, while Morris prodded teabags in chipped mugs and wittered contentedly. This was his sanctuary and Evans and Clarke allowed him to come and go as he wished, recognising what lay waiting for him in his own room. As he handed over the mugs and offered round the biscuits, he almost tripped over Evans' football boots and commented that at least he'd be able to put his boots away for the rest of the school year come Christmas. Clarke asked Evans what "gay" sport he'd be doing next term and a predictably immature exchange followed, interrupted by Morris remarking that whilst Clarke playing for the 1st XI was remarkable enough, it would be as nothing compared to Evans ever playing for the 1st XV.

Ten minutes later, the three of them were walking across the grass, leaves clattering and chattering around their feet, towards the hallowed turf of the 1st XV rugby pitch, which Sir Reginald insisted remained unadulterated throughout the year; its grass tended with more care than the 1st XI cricket pitch, its lines painted fortnightly, the posts sticking two fingers up at any sport that dared to distract pupils from the great game.

Morris handed over the rugby ball as he would an injured hedgehog and the conversion challenge commenced.

When pre-season rugby training commenced, Mr Rodgers took Clarke to one side to tell him he would be 1st XV captain the following term.

"There's no one better suited," Mr Rodgers urged, filling the stunned silence. "I may be the master in charge but this is going to be our team, not mine, so feel free to contribute whenever you want, on whatever you want. Selection. Tactics. The lot."

Those bold assurances of mutuality were tested to their limits a couple of matches into the spring term, when Clarke requested that Evans be brought into the team as a specialist kicker.

"May I remind you that this is Rugby Union, Clarke, not bloody American bloody Football. Our players don't flit on and off the pitch, any more than they wear girly padding and helmets. They are part of a team and it's not fair on the other fourteen players to carry a lightweight like Evans just so he can grab a spot of glory every now and then."

"I don't want to kick," persisted Clarke. "I've had a crisis of confidence recently. In any case, it's too much to take on, what with the captaincy and everything."

"Not to mention him being a walking gap in our defence," ploughed on Mr Rodgers regardless. "Fancy worrying about that all game as well?"

A fairly damning argument for the prosecution, but Clarke was not to be denied.

"He'll score more points than he'll lose us."

"Christ. He'd have to be a bloody outstanding kicker," said Mr Rodgers, rather enjoying the liberating language he felt this master-captain rapport permitted and pondering the insertion of something a little stronger.

"He is," replied Clarke, increasingly disconcerted by Mr Rodgers apparently mutating from distant, slightly ponderous history teacher to chummy, potty-mouthed pseudo-mate.

Mr Rodgers was thinking. Clarke could tell because his fingers were stroking his chin and one eyebrow had risen. Sure enough, "Your call, Clarke. You show me he's as good as you say and, well, fuck it, eh?" said Mr Rodgers, deploying the 'F' bomb for the first, and last, time in front of a pupil. They both very much wished he hadn't.

Clarke prevailed and left Mr Rodgers wallowing in a severe bout of post-"fuck" regret. At least he would have a friendly face during training, matches and, most of all, the coach to away games.

To date Clarke had elected for a distant style of leadership that had seen him seated at the front of the coach in the company of Mr Rodgers and Fulmington, the fleet-footed Wagner fanatic and reluctant winger who had been born aged forty-five, found school a tedious interlude to be endured before becoming a barrister, and who detested the caveman antics of his teammates on and off the field, whilst enjoying the more naked aspects of changing room life. Neither companion enhanced Clarke's credibility with the team, or added weight to his commands on the pitch.

But the alternative was far worse. Highlights in the rear seats included Henderson inserting twenty-one ha'penny coins in his foreskin, Marsh urinating in a bottle and drinking it down, fist punching the air in celebration of his pyrrhic victory, and Durbridge setting the most-audible-burps-in-a-minute record, despite his mouth filling with bile ten seconds before time was up.

But in Evans, a boy who loathed rugby players, he now had a companion. Eyebrows and the corners of their mouths would rise and fall throughout each journey as the cretinous musings of the moron contingent wafted over them like methane from the congested bowels of the rear of the coach.

"Don't worry," Clarke fraudulently reassured Mr Rodgers, as the team warmed up for a reluctant, slender, contact-averse Evans' debut at outside-centre, a position normally the preserve of a tough-tackling, hard-running brick outhouse.

"Easy to say," replied Mr Rodgers, with justified apprehension.

"Fuck it, eh," said Clarke and mortified himself by throwing in a playful wink.

"Double detention, Clarke," said Mr Rodgers, horrified. "*What?*"

"One for swearing and another for that ridiculous wink."

"But—"

"No buts, Clarke. There's a line and you've stepped over it. Have you a problem with that?"

"No," said Clarke, wondering at the inequity of stepping over a line that appeared to move at Mr Rodger's whim.

"Good," said Mr Rodgers, who, after failing to rise to the occasion for Mrs Rodgers the night before, was already regretting taking out his frustration on Clarke, for whom he had a genuine soft spot; though not soft enough to be winked at in that repulsive manner.

*

An official Nethercott tradition was the settlement of inter-pupil grudges through a formal request for an invigilated boxing match. The grievance would be presented to the master, and if approved as being of merit and a fair contest, a challenge would be issued and posted on a notice board. The challenged pupil had three days to accept, or not. If accepted, a three-round bout would take place with boxing gloves before an audience of their peers, a large crowd a certainty. If he refused the challenge, he committed to a meeting with the Head of Year and the other pupil to resolve the matter. Whether or not this worked was beside the point. In ducking the fight, he had effectively lost and gained a host of derogatory new nicknames. A tried and tested tradition dating back over fifty years.

An unofficial Nethercott tradition was for the two parties to meet behind the sports hall after school and thump the shit out of each other with bare fists until one surrendered or was incapacitated. Or the spectators stepped in to end it.

The spring term saw one official and five unofficial challenges. No-one could have imagined that the latter would include a Marsh-Morris bout; and one initiated by Morris at that. When asked why, all Clarke could elicit from him was that he'd had enough and something had to be done.

In the days leading up to the allotted time, Evans dismissed the whole affair as a prank that would never materialise. Clarke too was dubious and envied Evans his casual indifference, but there was something about Morris's disposition, a resolute desperation, that left him fearing the worst. Morris remained unswayed by Clarke's near-constant, badgering concern, though he secretly relished it.

"Why are you doing this?"

"It's between me and him."

"Why don't you do it the official way?" Clarke asked. "With a proper challenge."

"They'd never allow it to happen. We're hardly well-matched."

"Doesn't that tell you something?"

But the boy was not for turning.

The book had Morris at fifty to one. Clarke played the contest through in his head more than fifty-one times during the build-up. Morris lost them all. And when he did finally succeed in concocting a Morris victory in his imagination, it necessitated so many fanciful twists and turns that it had lost all persuasiveness long before Morris revealed his black belt in karate and snapped Marsh's head back with the heel of his out-thrust hand.

It was a Tuesday afternoon after school in late February that saw a crowd gather in the encroaching dusk on the patch of grass behind the sports hall. That the actual fight lasted longer than five seconds owed nothing to Morris's combative qualities and everything to Marsh's dilemma as he calmly stepped aside from Morris's initial foray: a frantic charge, arms whirling like an out-of-sync windmill. A cheer erupted and it dawned on Marsh that whilst he could never technically lose, the concept of victory might prove rather nebulous. He'd sat through enough martial arts films with his stepfather to know that for the fight to be a decent spectacle, it needed to last a while and see-saw between the protagonists. Hitting someone so pathetic would make him look like a bully. Getting caught by a punch or two, or the fight lasting longer than a minute, would be a technical defeat. So comedic it had to be. Unfortunately, this didn't play to his strengths. His idea of funny involved slapstick and someone else's pain. Witty word-play caused his eyebrows to furrow; for him the true essence of comedy lay in an inappropriate fart or burp, and the louder, the funnier. Consequently, he found himself in something of an irritated quandary as he contemplated Morris's flailings, like someone lying back in a lovely hot bath only to hear a moth launch its first irritating attack on the light bulb.

Ruminations concluded, he frowned, gave a slight shrug… and thumped him.

Not particularly hard, but enough for Morris to collapse in on himself and sink to the ground. Marsh stared down at the puddle of flesh and worked on a contemptuous sneer. Once he had it in place, he played the audience like a gladiator seeking the mood of the Colosseum before finishing off or sparing a vanquished foe. The crowd played their part in the pantomime with boos, laughs and jeers. Shifting glances and a change in communal tone alerted him to the slow, unsteady rise from the ground of Morris, albeit a wobblier version. He'd had enough of this and when Morris leant into a totter that compelled his body towards him, no quandary remained. His outstretched arm and open palm were enough to halt the charge and hold Morris still, aside from those two spindly arms circling uselessly. He pulled back his elbow and clenched his fist, but as he started to propel it towards Morris's still defiant face, he felt fingers clasp his arm firmly and a voice in his ear.

"Enough. No more. Leave it."

*

On the rugby pitch, the team had soon fallen into a pattern that brought out the best in Evans. If Nethercott had the put-in or throw and a kick was the elected option, Evans would move across and take up a position about five yards behind the scrum or lineout. The scrum-half would throw the ball back and with the entire team between him and the opposition, he had enough time to place his kick unharried, ridding himself of the ball quickly enough for any physical assault on him to be unlikely, or a clear foul. It wasn't pretty, but it was very effective. Win the ball and the pack could be fairly sure they'd have a casual stroll thirty yards up the pitch. And if they got inside the twenty-two, the drop kick option proved a near-guaranteed three points, as was a penalty kick anywhere north of the opponents' ten-yard line. With effort rewarded so readily, the pack responded. Tries may have been scarcer in those early exchanges, but with the steady stream of three-pointers invariably building up a clear half-time advantage, the backs were given their head in the second half and tries were easier to score against a tiring team resigned to defeat.

For Clarke, however, the constant invigilation and manipulation was exhausting. At every whistle he had to assess the situation and, more like a quarterback, call the play. And it fell to him at full-back to cover any opposition break through the three quarters, who were a boy down with Evans seldom present in body, and never in spirit, when it came to tackling. But if he ever needed strength at the home games, he had only to glance to the touchline, where Morris would be standing, shivering and shifting his weight from one foot to the other, that look of part disgust, part fascination on his face; flashing him a smile or a clumsy thumbs-up. And with every glimpse of his friend, his resolve would strengthen.

*

On the amateur dramatic front, Clarke's first direct involvement in that year's production was to attend the final night's performance of *The Mikado*. It did nothing for him and he was unimpressed with the scenery. He glanced around for Wolsey with what he convinced himself was casual indifference, but she was nowhere to be seen and he was back in his room by ten.

It was after midnight when Evans returned in high spirits with tales of bad behaviour, much of it his own and a lot of it involving someone called Georgina. Clarke feigned indifference, but he was intrigued and titillated enough to readily acquiesce to the invitation Evans had wangled for him to Georgina's Easter weekend party at her parents' Surrey mansion.

In the days that followed it was fear rather than excitement that gripped Clarke; his first extra-curricular mixed party, that traumatic last night at Aspire excepted. His apprehension straitjacketed the intervening weeks, though he did his best to be optimistic: it would be mainly girls there, which had to be a plus, and they behaved much better than boys, so it would be far more civilised; especially with the safety net of her parents in attendance to ensure good behaviour. If nothing else, he reassured himself, this would be controlled, invigilated access to girls and that couldn't be bad.

*

On the eve of the party, the first weekend of the Easter break, Clarke arranged to meet up with Evans at Waterloo station. He was disappointed to find they had company – the entire 1st XV pack amongst them – dismayed that they were already quaffing alcohol, and horrified when they bundled their bodies, rucksacks and sleeping bags into a smoking compartment of the train and all lit up. He reluctantly sipped at a can of warm cider, refused an offer of a cigarette, was called a "gay poof" and had to smile back at a wall of guffawing faces, his one ally lost to the crowd. Things could only improve.

Georgina did indeed live in a mansion, complete with entry gate, sweeping drive, tennis court, stables and a swimming pool. That part of the bargain was met. But the clause about her parents being in situ was not. They were in Antigua. Clarke's heart sank, then resurfaced on hearing that Georgina's elder brothers, Hugo and Edward, were in attendance, presumably to ensure law and order; names redolent of maturity and dignified authority.

News soon filtered through that Edward had passed out in an alcoholic haze; then Hugo drove past at speed on a sit-down lawn mower, shrieking and waving a near-empty bottle of whisky above his head. Clarke silently cursed the absent parents and abandoned all hope.

Three hours in and he was predictably in the kitchen. He'd tried the huge lounge, where the DJ had the stereo blaring and the lights flashing and the dancing was underway. But for all its shadows and noise he'd felt more exposed and on display than hidden. He'd tried wandering from room to room, giving the appearance of being purposefully in transit rather than desperately uncomfortable and alone. He'd tried the toilets, all three of them, several times each. But there was only so long he could spend in them at any one time and he was starting to exit to the same faces. He'd tried outside, but it started raining. He'd thought about leaving, but the taxis had taken a quarter of an hour to get them here from the station and he had no idea where they were.

Which left the kitchen, where he sat at the large wooden table and nurtured a glass of lager, regularly lifting it to wet his upper lip, but seldom allowing any into his mouth. People would wander in and engage him in inconsequential chit-chat and for those brief moments he was an integral part of the evening. Things looked up when a pretty blonde girl came in, got herself a drink and then actually checked herself from leaving and voluntarily took a seat opposite him. He offered up his musings on Fermat's Last Theorem for her consumption. She asked him if he fancied a dance, but instead he taught her how to play *Brussel Sprouts*. Before he realised it, he'd finished his drink, so he got them another. This was great. And he was winning five-nil. She even smiled politely at one of his word puns.

Then Bridges came in to ruin everything.

"Howdy pardner," was his opening shot, not the first reference of the night to the brightly-checked shirt, denim jacket and elaborate outsized buckle on his belt; fashion items selected by his sisters. One look at the outfit he had chosen had awoken a tide of protective pity and obliged them to stage an intervention. Glad of any interaction with them, he had surrendered to their superior knowledge and loaned clothing. "You look a bit like a cowboy," Belinda had said, and it sounded a good thing to look like.

He didn't bite and drew up the dots for another game.

"Give us a tune then," came Bridge's next stab; not the first reference of the night to the mouth organ poking out of Clarke's breast pocket. His idea, and one he was rather proud of.

"Not now… mate," the word sounding foreign and cumbersome in his mouth. "Maybe later," he added, not because of a busy itinerary, but because he hadn't a clue how to play the thing.

Bridges leaned over and looked down at the dots and curves on the paper between them. "What the fuck load of shite are you doing, you big nonce?" he enquired eloquently, before belching violently.

The girl stood up, smiled down at Clarke and said, "You coming?" He rose instinctively.

"Oooo, Clarke's got a girlfriend," interjected Bridges, and threw an arm carelessly around Clarke's shoulders. "Don't forget your mates, eh?"

Her eyebrows asked him again.

"I'll be through in a while," was his foolish, myopic response. The addition of a "love" was a moronic add-on, that earned him a pat on the back from Bridges.

She shrugged her shoulders and left.

"That's the way to treat 'em," said Bridges. "Rather have a beer than a bird any day of the week, eh Clarkie." A nickname at long last. His heart soared and he was swept along on a wave of testosterone that dumped him, fists aloft, on the dance floor in the midst of much of the 1st XV team in full voice. "You're everywhere and nowhere baby…" And there he was, part of a high-kicking circle of lads. His mates. "It's fucking obvious," they all bellowed, punching the air in that way groups of inebriated males have that celebrates the male bond while retaining maximum attractiveness to any girls watching. This was their mating dance and it stepped up a gear as the opening chords of 'You Really Got Me' riffed in and out came the air guitars. Guitars away for 'Jump Around', Clarke eventually getting to grips with the arm actions and simian antics that seemed to come so naturally to the others. Then came 'Smells like Teen Spirit' and they dissolved into a morass of banging heads and poorly-mouthed lyrics.

When 'Heart of Glass' started up, Clarke looked up from tying his shoelaces to find himself a solitary male, girls creeping onto the dance-floor. Panicking, he swiftly departed.

Too many in the kitchen. Toilets full. Still raining. He found himself in what appeared to be a library room that ran off the lounge. A couple of comfortable-looking armchairs sat empty, one in an inviting puddle of golden light deposited by a standing lamp behind it. He grabbed a book from a shelf and sank into the sanctuary of the chair. Instinctively he opened it up and began to read.

Twenty minutes into a chapter very boringly titled 'Jack's Garden,' he was still reading what appeared to be a very detailed description of a garden and the surrounding countryside. Nothing had happened. He looked forward and groaned on seeing that the chapter ran to page eighty-eight. And what a stupid pretentious name for a book. Why on earth had he picked this one? He searched for an alternative, maybe something promising a bit of smut, and noted as he did so that a Nethercott contingent – minus Evans, who he hadn't seen for ages – had formed in a dark corner of the lounge and were chatting excitedly with some girls. He was on the point of swapping the book when one of the girls broke away from the pack and came towards him. He reopened it and adopted a cultured look of concentration.

"Are you okay?" she asked, settling into the other seat.

"What? Me? Yeah, of course," he stammered, noticing that her skirt was riding up as she squirmed to get comfortable.

"My name's Rosie."

"I'm reading," he offered, superfluously.

"So I see," she said, smiling. Then she uncrossed her legs, looking away as she did so to acknowledge someone and he caught a flash of white amongst the tanned flesh.

"It's a book," his mouth said in a slur, distracted as his mind reconfigured what he had just seen and a pleasurable sensation lapped at his loins. "Er, I tend to get very involved in my books," he blurted, trying to rescue the situation. "Especially a book as good as this one."

She leant forward to peer up at the cover. He couldn't help but catch a look down the front of her top; all white lace and cleavage. He let out an involuntary groan, which fortunately she didn't appear to hear. He was thankful for the book to place over his lap.

"Mind if I have a look?" she asked, with a look of such innocence that he had handed it over before taking stock of his situation. He instinctively collapsed in on himself like a defective camp bed.

"Are you okay?" she asked, again.

"Yeah, of course," he said, again, sliding his elbows along his thighs to the knees and resting his chin on a hand. All topped off with a fascinated, intelligent look.

"You sure? You don't look very comfortable."

"I'm fine, honest."

She opened the book and started reading, giving him a much-needed opportunity to sit back and quickly adjust himself, which he effected with a cunning exaggerated yawn and stretch.

"Have you read much of his work?"

"Most of it. I love his… er… descriptive passages. They're very…er… enigma-like."

"Wow. You really know your stuff. What's your favourite?"

"Favourite?" his voice trilling all of a sudden. "So hard to say."

"You must have one."

"Of course. It's probably… er… that one?" he said, somehow making it a question.

"Other than this one, I meant, silly," she said, with a coquettish slanting of her head.

"Oh, right. That would be… er… Sex… I mean Sex… tet… er… City."

"That's a weird name for a novel. What's it about?"

"About? Right. It's about a family with six children and… er… describes them. Lots."

"Sounds cool," she said, leaving her lips in a tantalising open pout as she trailed off the word, eyes locking in on his once he'd hauled them up from her cleavage. "It's not listed in the bio."

"It's a short story. Ha. Yes, of course, a short story. Sorry. Can't remember which collection, I'm afraid."

"No problem. Fancy a dance?"

"Yes," he blurted, gratefully grabbing at an escape route.

"Come on then." She took his hand and led him through to the lounge. He shuffled after her like some mental defective, with a final restorative tweak of the crotch and a gaze at her bum.

"I love this one," she said.

"Me too," he lied. The track was 'A Forest', all twelve green vinylic inches of it. Had he known at the outset, he would have paced himself better. She had it off pat; elbows drawn in, forearms floating in front of her swaying body, the occasional swirl thrown in for good measure, her loose skirt rising to reveal an expanse of upper thigh, her body silhouetted beneath the thin cotton each time she moved between him and the DJ's lights.

The concept of dancing was proving elusive.

He was all right provided he didn't move his feet. He could sort of collapse his hips now and then and wave his arms round a bit, hitting as many notes with a clenched fist as he could accurately predict. It sounded like a bloody instrumental. He mixed things up with a few *moves* of course. The index and middle finger Vs dragged across the face. A spot of hand jiving. A twirl of his own, not to be repeated. Touch of the air keyboard. Then at least the singing started and he could earnestly mouth words he didn't know, using the customary tactic of saying each word a fraction after hearing it. On and on it went, until with much relief he mimed a dramatic drum roll and hit the crash cymbal with a flamboyant flourish to 'celebrate' what he antipated to be the final note, only to then have to repeat it several more times as it reverberated on interminably. He concluded with one that wasn't there, but turned it into a silent fanfare to greet 'Blue Monday'. Yet more heavy beats.

There was nothing else for it. Bring on the robot dance. Elbows tight against sides, forearms stuck out at ninety degrees, hands rigid. Arms up and down in short, stabbing movements. Jerk the shoulders. Turn torso one way, then the other. Serious moves. He even got a bit of a robot walk going.

"Fancy going somewhere a bit more private?" she fluttered and flattered up at him, braving the random gesticulations and sweat spray to get close enough to be heard.

Clarke nodded frantically and gratefully, his robot having mutated into a lurching zombie, body parts scarcely under control.

She took him by the hand and led him off the dance floor – he expected some good-natured rowdy banter from his teammates, but no one seemed to notice – through the library room, along a corridor and, unbelievably, upstairs. As they climbed the curving, ornate staircase it appeared to his goggling eyes that her hips had dislocated, such was the exaggerated sweep of her backside with each step she took, each one causing his buttocks to clench and his hard-on to wince.

She paused briefly on the landing, flashed him a conspiratorial glance and led him down a shadowy corridor. They came to a halt. Rosie put one finger on his lips and leant her ear to a closed door. She knocked and on getting no response, pushed the door open. His penis followed her in.

The main light came on to reveal a simply-furnished clutterless bedroom, with an en suite, that had that guest room feel and clearly wasn't used very often. Perfect. Rosie had moved round the bed and was fumbling for the switch of a bedside lamp. Upon succeeding she sat back against the pillows, swivelled her torso towards him, patted the bed and told him to turn off the main light and "Get over here." He did so, very quickly, hitting two items of furniture on the way before stumbling onto the bed.

"Sor—" he managed before she had fixed her soft, wet lips on his and launched a tongue offensive, her left hand working round his unguarded flanks and stroking his erection through his jeans. Fearing the worst, he grabbed her hand and held it up and away from his lap.

He felt awkward holding it in mid-air, like some formal dance position, so to justify his action and stop it scurrying back, he leant up and kissed a finger, then another, before alighting on her thumb. Working his mouth up and down its length, he nibbled lightly and groaned in a manner he hoped was erotic and suggestive. But suggestive of what? Repulsed, he discarded her hand, rolled on top of her and aimlessly pawed.

"I'm just going to freshen up in the bathroom," she said, coming up for air. "When I get back, I want you naked and I want you ready, if you know what I mean. I'll just go and lock the door. Wouldn't want to be interrupted." She flashed him the dirtiest of smiles, pushed herself off the bed, swaggered across to lock the door and then swaggered back, his eyes fixed on her the whole way. Just before she disappeared into the bathroom, she unzipped her skirt, eased it down off her hips, let it to fall to the ground, stepped to one side, bent down from the waist to retrieve it, and disappeared into the bathroom, closing the door behind her.

Wide-eyed and open-mouthed, Clarke had to shake his head to try and clear the vision of the straining backs of her thighs and buttocks. "Oh God," he spewed, tugging desperately at the belt buckle, releasing the button and zip of his jeans and yanking them down with his pants to relieve the pressure. Whisking them off, he extracted himself from his jacket and shirt and lay back to draw breath and regroup.

"Uhh," he said as a slither of light across his legs preluded Rosie's head poking round the door.

"Woah," she said. "Down *tiger*. Just checking you had *protection*."

"What?" he replied, concentrating on looking as relaxed as feasible sprawled on a bed with a straining, exposed hard-on under the gaze of a near stranger.

"Protection? Johnny? Condom?"

"Yeah of course," he lied, as she disappeared back behind the door. Or maybe not. Careful that his penis didn't come into suicidal contact with anything, he located his wallet and fished out the unused condom from the previous summer. He was surprised to note that condoms had a 'use by' date, concerned to note that that date had passed and even more concerned to note that the date had expired over a year before he'd used its former companion. "Fuck it," he said, appropriately.

The pressure between his thighs was almost unbearable as he slowly unravelled the condom over his quivering penis. Miraculously he reached base camp without emission and in celebration punched the air triumphantly, lay back on the bed, spread-eagled himself, and stared down at the one-eyed, nodding trouser snake looking up at him.

Then the door opened.

He looked towards the bathroom, but the door was still closed. A flash blinded him and as his vision cleared, he registered it was the other door, the main door – the locked door? – that had flung open and the picture it now framed was a cluster of faces, some familiar, some not. All laughing. His hands shot to his penis, admirably still standing to attention amidst the chaos, and his knees headed for his chin, before he realised what else he'd be exposing and keeled to the side into a confused foetal ball. Then the bathroom door did open and Rosie emerged. "No," he blurted, some basic chivalric instinct kicking in, his thoughts ludicrously only of her decency. But he needn't have bothered. She was fully clothed. As she milked the applause, she threw him the merest of glances. "Nice arse. Maybe another time." The audience engulfed her, a mass of smiles and back-patting, high-fiving arms.

Then the door closed, leaving him alone and confused.

How? The door had been locked.

Who? Just about everyone. Had Evans been part of it?

When had they cooked this up?

Why?

When he awoke the next morning, it was to a thumping, pulsing headache, an allergy to light and a foul-tasting tongue refashioned in rough leather. It was minutes before he could fully open his eyes, several more before he could move and a few more again before he could start to take stock.

On the plus side he appeared to be dressed, but just as he dared to venture towards a horizon of positivity, he heard a rumble of hooves and a herd of negatives appeared over the brow of a hill and thundered down towards him. He groaned long and loud.

He could remember next to nothing of the evening's events after his unwitting exposé, but with a steady stream of people happy to remind him, there was no hiding from his escapades. Strangely though, being caught by a dozen partygoers lying naked on a bed performing a horizontal star jump with a plastic-coated hard-on bobbing enthusiastically and expectantly for all to see proved to be one of his lesser concerns. In part this was because the incriminating Polaroid had been sabotaged by its flash reflecting in the mirror above the bed, rendering the image a splash of light with legs. But it was the breadth and extent of his subsequent antics, many of which the Polaroid did successfully freeze for posterity, that guaranteed his place in Nethercotian folklore.

Having eventually unclasped his eyes and fists to find himself alone, he had locked the bedroom door and had the wank his testicles demanded, a vindictive one that had him relishing the freedom for his left hand of not having to scrabble around for something to deflect, soak or fill. He dressed, took a deep breath, unlocked the door and surrendered to a cliché by getting rat-arsed, in his case for the very first time.

It started with cider, lots of it, but as the palate grew less fussy and rational judgment took a vacation, he drank whatever the imagination of his 'friends' saw fit to place in his hand. To begin with it was weird and wonderful alcoholic cocktails, but they soon moved him on to water from the swimming pool, water from the toilet bowl, water from the aquarium, water from the ornamental pond and some warm 'dessert wine,' courtesy of Marsh's urethra.

He gave a sustained display of enthusiastic break-dancing and mooning on the dance floor.

Not that it was all alcohol and dancefloor merriment. There was nourishment along the way. He ate his own bogies for all to see. He ate a whole pack of butter. He ate a tea bag. He licked the toilet seat. He ate Marsh's bogies. He ate a plant from the aquarium. He ate a raw egg. He ate raw chicken. He ate the cat's supper.

He rode the lawnmower.

He crashed the lawnmower.

Perhaps most damning of all, he delivered a succession of impromptu mouth organ solos to one and all; the joy of alcohol being not that it facilitated a new skill, but that it made him believe it had.

His final semi-conscious recollection had been of protective arms and patient, gentle voices in his ears. One male and known; the other female and vaguely familiar.

"Would you like a coffee?" asked the latter.

"No, I want beer," he slobbered.

"It wasn't a question. You're having a coffee and some toast."

"Didn't know you were here?"

"Got here late. Looks liked I missed the main attraction."

"What… who… oh right. Good."

"Got to see the encores though."

"Not so good."

He'd opened his eyes and peered woozily into the warmth of her smile before gagging, swallowing back a mouthful of sick and sliding away.

*

Revision was Clarke's stated excuse for stepping down as 1st XI scorer, as it was for spending all free periods and after-school time hidden in the deeper recesses of the school library or ensconced in his room.

The exams arrived, were endured and ended.

A week before the end of term Derek Clarke received a rare call from his son. At first he didn't recognise the calm, measured monotone that requested him not to turn up on the last evening of term, as was customary, but instead to pick him up the following morning at ten o'clock, the option of that extra night compulsory for staff, but reluctantly made available to the pupils, although the twenty per cent or so that did take it up did so for logistical reasons, rather than any great desire to prolong their Nethercott experience.

There was no need to come all the way up the drive. Just park in the first passing place a hundred or so yards inside the school gates. And please be there on time.

At a little after midnight on the last night of term, Clarke packed his case and humped, heaved and pushed it along eerily quiet and deserted corridors and down the stairs, cursing under his labouring breath at every door sill and raised piece of wooden flooring. The gravel yard proved easier than he'd feared, though noisier, and he welcomed the quiet, dark anonymity of the grass beyond. It was after one when he crawled, exhausted, into bed.

At breakfast the next morning he noted the presence of his quarries. Afterwards he lay on his bed for a while staring at the ceiling; outwardly calm, inwardly churning.

Winslow Marsh, also lying on his bed, was feeling rather maudlin and introspective. Such tender emotions were rare visitors and he would normally not hesitate in slamming a door in their face. But with his time at Nethercott Hall at an end and nothing more than a packed case for company, he invited the strangers in and permitted them to get comfortable a while. Much as he'd railed against what the school had offered, it had nonetheless been a place that had permitted him a free rein and fed him a steady diet of acolytes and fodder. Not to mention a surname regulation that had ensured a welcome sanctuary from the curse of his Christian name.

Quentin Badger wouldn't be leaving for a few days yet. He enjoyed the calm space that spread through the school as the students departed, and the opportunity it afforded for the leisurely ordering of the tools and props of his trade. He was making a start in the long, narrow, claustrophobic room that stored the school's theatrical costumes and props. With the last production a distant memory, there wasn't a great deal to do, but he enjoyed tinkering around with the ordering of costumes and it put off some of the more irritating tasks that lay ahead. A mug of coffee and half a packet of ginger nuts sat on the narrow work bench; a small radio trilled out something pleasant and classical. He whistled contentedly.

Scott Luxley couldn't wait to get away. The lot of the PE teacher meant there was nothing left to be done that hadn't been leisurely achieved in the plentiful gaps smattered through his working week. His dual role as geography teacher hardly interfered with his idle drift through the fag end of the term. To satisfy everyone, the school had to allow him at least five academic visitations upon the pupils each week. It elected to keep to that minimum and expose him only to the first year, pupils still too wet behind the ears to even consider questioning the knowledge and abilities of a teacher, particularly one so physically commanding and who greeted careless answers with mockery, and wandering attention with a lobbed board rubber accompanied by a comedy sound effect.

Once passing foot traffic had cleared, Clarke rapped repeatedly on the door of room twenty-two until it opened. It was the same fist that connected with the bridge of Marsh's nose, sending him staggering backwards. A follow-up blow put him down on the floor, to which he was pinned by a knee delivering the full weight of his assailant to his rib cage.

When his vision started to clear, it was to find Clarke's face only inches from his own, the words clipped, to the point and raining down flecks of saliva.

"Message received?" Clarke concluded.

Marsh nodded as best he could, eyes now screwed tight in anticipation of another blow, head twisting against the vice-like grip on his chin. He could taste blood. Had he heard a crack? Then the pressure lifted from his chest and he heard the door slam shut. He instinctively inhaled and yelped in pain.

Logic might have left Mr Badger until last. But with the middle finger of Clarke's right hand bruised and quite possibly broken, and his left arm incapable of delivering its extremity with any reliable and coordinated accuracy, he was giving serious consideration to a head-butt. That he had no idea of the precise mechanics of this particular assault weapon was disconcerting, but he concluded that even a botched attempt was likely to be sufficient.

And so it was, Mr Badger crumpling as much from shock as the blow delivered simultaneously by Clarke's forehead and nose.

Mr Badger abhorred violence, particularly against himself, and readily nodded his acquiescence to the ultimatum served upon him in a spray of blood and saliva, in the desperate hope that this nightmare might disappear and the grip on his collar that was driving it into his windpipe might relent.

Practice didn't make perfect. But with more venom, the element of surprise and a better technique – a forehead contact, unaccompanied by his nose, and a hearty follow-through – Mr Luxley was incapacitated long enough for Clarke to pin him down. Momentarily repulsed by the bloodied mess of skin, cartilage and mucus formerly known as Mr Luxley's nose, Clarke gathered himself and delivered the verbal element of his message.

With aching hand, bloodied nose and burgeoning headache, Kevin Clarke strode across the gravel and down the drive.

Derek had obvious questions he wanted to ask, but everything about his son's demeanour, as he tugged his case up to the car and hefted it into the boot, urged silence; which he maintained even as the first ambulance sped by shortly after they had joined the main road.

*

"Is Morris, I mean Charlie, there please?"

"Who's calling?"

"Hi, er, it's Kevin? Kevin Clarke?" Her breath, faint on the receiver. "From school. Nethercott?"

"Hello, Kevin. I thought I recognised the voice. It's been a long time. How are you?"

"I'm fine, thanks. How's Charlie?"

"Charlie's doing okay."

"That's good." He pauses to take a breath. "When you say okay…"

"He's a bit fragile, but getting by."

"Can I talk to him?"

"He's er… it's probably best that you don't. I'm sorry, Kevin. Goodbye."

And with that the line went dead.

*

(*A few weeks later*)

"Hello, it's Kevin Clarke here again and I would like, like very much to talk to Charlie please and if you won't let me talk to him, I'll…" he said, the words catching in his throat.

"Hello, Kevin."

"I really need to speak to him."

"Need?"

"Sorry. That sounded bad. It's just that I think about him all the time and I know I should have rung immediately but I did try last term and you wouldn't let me talk to him and then I've had mock exams and stuff and I…"

"Kevin."

"I just want to see him."

"Kevin," she said, her softening voice a counterpoint to his heightening falsetto. "Would you like to come and visit before you go back to school?"

"Really?"

"Yes, I'm sure Charlie would love to see you."

"Right, that's great. Yes. Good."

"One thing Kevin."

"Yes?"

"Just don't expect much. Okay?"

*

A blue Volvo swept into the station forecourt and pulled to a halt in front of Kevin. The passenger window slid down and Mrs Morris's face appeared at an angle just above the gearstick.

"Get in," she said breezily.

They exchanged pleasantries with the determined politeness of those avoiding an issue, his cheeks reddening at the recollection of standing, no more than half an hour earlier, in a rocking train toilet cubicle with his eyes and his dick squeezed tight, while his mind's eye morphed a vague recollection of Mrs Morris's face onto the body of some very accommodating centrefold. The end result had eventually done the trick, but borne scant similarity to the woman now sitting beside him.

They were travelling down a long country road when the car slowed. He searched for a driveway or a building as they came to a halt in a passing area. She turned off the engine, undid her seat belt and swivelled towards him.

"We're half a mile further along."

"Right," he said, warily.

"I just need to have a word with you before we get there."

"Right," he said, even more warily.

"I'd like you to tell me what happened in February."

"Happened?"

"Please, Kevin." She paused and bit her lip. "You're too young to understand what it feels like. To be a parent, I mean." Her voice oscillating now. "I was sorting through some old photos – I'll never forget the moment – when the phone rang and it was Charlie." A swallow. "And he said 'Mummy, I think I need to come home now.' I told him not to be so silly but he interrupted me and said 'Mummy…'" her eyes now moist and bloodshot. "'Mummy,' he said, 'I think I'm broken.'"

More silence. Kevin wasn't sure what to say, which was fortunate because now wasn't the time to say anything. She was merely composing herself before continuing.

"You'd have thought I'd have asked him what on earth he meant. I mean it didn't really make sense. But… but I knew. I knew instantly. I told him I'd be there that afternoon and I got straight in my car. As I turned off the road, he was sitting there by the school gates. The sight of him just knocked me for six. He got in and sat there silently. I asked him about his stuff and he just shrugged. We drove up to the school and I gritted my teeth, marched into the Head's office and told him I had Charlie in the car and was taking him out of school with immediate effect and that he would not be returning. We hadn't discussed it, Charlie and me, but I knew when I was saying it that it was true." She sniffed loudly. "I've never been Sir Reginald's biggest fan. The opposite actually. But maybe he saw something in my eyes that stopped him arguing. And to his credit, and I will always respect him for it, he said he understood and if we would wait outside his office, he'd get someone to get Charlie's belongings together. I told him we'd be waiting in the car and that Charlie had packed everything already.

And sure enough, within ten minutes someone loaded that stupid trunk into the car and we were off. He didn't say a word the whole way home, just stared out the side window. When we got home, he didn't move to get out, so we sat there a while. Then he said, 'Thank you,' and when I said it was no trouble, he said no that wasn't it. He wanted to thank me for not asking him why. For just accepting it. And I haven't asked him since. It's not like I don't want to know, but right now he needs me not to ask and I can't let him down. Ever again. He's not strong enough for that. Been through too much. Do you see?"

"I think so." *Not really*.

"But something must have happened. What was it?"

"I think it must have been the fight the day before."

"A fight? Charlie? With who?"

So he told her. About Marsh. Charlie sharing a room with him. Hating it. Probably just had enough and something pushed him over the edge. Made him desperate. Why else would he do something as suicidal as challenge Marsh? Marsh the thug; Marsh the bully. It was a stupid thing to do. He told her about the contest itself, if it could be called that; from the swipes at thin air to the final intervention.

"I'm pretty sure he wasn't badly hurt," concluded Kevin.

"He may be many things Kevin, but Charlie isn't stupid. He must have known he'd lose. So why would that be the final straw? It doesn't make sense."

"I don't know." And he didn't. He'd thought about it often enough. Asked around for any clues over and above the Marsh-shaped obvious, but he'd already survived almost two terms of him by then, so why snap all of a sudden? It hadn't made sense then and it didn't now.

After a short silence, her hand moved towards the ignition key, but she hesitated.

"Charlie's not well, Kevin. Not well at all. He probably won't seem like the Charlie you remember."

Nothing to say.

"And if I'm honest, Kevin… it breaks my heart. It really does. One day, when you have children of your own, maybe you'll understand. You look into their innocent eyes, all that unsullied potential, and all you want is for life to be kind to them. He was always a little different from other children. Fragile maybe. And it wasn't a problem to begin with. Up to a certain age it doesn't matter. Kids can get away with anything. But then peer pressure creeps in and some children stand out from the crowd. Charlie was like that. He used to get teased a lot. I'd sometimes wander down to his infant school during the lunch break and stand behind a tree spying on him. He'd run out into the playground with a look of unabashed joy for life and I'd smile to myself and my heart would lift. And if I could have frozen him then, frozen him forever, I would. I really would. But then with each rejected advance, every cruel indifference, every verbal taunt and shove out of the way, I'd watch the light in his eyes fade and all that enthusiasm ebb away. Until the bell went and he sloped back in a punctured little boy. And I'd stand behind that tree with tears running down my face and a knife twisting in my heart. And when I picked him up after school, I'd ask him how his day had been and he'd say it was great and talk excitedly of what he'd got up to with *all his friends* and I'd smile emptily at him and then walk into another room and break down all over again. It's tragic when it's any child. But it's soul-destroying when it's your own. There was one photo in particular that told me things had to change. It was taken at school at the beginning of his last term in year three. The smile was there as usual, but there was something strained and desperate about it. Something only a mother could see and enough to tell me he needed to be somewhere else. There were sixteen boys in his class that year at the school and he hadn't received one invite to a birthday party. Not one. And he must have known. Must have heard the other children talking about what they'd do at the next party, what they did at the last. Not one invite to go to play even. All that kindness and happiness to give and share and none of the little *bastards* were interested. And I just wanted to pick him up, wrap him in cotton wool and care for his every need until he grew up and could safely exist in a world that wasn't so cruel. But I couldn't, though I wish I had now; wish it with all my heart.

"So instead we took him out of the school and sent him to a prep school. He was still the same Charlie of course, but there were others there more like him. He didn't stand out anymore. Well, not so much anyway. He seemed much happier and when he said he wanted to go on to Nethercott like most of the others, we just went with it. Here was a chance to get him safely through to adulthood, when everything would be okay, he could be himself and that might be celebrated, not ridiculed. Seemed cheap at half the price. And we almost did it. Almost got there." Tear tracks lined her cheeks. "He always told us he was happy there. Was he?"

"Er… yes. I think he was."

"You don't sound so sure."

"He always seemed happy. He really did. We laughed loads."

"Thank you."

"For what?"

"Just thank you. You *were* a good friend to him. I do believe that."

"Were?" Kevin asked, thrown several ways by the intonation.

"Sorry. That's not fair. Don't listen to me. Guess I'm angry at a world that's let him down and you're part of that world."

"What does Charlie's dad think?"

"He's no longer on the scene. Probably for the best. As Charlie got older, his father got lazier at hiding his disappointment in him. His embarrassment. I got angrier and more protective and somewhere along the line we stopped communicating. Charlie didn't need pity. He just needed unconditional love and parents who accepted him and loved him for who he was. And if Charlie's father can't manage that, we're better off without him. We really are."

And with those faltering words, she started the engine and they moved off.

*

He found Charlie as she'd said he would, sitting in the conservatory; a sketch pad on his lap, a pencil in his hand and an artistically-clichéd bowl of fruit on the table before him.

"Hiya, Charlie," said Kevin with forced cheerfulness as he entered, only for the fixed grin to fade to a pout at the sight of the gaunt white face that was turning slowly towards him. The eyes were lifeless. He looked lost, dazed, confused. Like a ghost. Then from somewhere deep inside, a pilot light was lit and the Charlie he remembered flickered into view. A pale imitation maybe, but Charlie nonetheless.

"What you doing?" Kevin asked, moving closer under cover of a dumb question.

"Just sketching. What do you think?" he said, tilting the pad in Kevin's direction.

"Good," he lied. It wasn't, at least on any artistic scale he knew of. "Really good," he added, with guilty gusto.

"Thanks. I'm quite pleased with it," Charlie replied, and at once appeared to lose himself in some inner reflection.

An uncomfortable silence followed, minutes crawling by.

Kevin took a seat opposite. This was far more awkward than he'd expected. Charlie was now staring out of the window, apparently oblivious to his presence.

"Charlie?" Nothing. "Charlie?" A little louder this time.

"Huh," he replied, his head turning, eyes slowly focusing.

Kevin swallowed hard and forged on.

"What happened?"

"How do you mean?"

"What made you leave like that right in the middle of term? You didn't even say goodbye. Was it that ridiculous fight? If it was, I don't get it. You couldn't possibly have expected to win it."

"Of course I didn't. That wasn't the point."

"Then what was?"

"You. I guess."

Kevin, nonplussed, couldn't find anything to say that didn't stem from anger and this wasn't − couldn't be − the place for anger. So he waited.

"You should have heard the things Marsh said about you. You taking his position as goalkeeper. Then getting him moved in the rugger team to make way for Evans, your *bum-chum*. What a crap captain you were. What you and Evans must have been getting up to in your room. And the names he called you. I hadn't even heard of some of them."

"So what?" said Kevin, struggling to suppress his growing frustration.

"He had no right to say those things. You were doing your best, but he just went on and on. Every night I had to lie in the dark and listen to him slag you off."

"That's not enough to justify getting your head kicked in. You know it isn't, Charlie. I can handle Marsh." Thinking back to the bottled tackle in that game. "He's just a bully and a coward. All hot air."

"Maybe, but there was more."

"Okay, I get it. You had to share a room with him. No-one envied you that. But——"

"*Kevin.*" The first time Charlie had raised his voice; and all the more effective for it. "Sorry, but you really haven't a clue what it was like. You weren't there. It wasn't just words. There were other things… anyway you were in your room with Evans. Golly how I envied you both. But then I suppose that was pretty obvious, the amount of time I spent in there."

"We didn't mind."

"*You* didn't mind, you mean. I know Evans didn't really want me there."

"You're wrong about that."

"Am I? But anyway, that's beside the point."

Kevin ran his fingers through his hair before grabbing a handful at the back and twisting it in exasperation, searching for a way through; only for Charlie to beat him to it.

"You know I latched on to a lot of kids in those first few terms and you were the only one who stuck it out. The rest seemed repelled by me. Could probably sense my need. The moment they made other friends, they couldn't wait to get away. Can't blame them really. I say 'really' a lot, don't I? But you were different. I still don't know why you hung around. And every time things got bad, you were there and it didn't seem so bad. I felt able to carry on for a while. Ignore everything else."

"What *everything else*? I don't understand where you're going with all this. You never seemed that bothered by anything until that stupid room business."

Charlie nibbled at a nail, his eyes temporarily losing their focus again. His lips opened and shut a few times before he finally spoke.

"I wanted it to be you," he whispered.

"What?"

"I think, in fact I know, I needed it to be you."

"What *are* you on about? I still don't get what you're talking about. And speak up. I can hardly hear you."

"Who stopped the fight. Not Evans, of all people. I needed it to be you. And it wasn't."

"You mean that's what made you leave? Just that? That's not fair," said Kevin, measuring his words. "Is it?"

"No." And with an empty laugh, added, "Maybe not. But it's the truth."

"Why does it have to be about me? I was okay with it all. I didn't need you to bloody defend my honour or whatever it was you thought you were doing."

But Charlie's attention seemed to have wandered again, his gaze drifting to the window. He was repeatedly pushing his thumb nail into the back of his left hand, leaving a trail of white crescents in the skin. His left eye twitched intermittently, pulling up the corner of his mouth each time. When he did return his gaze to Kevin, it was through a watery glaze. And then, with the hesitancy and dread of a blind man being made to walk towards a cliff edge, he faltered tentatively forwards.

"Marsh knew things. Stuff you don't know. Never let me forget that he knew either. He saw me one evening.

After school. When he shouldn't have been there. But he saw things. Knew about other stuff."

"What do you mean?" asked Kevin, not there yet.

"Things."

"What?" Still not there; perceptive development arrested.

"If I tell you, you can't tell Mummy. You promise?"

"Yes," said Kevin, with an impatience he'd soon regret.

More fidgeting. More nail biting. And then Charlie seemed to inflate with resolve. His gaze turned to Kevin. His back straightened. And he began to talk.

The ten or so minutes of stumbling monologue that followed steamrollered through Kevin's defences, brushing aside his impatience before hurtling on and smashing the previous four years into hundreds of pieces; sharp little pieces that shredded memories and shared experiences, revealing them to be nothing more than a tattered illusory veil draped over a stark reality that had, it appeared, passed him by. And each time he thought it couldn't get any worse, it did. Much worse. Way beyond where his imaginings would have taken him even if they'd been given the freest of reins. He could think of nothing to say that felt appropriate.

"You're shaking your head?" said Charlie.

"Just can't believe I didn't notice what was happening."

"Why would you? Why should you? You had your own life to concentrate on."

"I know, but..."

"I set you up. With you by my side, I felt I could face anything. You were like a brick wall around me. And that worked for a long time. It really did. But then life sort of caught up with me and Marsh just kept on and on, knocking the bricks away one by one, and other... stuff, you know, had happened, and to rebuild the wall one last time it needed something huge and that's where you were meant to come in and yes I know it wasn't fair but that's just where I was at the time and when it wasn't you and I saw this sea of laughing faces and you not even smiling just shaking your head and walking away I knew I was lost. You didn't do anything wrong. I did it to myself."

Kevin salvaged a semblance of a smile from the self-pitying scowl that had been monopolising his facial features.

"You're not to say anything to anyone. Or do anything. No revenge. Do you promise?"

"They have to pay for what they did. You must agree with that," said Kevin.

"Maybe. But that's *my* decision to make, not yours. This is *my* business. You have no right to decide for me. I have to do what I have to do to survive all this. You understand?"

"Sort of."

"That's not enough. You need to promise me."

"Alright. I promise." Regretting his tone immediately and resorting to the safer ground of practicalities. "What about your exams? Will you be coming back for them?"

"No. I'm done. I was always on borrowed time. To be honest, it's astonishing I lasted that long. And I've got you to thank for that. I was struggling when you first arrived. Struggling badly. That I almost made it all the way through is a minor miracle. I'm not saying it was easy. It wasn't. But whenever I started to waver, you were there."

"I wasn't though, was I? Not always."

"But had you known, you would have been. I know that and ultimately that's all that matters. To me anyway. You have absolutely nothing to feel ashamed about. If there's a hero in my life, it's you."

Kevin would have replied but the tears that had crept from the corners of his eyes sporadically over the last quarter of an hour and been dismissed with blinks and stretches and faked itches had abandoned furtiveness and were brimming to a point of no return.

"Sorry. I didn't want to upset you, but I am glad I told you everything. Pity it hurts so much. And not just for me, eh?"

They fumbled through pleasantries a few minutes more before Charlie abruptly announced he was feeling tired and thanked Kevin for coming. They hugged awkwardly, laughing at each other's tears, then Charlie picked up his sketch pad and Kevin headed towards the door with guilty relief.

"You know, when I was younger," Charlie said to Kevin's back, "and things got really bad, I used to find myself a quiet corner, close my eyes and take myself off to a place in my head where I felt safe and secure. Out of harm's way. Until the summer term of that first year at Nethercott, that place was imagining myself sitting on my own in the tree-house out there in the garden on a warm summer day with a good book, the sun streaming in through the window, the sound of birdsong and bees and a light breeze rustling the leaves outside. It was my haven. A place only I knew about, and where I couldn't be found and teased and bullied and pushed around. But after that first summer at school, I didn't visit the tree-house again. Never needed to. Because you were there. Always. And I guess I just want to say thank you. For keeping me company all those times. I wouldn't swap them for the world and I'll always have those places to go back to. Sometimes it might be sitting on a bench on a balmy day by a cricket pitch. Sometimes it might be wandering through the school grounds on a long summer Sunday evening. Sometimes it might be just sitting talking. And unlike the tree-house, I'll never be alone."

Kevin made it through to the hallway before the first sob wrenched itself from his chest and released the intense pressure in his temples.

MAY 2007

TUESDAY

Having made it to his subterranean hideaway with nothing but a chuckle-accompanied "elementary, my dear Wilson" to endure, David unlocks the door, closes it behind him, turns the key and happily breathes in the familiar damp mustiness. With the light off, the room is not so much bathed, as sullied by the murky glow that permeates the grimy frosted glass of the long narrow window high up on one wall, occupying the ruler length or so of wall the room shares with the outside world; and through which, when it's open, disembodied salutations and banter, exhaust fumes, whispered gossipry, cigarette smoke and the myriad other sounds and smells of station life waft intermittently throughout the day.

On taking up his 'post' he'd inherited an 'archive store' crammed to the ceiling with boxes of superannuated bureaucracy and forgotten lives, broken fan heaters, castor-less chairs and all manner of obsolete technology. He'd spent a sweaty and unassisted week – reactions to his artificial insemination ranging from mild intrigue to outright hostility – shuffling along corridors and up and down stairs, relocating to a skip all the room's contents bar a desk, a couple of fans, the only functional filing cabinet and a metal waste paper bin. A chunky brown phone, an ancient computer and an even older printer were grudgingly relinquished his way, freeing up his allotted capital expenditure budget for an ergonomic chair, an ornate wall clock that doesn't so much celebrate the hour as quietly applaud it with a muted and melodic gong, a digital radio, another three filing cabinets and the assortment of coloured boxes, folders and wire mesh trays that augment the cabinets to house the filing system that powers his self-renowned detection technique. Making guest appearances from home are a few creature comforts: an old and faded armchair, a dartboard, his snooker cue in its long silver case, and framed signed photos of Ayrton Senna, Eric Bristow, Stephen Hendry, Phil Taylor, Jimmy White and Damon Hill.

Heroes and villains.

The phone rings.

"David Wilson."

"How's life in the hellhole?"

"Delightfully solitary. If I'm lucky they'll forget I'm here. How's things in the gutter?"

"I *aspire* to the gutter. Anything to break the never-ending stream of local-interest dross and inanity. Though I may have something a little out of the ordinary for you. If you're interested that is, and not already on the case."

"I very much doubt it, knowing this lot," he says, unable to keep the bitterness from his voice.

"Sod 'em. You're better than the lot of them put together."

"What have you got?" he says, keen to move away from the acute discomfort of praise.

"London buses mean anything to you?"

"No."

"That's why you've got me then, though it'll cost you lunch."

"Will it be worth it?"

"Oh yes. You'll love this one. Right up your street."

"Was that a joke?"

"I'll see you at twelve thirty at our favourite water-themed eatery to enjoy its ersatz rustic charms and *fusion* menu."

*

He never learns. Conned again. *Deep-fried brie and cranberry sauce* had sounded so appetising, but he should have known better; the limp and browning lettuce purporting to be a *salad garnish* a final insult. David tosses a blubbery globule around his mouth long after the cloying sweetness of the jam-like 'sauce' has dissipated. Rebecca looks even less enamoured with her choice of the unaccented *pate*, which she reports to have the texture of a stock cube and a taste put to shame by the slice of brittle toast that disintegrated on first, futile contact with the brown paste. A marriage made in gastronomic hell. As the plates are collected, she attempts some pate-themed punnery, only to receive a blank stare from the zombified waitress, doubtless lost in contemplation of a flatlined career trajectory; word play clearly not her thing.

They share a smile. This place never lets them down; its crass, national-chain *ambience* a constant source of wry amusement to be savoured in the knowledge that one of their employers is paying for it. Take a theme and run wild with it, basically. The walls are a veritable cornucopia of water-themed memorabilia and trivia born of far-too-generalised a remit and the consequent lack of any focus. An oar. A large brass bell. Various model boats. A captain's hat.

A canoe hanging from the ceiling. Random chunks of wood that once drifted. A ship's wheel hanging above the fireplace. A coracle mounted on a wall. The local bric-a-brac stores and car boot sales have taken a pounding. Not that anything can compete with the vast thirty-foot-high folly of the plywood waterwheel attached to the side of a building standing half a mile from the nearest body of water.

Rebecca pushes her glasses back up the bridge of her nose, scrunching her eyes closed as she does so.

"Ever thought of contacts?" he asks, voicing for the first time what he thinks every time she does it.

"Ever thought of a built-up heel for your left shoe?" What she thinks every time she witnesses his Chaplinesque gait.

He feels his cheeks flush and looks away.

"Look," she continues. "We both have our props and disguises we use as camouflage. Hide the real us from view. Mine are glasses, perceived scattiness and that extra ten pounds I lug around with me."

David senses there is a right thing to say at this juncture.

"What have you got for me then?" probably isn't it.

*

"Hello, my name's David Wilson. We spoke earlier?"

"We did?" She frowns distractedly, then crouches down to pick up a discarded purple jacket that has caught her attention.

"On the phone? About the incident on Saturday night. Well Sunday morning really," he says to the top of her head.

When she stands back up, a few wisps of greying hair hang down over her eyes.

"The more you spend, the longer they're at home and the less respect you get." She tries to blow the hair away and swipes at what remains with her free hand. Her eyes focus on him and his puzzled expression. "I'm sorry, but I haven't a clue who you are. Who did you speak to?"

"Mrs Carruthers?"

"Ah, that explains it. I think you'll find that's next door. Our new neighbours. We share the first bit of driveway. They took the old sign down. Didn't like being *Cosy Cottage*. Can't say I blame them, but it would be nice if they could make their mind up about an alternative and stick a ruddy sign up. We get their post most mornings. It'll be about the window, I suppose?"

"Yes. I'm very sorry. I just assumed this was the place."

"No problem. Fortunately, it's not us you need."

The door closes and he hears a muffled and weary, "Sebastian." He backtracks down the drive to a fork, shoes crunching on the gravel, and turns right. He rounds a slight bend to find another building, the evidence of a recent move littered in front of it. To his left is a patch of lawn, its centrepiece a toppled stone sundial.

The front door stands open. He tosses a tentative "Hello?" into the orifice. Nothing. He tries again, a little louder. And again, this time with sufficient volume to generate an echo and, in swift succession, a distant expletive, the slam of a door, footsteps on stairs and a gruff "Better be good." A red-faced, bulky man in his forties and ill-fitting overalls, flecks of paint dotted in his hair, appears.

"Yes?" he barks.

"Hi, I'm here about the incident on Saturday night."

"What are you? Another reporter? Some Neighbourhood Watch do-gooder?"

"I represent the police."

"What the hell does that mean? *Represent?* Anyway, the police have already been here, fat lot of good they'll do."

"Graham, leave him alone," says a woman half his size, appearing at his side. "Hi, I'm Diana Carruthers. You must be David. I apologise for my husband. He's too stingy to hire a proper decorator and too proud to admit he wishes he had. Not sure why he has to take it out on you." Graham Carruthers opens his mouth to protest, but an outstretched hand and a glare see the words catch and he huffily trudges off, the words *represents, police* and *huh* just distinguishable in his mutterings. "I'm sorry about that. DIY and Graham don't mix. Come on in."

"The police took the bloody thing away," she says a while later, as David peruses the surface of the tea in the mug clasped between his hands, wondering if it's loose leaf tea by-product or just dust. Packing cases litter what is clearly to be the living room, the two chairs they occupy and a large TV the only items to have yet escaped captivity. "Said they'd look for fingerprints." She catches the flare of his nostrils. "Oh. I see, that was just a line they fed me. How gullible am I? You don't hold out much hope, do you?"

"You never know. They'll do all they can."

"What does that mean?"

"Nothing will come from it."

"You know it happened just down the road as well?" He nods. "And that reporter lady said there were others a few miles away."

"I heard as much. You're the first I've visited but I'll be trying to talk to them all." Her lips constrict. "Look, Mrs Carruthers, in all likelihood the missiles will get passed around at the police station, there'll be a few in-jokes and then they'll end up in a storeroom somewhere.

There'll be no investigation and if there was to be a list of station priorities, which there isn't, well – this wouldn't even make that list. That's the truth of it. Now as I explained, I'm not an official police officer as such, but I do work there and I am interested in your case and I will be looking into it. No guarantees. I can't promise you anything, except that I will take it seriously. It's me or nothing."

"Sounds like you make that speech a lot," she says, smiling warmly.

"I do."

"Didn't fancy being a police officer then?"

"Actually, that's all I ever wanted to do, but it wasn't to be. So this is the nearest I get to it."

She picks up on his reluctance to expand and they fall into silence. He takes a tentative sip of the tea.

"Thank you," she says.

"For what?"

"For at least wanting to try."

He shrugs.

"What do you remember of Sunday morning?"

"I was in bed, obviously, drifting in and out of sleep. Graham snores in certain positions, so I seem to spend my nights pushing and prodding him until he shuts up. The security lights came on outside, but I took no notice as they've been doing that since we moved in and we've yet to get around to finding how to switch them off. Then I heard a dull thud, like when a bird flies into a window. I decided to go and have a look out the window and I was halfway there when there was this great crash. First thing I did was duck down to the floor. Then I crawled along to the window and when I plucked up the courage to look over the ledge, I saw this black shape entwined with the sundial. Horrible thing we weren't planning on keeping, but this bloke—"

"You're sure it was a male."

"Pretty certain. Stocky build and looked at least six feet tall. He really took a dislike to the thing, the way he piled straight into it. Knocked it off its pedestal and I couldn't even budge it the other day. He lay there a few seconds, got up, zigzagged across the lawn and careered straight into the hedge."

"Did you get a look at his face at all?"

"He had some balaclava thing on, so no."

"Did your husband see or hear anything?"

"No chance. He was dead to the world, and when he did finally deign to wake up, it was to tell me to *bloody be quiet.*"

"Mind if I take a look outside?"

The next visit, a hundred or so yards down the lane, proves less informative. He is curtly informed that having spent half an hour with a proper police officer on Sunday who clearly didn't give a toss, she has no interest in wasting more time with some "care in the community lackey" and if he wants to know anything, he can go back and ask his *colleague*. The one-sided exchange concludes with a slammed door.

Emerging onto the lane, and with the station holding negligible allure, he opts for the scenic route back and heads into the woods on the other side.

WEDNESDAY

DATE 2: GIZZ

"*Stand up if you hate Luton.*" It appears she has no choice so she stands up with everyone else, stopping short of singing along or the reverential stretching out of arms. She wonders at the need for constant repetition once everyone has assumed the vertical.

"*Cunts,*" bellows Gizz, laughing uproariously and looking around for approval. He gets two nods of acknowledgment, one more of a flinch; but a better return than he'd received from his initial scatterings of greetings as they'd edged their way painfully and apologetically between plastic seat-backs and reluctantly drawn-in knees before reaching their allotted perches. "Fuckin great bunch of lads here," says Gizz, in contradiction of all empirical evidence gathered to date.

"*Stand up if you hate Luton.*" Again? They're not even playing them.

Her bum's going numb. She shifts uneasily on the seat, the moulding failing to deliver on the implied customised comfort, only to sense Gizz may have mistaken it for excitement.

"Good, isn't it?" Oh dear, he has.

"Mmm, great," she tries feebly, and feels obliged to edge forwards. "Very exciting. Are they above or below you – us – in the league?"

"They're two points behind so it's a bit of a six-pointer. We got a draw up their gaff but recently – *oi you fucking long-haired lesbian cunt*," he shrieks at someone on the pitch, voice breaking as he delivers the final syllable, his face suddenly contorted, his mouth expelling a string of phlegm. The invective continues and their longest conversation of the evening is terminated.

"*Stand up if you hate Luton.*" Laura wearily rises to her feet.

Watford score. There is a nanosecond of silence as the light waves seek out brain cells, then an explosion of noise and a general lurching up and forwards, as if an electric shock has passed through all the seats. Shouts. Smiles. Clapping. An embrace from Gizz. She instinctively returns the hug and his hand seeks out her arse, his cheek grazing hers as she leans to the side, escaping what she fears may have been an attempted kiss. She's on the point of pulling clear when he releases her to hurl some abuse at the distant away fans.

"*Sit down if you love Luton.*" Really?

Gizz burps, pops in the last mouthful of his kebab, lets the napkin drop to the pavement, throws a "see ya" in the vague direction of the sweating lady lovingly ladling juices onto the turd-like, slowly-revolving dollop of brown matter, ducks under the awning and heads off.

She presumes she is to follow, the night still depressingly young.

THURSDAY

The local newspapers are his staple diet, and Thursday brings its usual four courses, although it's not until well into the afternoon that he gets to sit down and savour them. For once he's happy that they are near enough devoid of nutritional value.

He speedily logs what little else there is of any interest, then contemplates the much-anticipated article that has sated his appetite. He'd found it on page six – in what Rebecca calls the dead zone – wedged like a Tetris block between adverts for karate lessons and a local tanning studio. Now it sits on his desk, encircled by five small metal buses, their earlier arrival signalled by the clanking thump of a cardboard box dropped from waist height outside his door and a high-pitched "*playtime*".

He reads the article one more time before filing.

London Buses 5, Moor Park 0
by Rebecca Staniford

Isn't it so often the way with buses? A community can wait years and years to have them turn up on their living room carpets… then all of a sudden five are thrown through the windows of as many houses in and around the affluent Moor Park area in the early hours of Sunday morning. The unlucky homeowners were each rudely awakened by the sound of breaking glass to find a red concrete-filled model double-decker bus lying on their living room floor.

One of the victims, Diana Carruthers, told me she did see a figure fleeing her front garden but was unable to provide any clues as to his or her identity. 'We only moved in ten days ago and were attracted by the area's reputation for peace and privacy. This is not what we had in mind and one can only wonder at the kind of idiots who cause such wanton and random destruction.'

Police suspect the involvement of alcohol or drugs and believe the houses were randomly selected by a Saturday night reveller looking for cheap thrills. They would welcome any calls from potential witnesses.

Official police line: accommodating; helpful; interested; ongoing.

Unofficial line, delivered to David by the fast-tracking PC Smythe – pronounced Smith by him alone – earlier that morning: "a simple application of risk-reward principles and a negligible chance of a positive outcome make this a non-starter, I'm afraid. It's a fact of life. I know what life's like for the riff-raff who do this sort of thing, and it's so random and without thought that you cannot hope to catch them," his vocabulary and syntax yet again giving the lie to his oft-asserted claim of a shared life experience with the community they police. "The bastards," he'd added with a rapid shake of his head, a clumsy and uncomfortable addendum for the benefit of PC Hawes, who he'd noticed lurking nearby.

"What university posh boy here is trying to say, Sherlock," Hawes had grunted with his customary succinctness and disregard for tact and political correctness, "is that we've got better fucking things to do than cock around looking for a bunch of piss-heads who got tanked up Saturday night and took a justifiable dislike to some posh tossers and their fuck-off big mansions. And if it isn't them, it was the fucking gay-boys who mince about up there and I ain't frisking no meat-pushers on the off chance. Wouldn't know where they've been."

And with that thoughtful and egalitarian monologue, the impromptu crime-fighting think tank had concluded its business.

Reflecting now on that exchange and a few snatched words as he and Smythe had escaped, it added little to his current bank of knowledge, other than explaining the preponderance of used condoms that had littered his woodland walk; the Carruthers' due diligence appearing ever laxer.

He picks up one of the buses, its solid weight pleasing in his hand, and inspects it more closely. Ridges and jagged points of cement peep out from their red metal confines to scratch his palms and fingers. Most of the paint is chipped and caked in smears of cement, but the roof is positively pristine in comparison. On it, as with the others, has been crudely scratched the letters 'R.I.P.E.N.T.'

He returns to the page of hand-written notes.

5 addresses (see attached for addresses, occupants and OS map extract).

A and B situated 214 yards from each other in same lane. Houses all detached and secluded. Easy targets.

On other side of road from A and B is public woodland. One access route for motor vehicles, via rough track from main road on other side to car park in centre. Numerous paths lead off, a number of them to the vicinity of A and B. Woodland has reputation for homosexual activity.

C, D and E are all between 0.9 and 2.6 miles away, none of them within easy walking distance of each other.

Times of attack put at between 04.00 and 04.30 by victims, though precise times unclear. Most likely 4/5 attackers, though possibility of less if cars or motorbikes used. No engine noise heard by A, B or D. C and E each heard an engine rev and a screech of tyres. C thought car. E thought motorbike.

Missiles all similar bespoke design: toy bus filled with cement. Specifically made. Why these? Buses all mass-produced and available throughout London at many gift shops/stalls. Spoken to 4 toy shops in 5-mile range of attacks and none stock line. Dusted for finger prints but nothing of any use found. Gloves used?

MO: missile thrown through downstairs window and assailant then fled.

Only one sighting, briefly at A. Face covered by balaclava. Possibly injured making escape.

No evidence of any intention but damage to property. No attempted access. No theft reported other than attempted theft (vandalism?) of stone garden ornament.

Nothing left at crime scenes. Tour of woodland adjoining A and B 2 days later uncovered nothing of potential interest apart from a size 11 black leather shoe (right). Unlikely to be related.

R.I.P.E.N.T. Repent? Spelt wrong. Poor vocabulary. Alcohol. Full stops suggest an acronym.

This 2D representation of the case is his palette; and if he keeps adding facts and suppositions and studies them long enough, the answer may appear. A process of free association, like one of those mystery pictures that flings up a 3D image the moment the correct angle and focus coincide.

He can sense something lurking there, waiting to be discovered, and with that comes a mounting tide of excitement. For this is the *hit* he savours; the visceral thrill he gets when he knows he's onto something. Something missed by others, that he has all to himself, with no one to race against; no one to tell him what to do and when. A case deemed immaterial and unworthy by his venerable colleagues, their eyes seeing only paperwork and irritation, blinded by the victims' visible wealth to the logic gaps in the premise that has seen them dismiss the case as nothing more than drunken vandalism, the victims in some way deserving; not so much a crime as social comment and rebalancing.

His reverie is curtailed when his phone rings. An internal call.

"David Wilson?"

"Put your todger away and get the fuck up here. Match starts in under an hour."

Much as David would like to convince himself that his acceptance into the social strata of station life over the past few months had been down to professional respect or force of personality, there was only one key that had unlocked that particular door; and it's proving as problematic as ever to manoeuvre through the narrow corridors and tight corners of the building.

SATURDAY

Kevin's triggers are many and varied. The briefest of thoughts or images can flick a switch, sparking deep within whatever fusion of neural, psychological, endocrine and vascular forces launches that headlong stampede for the glans. Sometimes it can take more; a sustained sequence of contemplations nursed and relished during the day, the ultimate realisation all the more delicious for the wait. But mostly it's those late evenings spent lounging on the sofa with the remote control, roaming the stations for something – anything – that will titillate and arouse; give him something to work with.

And occasionally, very occasionally, he'll pull the bottom drawer of the chest in his bedroom right out, put it to one side and lift out the stash of magazines that have accumulated over the years since those first nerve-racked pubescent ventures into the carefully selected newsagent. That intense study of the contents of the lower shelves until you're the only customer left in the shop; then glance up, snatch, approach counter with one eye looking out for unwelcome intruders, place on counter with innocuous decoy magazine on top, throw in a packet of sweets for added camouflage, affect calm assurance, attempt to ignore percussive overdrive in chest and ears and still-shaking hand that passes across the money, lower voice an octave to acknowledge change, gratefully take hold of brown paper bag, exit, glance through magazine at first opportunity, get hard-on, go home, wank; that first release made all the sweeter, the girls all the more salacious, for the covert operation so recently and cunningly executed under the noses of a prying world; not to mention a youthful naivety that fails to recognise the purchase for the simple commercial transaction it was, nor the brown paper bag for the trumpeting fanfare of pornography that it is in the hands of any teenage boy exiting a newsagent.

And so it is that tonight finds Kevin tentatively inching himself back into the masturbatory arena; bruising still unsightly, but the pain easing. Propped up against the pillows on his bed, leafing through a batch of battered magazines. Mild fare. Nothing too strong. Suggestion always preferable to anatomical reality. Not for him the splayed frontage, like a rasher of bacon; a wound. And definitely not the splayed rear, reminding him of half a peach with the stone removed; not to mention the hygienic and mechanical practicalities. He's not interested in the *Barely Legal*, the *Over 50*, the leather-bound, the wives of readers, the submissives, the dominatrixes, the huge-breasted... none of the ever-growing number of niche-seeking absurdities and freak shows. He just wants a pleasing face, a body that curves in the right places and a little left to his imagination; someone to accompany him to wherever he feels like going and satisfy his needs; to use and then dispense with.

He flips through another, growing weary at the succession of empty eyes and forced smiles. Deflatingly aware of the deceit of it all. The gulf between the erotic delights hinted at and the reality of his own experience. Or maybe it's the ever-thickening quagmire he's been wading through since that awful night. Whatever it is, the pictures aren't working their snake-charming magic tonight. Desperation sees him take refuge in a story; the province of the flaccid or bored.

And under the title *Sixty 999*, he finds a touching and inspiring tale to restore any cynic's faith in the outstanding and selfless generosity of our uniformed emergency service heroes.

Lucie – irritating spelling but give the girl a chance – is working alone in the office late one night. What work that may be is not apparent from the accompanying photo, though a deadline is alluded to. Her desk is exactly what you'd expect from a props department consulting the manual under 'office': it is populated by nothing more than a computer, a keyboard, a desk tidy containing a couple of pencils and an entirely incongruous large blotter straight out of the nineteenth century, rendered all the more absurd by the absence of any blots, an ink pen or, come to think of it, any paper. Not entirely true. Juicy Lucie, the nickname a given, is clutching a batch of papers that appear to be blank, possibly explaining her quizzical look. She has pushed herself back from the desk and is slouched down in a large office chair, the edge of the desk wedged into the angle of a stiletto heel; knee tilting outwards; short skirt hitched up over top of obligatory suspenders; flash of taut gusset; straining white shirt unbuttoned to halfway down sizeable cleavage; pen inserted phallus-like between moistened and pouting red lips; free hand squeezing buggery out of some stress-relieving toy; pair of thick-rimmed glasses – refer to manual under 'intelligent' – over which she peers with that gormless/puzzled/constipated look that tells the aspiring wanker that she wants *it*; and very much wants *it* with him.

Kevin is intrigued enough to continue. Nothing better to do, anyway.

With the scene set, the drama can commence in the shape of a wisp of smoke coming from the back of the photocopier behind her – Kevin can picture some bloke crouched down smoking a fag. Cue photograph of Juicy contorting herself to lean over the combusting office equipment, sporting a look of growing panic; fingers held in front of gaping mouth. Acting her little socks off, though it's wasted given the reader's attention will likely as not be focused instead on the undercarriage of her splayed buttocks peeping out beneath the hem of her skirt.

What to do? Juicy dials 999 of course. Why turn it off at the wall and wait until tomorrow, when you can make a nuisance call? She's about to explain the problem to the operator when a loud flash and bang cause her to drop the phone with a scream. She rushes to the kitchen, fills a jug with water and throws it over the copier. Everything fizzles out, no mean feat given the quantity of splashback needed to wet her shirt to the extent that her pendulous mammaries and largely peripheral black bra are now clearly outlined through the clinging material.

She boils a kettle – as you do immediately after an electrical emergency – for a cup of coffee to calm her nerves, only for the office door to open, such ready access raising serious concerns at the out-of-hours security arrangements; although when it comes to distracting practicalities, nothing can hold a candle to the *dramatis non sequitur* that is the swaggering entrance of a fireman, a policeman and a paramedic. Although to his credit, the writer at least attempts a feeble stab at persuasive logic.

Hello love. We got here as fast as we could. The operator wasn't sure what you needed, so I'm afraid you've got us all. Hope three's not a crowd. How can we assist?

I'm in your capable hands gents, says our heroine. *What do you suggest?*

I think a thorough working over is going to be required, suggests Barry the fireman, his eyes taking a journey up and down Lucie's body, lingering at major landmarks en route. With an innocence Kevin cannot help but suspect she'll shortly belie, she points him to the malfunctioning fixed asset.

Anything I can take down for you? asks PC Dean Holmes with admirable attention to detail and procedural requirement.

I'd recommend you get out of those wet clothes before you catch a death – Kevin lets out a snort – says Terry the paramedic, effortlessly establishing his medical credentials.

Judging by Lucie's wide-eyed acquiescence, this torrent of double entendres is lost on her, so subtle has been their delivery. It is therefore entirely reasonable that she should unquestioningly ease the wet shirt over her head, the *damp material clinging to each delicious contour*, and *inch down* her skirt to reveal the matching set of see-through lacy bra and obligatory *skimpy panties*. Never a large pair of practical and comfortable cotton pants and an old faded bra that was the first thing to hand that morning. Not in Pornoland.

Whatever regulations have been tenuously adhered to so far, they are jettisoned out of the window as PC Dean starts disrobing and announces that he might have *just the tool for this job* to hand.

At this point there's the last photo: Dean's ripped chest like a washboard, Lucie sucking the end of one of his index fingers as the other works its way under the cup of her bra to tweak a nipple.

From here on in the story will inevitably *throb*, *grope* and *thrust* its way into no-go areas for photographic capture. Instead a series of fairly tasteful sketches punctuate the rest of the text and as he glances ahead, most are of Lucie pinned by, or skewered on, various hidden penises; make that cocks of course. Porno studs don't have penises. They have cocks. Or members. Or beef swords or bayonets. Or, Kevin's favourite, they have *thickly-veined stiffnesses*. And they're not after vaginas. Oh no. Nothing but *pussies* or *quims* will do.

Kevin can't help but wonder how many synonyms are going to be needed to get to the end of the impending cock-onslaught without obvious repetition. Sure enough, he snorts when the first *thickly-veined stiffness* makes an early appearance, boinging out of Deano's pants to be met by a gasp from Lucie, presumably of grateful anticipation, though Kevin suspects (hopes) that in the real world it might owe more to trepidation. Dean is commendably taking his public service remit very seriously. *Ooo, I like your truncheon*, says Lucie. *Is it for me? Reckon you can take it all?* asks Dean considerately, the charmingly flirty badinage sparkling merrily, the delightful young lovebirds tentatively getting to know each other as they embark on the path to a more meaningful multilateral relationship. *I'm going to fuck you good and hard*, chirps Dean, ever the romantic.

Seeing no reason to miss out, Terry and Barry have also undressed and are now looking for spots in which to park their respectively *huge* and *lengthy* erections. Lucie is keen to accommodate. What a lovely and generous girl.

Kevin is perturbed to see he is not yet halfway through and is contemplating skipping forwards to the denudement, if only to check she survives in one piece, when the door opens and who should wander in but… why, it's Jerry the alarm maintenance guy; the writer grimly clinging onto any vestiges of narrative integrity, though lacking the will to go back and mention an alarm going off in the first place.

Jerry doesn't drop his toolbox in amazement. Jerry doesn't apologise for intruding and leg it. Jerry doesn't check to see if Lucie is fine and dandy with this looming lance-fest. No, what Jerry does do, with commendable deadpan delivery, is ask i*s everything in hand?* Good old Jerry. Nothing like a euphemism to break the ice. *Ooo yes*, says Lucie, her fingers encircling the now *throbbing cocks* of Terry and Barry – Deano's thickly-veined stiffness is unmentioned at this juncture – considerately keeping them primed, presumably while everyone frantically debates logistics, struggling to recall basic geometry.

Meanwhile Jerry has stepped out of his overalls, which appear to be his sole item of clothing, to reveal a hairy chest that Lucie loves enough to disengage a hand from either Terry or Barry and run the freed fingers through the curls. He also has a *thick* cock; his second USP. Lucie announces she's never seen one so wide. He looks like Super Mario.

When there's a knock at the door, Kevin half expects Lucie to throw her hands in the air in exasperation and tell them all to bugger off, or at the very least form an orderly queue. And spare a thought for the poor guys trying to stay *huge*, *smooth*, *thick* and *thickly-veined* respectively, not to mention *throbbing*. But no. *Come in* beckons Lucie, keen to jump aboard the double entendre carousel. The door opens and in swings a lycra-clad bicycle courier. Fuck knows why he's here, and quite frankly, who gives a toss; so he doesn't even bother offering an explanation.

Nor need he worry about feeling left out as Lucie has, through the copse of quivering penile wands, seen something to take her fancy: the lycra-moulded bulge snaking its way down his inner thigh, *reaching almost to his knee*. It's Christmas come early for greedy Lucie, who eagerly unwraps her latest prezzie, tugging and pulling to release the *black mamba* from its polyurethane prison. Cue gasp from Lucie who informs Leroy (!!) that his is the *smoothest, longest cock* she's ever seen – poor old Barry, or was it Terry? Kevin doesn't care enough to check. Leroy replies that *it's all yours baby, if these guys don't mind sharing, that is.* They're in danger of having a conversation at this juncture, or would be if Lucie wasn't sword-swallowing, rendered speechless by the penis now in her mouth, which she is *sucking at greedily, moaning with pleasure.* The others take stock and pick an orifice each.

Happy days for one and all, though Kevin is fast coming to the conclusion that our Lucie is a bit of an air-headed, semen-coated slapper, and his imagination is giving up on the construction of any workable fantasy that doesn't make him want to retch. And even if he could succeed in separating Lucie from her philanthropic suitors, what has he got to offer her? These are not his people and Lucie is definitely not his girl for tonight, a conclusion his limp penis reached some time ago. He exits the story as Lucie is man-fully servicing all five at once – Jerry presumably having drawn the short straw as he merrily pumps away at her armpit – like some sick homage to Bert's one-man band in *Mary Poppins* or a sex-army knife in fully extended exhibitory mode.

He leafs back through the magazine, moving rapidly past *Collette,* who looks disconcertingly like Carl wearing a wig, before tenderly whacking off to a narrative-less blonde in gradually unfurling dungarees making a mess of the decorating without another bloke in sight. Just him and her; and very happy she is to see him.

There's a slight twinge that brings memories of an ambushing garden ornament distractingly to the surface, but that's a small price to pay for the reassuring feeling of being back in control.

SUNDAY

DATE 3: DEAN

"Twenty quid."

"What?"

"Okay, make it twenty-five."

"What *are* you on about, Dean?"

"To pick me."

"I do hope you're kidding."

"I know I've got issues and stuff, but they treat me like some care in the community project. I'm there every week but I only get to play a few times a season. I just want to show them. Thirty?"

MONDAY

A new working week brings fresh impetus. Nurturing the one decent cup of coffee he'll have all day, sourced off-site, David sets his office in motion and checks his emails, trawling through the uninvited, irritating and irrelevant. Scant fare in response to his request for feedback, save for a suggestion – one that generates a sigh – that he might wish to speak to Messrs Mills and Bowen.

Girding his loins and donning his thickest skin, he exits his bunker with trepidation and five minutes later is shuffling towards them with all the self-assurance of an inadequately armoured infantryman making his way across No Man's Land. They sit hunched over plates of full English, Bowen holding court as ever, the verbal flow uninterrupted by the inconvenience of eating; a sausage poking out of a corner of his mouth.

Bowen's anecdote comes to a spluttering, self-congratulatory conclusion and his fellow diners dutifully snigger. He runs a yolk-tinged tongue between greasy lips and spies the loitering David.

"Hang on, boys. Fear not. It's Sherlock Morse on the case." Neither funny nor clever, but David forces a smile and Bowen is very pleased with himself. Momentarily distracted by a baked bean's gravity-resisting progression down Bowen's glistening chin, David leaves himself open to yet more comedic excellence. "*What's-on* your mind, then?" Cue belly laugh, a prolonged preview of what awaits Bowen's stomach, then several recaps to enlighten the confused and milk the moment. David dives in regardless.

"Just following up that email I sent asking for some feedback from the two houses you visited."

"Easy tiger. Give us a chance."

"It's just I was thinking of maybe popping along later today for a follow-up chat."

"Ooo. Get you. *Popping* along. Anyone would think you didn't trust us proper coppers to do a decent job."

"It's not that. It's just…"

"Don't worry. You're welcome to them. Though I'd be lying if I said I hadn't considered *popping* back to see Mrs Forbes. She was well up for it." The titters this generates signal David's time is up. "Catch you later," Bowen adds, confirming David's imminent exit.

"I'll wait," David says, with a calm assurance that surprises all present.

*

Mrs Forbes is wearing a lot of make-up and a skirt that doesn't quite reach her knees. She doesn't like being called Mrs Forbes. She prefers Alice. He feels uncomfortable calling her Alice, so avoids calling her anything. He isn't sure what a well-up-for-it woman looks like, so is unable to interpret the smile Mrs Forbes offers him as she pours the tea. In his experience women tend to see him more in a maternal pat-on-the-head way. All he has to go on is the Mrs Forbes-related anecdote that was the price he had paid for overstaying his welcome in the station canteen.

Without ever appearing to have actually said or done anything specific, Mrs Forbes had nonetheless communicated to Bowen in no uncertain terms that she was trapped in a passionless marriage, starved of sex, 'gagging' for it and struggling to keep her clothes on. "You know what these posh birds are like; cold as hell to begin with, but once they thaw out they're as dirty as fuck," Bowen had waxed lyrically with the smugness of a man who had walked away with a carnal i.o.u. he was at liberty to cash in whenever he wished.

If Mrs Forbes is gagging for anything with David, she's hiding it very well as she takes him through her experience eight days earlier, any irritation at having to repeat herself not apparent. It rarely is, the public usually just relieved the police appear to remain interested in them; that a solution not only exists, but is actively being hunted down. Any guilt he feels as perpetuating that illusion is more than compensated for by the comfort he knows he gives. This is what he does.

Unfortunately, her recollections add nothing new. He nods occasionally, taking the opportunity, as he takes a sip of tea, to peep out over the inverted mug to give her a quick once-over. Her knees part slightly. She has a mole just above her knee.

"Would you like a tissue for that?"

He follows her gaze downwards and for a panic-stricken second misinterprets the splatter of dark stains slowly spreading in his crotch.

"You've spilt your tea. Don't worry. The mugs look good and cost a small fortune, but they're not very practical. Here, take it." Their fingers brush as he takes the proffered tissue from her. There is the briefest glimpse of a bra strap.

"Nothing else you can think of?" he stammers.

"Sorry, no. It was all a bit chaotic, I'm afraid."

A pregnant pause ensues, and when she fails to fill it with an instant de-robing and offer of intercourse, he takes it as his cue to leave; only to be thrown again when, as she shows him out, her hand rests briefly on his elbow as he steps past her into the garden. And did she have to stand that close? As he walks down the drive he wonders if that was a gift horse not only looked at, but given a full dental examination before being locked back in its stable; or not?

All very confusing, if a little thrilling.

The breakthrough comes at the second house he visits.

Mrs Robertson's weary rotundity ensures sexual chemistry is not a factor in their conversation, allowing David to concentrate on the matter in hand and forage further. He mentions where he's just been and is informed that, "Yes, Alice said you had called."

"You know her?"

"Just from the school. Our boys are in the same year. Not really friends or anything. Bit of a coincidence all round. Four of the five, it was five, wasn't it?" He nods. "Yes, four of the attacks on parents at the school. Just a coincidence I'm sure, there's enough of us round here. But a bit spooky, don't you think?"

He does, and confirms with her the identities of the other parents; Mrs Carruthers the odd one out.

"I did mention it to the other policeman, but to be honest he looked like he couldn't wait to leave."

"I'm sure that wasn't the case, but I can assure you that I am very interested in anything you have to say."

This brings a smile to her face and she crosses the room to fetch a framed photograph. David looks down on the decidedly unappealing face of a young male riding the cusp of adulthood and falling into the surly, awkward no-man's-land between the cuteness of childhood and the ease of maturity, where the tectonic plates of the face shift features in a molten landscape; the type of face you would want to slap repeatedly, then wash your hands.

"Very nice," says David, unsure what you do say at such moments and immediately worrying that his hastily-chosen words sound ridiculous in the face of such unsightliness, not to mention a little creepy.

"Not really," she says, with evident regret. "Used to be my lovely little boy. Now he's just a bloody oik. Only a mother could love a face like that. Or so they say."

David selects silence as his response, and is saved by the sound of footfall on stairs, heralding the entrance of a girl of about seven or eight.

"Ah, here's Lily," says Mrs Robertson, with an outpouring of unbridled joy for the antithesis of the face that sneers at David from his lap. He places the frame on the table, face down, and says hello.

"This is PC... sorry, I forgot your surname."

"David will do," he says, and flashes his friendly smile.

"He's a policeman and he's just here to ask a few questions about what happened last week. Nothing to worry about."

But the smile has vanished from Lily's lips and she buries her face into her mother's jumper.

"Come on, dear. There's nothing to worry about. We just want to make sure the naughty people who did it get caught."

When Lily's face reappears, the panic is clear to see.

"What's the matter, Lily?" asks her mum.

"I'm sorry. Don't let him take me away."

"What *are* you on about?"

"Promise?"

"I'm sorry about——"

"*Promise?*"

"Of course I promise," interjects David in his child-friendly, late-night-DJ voice.

Lily looks up at her mum. Receives a nod and a smile. "I'll go get it," she says.

She arrives back downstairs with her hands behind her back.

"It was stuck to that bus thing. It looked pretty, so I took it off when no one was looking and... sort of kept it. Sorry." She produces something from behind her back and hands it over to David. He accepts it as if it were some fragile butterfly.

Bingo.

He's at the door on the point of departure when it opens and in slouches the 3D version of the delightful Master Robertson. The camera hadn't lied. His mother summons up an, "Oh, hi there. How was school, love?" He grunts, "Pathetic," presumptuously dumps his school bag at his mother's feet, throws his blazer into a corner and lopes into the kitchen; his mother observing his departure with barely disguised relief, her face etched with disappointment.

"I'm sorry. Manners don't rate very high in the *cool* stakes when you're that age. He's a lovely boy under all that attitude," she says unconvincingly, desperately drawing on dwindling reserves of maternal pride. Above the clamour of rattled fridge contents, slammed cupboard doors and abused packaging, the occasional "oink" is clearly to be heard.

David spares her any more pain and embarrassment by politely taking his leave, smiling broadly at Lily and emerging into the weak wash of late afternoon sunshine.

TUESDAY

It's not until after midday that David escapes a succession of pointless meetings; pointless because they don't relate to him. Not that he can win. If he didn't attend, they'd all have a good chunter about it, yet when he does, he's peppered with sideways glances and there's an audible resentment at his presence.

But today has been different. The meetings were still of negligible relevance to him, dealing as they did with actively-pursued cases and general station matters, but for once he hadn't felt like an extraneous irritant. People talked to him. He'd been saved a chair. There was even physical contact.

Acceptance; although a cynic might hazard a link to the cup semi-final this evening, the station's first ever.

But for now, the rest of the working day is his to luxuriate in.

And why does he do what he does?

This is why.

Before him on his desk sits the bounty from the past week's sleuthing. Centre stage are the five buses.

To their right is a single black shoe, an intriguing though quite probably irrelevant discovery on his tour of the woods across from Mrs Carruthers' house. To the other side is a playing card: the five of spades, its rear a checked red and white, bar the rough-edged hole in its middle where it was glued to the bus, a clear hard residue on the nearest bus laying testament to that.

It's the card that excites him most; the real treasure. A prized addition to the collection, another link in the chain.

He picks up the phone and taps in the number.

"Rebecca Staniford."

"Hi. It's me."

"Hello me."

"Can you do me a favour?"

"And there I was thinking you might just want a chat."

"Eh?"

"Never mind. Shoot."

"What?"

"Just say what you want."

"I need you to check a name for me. Probably deceased, sometime in the last few months."

"What's the name?"

"Ah. That's the problem."

*

Nielson, the captain, nods in the direction of a group noisily playing cards.

"That's them. Cocky wankers," he says under his breath as they move over to the bar.

David casts *them* a cursory glance. They don't look that impressive slouched in their chairs, hurling good-natured abuse at each other. They certainly don't look chastened by the events of the league encounter back in November, before David was recruited, when a five-nil mauling at their hands had seen two of the opposition slung into a cell until the night duty sergeant intervened to prevent a public relations nightmare. Not that there hadn't been provocation: frames played with pool cues, constant sniggering, shots played with eyes closed and so on. The tipping point had come in the final frame when their player had accompanied every shot with an audible pig noise as cue hit ball.

"What you having, Dave?"

David winces and asks for a pineapple and lemonade. Behind him the banter continues apace. He may be wrong, but the matter under debate appears to be about which snooker player, past or present, they'd most like to receive a blow job from; Kirk Stevens and Tony Knowles getting repeat mentions.

"Yes," says the barmaid, reading his pained expression. "That's exactly what they're talking about. Ignore them and think yourself lucky you haven't had to put up with this drivel day in, day out. Legends in their own minds. If life was fairer, they'd be rubbish at snooker, but there you go." He smiles back weakly.

The station's team comprises two half-decent players, two very average players and David. The tactics formulated in the minibus for the best-of-five encounter are simple: David plays the frame after their opponents win their second frame. This is two rounds further than they have ever reached and they now need to win three frames against a team who are the reigning cup winners and have only lost two frames all season in twenty-two league and six cup games. Their progress has resulted in celebrity status at the station.

David doesn't do conflict, so he's pleased to see the opposition on best behaviour, even magnanimous in defeat as they lose the first frame easily, their player looking so nervous he's virtually incapable of potting a ball. The next player is clearly decent, but Nielson plays way above himself, knocking in a forty-one break and then prevailing in a tight, safety-dominated end game. David flinches as Nielson forgets himself and punches the air, but his opponent summons up a smile with his handshake and the tension dissipates. The reports appear to have been exaggerated.

Or maybe not.

A clinking of metal heralds the entrance of the opposition's third player. The handcuffs are removed to enable him to play but the leg irons stay on, necessitating much use of the rest as he proceeds to knock in a faultless eighty-three break; which would be begrudgingly enjoyable to witness were it not for the fact that he's playing Benson, a man who even in his lighter moments is never far from psychotic meltdown. He dislikes losing intensely, but losing and being subjected to this piss-take is enough to send his face into a swirl of emotive magma, lips squirming and straining to contain the words that fight for air play, their utterance an inevitable precursor to a physical onslaught. Only a literally hands-on approach from his captain caps the crater and averts the eruption.

"No problem, mate," says the opponent when his handshake is refused. "Just a bit of fun, eh? No harm meant." Still pushing it, but he's permitted to leave the room in one piece, and David lets out a breath.

Hopes of an isolated incident are dashed with the entry of a bloke dressed in striped T-shirt, sporting a mask and carrying a bag on which the letters S, W, A and G have been crudely etched in thick black ink.

Mills and Bowen, ostensibly here to offer their moral support, smile weakly. But when the mask stays on and the opponent gleefully whacks the cue ball into the pack, sending the reds to all corners of the table, they make for the bar and David fears the worst.

The semi-final goes to the last frame and David takes himself away to prepare for battle in a distant corner of a now-packed room. He surveys the unfolding pantomime. "*Enough*," bellows a voice with an authority that briefly curtails the furore. It takes David a few seconds to recognise the voice as his own, and a few more to overcome his astonishment; which is as nothing to that of his team and supporters. And while he has their attention… "Right. You've got a choice. Either you all just clear out of the room or I concede this frame. And I mean *all* of you. If we're going to win this match, I want to win it fair and if we lose it… well at least I'll be able to look at myself in the mirror afterwards. But this…" He waves a hand in a sweeping arc. "This is pathetic. Just go. The lot of you."

The ensuing silence starts to erode whatever inner strength propelled the outburst, so he takes refuge in some intensive cue tip maintenance, his hands shaking. After what seems to him like an eternity there's a movement in the ranks and the assorted spectators shuffle slowly out of the room; the only sounds those of heavy boots peeling off sticky carpet, riot shields clunking against the sides of snooker tables, a canine whimper or two and a succession of dull thuds as a dropped helmet bounces along the floor.

It's only when he's sure they're all gone that he looks up from a ridiculously over-chalked cue tip and meets the studied gaze of his opponent. He returns the smile, more from relief than amusement, and tries to quell the tremors still vibrating through his body.

"Hi, I'm Kevin," says his opponent and they shake hands. "Do you need a minute? Or should we just get this out of the way?"

When they emerge over half an hour later, David stops in his tracks as he struggles to assimilate the chaos before him. Various scenarios had presented themselves for his grim contemplation in the more passive moments of the frame, all of them enough to send a shiver down his spine and into his bowels; but this isn't one of them. Nothing like it. Discarded police jackets, helmets and other riot paraphernalia litter chairs and floor space; the detritus of an all-round back-slapping, alcohol-quaffing, card-playing love-in that sees David's jaw drop, its centrepiece Benson and his opponent, arm in arm, one leg each on the table before them, light glinting off the irons that bind them.

David accepts the offer of a drink from his opponent and has it in his hand before anyone thinks to ask about the result. He accepts the pats and words of congratulation, but can't escape the nagging feeling that his opponent just might have chucked the frame.

The pantomimic revelry is in such full swing, that the hunched figure sporting the balaclava attracts no attention as it slopes through the front door and makes a beeline for the bar, where Steve stands keeping track of the large, and getting larger by the minute, IOU that is the price of peace. The interloper's right hand disappears up the left-hand sleeve of his jacket and re-emerges clutching the handle of a knife, which he brandishes out towards Steve, who gives no indication at all of having seen it.

"This is a hold-up. Give me the money," comes the slightly muffled ultimatum.

Steve continues to count the notes, apparently insensible to the threat implied by the wavering steel blade less than a foot from his chest.

"I said give me the fucking money."

"Oh, didn't see you there Eamon. How's it going?"

"What?"

"How's it going, Eamon?"

"Fuck off. I'm not Ea— I'm not who you said I was. Give me the money."

"What can I get you, Wayne?" enquires Steve casually of a new arrival at the bar, dragging along his manacled new best friend for the ride.

"Five pints of lager and a pint of bitter please, Steve. Hiya Eamon, long time no see."

"Hiya W— *fuck*," comes the shrill and exasperated response. "How many times? I'm not him."

"Right. Who are you then?"

"*What*? I'm not going to tell you. Why do you think I've got this sodding thing on? It's so you can't recognise me."

"Must be hot in there."

"As a matt— *enough*," he screams. "Steve, just give me the bloody money and I won't…"

"Won't what?"

"Do you."

"Do me."

"Yes."

"No."

"Look mate. I really need this. Please just give me the money."

"You know I can't, and we both know you won't do anything with that."

"I will, you know."

"No, you won't. Have you met Wayne's friend here? He's a copper and he's brought along a few of his colleagues."

Eamon jerkily surveys the room, then turns and looks up into a smiling face that promises anything but shared mirth.

"Or you can take this tenner and fuck off," offers Steve, succumbing to a moment of sympathetic generosity.

Eamon grabs the money and fucks right off.

*

Kevin's thoughts are too jumbled to permit sleep, so he reclines on the sofa and brings up the menu. He's soon watching a favourite episode, the innocuous lift music and incessant stream of instructions a distant backdrop to the straining curves, flexing buttocks and splayed crotches that empty his cluttered mind and see the head of his penis poke out from the folds of his dressing gown like a naked mole rat emerging blinking into the sun. *Aerobics Oz Style*. It never fails. When the one who barks the orders and is almost twice the age of the others – though fair play to her, she's in good nick – starts hogging the camera, bringing with her the spectre of stretch marks, cellulite and other 'older woman' issues he doesn't really understand, he switches to that most reliable of inspirations: *The Kovac Box* (currently ranking very highly in a top ten of screen backsides alongside the likes of Sigourney Weaver in *Alien*, Vera Farmiga in *Running Scared*, and the ever-present, ever-pert, Elastigirl). He watches the twenty or so seconds from phone ringing to shower several times before stop-starting it into a favourite celluloid still. He doubles up two sheets of kitchen paper and folds them into a neat rectangle which he places on the arm of the sofa. He drinks in the white cotton clinging to the smooth, tanned curves of her derrière, lets his imagination conjure up the undoubted magnificence of the view from behind denied by the camera angle and lets his hand get to work. That she will very shortly fall from a balcony and lie splayed in a pool of spreading blood is of no concern in that moment; she and her fate – he never watches beyond this point – are discarded along with the sodden wad and its expiring gelatinous content.

WEDNESDAY

The price Rebecca sets for what he wants, or at least the promise of it – she was mischievously light on detail – is lunch. He'd pushed for her to tell him on the phone but she'd remained adamant. So here he is, winding his way through the cluttered restaurant to where she's sitting in a booth. She fixes him a smile and he does his best to hide his resentment at having his routine dismantled at such short notice.

"Cheer up. I know this is your idea of hell, but I promise I'll let you get back to your burrow once I've pigged myself senseless."

"No, it's fine. Does me good to get out," he mumbles unconvincingly. She looks different somehow. Almost glowing?

As they peruse the menus David can't stop himself mentioning the extortionate price of the starters, only to then feel guilty as Rebecca frowns and turns the page to the main courses; though not guilty enough to send her back.

It's her hair. Maybe.

After an uncomfortable silence, and with the resigned air of a comedienne whose opening gags have drawn underwhelming applause, Rebecca shuffles the running order and skips straight to the failsafe material.

"It wasn't easy, but I think I've got your man."

"Really?" More emotion in one word than he's summoned in the previous five minutes put together.

"Gosh." She looks theatrically over her shoulder. "Thought someone interesting had walked in for a moment. Now where were we?" she continues, unable to prevent a smile at his obvious unease, her left hand working to free an ear-ring that's snagged on her collar. An elaborate coiled metal effort. Some Celtic design? He can't recall ever seeing her with anything other than a stud previously. "The 'E' threw me for a while but I'm pretty certain that 'E.N.T.' is one Edward Norris Taylor. Known by one and all as Teddy, hence our missing him to begin with. He died about three months ago. Found lying dead in the road no more than fifty yards from his home. Massive heart attack. We covered it at the time and I spoke to the reporter this morning. Turned out he was a bit of a local hero; decorated World War II veteran no less and chairman of the British Legion to boot." With a flourish she sits back and crosses her arms.

David tries to squeeze enthusiasm into his facial features and discovers that he can move his ears backwards. That triumph is but fleeting, his initial excitement ebbing away – how on earth does any of this connect with the vandalism? – and his mind turns to how he can diplomatically enquire if there might be another 'E.N.T.' anywhere in the archives. He's fumbling around for some tact when she laughs.

"Don't worry. I have more. Your face was a picture there for a moment. Sorry, I'm waffling. I promise I'll earn my lunch."

And, after gulping down some air, she does.

As places go to take your final breath, this might be as unglamorous as it gets, thinks David as he stands at the street corner with nothing but a pillar box for company.

This was a man who, in 1944, had volunteered to remain in a crumbling wreck of a building and draw enemy fire while his colleagues, seriously wounded among them, made their escape. For over seven hours, running from one window to the next, he fooled a vastly superior German force ensconced on the other side of a town square into overestimating the number of soldiers they were up against and delaying an attack until reinforcements arrived. When his ammunition finally ran out and the Germans surrounded and tentatively entered the building, they were astounded to find Private Taylor reclining on a bullet-ridden chaise-longue, puffing on a cigar and toasting them with a bottle of warm Pilsner. He was posthumously awarded the Conspicuous Gallantry Medal for the selfless actions that saved eighteen lives that day, only to turn up in a liberated prisoner of war camp a year later.

The rest of his life had been far more conventional, Rebecca summarising it in under a minute, but he'd blossomed again in his seventies and eighties, gaining some renown as a local campaigner. Rebecca has reeled off some of the issues that had exercised him, leaving the best to last, just as David was starting to fear this lunch was all one big joke at his expense.

Teddy had grown more and more irritated at the vandalism of bus stops, the glass an apparent magnet to the senseless morons who felt compelled to smash it. A regular user of buses, he took up every instance with the council, pressuring them to replace the entire structure with something that couldn't be broken. He'd failed of course, the council unable to see beyond that year's already asphyxiated budget, nor sure enough of re-election to entertain any form of long-term initiative, particularly if it might be another regime who stood to benefit.

It was here that Rebecca had gone the extra yard, speaking to someone she knew at the council and getting hold of the dates of reported vandalism on bus stops in the area. Teddy Taylor had left the Legion shortly before ten on the night of his death and, as always, walked home. An incident had been reported around that time along the route he would most likely have taken. Time of death had been between ten and midnight. The body hadn't been found until the morning after a cold night, preventing a narrower time window.

David follows the route on the map Rebecca gave him after lunch and stands at the now-intact bus stop. The British Legion is only a few hundred yards away. Running along either side of the road are lines of terraced housing, save for the innocuous entrance to the scene of Tuesday night's sporting carnage, belying a Tardis-like interior and its twenty snooker tables. Did anyone see anything? Had anyone asked? Not according to the council when Rebecca had enquired. This sort of thing happens all the time and they've long ago given up bothering to look for culprits unless they fall into their lap.

But David has his connection.

And with Rebecca sworn to secrecy, he can pursue it at his leisure.

*

DATE 4: CHRIS

It's a lock-in.

Armies are amassed, tactics formulated and dice grasped in sweaty palms; the battle for Middle Earth, or whatever the hell this primary school art project monstrosity they are seated around is meant to be, is about to commence. *Why don't you all just grow up?* Nonetheless she summons up a shrug and a smile she hopes doesn't look as inane as it feels. It's only half past seven, she contemplates with dismay.

"You can have the first throw," says the timid waif to her right.

"Are you sure?"

"Mmm. Maybe the second throw."

"Right. Okay then." A blow, but one she'll recover from.

The dice skittle and scatter across the undulating landscape, this kingdom where they can be kings, and wipe out a whatever of whatevers. Orcs? Goblins? She's fast losing the will.

"Sorry," splutters the thrower, doubtless wishing he'd been looking at the table rather than at this strange creature who is generating such weird sensations and throwing the usual group dynamic into disarray.

*

"What?" Rebecca had asked, after another lingering look of puzzlement.

"Nothing."

"Rubbish. Spit it out."

"Why are you… orange?"

"What?"

"You look all orange," he'd blundered on. "Or like you've been standing over a bonfire for a while."

"Why David, thanks for that. It's tanning cream actually and the label said I'd have that straight-off-the-beach-healthy glow."

"Mmm. More like radioactive I'd say," had come the response, very fucking pleased with himself, before her expression had put a stop to that. "It's just I thought you had a smudge of soot above your eye there." His finger poking inches from her forehead, making her feel like some freak show exhibit in front of a group of schoolchildren.

"It's called make-up," she'd informed him through gritted teeth.

She replays the conversation, spitting out certain phrases through the soap lather. She rubs and rubs, then splashes water over her face before standing blinking into the unforgiving mirror at the white, blotchy expanse that is the reality of her face. Then she tosses the alien tubes of make-up and their false promises into the bin and heads for the refuge that sometimes only a packet of Jaffa Cakes can offer.

THURSDAY

"The stupid cow," David forces out through clenched teeth, the newspaper spread out on the table before him. He snatches up the phone and punches angrily at it.

"Daily Prophet."

What?

"Rebecca?"

"David?"

"What did you just say?"

"Ignore it. A little in-joke. Relieves the boredom for us whacky journos as we summon up the energy to start on next week's edition."

"I'm not happy with you," he says, irritated that his words sound so feeble.

"Oh dear. What have I done now?" Not taking this remotely seriously.

"I told you very clearly that I wanted to keep this between us, not bring in anyone else. And what do you do?" Pause for effect.

"Am I supposed to answer that?"

"You go and start a bloody *Save our Shelters* campaign and invite the world and his dog to ring in. What came first, the idea or the acronym? Don't you want to get to the bottom of all this?"

"Er, yes. That's why I started the campaign, Sherlo— sorry. Look, David, at least be honest with yourself. When it comes down to it, this isn't really about solving anything. It's about nurturing something for yourself; your obsession. And you just don't want anyone to jump on your ride."

He slams the phone down.

FRIDAY

"Meet me at the bus stop at half past eleven."

And she's hung up before he has a chance to speak. Sod her. He will not be ordered around. Not by anyone. Certainly not by her.

*

David approaches with a walk carefully designed to convey that he is still angry, has certainly not forgiven Rebecca and, while he may well be here as and when requested, that is only because this is precisely where he wants to be at this time.

Unfortunately, she clocked him as soon as he rounded the corner and before he was ready. He'd been glad of the first ten yards to put 'the look' in place, but the remaining ninety are proving excruciating as his resolve weakens, not helped by a ridiculous "cooee" hurled down the street, and as he draws near he forgets what is meant to be doing what and it all dissolves into a hobble and a petulant scowl, the cutting comment formulated earlier now escaping mental recall.

"Ahh. Who's a little sulky chops?" she smirks. "Follow me, Mr Grumpy." And with him floundering for a response, she spins on her heels and he has no choice but to follow her up the path to the door she's knocking on.

"Hello, Mrs Bradley," she shouts breezily to the elderly woman who opens the door. "This is the policeman I told you about."

"Doesn't look much like a policeman."

"Well actually, er, madam. I'm not really…"

"I'm eighty-three."

Momentarily thrown, David looks helplessly to Rebecca.

"Can we come in, Mrs Bradley? David here would love to hear what you told me yesterday, wouldn't you, David?"

He gives up the struggle and follows them into a beige, antimacassar'd, ornament-crammed grotto, only to promptly be marooned in the middle of the room as Rebecca disappears in pursuit of their proudly-octogenarian hostess with an offer to help make the tea.

They return to catch him deep in contemplation of the artistic merits, not to mention proportionality, of an object that comprises a large clam shell mounted on a wooden base on which also sits a cat playing with a ball of wool, a miniature water wheel and a polished green precious stone. Lest his mind be read, he guiltily replaces it on the mantelpiece and turns to find Rebecca patting the sofa cushion beside her as their hostess sets about pouring the tea with a palsied enthusiasm that promises spillage. Short of perching on an arm rest he has no choice but to comply. He feels like a ten-year-old.

"You look very young," says Mrs Bradley, unhelpfully. He forces a smile and reaches to take the proffered beverage before the saucer overflows.

"Thank you," he says, and selects a fig roll from the retro biscuit selection. He turns to Rebecca in desperation.

"Mrs Bradley, sorry to ask you to repeat yourself, but I'd very much like David to hear it from you… what we talked about?"

"Just children," she says looking over at the window. "All that money lavished on them and so little respect. My Bertie would have… well… I just don't know."

"Should I fetch you a hanky?" asks Rebecca.

"Thank you love, but I've got one." She removes a ball of tissue from under the cuff of her sleeve and dabs gently at her eyes.

"Take as long as you need."

"I'm sorry love. Just comes over me sometimes. When I see the way schoolchildren are these days. Makes you worried to go out at night sometimes."

"Did you say schoolchildren?" asks David, a distant bell ringing.

"The boys I saw breaking the glass that night."

"That night?" Getting louder.

"The night that poor man died, or so young Rebecca here tells me."

"About what time was this?"

"Must have been about just after ten. That's when I tend to get ready to go up. Group of five or six of them messing about. Then one of them disappears and comes back with what must have been a rock or a brick, as the next moment there's this loud crash and glass all over the ground."

"What happened then?" asks David, now leaning forward almost onto his knees.

"They were laughing. All that mess and they were laughing. Then I heard a man shouting at them. He was giving them a right ticking-off. Rebecca here thinks it might have been Mr Taylor."

David glances at Rebecca.

"I don't know the name of the school but there can't be many with that colour blazers."

"Hang on Mrs Bradley. Wasn't is a bit dark to be sure of any colours?"

"Not then. But I've seen that lot hanging around there before."

"The same boys? Are you sure?"

"I may be getting on young man, but I'm not stupid."

"I'm sorry," says David, sinking back into the sofa.

"What colour were the blazers, Mrs Bradley?" asks Rebecca, her gaze fixed on David.

"Purple. Horrible colour really for boys. Never in my day. I'm eighty-three, you know."

His mind is struggling to assess where this news gets him as they step onto the pavement.

"You're right, of course," Rebecca says. "That *SOS* stuff was clearly a *stupid* idea. Won't get us anywhere. Silly me. I hear that new Greek restaurant is nice. Maybe you could order some hubris to go with your pitta bread."

SUNDAY

Kevin's face is aflame by the time the doors slide open and they approach the entry barrier. He hides his nerves poorly with a stream of randomised drivel that Pete mistakenly pursues, before undermining the intended casual anonymity by exclaiming loudly, "Kevin, what the fuck are you on about?"

Kevin counters with a relaxed laugh rendered tremulous by his still-rattling nerves before it is truncated as he pushes with the inside of his hip against the barrier, a split second before his card swipe renders it push-againstable. The performance is worthy of a bow, but he overplays that as well as his upper body snaps down over the metal bar to the accompaniment of a loud grunt and an expelled warm sirocco of partially digested meat-lathered couscous that is the gift that appears to keep on giving from last night's misguided visit to Watford's first – and last? – Moroccan restaurant.

Pete sighs and leaves Kevin to mop up the shattered remnants of his dignity before a sizeable audience of puzzled staff and members.

Kevin wincingly regains verticality, tentatively negotiates the barrier and shuffles towards the sanctuary of the changing room.

He'd have drawn less attention had he strolled into the gym playing a French horn.

The best behaviour he's sworn himself to on this return to the scene of his last humiliation – or at least his last gym-based humiliation, before today that is – is inevitably compromised, the honey trap taking the form of a derrière of breathtakingly hypnotic undulations; like some perpetual motion wave machine lapping rhythmically at his genitalia as it powers the legs of the cross-training brunette at two o'clock. The downside is that an intended five-minute jog is turning into a ten-kilometre slog and the resulting fatigue sees his furtive glances lapse into one long heavy-breathing, slack-jawed gawp. Sensing the weight of a gaze from the man on the machine to his right he drags his eyes from their salacious feasting and flashes him the complicit sneer of the fellow ogler, before the very real risk of coronary arrest and/or an impromptu crumpled dismount necessitates prolonged depressing of buttons. Easing into a welcome warm-down stroll, he prepares for a more leisurely posterior appraisement, only to observe his recent neighbour dismount, stroll over to the object of his overt lechery and engage her in conversation, before flashing Kevin a look that he struggles to interpret, although it's definitely not inclusive.

There are a number of appropriate options open to Kevin at this juncture. A wink would be very near the bottom of that list. But then hindsight is a wonderful thing, and of scant use to Kevin as he recoils from the sheer enmity his wink engenders.

With commendable compensatory foresight he deciphers the warning signs – more Dora The Explorer than Alan Turing – and beats a hasty retreat for the changing room. As he passes Pete, he announces he's off for a swim.

There are many reasons why Kevin rarely swims: water up his nose; chlorine in his eyes; liquid lodged for days in the inner recesses of his ears; floating, nattering hairdos clogging the lanes; the failure of far too many to observe the simple protocol of the clockwise use of the non-recreational half of the pool; and the knowledge that if even twenty per cent of the other swimmers deposit even ten per cent of the phlegm and snot that he routinely coughs up and surreptitiously deposits in the water, then short of a fine sieve and full transfusion every few hours, he's swimming not so much in a pool as a tepid mucus-infused minestrone. And that's before he even starts considering what other secretions and waste products he might be bathing in.

Not that he is defenceless.

He has four weapons in his armoury: goggles, nose clip, ear plugs and a profound but blind faith in the all-conquering sterilising qualities of chlorine. He dons and inserts the protective equipment and sets off.

Three strokes later the nose clip slides down and off his sweat-lubricated nose. He makes a grab for it but misses, forgets to blow out through his nose and stands up spluttering. A noisy nasal evacuation ensues. Pinching his nostrils tight he dips his face below the surface. He is pleased to locate the clip wafting along the floor a few yards away, but not so pleased to see what appears to be a length of tissue and what is definitely a used plaster also suspended in the water. On the fourth uncoordinated dive/sink he succeeds in grabbing the clip and after some vigorous nasal rubbing, attains friction and is able to set sail again. Only this time the goggles let in water and twice require servicing. Twenty metres has never felt so long. It's only as he reaches the end of his second length that he realises that the ear plugs are absent. The option of looking for two tiny gel discs is easily denied, so he recklessly abandons his ear canals to the vagaries of chemically-infused water and ploughs on.

As he empties and demists his goggles for the umpteenth time, he catches sight of an Adonis emerging from the changing room and pausing for maximum effect. And it's hard to deny him the glare of the spotlight. The bastard. The good-looking, perfectly-toned, muscle-bound bastard. Kevin leans back into the corner of the pool and awaits the oh-so-predictable pantomime of the aquaphobe. Sure enough, the bloke sits on the edge and tentatively dangles his feet into the pool, which he eyes with distrust. Eventually he slides down into the water, lets out an audible shiver and hugs himself. Finally, he not so much launches himself, as topples forwards and, head swinging manically left and right like a tennis spectator on fast forward, flails his way up the pool. The effect achieved is that of drowning-man-swept-along-on-rip-tide. He finally makes the other end, leaving behind him a wake of foaming water, waves still slapping against the sides of the pool. He takes a couple of minutes to recover, before pulling himself effortlessly from the water and swaggering back to the changing room; his work done. The embodiment of what women desire. Or at least what Kevin assumes they do. But then what does he know?

He goggles and clips up and consoles himself with the sure knowledge that for all his enviable physical advantages, the bloke will forever look like a twat when in water. Scant comfort, but enough to propel him forwards with exaggerated precision and stylistic flourish.

His reward for nineteen laboured lengths is five minutes in the sauna. He's relieved to find it empty and lies down on a bench, the heat of the wooden slats burning the back of his calves for a few seconds. He lets the rest of his body relax and subjects further small areas of skin to a fleeting scalding. It's hot. Very hot. The secret is to think cool thoughts. He closes his eyes and transports himself to an air-conditioned room. An air-conditioned hotel room. And he's not alone. A maid. Offering to turn down the covers for him. Leaning provocatively over the bed. Asking if there's *anything* else he needs, as she's about to go off duty. "*Anything,*" she repeats with maximum insinuation, flashing him a dirty look as he... the clunk of the door and a gush of cooler air snaps him out of his randy reverie and the jolting realisation that he has an erection sends him rolling away from the intruder and onto his side; nose and penis bisecting the angle of bench and wall, the meeting of new areas of flesh with the heated wood an assault on so many fronts that it generates an "aaarrrgghh."

"Are you okay?" asks a female voice, its tone one of tender concern.

"Fine thanks. Just a, er, a Pilates exercise." Those last two words evading the clutches of quality control, compelling him to elucidate further in doomed pursuit of authenticity. "It's all about the core." Which sounds ridiculous. "It's a routine I do." The ensuing silence is awkward, his words so painfully unconvincing that surely more is required. He sets about creating a series of what he believes Pilates moves should look like, the common, and much limiting, denominator – other than their not being Pilates moves – being that none of them can reveal the erection that is stubbornly refusing to go away. Left leg up, out, back and down. An arm flails. And... repeat?

He tries to empty his mind but it's filling uncontrollably with the wrong images. Either he's back in that hotel room, his fingers buried in the nooks and crannies of a nubile domestic worker, or he's in this sauna, alone, with the as-yet-unseen female sitting there just a few feet away. He can hear her breathing, getting quicker, almost panting, in a bikini, the two of them, a woman, in a bikini… She's shifting, moving? Coming towards him? Whatever parts of his body that aren't rigid tense. She's definitely moving…

Then the door opens with a slight suck and a wash of cooler air fans his back. He's alone again, with an unabated hard-on; and he's feeling a little giddy.

Feeling a lot giddy.

A noise like waves crashing on rocks fills his ears and a blanket of darkness descends towards him and he knows he's going to succumb if he doesn't get the hell out of here so he's trying to stand and his eyes are filling with a myriad flashing lights and a piercing ringing assaults his ears and the darkness is almost upon him and he feels nauseous and his knees are buckling as he pushes at the door and the floor tiles are rising up to meet him and…

When he regains consciousness, it takes him a few blinking, startled moments to determine that he is lying on the blissfully cool floor just outside the sauna, looking up into the concerned faces of assorted strangers. He waves an arm – part dismissive, part reassuring – and pulls himself up into a seated position against the wall.

"I'm fine. Really, I am. I've had a cold lately and it appears I'm not over it yet. Sinusitis probably. Plus I didn't have any breakfast." His imagination exhausted, he waves his hand in the air again. "Really. It's nothing to worry about." He bows his head, the fussing abates, and gradually they all abandon him to his embarrassment.

Almost all. There's a lingerer, one with the patience to wait for him to look up. Which eventually he does, to find, atop a rather plump body, a flushed cherubic face sporting a worryingly proprietorial look. Her lips move and he emerges from his daze to catch the last few syllables: "…lattered."

He frowns at her.

"Our little secret," she says in a voice strangely familiar, tapping her nose with a bulbous finger and briefly glancing downwards. Then she stands, flashes him a conspiratorial look and leaves him with a view of the not inconsiderable lateral sway of her departing buttocks ruminating in the confines of a bathing suit several sizes too small. The combined effect of it all is to chill him to the marrow.

*

DATE 5: RAY

"Hello."

"Er, hi Laura."

An awkward silence ensues as they each shift their weight from one foot to the other. Then there's a tug on his sleeve.

"Yeah, right. This is Julie."

"His *girlfriend*," states Julie. If looks could kill…

"I, we thought we might go to the cinema. Julie wants to see the latest Clive Owen film."

"I think that's a marvellous idea."

MONDAY

If David's in-station popularity had been measured on a heart rate monitor, they'd have turned off life-support months ago; the constant drone of anonymity the soundtrack to his barely-abided existence. Presented with a rare window of opportunity afforded by Tuesday's last-gasp victory, David determines to open it wide.

And once more he finds Bowen holding court in the canteen. He instinctively pulls back to wait his turn but is promptly hauled in amidst a barrage of back-slapping and complimentary anecdotal involvement. He sheepishly endures the strange experience and it's only as the others drift away that he broaches the subject.

His new best friend is more than happy to oblige, the glint in his eyes for once of no concern to David.

*

DATE 6: WAYNE

"Might as well agree up front. Are we gonna fuck now, or build up nice and slow for later?"

"What?"

"Fuck? You know. Shag? Rut? Horizontal jog…"

"I know what you mean."

"Thought you might." He lets out a knowing snigger. "Well then? Now or later?"

"Er, neither?"

"Look, love. Forget your WMDs. Waste of time looking for them if you ask me. Why don't you go in search of the WMF we both know is hiding here somewhere? I'm sure something will *come* up." And when she doesn't react, he delivers his punch line. "Weapon of Mass Fucking is what I'm talking about, and it's primed to detonate anytime you want, darling."

"I think I'll leave it for someone else to disarm."

"Your call, but I'll warn you now. Doesn't matter whether we do it or not; I'll still be telling everyone we did."

"Are you serious?"

"What do you think?"

"*Riiight*. And will I have enjoyed it?"

"Yep. Loved it. Begged me for more. Gagging for it. A right little gusher."

"*Gusher*?"

"Gusher."

"And you're okay with all that?"

"Me? No problem. I've got an image to live up to."

"What about mine?"

"I've got a huge cock. Fucking donkey kong."

"Words fail me."

"You wouldn't be the first love, believe me."

TUESDAY

David has to give the kid some credit. Whatever he's feeling inside, the outside is all sculpted, lanquid indifference. As agreed, the duty sergeant leaves the boy in reception and shows Mrs Robertson through to meet David in an interview room. Mr Robertson is too busy at work to get away, she tells him, averting her gaze as she does so. David fills her in on what he's intending. She blanches, then becomes tearful, before summoning from deep within the courage to give her agreement. David gives her assurances he has no right to give her, particularly as he won't even be in there. It'll be Mills, Bowen, the duty solicitor and sixteen-year-old Sean Robertson. The station's two loosest cannons, under instruction to make this spoiled brat suffer; teach him a lesson. What can possibly go wrong? The mother's trembling body and brimming eyes only serve to increase his concern, but the time to call a halt has passed.

Lacking the emotional range to offer anything she needs, he abandons her to a solitary vigil in reception.

For over half an hour he pretends to read notices, wanders up and down corridors, asks questions the answers to which he doesn't hear or care about and swallows tea and biscuits without tasting them; all the while steadfastly avoiding eye-to-eye contact with the woman doing pretty much the same in reception. Only it's *her* son in there. He can't compete with that. So why does he feel so nervous? However much he tells himself it's about the mother and her son, he knows deep down it's more about his own obsession. Rebecca, as ever, had been spot on.

He exits the toilet just in time to catch the reception-bound procession. He moves around a desk for the best vantage point and sends a paper cup flying, the dregs spreading over an unfeasibly large area for so little liquid. He pulls a ragged and soiled lump of tissue from his pocket and dabs it into the centre of the puddle. It is saturated instantly without any discernible impact. He looks up and leans forward in time to see Mrs Robertson rising to her feet shakily and facing her son, her face tortured with trepidation. His head is bowed as he walks in. He wavers for a few seconds, then slowly looks up. His face is red and puffy but he's holding it loosely together; that is until he meets his mother's gaze, at which point his features crumble and he lurches into her arms, the word "sorry" repeatedly discernible amongst the outpouring of sobs. Mrs Robertson's eyes are squeezed shut. Then they flicker open and she's staring straight at David. Her lips form a reluctant smile, and mouth the words, "Thank you." David nods with relief, then looks down, not in any polite deference, but to ascertain the source of the dampness on his upper left thigh.

A trickle of liquid has detached from the main body and made its way across the desk top in order to conduct some basic chromatography on the material of his trousers. He pulls himself away with a groan and inspects a dark stain. It looks like he's just had a lap dance, he guesses. The need for tissue increases exponentially, but upon hearing Bowen take his leave with a commendably harsh-but-surprisingly-compassionate, "I hope lessons have been learned here; you'd better take your son home," a greater need takes precedence and he rushes across the room to head off Bowen and uncover the facts.

As he rounds the corner into the corridor, he remembers the offending stain and automatically moves to cover it with his left hand. That feels unnatural so he loops his thumb over his belt, tugs it downwards as far as he can and goes for a hanging hand casual look. The rest of his body struggles to adapt and lurches into an apelike lope that David swiftly corrects into more of a bent-over swagger. The lesser of two evils. Maybe.

Unbeknown to David, Bowen is coming off a twelfth viewing the night before of *2 Fast 2 Furious* and is a connoisseur of Paul Walker's method acting and his effortless transformation into a pseudo-black, complete with authentic dude-strut. So when Bowen sees David coming at him like a true bruvva, he goes for the appropriate greeting.

David is perplexed to see Bowen's right arm shoot up like he's about to do that silly Morecombe and Wise dance. When Bowen shifts his right shoulder forward David instinctively both flinches and puts up his own right arm, whereupon his hand is grabbed by Bowen and he's pulled into an awkward shoulder bump.

"How's it hanging Davo?" asks Bowen.

"Good, cool, yunno," stumbles David. "How did it go in there?" he adds, hoping that an injection of syntax doesn't curtail this vibe thing they've got going on here.

"Cushtie man. We played it nasty cop, nasty cop, got him crying like a little baby and then he couldn't wait to dump his mates in it. Full confession. The lot. He reckons they done at least a dozen. Bit of a crack and all that bollocks. They hang round together in the evenings and he says they got bored one night and did the first for a laugh, then got into the habit. Spoilt public school wankers. I'd blame society, if I gave a flying fuck." David forces the required chuckle. "Anyways that night he says they did the bus stop and next thing there's this old geezer giving them a bollocking. He says they gave him some verbals but swears they didn't do nothing else." David's nose wrinkles at the double negative. "I believe him. He was in a right state by then. Looks like the old codger wandered off home but the stress did for him and he had a coronary before he got there."

"How many of them were involved?"

"Five that night. The four whose houses were done and some other kid, er…" he reaches for his notebook. "Some poncey name."

"Sebastian?"

"Yeah. Fuck. How did you know?"

"Mistaken identity; he lived next door to the other house."

"Morse strikes again."

"Are you taking any action against him?"

"Haven't decided yet. Reckon the message got through all right and we'll be paying the others a visit and telling the school, so they'll be in enough shite as it is. No point in adding to the paperwork if we don't have to, and there's no way we can do them for the old geezer croaking. Main thing is we get to put it to bed and look good. I'll make sure you get your fair share of the credit."

David doubts it, but that's not what he's after.

"So that'll be it then?"

"Yep."

David clenches his fist in celebration at having it all to himself once more. Bowen clearly mistakes it for another gangland greeting and they come together in some god-awful mess of limbs and clashing torsos that ends with Bowen's notebook falling to the ground. David picks it up for him and finds Bowen intent on his crotch stain.

"Er, accident with the tap in the... er... bogs," he tries, dumbing down uncomfortably.

"No problemo Davio," Bowen replies with a wink and a tap of the nose. "Secret's safe with me, mate. Just remember to take it out next time you whack off, eh?"

David doesn't even bother searching for a response and heads for the toilet, face burning, Bowen's laughter echoing after him.

*

The Chief Inspector surprises David with the simultaneous knock on the door and entry that is beholden to the mighty.

"Wanted to congratulate you on the bus stop case. Excellent work, David. That's just the kind of result that'll shut them all up. I had a call from the mother and she was full of praise for you. Said she feels like she's got her son back. Sterling effort all round. What's all that?"

David stares stupidly at his secret collection. The gallery.

"Just some bits and pieces."

"Working on a *case*?" Unable to suppress his distaste at the inaptitude of the word.

"No. Not at all," stumbles David. "Some leftovers, that's all. Heading for the bin, no doubt."

"*Right.*"

"Uncle Malcolm?"

"Yes."

"What's the force's view on vigilantes?"

"Vigilantes? Officially? The thin end of the wedge. Totally unacceptable. There lies anarchy if we don't nip it in the bud. Who are they to decide what people can or can't do, and what punishment they deserve? We have a police force for a very good reason. Leave it to us."

"And unofficially?" asks David, feeling excluded by that 'us'.

"I'd be lying if I said there wasn't a little piece of me that doesn't cheer a little when I hear about some scum getting his comeuppance. An element of the vigilante in all of us, I guess. The bit that wants to forget the rule book and dish out some proper punishment. Ignore due process and cut to the quick." Pause to savour. "But that's a dangerous road to go down. Very dangerous. Why do you ask?"

"Oh, no reason. Just an article I was reading the other day."

"Very good," he says, shrugging it off as if random questions are par for the course. "As I said, excellent work, David. Jolly good stuff." And he's off.

David sits back in his chair and smugly surveys the tantalising fruits of his labours, indulging in deliciously teasing flights of fancy.

Just before he leaves, he picks up the phone. He gets her answer machine. Resisting the temptation to hang up, he waits and leaves a message.

"Hi, just me. Wanted to fill you in on developments and well, just say… er… thank you." Pause. "And sorry." He hangs up, feeling stupid.

FRIDAY

DATE 7: KEVIN

He looks pale, uncomfortable and close to panic. There's sweat on his forehead. He's pulling nervously at the collar of his shirt and sticking his chin up and out, clearly irritated by the knot of his tie.

"Come on. We'd better be going. The table's booked for eight," he blurts.

"If I ask you a question, Kevin, will you give me an honest answer?"

"I'll try."

"If I wasn't here and you could do whatever you wanted tonight, how would you spend it?"

"You really want to know?"

"I wouldn't ask if I didn't."

"I'd have a nice hot bath; get the smell of the betting shop out of me." Unnecessary detail. What *does* a betting shop smell like? "Wrap up in a dressing gown. Then I'd order a curry, home delivery of course, and open a lager before settling down on the sofa for a couple of DVDs. I'm working through a pile of… er… special interest films. After that I'd make myself a hot chocolate, watch some crap on the TV and then bed." He blushes. (That had been a slightly abridged version, omitting two definite wanks and the potential for a third). "You did ask," he adds, clearly feeling foolish; fiddling with a shirt cuff.

"No restaurant meal?"

"Er, no."

"You know what," she says, removing her coat, flinging it over the back of a chair and kicking off her shoes. "That sounds pretty damn perfect to me. So do us both a favour and get out of that bloody suit. You look like you're allergic to it. Go and have your bath. I'll order the curry and watch some crap on the box. You soak away and then we'll eat, watch your DVDs and vegetate."

"Are you serious?" The release of relief evident.

"Totally. Sounds great to me. Minus the bath and the bed bits, of course. I'll let you go solo on those," she adds, with a reassuring smile. "Over the past few weeks I've been paraded as a trophy, offered a bribe, had my thighs stroked, been offered an allegedly huge dick… what?"

"Nothing."

"You're smiling."

"You don't want to know."

"Which means I do. Spill it."

"No, really."

"*Kevin.*"

"Allegedly," wavers Kevin, a hint of mischief now in his eyes. "Allegedly, and these are Wayne's words remember…"

"Oh great." She shakes her head. "Go on."

"He says you're the… er… the wettest bird he's ever had."

Not wishing to dwell on the thought any longer than necessary, she resumes her tale of woe. "As I was saying. I've been *offered* an allegedly huge dick, had the c-word bellowed in my ear, frozen my arse off, had my first and last donner kebab – just what is that stuff? – had my backside fondled accidentally-on-purpose, met a jealous girlfriend and spent three hours I can never get back locked in a room with Watford's nerd collective while they acted out their sexual frustration with models of goblins. After that little lot, your proposed itinerary sounds like a Caribbean cruise in comparison." On balance it's a compliment, not that he seems to have noticed; doubtless too busy working through a montage of mental images. "Seriously, Kevin. Right now, there is nothing I would rather be doing. Give me the number of the restaurant so I can cancel. Then go and run that bath."

As he leaves the room he doesn't simply turn right, but achieves the same goal with a two-hundred-and-seventy-degree anti-clockwise swivel on the ball of his foot that lands him in a sneering James Bond opening credit pose, gun courtesy of two pointed fingers and a cocked thumb, which he holds for an uncomfortable few seconds before striding off.

Stranger and stranger, she thinks. *Why can't anything ever be normal?*

"Maybe you should choose a film, or we could watch TV."

"Kevin, pick up the film you were going to watch and stick it on. I don't care what it is. This is your evening."

"Okay, but you should know…"

"Kevin. Shut the fuck up and put the film on."

The black cop is chasing the woman. She ends up cornered in some disused building and he appears at the window pointing a gun at nothing in particular.

"Hold it bitch, you're not going anywhere," he says in an unflinching monotone, a pause between each syllable, displaying the instinctive acting ability of a steel girder.

"Right. You can now unshut the fuck up. What the hell is this crap?" she asks incredulously.

He can't keep the smirk from his lips and she can't recall him being this relaxed.

"It's a little-known classic. *Bad Girls' Dormitory*."

"It's rubbish, is what it is."

"Yep."

"And?"

"What?"

"Why?"

"You said you wanted to."

"You know what I mean. *Why*?"

"If you must know, I'm working on getting together a list of the worst films ever made. Everyone has their favourites. *Citizen Kane. Shawshank Redemption. Pulp Fiction.* And so on. You know, the usual suspects." He pauses, apparently for a reaction from her, but she's not sure what, so she waits until he continues. "I'm not interested in that. The other end of the spectrum is far more interesting. I'm not talking about the obvious, knowing kind of rubbish. *Attack of the Killer Tomatoes, Alien Apocalypse* and the like, though they have their own charm and I must admit to still holding on to fond fantasies of genuine artistic intent for the latter and Bruce Campbell is a total fucking god, of course." She hasn't a clue what he's on about, but this is the most animated she's ever seen him and she finds herself smiling as a result, then hoping he doesn't misinterpret; though he appears oblivious as he careers on. "No, they meant to play it that bad, so it can't count. Now this," he says with a nod in the direction of the umpteenth snarly canteen stand-off. "This is something special. This is proper adulterated crap. People have come up with a concept, written it, pitched it, gotten some idiots to put up the money and then a bunch of consenting adults have spent several months in all seriousness filming the bloody thing. Did they recognise its excremental quality or not? Who knows? But here it is for all posterity; their laboured, amateurish efforts captured for time immemorial. Or at least until Amazon runs out of stock."

He takes a breath and the lull is filled with pained moaning that draws their eyes back to the screen.

The follow-up, to which she naively consents, displays the 'full' thespian range of Steven Seagal in a staggeringly stupid tale of a wronged ex-special forces officer with immobile facial features mumbling gibberish while shuffling about in a long leather coat and launching his body double at a succession of baddies. She mentally treads water to the bitter end. It's well after eleven.

"I'd better be off."

"Oh. Right."

"Have you got a favourite film? I mean a proper film?" she asks, looking for her coat.

"Of course."

"And a top ten, I bet."

"Yep. Well eleven, actually."

"Eleven?"

"Eleven."

"Why am I not surprised. And you can probably name them straight off?"

"Of course. *Harvey*, *A Very Long Engagement*, *Life is Beautiful*, *Kind Hearts and Coronets*, *Evil Dead 2*, *City of God*, *Apocalypse Now*, *Good Will Hunting*, *American History X*, *Rounders*, and *Pulp Fiction*."

"In order would have been even more impressive."

"They were."

"What a guy."

"Sorry."

"Don't be silly. I'm only joking. Verging on the nerdy I'll admit, but not without charm. Bet you've got them all on a separate shelf."

"Of course."

"*Evil Dead 2*, you say."

"Yep."

"Go on then."

"*Groovy*."

SUNDAY

Kevin tries to ignore the ringing. Hopes it will stop soon. Attempts to concentrate on the matter in hand. But it's no use and he irritatedly curtails his pursuit of fleeting abandon.

Emerging from the showers into an empty changing area, he fears that a habitual indifference to fire alarms after countless tests and half-hearted fire drills may have resulted in his being the only person stupid enough not to have left a combusting building; a feeling that only grows as he rushes along an empty corridor and through a deserted foyer.

Looking on the bright side, someone else has a towel with them. Optimism is tempered however by the fact that it hangs over a shoulder, and is being used to absent-mindedly dab at a damp head of hair.

Kevin also has a towel.

Unfortunately, a towel is all that Kevin has.

There are some fifty people assembled on the pavement opposite the entrance. They are being thanked for their patience during a successful drill and told they can all go back inside in five minutes by none other than *Grant – Assistant Manager*. Kevin is sorely tempted to raise a hand and challenge the alleged success of the exercise on the basis that if everyone has acted in a genuine fashion, how come all bar one miraculously found the time to get dressed before exiting.

But he doesn't. He just feels sorry for himself. Anyway, who needs cluttering, constrictive layers of clothing when you can make do with a sodding, sodden piece of material that is more hand towel than bath sheet? His fingers are aching from the tightness of the grip on the one thing hanging between immodesty and simply looking like a twat. Standing here in pallid, goose bump-ridden humiliation; everyone either looking at him or looking like they're trying to look like they're not looking at him. Except Pete, that is, who is standing far enough away to be outside Kevin's aura of mortified ignominy, thereby escaping embarrassment by association, and is finding this all highly amusing.

MONDAY

An expanse of idle afternoon stretches out before David, and for the umpteenth time he reverentially eases the leather-bound file from the bottom drawer of his filing cabinet and winds his way slowly and deliciously through its hoard of prized exhibits, as much to admire its beauty as with any hope of substantive progression. Between brightly-coloured dividers sit punched clear plastic pockets, each containing a playing card and marked with a small coloured sticker matching the colour of the tab on the divider. Behind each pocket are the pages of detailed notes, diagrams and photographs which he hopes will one day speak to him in a language he can comprehend, revealing their secrets.

As he turns over the brown-tabbed divider − his little joke − he wrinkles his nose as he always does, reminded of where this one was found. Not that you can smell anything now. The queen of spades. A pun in there somewhere.

And the others?

The four of diamonds found in a fruit bowl on a table in a conservatory, albeit one without walls or a ceiling.

The jack of clubs found by the roadside near a patch of oil that had sent a motorbike into a slide that had put its rider in hospital with a broken leg, dislocated shoulder and severe bruising. This one deliberate sabotage, not a harmless prank. Or maybe nothing more than mere coincidence.

The queen of diamonds under the windscreen wiper of a Cayenne found standing on piles of bricks, its lights broken, windows cracked and paint fighting a losing battle against acid.

The ten of clubs – a weird one this – found sticking out of one of four patches of concrete laid across driveways one night and in which had been set fast all manner of wooden shapes, later determined to have been fence ornaments, plus some lethal-looking metal scraps and spikes. Interpretation further compromised by the front lawn of each garden being strewn with the contents of the wheelie bins of their neighbours. Not to mention the son of one of the families being attacked by multiple assailants the following evening on the way home from school and pelted with wooden baubles. Enough to leave him bleeding, bruised, nursing a broken finger and afraid to go out. The elements at odds with each other: the rubbish suggested inebriated opportunism, the concrete would have required a good deal of planning and coordination to execute, whilst the attack was personal and violent.

Connectors everywhere; yet no pervasive commonality to direct him.

And now this five of spades that has arrived by bus. Again, no fingerprints. The same design as the others on the back. A calling card, no doubt. But whose? This one reeks of vigilantism.

And if he were to view all the others in the same light…

TUESDAY

"You likie this, no?"

"Er, yes."

Not really. And what's with the accent?

"You wanna fucky-fucky wid me?"

"Mmm."

"My nipples rock hard. You wanna suck dem?"

"Mmmm."

"Ee, I'm sooo hot, baby." There's that hint of Geordie again, peeping through the East European drawl. Very disconcerting when you're trying to conjure up a picture of Horny Helga, the goat herder, lying spread-eagled on a haystack.

Phone sex is Kevin's go-to stimulant in times of most need. It never fails; until tonight, that is, and this nagging struggle with authenticity.

"Where are you from exactly, Helga?" Kevin asks.

"Oo… er… I from Romania." Sounding like lyrics from a Wurzels song.

"Really? I went there once. To the capital actually. Now, what was it called?"

"I from the countryside. I milk zee goats and then I milk zee men. I maka zee men cum. You like coomin?"

"I prefer cinnamon." The feeble joke is immediately regretted. "What's the weather like over there?" he tries, for the want of anything else to say.

"The... de wedder?"

"Yes."

"Oo, it's like me, baby. It be wet and hot over 'ere." She appears to have relocated to the Caribbean. "But zee men dey are so boring and ugly. I need real man to make me cum. You wanna make me cum, big boy? I bet you real big boy."

"Mmmm, I'm huge," he offers half-heartedly and then, feeling guilty, throws in the occasional "er" and "um" as she embarks on a series of random vowel sounds.

He knows he's onto a loser when each "oo oo oo" is followed in his mind by "the funky gibbon," every "oh, oh, oh" by "it's magic" and every "ee" demands a "by gum."

His dick feels like a newly born hamster nestling in his palm. He's about to put them both out of their misery when he hears her say "Kishinev." And in a flash of credibility she's lying before him, as Romanian as a Romanian can be, goats an entirely rational given, looking up at him with *that* look on her face; and the details cease to be important as the wave approaches and by the time the word 'Budapest' emerges through the pre-ejaculatory smog, he's too far gone to care.

WEDNESDAY

"Thank you for calling me back, Mrs Warburton. I wasn't sure you'd remember me."

"How could I forget? A drop of kindness in a sea of indifference."

"Yes, well. That's very nice of you to say so."

"Not that it did much good, of course."

"No… er… sorry."

"But it was appreciated nonetheless."

"I was wondering," says David, keen to get to the point, "if I could just ask you a follow-up question about… the unfortunate incident."

"Go on."

"Do you remember anyone before that night who you'd had an argument with, possibly about the dog? Maybe its… er… toilet habits or something like that?"

"Sorry. No."

Bugger.

"No problem. But if you do by any chance recall something, however insignificant it might seem, please just call me."

THURSDAY

The match flashes by: five one-sided frames, five graceless victories, five more disgruntled opponents shaking their heads and looking forward to a season without this bunch of cocky sods defecating all over them.

Normally a home game descends into alcohol and cards at this juncture. However, there is more important business to attend to this evening, as the Magnificent Seven gather to hear Laura's verdict.

"Okay lads, let's see if she's up for more with yours truly, or if one of you lot's gonna get some of my sloppy seconds," says Wayne, serenading her approach towards the assembled suitors.

"I'd like to thank you all for some lovely and… *interesting* evenings, and it was fascinating to get an insight into what makes you lot tick."

"Blah, blah, blah. Why don't you just cut to who's going to sample the wares, love."

"Thank you, Wayne. You really are a treasure. So very touching."

"I'll touch——"

"*Enough*, Wayne."

"I was just saying…"

"Well don't. Anyway, moving on, I'm not going to go into any details here because as far as I'm concerned, they were all private." Pause for a stare at Wayne. "And contrary to what you may have heard, I survived all encounters without *any* physical intimacy, save for a high five part way through *Evil Dead 2* − don't ask − having a knee stroked by a drunk and sweating magazine editor and a brief hug from Gizz." Pause as Gizz rises to his feet, arms outstretched, giving it the big come on. "I'm so glad it meant that much to you, Gizz." Further pause until he runs out of steam and a barrage of abuse sees him sit down. "In seventh place… only joking. The winner is − for a lovely, if slightly weird, night in − Kevin."

A shocked silence ensues, as if no one even knew he'd been a competitor. Jaws sag, none more so than Kevin's, before mouths close and the cry goes up for a curry on the victor and the motion is carried.

Laura politely declines the offer and leaves them to it.

FRIDAY

"You didn't have to come all this way. I could have told you on the phone."

"It's no problem, Mrs Warburton. I prefer doing things face to face. And it gets me out of my office." He smiles, and for a second she lets her façade slip. Then resurrects her first line of defence.

"Come on in, then. You'll be wanting a cup of tea, I suppose."

"That'd be lovely."

"It came to me last night as I was trying to get to sleep. It doesn't get any easier, you know," she says as they take their seats at either end of the sofa. His eyebrows ask the question. "Sleep. When you get to my age, the regrets and the losses weigh heavy on the mind. I'm not scared of dying, but I'm not much looking forward to the journey getting there." She looks down at her hands, before collecting herself. "Anyway, where was I? Oh yes. It was quite a long time before. Maybe that's why I didn't think of it the other day on the telephone. There was this young man who shouted across the road at me. Dogs will be dogs. When they're ready to go, they're ready, if you know what I mean." He doesn't. Then he does. "Well I was taking Mitzy for her walk and she needed to go. I let out the lead so she could do her business. Anyway, the next thing I know there's someone shouting at me. Very irate he was. To begin with I was a little scared, I have to admit, and thought for a moment he might come across the road, but I knew he wouldn't so I just walked on. He called after me but I honestly can't recall what he said. I doubt it's relevant, but you did say you wanted to know anything, however insignificant. I suppose you think I've wasted your time."

"Not at all. That's very useful."

"You don't think he was involved do you? He really didn't look the type."

"You remember how he looked?"

"Not really. He was tall. Brownish hair. I'm sorry, that isn't very helpful. He just looked... normal."

"You said you knew he wouldn't come over. What did you mean by that?"

"One look and I knew he didn't have it in him. Sometimes you can just tell."

"Just one more question," he asks as she opens the door for him. "Did you pick up the dog... doggie... doings? You know, the..."

"The poo? Of course not. I always leave them as a little treat for the foxes."

*

Kevin is not in his element here; thudding bass-dominated music, 'beautiful' self-celebrating people and that Friday evening sense of release. Laura disappeared a while ago to scrimmage at the bar for a second drink, leaving him alone with half an inch of tepid lager and his thoughts; chief amongst them the perilous state of his guts.

The previous night's curry had predictably deteriorated into a macho eating context. They were dealt the vindaloo, raised it to a phall and then re-raised their hosts to further heights of chilliness. The kitchen had proven more than up to the challenge, not that they had thought so as they departed in the early hours. Through lager-infused eyes they had interpreted the smiles on the faces of the waiters as grudging respect, not those of assassins, content to pay the long game.

Kevin had woken that morning with a mouth that tasted of mould, a yellowy stain around his mouth like hastily-applied lipstick and a general body odour that laughed in the face of deodorant. He tried a shower, but it still felt like the curry was exuding through his pores. The hazy morning-after logic that deduced what he needed was an Egg McMuffin, hash brown and fizzy accompaniment proved misplaced; an error further compounded by a stubborn refusal to deviate from the habitual Friday lunchtime 'treat' of jumbo battered sausage, baked beans and curry sauce.

It had been just after three when Laura had popped her head into the shop and reminded him of their date that night. Any alarm at impending disaster had failed to register against a chorus of cat-calls and a rapid elevation of his kudos in the eyes of the local detritus, whatever that might be worth.

Now here he sits, contemplating on the one hand the immense quantity of crap he has ingested over the last twenty-one hours, and on the other the marked absence of excretory substances produced in retaliation to the gradual self-inflicted poisoning his body has endured;

three urinations to be precise, the first one akin to passing acid. Other than what he's sweated out, that leaves a great big pile of slowly composting stodge working its way through his digestive system. He's made several straining, red-faced efforts to rid himself of the burden, but to no avail; his body noisily registering objections by way of a succession of groans, rumbles and internal farts; the occasional jab of pain; a constant unease. Each bubbling commotion implies a release of gas and if it's not coming out, where the hell is it going? And now he's only added to the problem by sloshing a pint of fizz down his throat and then moronically agreeing to another. The issue needs forcing and he's on the point of retiring to the toilets for a spot of aggravated eviction, when Laura returns.

"That was fun. There you go," she says, placing a glass on the table. "I made it a half as it was taking so long and we need to be leaving soon. It starts at quarter past."

"What does?" he asks, trying to hide his relief that the lengthening awkward silences – save for gastronomic gesticulations and intestinal indiscretions – are soon to end and the evening now has a momentum that will hopefully afford him the spaces and distractions in which to fartily and burpily tread water until his body consents to voluntarily let go of its burden.

"Your reward for victory is a night out with me doing what I enjoy the most. Correct?"

"Yep."

"Well you'll have to wait and see then. Come on, get that down you."

Kevin forces down a long mouthful, only for half of it to immediately regurgitate back into the glass. Losing his appetite for this spittle shandy, he abandons the glass and reaches behind for his jacket. Laura's already heading through the throng, attracting more than her fair share of lecherous glances, and it's with something of a swagger – for all manner of reasons – that he follows her out.

Stepping out onto the pavement, they head off in a direction of her choosing. A few turns later and they're walking down a quieter street, Kevin none the wiser about the destination, when she stops abruptly. Before them stands a balding, slight man with his hands tucked in the deep pockets of a bomber jacket.

"Shit," she mutters under her breath.

"Laura," says the man.

"Go away."

"Come on Laura, stop this. Please."

"Me stop? *Me?*"

"Why are you doing this to me?"

"You did it to yourself."

Kevin's head twitches between them; a spectator unsure of the rules of what he's watching.

"Who's this?" he contributes.

"You seeing this bloke? He your latest? Watch her mate. She's——"

"Just go away, will you?" says Laura, her desperation clear.

"You'd like that, wouldn't you? You bitch."

"Right. I've had enough."

"*You've* had enough? You *utter cunt.*"

"Oh piss off."

"I'm going nowhere."

"I'm calling the police."

"Come on." A softening in his tone. "Give me that phone. I just…"

"Get off me. *Kevin.*"

Hearing his name shrieked jolts Kevin out of his confused stupor and compels a switch from observer to participant. This bloke is abusing her. His hand grabbing at her sleeve. Making her upset. Using the c-word. The obvious distress in her face. The contorted anger on his. Something wells up deep within, something base and primitive, propelling his foot forward and his arm into an arc that lands his fist clumsily on the side of the man's head, sending him stumbling backwards and to the ground.

"Laura. Please," the man pleads, his hand tentatively feeling the side of his head. He's about to say something else, but Kevin is now standing over him, fists clenched. "All right. Take it easy. I'm off mate. I just wanted—"

"Just *go*," Laura bellows. And when Kevin looks back down, the pavement is clear and the man is staggering away down the road. "Thanks." Her voice now soft, grateful and affectionate; a hand placed tenderly on his arm, her forehead resting on his shoulder.

"You okay?" His voice firm. Dominant. Protective. Strange feelings course through him; strange and intoxicating. He could get to like this. He places an arm around her shoulders and pulls her to him.

"I'll be all right. He just scares me."

"Who was he?"

"Can I tell you later?"

"Sure. Come on. Let's go. Where to?"

"I'm not really in the mood anymore."

"How about we just go for a coffee? We could both do with one after that."

"That'd be perfect. Thank you, Kevin. I really mean it."

He picks up the coffees and walks over to where Laura sits tearfully in a deep armchair, still visibly shaken.

"There you go."

"Thanks," she says, sniffing loudly. "You shouldn't have had to get involved in that. I'm sorry."

"No problem. What are... er... friends for?"

"You're sweet."

"Who was he?" he asks with feigned indifference, unsure of whether 'sweet' is what he wants to be.

And with breaks for sobs and sniffs and distracted gazes into the distance, she tells him the whole sordid story.

"He's my brother-in-law. A few years ago, I was living at home and my mother met the next in a long line of Mr Rights who always end up as Mr Wrongs and invited him to move in. He was a lot younger than her and wasn't working; said he was an out-of-work actor, not that he seemed to care much about looking for work and was vague whenever I pushed him on what he'd been in. His real love was *theatre* of course. A real luvvy. Have to give him his due though, he put in a bloody good performance with my mother. Had her totally fooled. She got to feel desirable and ten years younger and he got to lounge around rent-free watching TV all day while she went out and earned the money. I was doing bar work then as well, so my hours were all over the place. He was politeness itself when mother was there, but the moment she left the room he'd leer at me and make smutty remarks. Nothing too obvious, just little innuendos that he'd wriggle out of with mock horror and offence if I ever took him up on them.

"Anyway, after a few weeks came the first clumsy grope and that was enough. Told my mother I was moving out and off I went. I thought about telling her everything, that it was him or me, but the truth was the person I really needed to get away from was her. They deserved each other. She booted him out soon after."

Kevin instinctively places his hand gently on hers. He has his concerned face on.

"My sister Jenny had moved out when she got engaged, years before. Said it was the best thing she'd ever done getting away from *her*, and she was always telling me I was mad to stay there. I had nowhere else to go, so I called her up and she said no problem, I could stay at their place. Them being her and Clive, that creep you just met. They'd got married a bit before and Jenny was pregnant. She said it would be nice to have some company while she got fat and ugly. They had a spare room, I paid a bit of rent and it all worked fine to begin with."

She pauses and Kevin swallows, unsure where this is going and how far out of his depth he's straying. He's pretty much exhausted his compassion stockpile with a stream of comforting letter sounds, some facial contortions he hopes translate into empathy and a great deal of tissue passing; and the worst is clearly still to come.

"Then one day…"

"You okay?"

"I'm fine. It's just… difficult."

"I know." Which sounds stupid. Just what *does* he know? "Take your time." He hands her another tissue and she bunches it up with all the others she's yet to use.

"It started with little things. I found my underwear drawer open when I was sure I'd closed it. Things weren't where I remembered putting them. At first, I thought it was just my imagination. Then one day, sometime after Jenny gave up work and when she'd gone upstairs for a nap, I walked into the utility room when he was putting the washing on and found the creep standing there with his face buried in a pair of my knickers."

"Mmm." Poor choice. "Disgusting." Better. He resists the obvious follow-up question.

"It got worse. I'd get my laundry back and a pair of my knickers would be missing. I'd ask Jenny casually to check if she had any of mine, but once she'd said no, what else could I say? I did accuse him once when Jenny was out. But he just smirked and denied it." Kevin shakes his head. "And then there was the bicycle seat." Kevin drags his eyebrows back down and forces them into a frown, hoping it will convey an appropriate sentiment. "When I asked him what the hell he was doing, he just laughed and said he loved the smell of leather."

Fair play to him. A decent enough answer, although leather has caused Kevin no end of practical concerns over the years. He never could get aroused at *The Girl on a Motorcycle*.

"Then I came home early one day." *Christ, there's more.* "I let myself in and was going through to the kitchen when I heard this grunt come from upstairs. I knew Jenny was out as I'd been on the phone to her only five minutes before. I thought I'd catch him with someone, get rid of the sod, but the grunting had stopped by the time I got to the landing. Then the door to my room opened and he walked out bold as brass, saw me there, grinned, told me I'd just missed the fun and as he walked past, he wiped his hand on a pair of my knickers and dropped them in the dirty washing basket."

"You mean…"

"Yes, Kevin. What do you think I mean? He wasn't cleaning the bloody window with them."

"That's terrible," he manages.

"It never stopped. He'd whisper that he thought about me when he masturbated. That Jenny wasn't interested in sex anymore and he needed it all the time. How big he was. What we could get up to. We'd be watching a film together, the three of us, and Jenny would be sitting on the floor resting against the sofa between his legs and he'd be lying back stroking himself and leering at me. I could see it bulging in his trousers. Urghhh." They both shiver; her with disgust, him libidinously. "When Jenny gave birth, she had to stay in hospital a few nights and I ended up staying at a friend's place, I was so scared of what he'd try on. I hoped it would get better with the new baby. Maybe give him some perspective. Make him realise what he was doing." She pauses.

"And did it?" asks Kevin, relishing the confirmation that this kind of stuff actually happens outside the conjurings of his imagination.

"No chance. Touching my arse when he went past. Brushing against my breasts when he reached across me." *Lucky sod.* "Never enough to say anything. He'd just have denied it; made me look like I was imagining things. I just had to put up with it all. His eyes poring at me the whole time whenever Jenny wasn't looking. Then he started telling me he loved me. How he'd leave Jenny if I wanted him to, so we could be together. Said he knew I wanted it as much as him. He was crazy. Out of control."

"What happened?"

"I left. Got up one day and decided I'd had enough. Told Jenny I thought they needed some space to be a family together. She tried to persuade me to stay. Poor girl hadn't a clue what he was like. I came so close to telling her, but she had to find out for herself. To give them any chance, I had to get out. So I did."

"And he didn't like that?"

"Not one bit. Been following me around ever since. I settle in somewhere, he tracks me down and gets in contact. Letters usually. I've already had to move once since I got here. Then after a while he plucks up courage and, like tonight, just appears. Nothing violent... until now."

"Are they still together?"

"As far as I know. I meet up with Jenny every now and then, but never at their house and never when he's there. I've got a lovely niece who I've only ever seen a few times." She's close to losing it now, and Kevin's hand flutters through the air like a drunk moth before resting on the neutral ground of her forearm.

"It's stalking, Laura. You should report him to the police."

"How can I? What will it do to Jenny? It'll tear them apart."

"You're too kind. That's your problem. But surely it can't go on like this."

"It'll have to, I suppose."

"I wish I'd kept hitting the wanker."

"No. He's not violent or anything. More pathetic. I don't think he'll ever do anything to me. He's just deluded and won't let go. I keep hoping he'll get the message or get bored. That was only the third time he's actually approached me. Don't suppose he'll try it again for a while, thanks to you." She places her hand on his and smiles up at him. "My hero."

And Kevin feels like *someone*, like he matters; a feeling he hasn't had in a very long time, since that final day at Nethercott when he last threw a fist in anger.

"I'll walk you to your door," Kevin had said, a touch masterfully to his own ears; and here they are.

"Why don't you come on up for a while. It's still fairly early."

He follows her up the stairs and loses himself in the gentle sway of her hips. A display for him? Is this going where he thinks it is? *Bloody hell.* His mind swims with potential opening moves to make as soon as they're inside. He needs to take control. Be tender yet forceful. No, not forceful. Protective? No, dominant.

She opens the front door of her flat and he follows her into a small hall. She's taken off her coat and is standing there with an expectant look in her eyes. This is his moment. But his feet won't move.

"Your jacket?"

"Oh, right. Yes. Of course." He takes it off and she hangs it with hers from a hook, leaning up and away from him as she does so. He takes another long look and is overcome with an unmistakable and irresistible wave of imminent rectal evacuation.

"Can I use your loo first?"

"First?"

"Now. Right now. Please." More than a hint of desperation in the plea.

She frowns as he shifts his weight from one foot to the other and barely suppresses a whimper, then points vaguely towards a narrow corridor leading off the hallway. He exits the hall with as much nonchalance as his internal turbulence will allow and then, once out of her sight, legs it down the corridor.

Less than a minute of frantic clothing removal and blissful release later, Kevin has much to contemplate.

In the first place he is sitting on a toilet seat that has not been fastidiously washed down; and he never sits on a seat that hasn't been scrubbed spotless.

Secondly, he appears to have given birth.

And thirdly, the smell is truly terrible.

Looking down between his thighs he stares at what he fears may be the tip of a feculent iceberg. He feels thoroughly and disconcertingly eviscerated. And a stone lighter. He glances behind him and is relieved to see an aerosol can of air freshener. Looks like the same one he has at home. Blitz the behemoth. He sticks it down between his legs, depresses the nozzle and proceeds to coat his scrotum.

"Aaarrgghh," is the auditory accompaniment to the icy coating of his balls. "Shit." He twists the can round as best able and this time directs the spray down. Then studies it – *Woodland Glade* – and sniffs. He's not getting that.

He tentatively daubs at his testicles with tissue paper, cleans up and flushes. Then he flushes it again. And again. Not so much wedged as screwed in, like some faecal tic, and it's not for budging. Kevin looks around for available tools, but he's not exactly spoilt for choice. Adaptation required.

Two further flushes and some clumsy sawing later, the 'body' has been dismembered and now lies safely the other side of the u-bend. Well almost. He has a not insubstantial floater, its bobbing jauntiness mocking him as his desperation plummets to new depths. He piles a fistful of toilet paper on top of it and flushes again. The paper catches as intended, but to no avail. Must be full of air. Another bigger ball of paper. Wait for bubbling and hissing in cistern to subside. Taking an eternity. Press the flush. Damn, too quick. Wait. Throw in a bit more paper just for good measure. Press flush again. Clogged, glugging noise. Nothing's budged. Bugger's blocked. *Fuck.* He wants to cry. He closes his eyes, tilting his head back, and when he opens them, he sees his only apparent option.

When finally he exits the room, he closes the door behind him, waits for ten seconds and then pops his head back in. Mmmm. Shite-with-a-hint-of-potpourri. Well, shite actually. He's contemplating further remedial work when a cough sends him jumping out of his skin.

"Shit, you startled me."

"What are you doing? I thought you'd run out on me there, you've been so long."

"Sorry. Er…" A frantic search raging in his befuddled mind for the words that will satisfactorily explain what must have been well over ten minutes in her bathroom, without mentioning any of the pertinent facts or alluding to the aroma that's leaking under and around the door, the handle of which Kevin is forlornly tugging at in the vain hope that it might, allied with his mental desperation, create some form of unlikely airlock. His mouth delivers the abject end result. "I'd leave it a few minutes if I were you." Not so much eureka as nineteen seventies sitcom. "Curry last night," he adds idiotically, ramming the final nail into his own coffin.

Coitus annihilatus.

Kevin doesn't feel like any more coffee, but it comes gift-wrapped in an odour that might just compete with the pervading excrementitious smog that has settled over them, undimmed by the fifteen or so minutes since their reparation to the living room. So he endures its bitter assault on his taste buds for the greater good, wafting the steam towards Laura every time she looks down or away. They chat a while. Not surprisingly she's still very shaken and he's hoping her mind is elsewhere. He delivers a steady stream of fatuous monosyllables and facial expressions to evidence his compassion and disguise his own emotional disability.

"Not exactly the evening I had planned," she says, with a sniff and a smile. "Sorry."

"Don't be silly. It's fine. Not every Friday night I get to play the hero and scare off a pervert."

She smiles back weakly and it hits him that any *moment* there might have been has passed and his time is up. Vini, vidi, shitti.

"I'd better be off," he says, rising to his feet. "You sure you're going to be okay?"

"I'll be fine. This has happened before and I know how it plays out. Doesn't stop it being upsetting though. I've done nothing wrong, yet everywhere I go he follows and tells those lies. He's too pathetic to do anything drastic, but he just never lets up. I'm so tired of it all." She stands and leans into him. "Thank you," she mumbles into his chest. Instinctively he throws his right arm around her, the left hanging uselessly by his side. Feeling awkward, he contemplates going for the full hug, but his loins don't speak the grey language of platonic intimacy; the mere pressing of her body against his enough to set the tsunami in motion and he can instantly feel the front of his trousers taking the strain. He flinches back and turns away, right arm still in place. For a second they stand there awkwardly, then break apart and Kevin takes refuge in functional detail.

"Now, where did I leave my jacket."

No response, and when he looks at her, he sees the hesitation and quiet desperation in her eyes and every chivalric urge in his body comes clamouring to the fore.

"Are you really okay?"

"I was wondering," she says, looking down at her fingernails, "if maybe you could stay, just for tonight. I don't want to be alone – you know – after what happened earlier." She glances up from her hands and so obvious is her vulnerability that he knows he'll do whatever she wants him to. "And…" she trails off.

His mind is zigzagging crazily, a persistently-growing tumescence only adding to the inner confusion. He pulls himself together. "Sure, no problem," he manages, drawing strength from her helplessness.

"You're very kind," she says. "I'll sleep easier knowing you're out here. Let me go and get you some bedding. Stick the telly on, if you want."

He does so and settles back on the sofa, glad of the distraction. Not that it distracts him for long. Laura's bedroom leads off from the lounge, its door a few feet to the left of the TV. The door stands about six inches ajar. He's aware of movement to and fro but respects her privacy and doggedly glues his gaze to the semi-circle of smug self-appointed critics successfully turning all they ponder into tedium. This he manages for a few minutes. Then he lowers his chin to his chest and glances up briefly under cover of his eyebrows. She's standing facing away from him, feet apart. She's already taken off her jeans, her clinging top struggling to maintain coverage of the pleasing swell of her backside, the nursery slopes tantalisingly visible. He swallows drily. She leans slightly forwards, crosses her arms over, grabs the hem and with a delicious wriggle tugs the top up and over her head. Kevin lets out an involuntary moan of anguish before clamping one hand over his mouth, the heel of the other pressing down on his crotch in a misguided attempt to stem the tide. As she fiddles with the catch on her bra he drinks in the magnificence of her buttocks, their curves pushing at the white, lacy proof that real women do indeed wear impractical underwear out of choice. It can't get any better than this.

But then it does, as she removes her watch and leans over the bed, resting one knee on the mattress for support, to place it on the far bedside table. If Kevin could ever stop time, this would be the moment. Visual perfection, everything just tensing and stretching and straining and bulging in perfect symmetry. Finding himself caught between acute pain and pleasure, Kevin's teeth grind and his toes curl up. A groan leaks out. Then she stands up, a nightshirt in her hands and he senses the end is nigh. He leans forward, eyelids flicking up and down like the shutter on a camera as he desperately tries to etch the view into his memory; create a photo album for future reference and savouring. She reaches up, shifts her weight to one hip, generating another gorgeous ripple of exposed flesh and then the nightshirt cascades down her back, bringing the show to a close.

He sits motionless, the ten per cent of his blood supply not partying in his penis seemingly incapable of generating any movement. Then the rational part of his brain flickers into life and he has the remote in his hand and his eyes on the screen as the door swings open and she comes in carrying his bedding.

"There you go."

She hands him the pile and hesitates.

"Sure you're okay?" he asks.

She nods. He smiles. She reaches down and gives him a peck on the cheek. He smells a whiff of perfume he hasn't noticed before and accidentally-on-purpose catches the briefest of glimpses down the front of her T-shirt, completing his voyeuristic full house for the night. Then she's walking back to her room, throwing a "goodnight" back over her shoulders and closing the door. He's left slack-jawed, rigid-penised and with a scrotum that feels fit to burst. He closes his mouth, ponders the options for a millisecond, staggers awkwardly to his feet, keeping all pressure off any possible trigger, and lurches along the corridor to the bathroom, where he frantically grapples with his belt and zip to release himself, savouring that first boing of freedom. For a brief moment it occurs to him that the mere passage of air might in itself be enough of a tipping point. The practicalities of a tissued safety net ignored, he reaches down and summarily and vigorously wanks himself off.

It's over in seconds, the displacement and discharge of fluids leaving him light-headed and leaning against the basin for support.

After mopping up – he's never seen so much of the stuff – he tidies up his clothing and returns to the sofa for some rest and relaxation. He slumps down and breathes out loudly.

Every high tends to be followed by a proportionate low, and it's barely ten minutes before a wave of tiredness sweeps over him. He turns off the TV, putting some tuneless latest-thing and their thinly-disguised plagiarism out of their misery and manipulates the sheet, blanket and pillow into something loosely resembling a bed. He takes off his jeans and jumper, plods across the room to turn off the main light, then attempts to adjust his seventy-five inches into a shape that fits the contours of a two-seater sofa.

The desire to leave the foetal position and simply stretch out sees the floor becoming a more and more attractive option. He's about to decamp when the bedroom door opens slightly and leaks out an apricot glow cast by a bedside lamp.

"Are you awake?" Laura whispers.

A logical silence suggests itself, but the words "Just about" leave his mouth. "Trying to get comfortable," he adds in a drawl he hopes speaks of tiredness and inactivity, not exuberant ejaculation.

He looks across the room and observes that beneath her tousled hair the previously resented shirt is revealing itself to be somewhat transparent. Regrettably, he sees this with the apathy of the very-recently-evacuated.

"Kevin."

"Yes."

"I don't want to sleep alone."

"Oh. Oh, *right.*" *Christ.*

"Only if you want to."

"Yes. Of course." His voice shrill. "No problem," he lies. "And I promise I won't try anything on. I won't let you down."

"No. You don't understand." *Oh dear God.* "I want you to make love to me." *Nooooooooo.* "And I want you to do it now. Come." *Thank you, fucking life.*

He climbs to his feet and trudges towards her outstretched hand with the doomed resignation of a condemned man, fated to disappoint yet again, another chapter in his pitiful sex life about to be written. Hero to zero in an hour. She takes his hand and leads him towards the bed, the sway of her hips mocking that of his limp chipolata which, if anything, is getting smaller, red blood cells abandoning a ship they know is going down; the novelty Scooby Doo boxers the least of his worries.

He makes a desperate rush for a lifeboat.

"I respect you too much for this." *Nice.*

"I don't need you to respect me, Kevin. I just want you to fuck me."

A whimper exits his mouth like a fart from a clenched backside. Plan A isn't working out. But he won't give up.

"But after what you've been through, I want to prove there are blokes out there who don't just treat you like an object. Who treat you right." *This is pathetic.*

"Kevin?" She's now kneeling before him on the bed, chin lowered, eyes looking at him through fluttering eyelashes. Impossibly sensuous and sexy. Impossible to satisfy.

"Yes?" Then, lowering his voice a couple of octaves, he tries again. "Yes." This time forgetting the question mark.

"Do you find me attractive?" Her moist lips pout.

"Of course I do," he replies dispassionately, the preferred answer of "I'd fancy you a lot more if you could give me an hour while the cistern refills," not a viable option.

"Does this do anything for you?" she asks and the shirt is whisked off and dispensed to a distant corner.

"Oh yes," he objectively concedes. *And yet at the same time… it appears not.*

But there is hope.

Because he does have the knowledge.

He does possess the tools.

Maybe she can read his mind; knows how this has to play out. Because when she lies back against the headboard, teasingly allowing one knee to fall outwards and running the back of her fingers down the taut white gusset, the nails audibly raking across the lace, her choice of words is exactly the cheesy nonsense he needs to hear if he's to forget what he has been, how the others made him feel, what he fears he is, will always be; the dysfunctional failure. And become what he needs to be to get through this nightmare. Because when a girl splays her legs and says, "Hey Shaggy, why don't you leave Scooby outside. Are you going to fuck me or what?" you just have to be in Pornoland, and no one knows Pornoland and the rules that apply there better than The Shagmeister.

His mind is suddenly clear.

He contemplates the battlefield with the tactical acumen of a cunning First World War general. The threat of imminent copulation – or in his case, not being physically able to – must be averted at all costs. Honesty is not an option. This is a first: an attractive female who simply wants to have sex with him. He's not second choice this time. There is no set-up. He has to go through with this; he has to satisfy.

She appears ready and increasingly impatient. He's wearing baggy 'comedy' boxers, though at least they're helping disguise the fact that he's packing more of a cock-sock than a cock-rock. He needs to delay proceedings long enough for inflation to commence and judge entry to hit that window of opportunity when it's erect but screaming *not again*, thereby maximising the time in before succumbing. So, all he has to do is draw this out for twenty or so minutes. And to do that he's going to need the full armoury of pre-ejaculatory moves garnered from his vicarious solo sex life.

"Sure am, baby," says the Shagmeister in a voice of unwavering and emboldening certainty. Bending forwards, he pushes his boxers down to his ankles, steps out of them and without standing up, shuffles forward at a right angle and tumbles onto the bed, aiming at a foot. He falls slightly short and has to slither the last few inches, but once there he readies himself for some sexy foot action, whatever that might involve. He's never understood this bit, but he's lost count of the number of times he's watched a man salivate over a foot with clear delectation while its owner writhes and moans in ecstasy. There has to be something in it. He pops a big toe in his mouth and… then what?

While he's contemplating the lick/suck/in-and-out dilemma he glances up over the landscape of Laura's body and sees a curious look on her face. Kevin might worry she's feeling uncomfortable. But the Shagmeister knows she's loving it. It's a wince of pleasure. He tentatively places his tongue against the pad of the toe and moves it around. Nothing too unpleasant. A little earthy maybe, but it's fine and he gives it a tentative suck. Not too bad, so straight into a little pneumatic in-and-out. The toe next to the one in the saliva spa bath is wriggling against his cheek, begging for attention. Time to move on. He gives the big toe a last lingering suck, his mouth detaching with an audible pop, before diving in on piggy number two. Not so easy to access. He does the best he can in such limited space, but he's growing bored; all feasible permutations of lips, toe and tongue exhausted a digit ago. He half-heartedly drawls his mouth along the tops of the other three toes like an amateur pan pipe player and heads onwards and upwards.

He kisses the top of her foot, his nose tickled by the short hairs, and then the ankle, then the skin a centimetre up the front of her leg, then the skin an inch higher, and so on, massaging the back of her leg with his fingers all the time. He's procrastinating on safe ground here, dreading the territory that lies ahead, as familiar to him as the back of his own head.

Think 'vagina' and what does he visualise? An oyster lurking in its shell. The top of an opening egg in *Alien*. Folds. Hidden recesses. Trapped secretions and odours. Mystic depths.

He tries to distract himself with the knee he's alighted on… just a thigh away. But the knee doesn't lend itself to dawdling foreplay and after one aborted attempt to suck her knee cap, curtailed by a sore jaw and his tongue running over the unmistakable contours of a scab, he reluctantly plants his fatiguing oral organ at the base of her thigh and messily meanders northwards like an inebriated slug.

The thigh proves far more enjoyable: less unforgiving bone, more fleshy curves and slightly doughy skin. He contentedly nuzzles and kneads, relaxing in the knowledge that he has left behind the realms of the fetishist and is now ploughing the more fertile, much described and oft witnessed fields of conventional foreplay. A faint frisson is generated in his crotch, the relief quickens his passage and he's homing in on the abyss when Laura's hands clasp each side of his head and she's pulling his face up and over her body. Porn convention dictates that she now shoves his face into her crotch and instinctively he holds his breath for an initiation in the art of genital potholing. But as the latticed landing zone sails far below, he realises that's not on her agenda. This acceleration cannot happen. He's nowhere near ready. He yanks his head clear, takes a deep breath and prepares to dive.

"No, I'm not comfortable," he hears her say.

"I really want to," says The Shagmeister dominantly; then in deference to Kevin adds tenderly, "I wouldn't if I didn't want to." And before she can stop him, he throws his head downwards, giving his nose a whack on a bone he hadn't expected to be there.

Recovering, he soon realises that just licking the lace isn't going to work. His tongue is very quickly sore and it scratches his nose. A muffled noise from the top of the bed implies he must be doing something right, but this has to stop and he dives into the pillow of an inner thigh and generally slobbers around while he ponders an alternative plan of attack. Resolving to tease and yet further delay, he kisses the skin just to the safe side of the elastic. Then moves his way along it like a snuffling fox working his way round a hen coop probing for weaknesses, though in this case the fox isn't that hungry and would probably ignore an entry point even he came across one. Along the way the terrain alternates between smooth and stubbly, the occasional wisp of escaped hair tickling his lips. He's relieved when the lace runs into a soft silk that positively invites contact, so he kisses that instead, only to find it promptly taper to a thin strap and fall away at her right hip. He follows it down until his face is wedged into the angle between sheet and buttock, an unspoken hint for Laura to roll over. When she doesn't budge, he places one hand on her hip, the other under a leg and heaves her onto her front.

They emit synchronous grunts.

Now what? He plants a knee either side of her legs. Her pants are not symmetrical on each buttock, so he takes the opportunity to straighten them up. He gives the right one a grope and a wobble. Then the left.

Then both together. He repeats the sequence, though this time the double handful feels so nice that his hands get a little carried away and he lets slip a noise that sounds worryingly like "whoarrrr". He withdraws his hands and re-establishes the symmetry lost in his frantic manipulations of the glutei maximi spread beneath him; then contemplates with mounting panic the barren wilderness of his sexual repertoire.

Fortunately, Laura takes control.

"Take them off," she says into the pillow.

He places his palms on either hip and slowly starts to roll her pants down. She lifts herself helpfully and they form a nice neat roll of material, reminding him of doing the same with his socks in tedious school lessons. Determined to keep the roll going as neatly as possible, he pauses a few times to balance off and tidy up. The left side has moved ahead of the right and he pulls it up a little. He's appraising his work with disproportionate pride when Laura mutters, "For fuck's sake," and her hand grabs the pant-roll and attempts to push it down her legs. Kevin takes the hint and together they clumsily remove her underwear. He finds himself kneeling above her, one knee now between her thighs, and looks down with fascination at Laura's bottom shuffling towards his knee. Once reached she closes her thighs against it and starts to grind herself into him. Slowly at first. Rotating as she does it. Then faster. Occasionally pushing harder. Then slow again. He is spellbound. *Is that a pimple?* says the voice. No. *Yes it is.* All right, it may be. But look at that... *fair point.* And together they watch mesmerised; all three of them. For the one-eyed battle-weary soldier is at long last showing a passing interest, turgidity a now viable adjective; rigidity a distinct possibility.

"At last."

"What?" she says, rising on to an elbow and twisting round. His denial is lost in a blur of limbs as Laura continues the revolution until she's on her back, legs now either side of his knees, her eyes meeting his and bringing into startling focus the reality of his situation: him naked on a bed with a naked woman, legs akimbo, her expectant of satisfaction and him in possession of a penis that is at best lolling. He can make it jump slightly with a clench of the buttocks but that feels more like a party trick than a call to action. Her eyes wander along his outstretched right arm and alight with a frown on a hand that still clasps the limp carcass of her underwear. Gawping like a fish he clamours for precedent.

Then recalls with a rush of relief that this is a staple porno scene: cocksman pulls off her panties – always far too early in the skirmish for Kevin's liking – and before discarding subjects them to the kind of nasal appraisal a sommelier might give a glass of high-quality red, their denuded owner incredulously more turned on than horrified by the sight of it. It never does much for Kevin, who can't help but come to the deflating conclusion that the bouquet has to be less alpine meadow, more manky latrine.

Nevertheless, he fixes the smile of the knowing and, throwing in a wink for dubious measure, brings them to his face and smears them slowly across it. Instinctive revulsion sees him attempt the not inconsiderable feat of blowing air steadily out of both nostrils whilst at the same time emitting various audible indicators – he hopes – of olfactory relish. He's far from convinced that the resulting spluttering mumble has done the trick, so he throws in an enthusiastic, if breathless, "Delicious," for validatory effect. Judging by her squirming and pinched face it's mission accomplished and, like a matador playing to the crowd, he sticks out his chest, twirls the pants on a finger and throws them theatrically over his shoulder. He's dimly aware of something heavy toppling over, rolling across a surface and falling to the ground with a dull thud.

But it's going to take more than a puffed torso to seal this deal and the moment of triumphant bravado evaporates with the realisation that he's showcasing what he's not packing just yet. The answer is staring him in the face. Sucking in a deep breath of resolve – and precaution – he takes the plunge.

A softer landing this time and drier than anticipated; somewhere between springy moss and his Auntie Pat's fox terrier. The hairs are a little like wire wool, though much softer, and all in all he's pleased to find that it's not too bad a place to be. He has a little nuzzle, punctuated with the occasional tentative kiss and fearful tongue probe. She appears to be closed to business… but then again, he might be lost. He forages some more. He says, "Mmm." He kisses. He says, "Oo yeah," and wishes he hadn't. He probes. Reverts to, "Mmm." Nothing. Definitely lost. Time for a visual survey. He pulls his head back, but the light is so poor that all he can determine is an area of forestation in a moonlit valley. He pushes her legs wider apart and there is a faint glimmer discernible. Keeping his eye on the spot he has a poke around. Bingo. His finger disappears into warm wetness and he unintentionally lets out a gasp. He tentatively pushes the finger in further and it emerges into what feels like a cavern.

Fortunately, he's read enough *Men's Health* articles to know that he needs to head for the G-spot, whatever that is. He dimly recalls that it's on the wall of the vagina, a couple of inches in. Unfortunately, he doesn't know in which direction, so his fingertip works round in an approximate circle, like a wonky compass. He can't detect anything that feels remotely like a spot, let alone the mythical short-cut to ecstasy. For a moment he thinks he might have struck gold as she lets out a gasp, but he has to concede it may owe more to an awkward wristy manoeuvre as he tries to ensure the tip of his finger maintains in contact throughout its revolution.

Nothing discovered, he gives up and waves the finger in the vaginal void, more in hope than design.

Now what?

A red light bulb clicks on above his head and a doubtless inaccurate statistical recollection flashes through his mind: only one in ten women can come through penetration alone. *The clitoris. Of course.* Now he just has to find it.

In his desperation he recalls the once-read and never-forgotten words from some porno yarn: '*He pulled back her labia and out popped her clitoris.*' Worth a stab, though it might help if he knew what a labia was. He rummages around with his fingertips in some clumsy homage to Basil Fawlty looking for duck in a trifle. But nothing pops out. Then a hand grabs his wrist, fingers seize his forefinger, work their way to its tip and guide it to a small raised nodule. He's too relieved to resent this slight to his knowledge and celebrates with some enthusiastic jabbing and flicking. The hand grabs his wrist again and a voice says, "Gentle."

Bring on the tongue. With trepidation he relocates the target spot with a finger, lowers his head and traces his tongue down the last inch or so of digit until it alights on what has to be the clitoris. He runs his tongue over it and is minded of the flaps of skin just inside each corner of his mouth that he finds himself nibbling on in times of absent-minded distraction. Again, he finds his options limited and quickly exhausted. It's *Men's Health* that again comes to the rescue with its unforgettable hint for just such a moment: '*Hum during cunnilingus, as the vibrations enhance the sensations for the woman.*'

He closes his lips over her clitoris and emits a low constant drone. To introduce variety, he experiments with tone and lip positions, achieving an effect somewhere between a restless wasp and an amateurishly-played kazoo. Inevitably he drifts into humming tunes. 'Land of Hope and Glory' generates some serious vibrato whilst the theme tune to *The Great Escape* offers a pleasing range.

Clitoral options exhausted for no discernible advantage, his aching tongue blunders away from it and stumbles into her vagina. A wave of terror hits him, but he's clearly been doing something right, though self-congratulation is tempered by a recollection of Wayne's ringing endorsement of her lubricatory prowess. With the trepidation of a nervous child about to bob for an apple, he takes a deep breath and explores, messily and noisily; akin to eating a slice of water melon without using hands. He doesn't recall the lurching porn soundtracks ever being drowned out by the slurping noises currently assaulting his own ears; only feminine sighs and masculine sexy-lines.

Of course.

"Woowherewaby," he says moistly. (*Oh yeah baby*).

Slobber.

"Brurrruvully," he says drippingly, always the romantic at heart. (*You're lovely*). Then steps it up a gear. "Armdoeingdoougduerweelwerd," he reassures her tenderly. (*I'm going to fuck you... er... real hard*).

He pauses to drag his sodden chin messily across his own shoulder and pull at a couple of hairs stuck between teeth.

"Fucky fucky," he says mid-hover, for reasons known only to The Shagmeister. The harsh, dry, coherent syllables clatter around the room, but seem to spur Laura into action. Some sort of judo ground move sees him on his back, her astride him and reaching over to pull open a drawer in the bedside table. He's about to latch onto a dangling teat when it's snatched from his gaping mouth and she's telling him to, "Put this on." He apologises, for absolutely no reason. She makes a noise of irritation. He tugs open the packet and fumbles the condom onto what is, it only now occurs to him, a splendidly-erect penis.

The moment of self-congratulation is curtailed by a hand on his shoulder and his head is pushed back roughly onto the pillow. Now she's moved up his body and eyes closed, face contorted in grim concentration, starts to grind her crotch into his stomach. He obligingly squeezes whatever he can get a grip on, if only to feel involved. Then with a grunt she pushes back her hips, reaches down between her legs, grabs his penis and pushes it into her, the insertion squeezing out the saliva and drivel he's just been splurting into her with a farting noise that mockingly, and with no less clarity, regurgitates his own sweet nothings. Kevin pretends he hasn't heard it and she mumbles a disclaimer. Then she's leaning over him.

He reaches round for a buttock but she pushes his arm away. The other hand is similarly deflected from a breast and then the wave approaches. As her hips start to thrust, he is far from idle, frantically conjuring up mental pictures of elderly relatives, before embarking on the seventeen times table… and starts to come on seventeen. For the third time in his life he does his best to conceal it, though in truth she appears a little lost in her own world and gives no sign of having heard his strangled whimper. Her face burrows into his neck and emits rasping, irregular gushes of breath on his skin. He meets her thrusts with his own. There's a loud click of enamel and she tells him to, "Stop shrugging your fucking shoulders." He apologises. He keeps on apologising and she tells him to, "Just shut up." He apologises again, then starts to apologise for apologising, but catches himself before another admonishment comes his way. Despite the heavy breathing and grunts assaulting his ear and the large proportion of their respective skin areas clinging clammily to each other, he feels extraneous; more *done to* than *doing with*. He almost forgets to throw in his own feigned groans of heightening pleasure. And in the moment he senses her tighten, shudder and exhale, he feels utterly and unexpectedly alone.

Later, as Laura pushes the hair band back over her hairline and reaches for the tub of cream in the bathroom, questions bombard her.

Has she just been with a master craftsman?

Or a sexual retard?

What is that globule clinging to the mirror?

And where's her toothbrush?

Meanwhile Kevin is near enough skipping down the road.

In truth he'd been relieved when Laura had suddenly remembered she had to leave early the following morning and suggested it might be easier all round if he woke up in his own bed. She seemed disappointed about it, but it was well after one o'clock and far better to go out on a high than over an awkward breakfast. *Quit while you're ahead* he says to himself, his face cracking into a self-congratulatory smile. In one evening, he's defended Laura's honour, had his first fight for well over a decade – and won it – and more than held his own in consensual sex with an actual woman. In fact, he'd been pretty damn good. A corner turned; past traumas now well and truly exorcised.

He punches the air and heads into the night.

A new man.

SATURDAY

Laura pulls the drawstring tight, throws the bag over her shoulder and heads down the communal stairs and out the back door. And almost steps in what appears to be a large clump of sodden and soiled toilet paper. More than soiled; there's something lurking in there.

She shakes her head and steps over it. Gives it a wide berth on the way back, pausing to give brief consideration to the notion of doing the *right thing*. Then she catches a whiff and it's enough to banish conscience and send her through the door.

Someone else's mess. Someone else's problem. Sod community spirit. Welcome communal living.

SUNDAY

As a paid-up member of the sexually active club, Kevin can face down the gym and all that unfortunate *history*. And with virility coursing through his veins he attacks the machines like never before, pushing himself on to higher weights and greater reps. He savours each muscle flex. He welcomes the burn. He relishes the sheen of sweat that coats his flushed skin. He still takes in the eye candy, but now feels legitimised in his voyeurism, rather than covert; a bona fide *player* now.

It's a pity Pete's not here to share in his revelatory joy.

And it's a shame that Carl is; on one of his rare visits, almost as if he senses a loss of ground and has arrived for a spot of reannexation.

But he's picked the wrong day for colonising this particular territory. Because today, Kevin owns it.

So it's with libidinous smugness that he reclines redundantly on one of the machines, mesmerised by the hypnotic poetry of the woman some ten feet away from him who, legs astride, is performing a series of deep squats, the kettle weight clasped in both hands all but touching the ground at the bottom of each dip; the attainment of the desired ninety degree angle between calf and thigh causing the black material of her tights to turn grey and then translucent to reveal a rather splendid pair of straining, splayed buttocks. Kevin is perturbed at the probability that she has no underwear on, only to then make out a thin fishtail of darker material rising from the northern tip of her cleavage, a lesser of two evils that he's grateful for.

The only blot on the pleasingly undulating landscape is a small square of washing instructions, an interjection of asymmetry and practical mundanity that Kevin can do without as he conjures with his mental story board.

But at least there's a degree of subtlety − and respect − about his own ogling, unlike Carl who, though sitting much closer, is giving the casually-entitled appearance of sitting in a booth in a lap-dancing club savouring a private 'performance'. Kevin's resentment builds, and with it an internal outcry − any nagging hypocrisy smothered by burgeoning outrage − in support of this woman's right to be free from such blatant and degrading objectification. He looks around for an irate, muscled boyfriend heading Carl's way, but the entire room appears oblivious to this visual molestation. *Is there no justice?*

He's barely able to contain a cheer when she swivels on her heels to catch Carl *in flagrante delicto*.

Gotcha.

Yet if anything his smirk only widens. There's a delicious moment when her face tightens and Kevin can visualise the imminent conjunction of weight and Carl.

"Can I help you?" she asks tersely.

"No, I'm fine, thanks." *Cocky bastard.*

"It's just you seemed to be staring." Icy cold. *Nice.*

"Can't blame a guy for admiring the view." And, having dared to venture the corny verbal equivalent of a wolf whistle, he gets to his feet, starts to turn away, checks himself, and delivers – Kevin recognises all the signs, so can see its approach – his *coup de théâtre*. "Oh," he commences, pausing with relish to construct a tried and tested lascivious grin deserving of a slap and which Kevin, just once, would love to see demolished, "make sure you look after those tights. Machine wash at no more than forty degrees, no bleach, tumble dry and iron on low heat, and it should be fine to take to the drycleaners. Might even make their day." A tongue tip appears briefly before being withdrawn between lips he permits to stay apart. And he's away, without even a glance back.

Kevin swallows and studies her face with the intensity of a rescuer staring at a pile of post-earthquake rubble, desperately hoping for some sign of the justified indignation that might propel her to appropriate and summary retribution.

Instead she looks confused, then enlightened as she slaps a hand on her backside and gropes around – not unappealingly – until she locates the label. She flashes the self-indulgent smile of the flattered and in a tone more playful than castigatory, issues the ultimate in self-defeating admonishments.

"Cheeky sod."

It doesn't matter how many times Kevin sees this ensnarement play out, it still sickens him to the core. And however hard he tries to persuade himself that it's the victim he empathises with, the truth is that he sympathises only with himself.

He'll have to tell Carl everything now, if only to make a vain stab at parity.

MONDAY

Rebecca arrives at the restaurant *au naturel*, all bar the most basic of beauty products discarded after that disaster last time. She feels exposed, but there's an honesty about it that feels appropriate for a first luncheon date not proposed with an agenda in mind.

A condition-less meeting might be considered by some to be... what?

Very confusing.

Without the direction, definition and, above all, rationale that the usual trade-off provides, the conversation is staccato and the silences many, although she's pleasantly surprised to find they feel more comfortable than awkward. And with this being his idea, she's content to wait for him to verbalise whatever it is that's behind that sparkle in his eyes; although the near-constant smirk soon starts to irritate. She's on the verge of telling him just to spit it out when he finally takes the plunge under cover of the arrival of their main course.

"I need to tell you something."

"Okay."

"I've been wanting to for some time now but it never felt fully formed, so I've kept it to myself." *Blimey.* "I know I'm often a victim of flights of fancy." *You are?* "But I realised last week what it is that's been nagging away all this time and the pieces finally fell into place." She pauses mid-mastication. "Thanks to Mrs Warburton." *Oh.*

"Who?" she asks, and swallows.

"Mrs Warburton."

"I know that's what you said. I meant who is she?"

"She's the lady who had hundreds of dog turds put on her lawn."

"Now I am *totally* confused."

"Sorry. I should make myself clear."

"That would be nice," she says, her patience waning.

"This has to be totally secret between the two of us. I haven't told anyone else and I'm not planning on doing so until I'm absolutely sure. But I have to tell someone."

"Well go on then." He hesitates. "David, your secret is safe with me. I promise."

"All right." Pauses. Takes a breath. "I think there is a team of vigilantes operating in the area." Another pause, this time for effect. Short of slapping her hand over a wide-open mouth, Rebecca is unsure what she can offer. She settles for a raise of eyebrows. "I don't know how many, but there are definitely at least four, probably more. I've got a few loose descriptions but no more than that. They don't go for anything major, more local nuisances and anti-social behaviour and their punishment always suits the crime in some way. That whole bus-through-the-window thing was the latest, I think. Oh yes, and they leave a playing card at the scene every time."

This time it's she who hesitates, trying to process the rambling stream of barely-formed consciousness.

"Too much?" he asks.

"Too little," she answers. "Start on your food before it gets even colder and take me through it in detail. Tell me everything. I'm in no rush."

"Why me?" she asks as he breathlessly concludes and they're waiting for the bill.

"I just wanted to share it with… with someone, with a, with, you know…"

"Er no, what?"

"A… friend."

"Did that hurt?"

"What?"

"Never mind."

It's progress, she supposes. Of a sort.

TUESDAY

Kevin does a double take.

It's definitely him. Sloping into the shop and heading for a distant corner.

What the fuck?

This can't be good. The last time they met, Kevin's reaction had been instinctive, dictated by primaeval urges. Now, with time to think, and despite his home advantage, he can feel the balance of power shifting as worst-case scenarios taunt him. He's stockier than Kevin remembers. Looks like he can handle himself.

They make eye contact and he gets a read on his opponent. Resolve, yes. But he's not getting threat. And by the time the trespasser plucks up the courage to head over, Kevin is bristling and ready for conflict.

"What the hell are you doing here?" whispers Kevin.

"Pardon?"

"What the hell are you doing here?" he repeats, this time too loud. A few heads turn.

"I need to have a chat, that's all."

"You're lucky there's this screen between us, I can

tell you," says Kevin, very glad of the screen between them.

"I'm not here to make trouble. Promise. I just want five minutes of your time."

"Can't you see I'm busy? There's a race about to start."

"No there isn't."

Fair point. It's not even half ten. Kevin shrugs the shrug of the logically defeated, tells Maggie he's popping out for a few minutes, endures a rambling paragraph of babbling inanity and steps out onto the battlefield.

"It's Clive by the way," his opponent says and offers a hand. Kevin hesitates a second, then engages.

He wins the handshake and takes further confidence from the five or so inches he has on the bloke; not to mention the knowledge that he's been where pervy Clive never has.

"Fancy a cup of coffee?" asks Clive, his conciliatory manner continuing to undermine Kevin's predisposed antipathy.

"Not in here. It's crap. Come on, there's a café a few doors up."

Once there they order, agree to split the cost, find a seat and share an amused look as they unavoidably eavesdrop on a nearby table's moronic exchanges. Kevin is finding it difficult to dislike Clive as much as he feels he should, so brings an abrupt end to the bonhomie before he loses all advantage.

"Right, what did you want to tell me?"

"It's about Laura."

"Thought it might be," he says in a sarcastic tone immediately regretted.

"Are you and her…?"

"Yes," replies Kevin, a little wishfully given how lukewarm she's been with him since Saturday morning. "What of it?"

"What's she told you about her and Jenny, her sister that is, and me?"

"The full story."

"I doubt that. More likely whatever suited her purpose."

Kevin gives him a patronising shake of the head, then hits him with an explicit resumé; gets to throw in and relish some favourite words that usually can't get an airing without making him feel self-conscious, each of them authenticated by finger-wiggling quotation marks.

Clive maintains an expressionless silence.

Hears Kevin out.

Then looks up.

And hits back.

*

The parallel with that morning isn't lost on Kevin as he approaches the bar, dreading what lies ahead; praying she'll readily put the lie to Clive's version of events.

"Hiya, there's not a game tonight is there?" she says breezily, disarming him with a smile.

He surprises himself when the words, "Clive came to see me this morning," escape his lips. He sees the look of wounded fragility on her face and knows he's been had by that chancing stalker; that she's the only victim here, that she needs him and once more he's her protector, that this can be a shared reference point from which they can grow together. It's all he can do not to vault the bar and take her in his arms.

"What did he say?"

"A load of old rubbish really. He said you tried it on with him and when he turned you down you went to your sister and told her... well, a pack of lies is how he put it. She threw him out. He thinks you were jealous and wanted to break them up. He says he begged you to tell your sister the truth, but you refused and then just left, telling her he'd made your life a nightmare. He said the only reason he follows you round is to persuade you to come clean so he can see his daughter more than once in a blue moon."

He sucks in his lips and gives a shrug that tells her whose side he's on and what he thinks of Clive's version of events. She returns the shrug and he's about to make some jokey comment to relieve the tension when her expression hardens and he realises with a crippling rush of déjà vu that once again he's got it all wrong.

Please no.

"I'm sorry, Kevin."

"Don't be s—"

"*Kevin*. Just be quiet please. Look, I'd love to tell you it is a pack of lies, but I can't," she says, the words like knives, driving home all his worst fears. Reopening wounds.

"*What?*" he flails.

"I did what he said I did. And probably worse. None of it would have happened if we'd just had a shag. Once would have been enough for me. I probably wouldn't have said anything. Quickly got bored and left them to it. I never fancied him or anything. I just needed to know I had it in my power to wipe that smug grin off Little Mrs Perfect's face whenever I wanted. But he wouldn't play ball, the self-righteous prick. So I took their idyllic little world and messed it up a bit."

"A bit?"

"Not my problem."

"And doesn't that bother you?"

"Why should it? It's what I do."

"It's what you *do*?"

"What I am."

"What the fuck does that mean? What about… you know, what we did that night?"

"Look Kevin. You're a nice guy. But it was just sex, that's all. Fucked-up weird sex, I'll give you that, but just sex nonetheless. It's not like we're a couple or anything."

"Aren't we? That's all it was to you? And to think I sat there this morning defending you while smugly telling myself that Clive's amateur psychology was a load of old crap."

"Go on then, I'm fascinated. Let's hear what he had to say."

"He said you and your sister had a shit childhood actually. That your mum… er…"

"Fucked around?"

"Yeah. He said your mum had a never-ending stream of blokes in the house. Didn't care what she got up to or what you saw. That some of them even… um… tried it on with you." He pauses, but she's not giving. "That your sister left home as soon as she could, leaving you there on your own with your mum. Clive said she always felt guilty, but she had to get away and you were too young at the time to go with her. They both know it must have been bad for you. That's why they offered to let you live with them. Your mum didn't like it. Kept ringing up. Even claimed you'd been sleeping with her latest boyfriend and that's why he'd left her." Another pause, but again he can't read her expression, so he ploughs on. "They didn't believe her at the time, but Clive does now. He reckons you watched your mum use her looks and her body to keep men interested, and at the same time you watched the way the men used her and then just walked away. He said you hate men but you hate yourself just as much. That you crave their attention because that makes you worth something but at the same time you need to control them and make them suffer. That's it basically." The eyes he stares into are cold and dead. He feels compelled to challenge her dispassion. "Says you're fucked up, basically." He desperately wants a reaction; an exchange of any kind. But instead she probes the inside of her cheek with her tongue and allows her gaze to drift over his shoulder. "Say something, Laura. Surely I'm worth…"

"Worth?"

"You know what I mean. I'm not…"

"Not what?"

"Not like those men."

"You're exactly like them."

"That's not fair."

"All right, you want me to say something? Well let's just say Clive is a lot more perceptive than I'd given him credit for."

Kevin contemplates the carnage.

"Kevin?" A definite softening in tone.

"Yes?"

"I'm bad news."

"It's just that I think you're being too hard on yourself. I think we should at least…"

"You're forcing my hand."

"Please, Laura."

"Kevin." Deep breath. Not a good sign. "I used you to piss off the others. Do you really think I'd pick *you* to have sex with? Had it been about attraction I'd have picked Carl. If I'd wanted a quick fuck it would have been Wayne, though he was just a little too cock-sure. They both knew that. Knew what was going on. You didn't. That's the point Kevin. It's all a game. Otherwise I wouldn't have picked you. I mean, why would I? What with your OCD, your odd little jigs and comments and that creepy collection of Australian aerobics DVDs."

"That's not what you think."

"We both know it is. You have the cheek to sit there thinking I'm messed up. Look in the mirror, Kevin. Guess that's what made you the perfect choice, though you took your bloody time about it. I had to pull out all the old tricks. Thought you'd never get round to it. Then I had to put up with all that prodding and sucking and kneading and sniffing—"

"*Sniffing?*" asks Dean.

"*Dean*. What the *hell* are you doing there? Just fuck off, will you."

"I only wanted a... never mind. Sorry, Kev mate. I'll leave you two lovebirds to it."

They watch him shuffle away with the air of a man who realises he lost the fight, but dodged a bullet.

"I mean what the hell *were* you doing that night?" she picks up again. "It made me feel like a piece of meat a dog had found. And those ridiculous boxer shorts?" He can feel his face crumple. "Oh dear, did you think you'd seduced me?"

"I just thought... it kind of happened," he stammers.

"Only because it suited me to let it."

"Have you *anything* nice to say about me?"

"I don't do pity. And I may hate men, but no more than you hate women."

"I don't."

"Deep down you do. Or maybe you're just scared of them. Probably both."

He can find no words.

"Welcome to the fucked-up club," she adds, then turns away to serve someone.

*

Kevin sinks into the heat, closes his eyes and ponders the day's exchanges. He'd gone into both as odds-on favourite and still lost each time. Some bookie.

But then he's not really a bookie, is he, any more than he's a boyfriend.

Which leaves what, exactly?

KARMA GARDA

"Another couple of pints, Breandan love?"

"No ta. Duty calls. Maureen's hosting a birthday party for wee Shauna. Full house expected, so we'd better be getting back."

"Ah, bless you. You helping out as well, Conor?"

"Indeed I am."

*

The place is heaving. Wee kiddies running about the place screaming and shouting. Their mothers taking a break, sitting in groups nattering, drinking tea and stuffing cake down their throats; the few fathers who couldn't find reasons to be elsewhere loitering in quieter corners, drinking beer.

His beer.

A *lot* of his beer.

And in the middle of this human chaos is Conor, lying on the sitting room floor, his big distended belly a mound – it reminds him of those ant hills you come across in the woods; of one in particular that they'd once made imaginative use of many years ago, back in the day, when pretty much anything went and a lesson taught was always a message sent – on which a succession of ebullient toddlers repeatedly and heedlessly hurl themselves, their laughs and shrieks only fuelled by Conor hamming it up, grunting and groaning loudly in fake pain.

A young bloke brushes past him, drink in hand, connecting sufficiently firmly with Brendon's upper arm so as to cause a spray of liquid to leap from the lip of his own bottle. He feels specks lightly sprinkle his face and watches as the spillage soaks into the carpet. His carpet.

"Hey, watch it why don't yeh…" starts his unwitting assailant, only to halt in mid-sentence as he looks up. "So sorry Mr O'Riordan. My fault completely. Really sorry. Can I be helping yeh tidy up an' all? Oh God, I am so…"

"Dat'll do, Brian. We're fine here. Be on yer way now."

Shaking his head ruefully, he watches the eejit head for the sanctuary of a distant corner, before a series of pants and wheezes preludes an arrival at his side.

"Been having a nice time, have we, Conor?" he asks, without looking at him, instead maintaining his steady glare at Brian's fleeing form just long enough to meet the first glance back over his shoulder. Relishes the resultant shrinkage; the colour draining from the lad's face.

"I'm too old for diss shite. Young Brian been causing any problems?"

"Ner. All sorted now."

"Enough to make you weep, isn't it? We've given birth to a generation soft as shite. If it ever kicks off again, we're all fecked."

"About dat. I've had a wee request from *over there*. Looks like Mick and Paddy could be coming out of retirement for one last hurrah. Bit of a swansong, you might say, dodgy accents and all. You up for it?"

JUNE 2007

It ends with a handwritten message on a card in an envelope on his doormat.

Hello Kevin, or rather goodbye, because I'll be long gone by the time you read this.

This isn't like me. Not the doing of 'my thing' and then disappearing. That's entirely typical, I'm afraid; though I did hope to last a little longer this time. But sooner or later I always revert to type. So don't take it personally. But this, this sentimentality... well it's very much not me and a bit disconcerting, I can tell you.

Your experience of me is what I do Kevin. Rather than confront what I am and ask awkward questions of myself, I hide from them by deluding myself that I'm in control and I do that by looking to control others... well, men basically. I'm really rather good at it. That was one thing my useless, self-obsessed mother did teach me and like her, I draw men in and then play with them like a cat plays with an injured bird. They're my fall guys and when occasionally one gets too close for comfort, I have to protect myself and there's only ever going to be one casualty. Normally that doesn't bother me but this time it has. Which is a compliment, believe me, as is this explanation, something I've never felt the need to bother with before. As I said, all very disconcerting.

I said some very nasty things to you. I know it's a cliché but sometimes you do have to be cruel to be kind. And I was cruel to you. Very cruel. And the kind bit? Well you're going to have to take my word for that. But I could see you adding two and two and getting a lot more than four and I had to ground that flight of fancy before it could take off. Limit the damage. And the harder you made it and the more you fought back, the meaner I had to be, in both our best interests.

Kevin you're one of the good guys. I'm sure of that. And I'm equally sure that along the way people have hurt or misunderstood or let you down and unless you confront that, they'll always win and you never will. You'll keep picking the wrong person and it will always fail. So please do something about it. Yes, I'm a total hypocrite, but the advice is good.

One last thing. I can honestly say that our first Friday night was one of the most genuinely enjoyable I've ever spent and I thank you for that. And that second 'date' may have featured some of the most left field foreplay I've ever experienced, but you were a gentleman and in case you're wondering, whilst it sure as hell took a long time coming, the orgasm was genuine.

You're far better than the others and worth ten of me. But until you realise that and conquer those demons, you'll always be an easy mark.

Be better than that. Be better than me.

Look after yourself Shaggy.

Laura

*

"To conclude, I have nuttin against yer man Mr Shakespeare, even if he is a touch overrated."

"Mmmmmmm." The repetitive protestation is curtailed by a slap across the side of the head with a book.

"Shut it. If I wanted a conversation, I'd remove dat tape. But I don't, yeh see. Diss is more in the way of a sol... a sul... what's the word I'd be looking for, Mick?"

"Feck knows."

"Helpful as ever."

"Uuuuuuuuu."

Tempted by another slap, but instead he peels back the tape slightly to allow the lips to part.

"Soliloquy?"

"Dat's de one." He replaces the tape and smoothes it down. Looks distastefully at the snot on his fingers, back at the offending nostrils, reconsiders that second slap, but makes do with a slow shake of the head that he knows hints at far worse. "But diss," he says, brandishing the copy of *A Midsummer Night's Dream*, "is complete and utter shite. Load of poncing about basically." He stares into the distance and cracks his knuckles for maximum effect. "Yeh like horror films, wee fella?" Nothing like a tangential detour to scramble a brain.

Rapid shake of the head.

"Didn't tink so. Well dare was diss one made years ago. Yer man Vincent Price was in it, yeh probably don't know him, and he was playing diss actor who got the hump and went around murdering people he had grudges against in real violent and grisly ways, all inspired by de plays of Shakespeare. Gave me some creative ideas for appropriate... how should we put it? Reparations. '*Out vile jelly!*' and all dat kind of stuff. Very inspiring at times is yer man Will." He waits until the eyes tell him the implication has hit home. "But we was told it needed to be diss one. Very disappointing. Feckin fairy on the front, I ask yeh. What kind a shite is dat? So I guess yeh got lucky dare." Sees the relief; a flicker of hope. Allows it to be nurtured. "Plus doing something over-*elaborate* to a wee slip of a ting like yourself might reflect badly on men like ourselves who take pride in our reputations. Not dat dare wouldn't be a long line of people patting us on the backs for dispatching a kiddy-fiddler like yer man here, eh Mick?" The bulging eyes and increased volume and insistency of the wordless babble emanating from behind the strip of tape tell him the message is getting through. Time to up the ante. "I mean don't get me wrong. We're still going to hurt yeh and hurt yeh pretty bad. A few breakages. Some lifelong mementos of our quality time togedder for yeh to cherish. Got our reps to tink about after all. Not to mention our insurance policy against any bleating. But we *are* going to take yeh permanently out of the game fella. Can't have yeh plying yer perverted trade no more. So we'll be assisting in yer enforced relocation to a more sheltered environment. Let other less principled individuals dan our good selves and with nought to lose mete out some more drastic retribution. Not our usual modus operandi, I'll grant you, but adapt or die, so to speak. And diss is where I hand over to my systems expert."

"If I could find de feckin on-switch."

"When I say expert, I might be overstating tings a touch. What I really mean is he's da one of us two who knows most about dem tings, and I know feck all."

"Got it. There yeh go."

"Guy's a genius. And?"

"Need a password."

An enquiring look receives a frantic shake of the head, revealing they've struck oil; and warrants that slap.

"We can do diss easy or hard. Yer choice."

*

"Hello."

"Mum. It's me. Kevin."

"It's not my birthday is it?"

"Er… no… look…"

"I'm just joshing. It's nice to hear from my little boy."

"Mum. I need to have a chat with you."

"That's fine. I'm meeting Belinda for lunch but that's not for another twenty—"

"No. I need to see you face to face sometime."

"Gosh, that does sound serious."

"Mum, please."

The 'neutral venue' that had sounded so melodramatic on the phone is a necessity. He couldn't have guaranteed more than ten minutes in the frilly, pink nest without feeling nauseous, or being interrupted by a sister popping in for a *little natter,* or to drop off one or more of the tribe of precious little grandchildren for some free child minding – the greedy scrabbling for maternal attention an unacknowledged battle to right perceived childhood iniquities and imbalances that would be dismissed with horror were they ever to be aired – or to discuss celebratory logistics for the next in the unending stream of birthdays and Easters and school plays and christenings and Halloweens and sports days and Mothering Sundays and ballet productions and Christmases and house-warmings and pancake days and assemblies and… whatever else they could use as a reason for their coven to congregate.

The removal from her natural environment has proven easier than he could have hoped for and, as he steers her to a quiet and partially-hidden corner of the coffee shop, he congratulates himself on a first step achieved without a hitch.

Now for the leap into the unknown.

"This is nice," she says, not meaning it. "Do you come here a lot?"

"Yes," he lies.

She takes a bite of her cake.

"Mmm, very tasty." The flared nostrils and pursed lips giving the lie to the compliment; the subtext *I could make much better*. And sure enough, this self-constraint doesn't hold for long. She just can't stop herself.

Kevin leans forward over the table and stares down into the rising steam, rocking gently back and forward, hands clasped tightly out of view, fingernails threatening to puncture skin; teetering on the parapet, paralysed.

"…over orange peel any day of the week," concludes the culinary monologue he has zoned out of. He tugs at a hangnail, flinches and watches as a bead of blood inflates, vibrates and then breaks, running over the side of his finger.

"Are you all right, Kevin?"

"I'm fine. Look…" Deep breath. "Do you hate me, Mum?"

"I beg your pardon?"

"Have you ever wished I'd never been born?" This second question asked without having drawn breath after the first.

"What a ridiculous question. Of course I…" Her facial features freeze, contorted into an expression stranded somewhere between horror and disgust, her eyes fixed on his. He can feel that knot of resolution he's been determinedly constructing for days unravel like some cheap magic trick before her gaze, and the regression builds up momentum. He's on the point of disintegration when there's a flicker at the corner of her left eye and a near-imperceptible softening of her countenance before her lips close gently together. And in that brief instant comes the epiphany that there's no external focus in her stare. It's not about him, this moment; it doesn't concern him. He could grab the cutlery and exhibit percussive excellence on the table and she'd probably not notice.

Her lips move but all he catches is the faintest of hisses.

"I can't hear you."

"I said sometimes," she repeats, in little more than a distant echo of her normal voice. "Not the hate. The wish though. Sometimes. Very rarely. During the worst times. But, sometimes, yes. God help me. It's nothing personal though." She emits a shrill, nervous ghost of a laugh and smears crumbs into her plate with a fingertip.

"Nothing *personal*?"

"I know. Sounds silly doesn't it."

"Aarrgh. I'm just so *bloody* confused."

"*Language*, Kevin. I'm still your mother." The stern tone contradicted by a smile. He can't help but smile back and that rarest of things, a shared moment of equality, seems to lift a load from her shoulders.

"I don't think you ever had a chance, love. It was never about you. That's what I meant when I said it was nothing personal."

He lets his face do the talking, forcing her to continue.

"You don't remember finding me on the floor upstairs that day when you were little, do you?"

"Yes, I do. You'd fainted, or something."

"It was a little bit more than that, love."

"How do you mean?"

"Your father was away at the time. I asked him not to go. Said I didn't feel right. Meant that *it* didn't feel right. Should have said that, but I thought he might care more if I made it about me. Silly really, but I was that naïve. So off he went."

"You said '*it*'."

"I was pregnant. Had the first scan a few weeks earlier. Some company at the hospital would have been nice, but there you go. A little girl. And I wanted this one, I really did. Surprised myself after... well..." Pause.

Eyes welling up. Questions. So many questions. But now is not the time. There are moments to shut up and listen. "Clean bill of health, wouldn't you know." She emits a loud, wet sniff. "I was so made up, I broke the rule and rang him at work. Silly me. Most definitely a no-no. The response I got from him, you'd have thought I'd just ruined his day. Looking back, he was as good as gone by then. I was asleep when he got home and he'd left most days before I woke up. That's enough, Angie. Sorry, talking to myself. First sign of madness, they say. But I promised myself I'd never talk him down. Be above all that stuff. Be better than him." She takes a breath. "How is he, by the way?"

"Okay, I think."

"Do you see him often?"

"No, not really. When it suits him."

"Is he still…"

"Yes."

Another pause, one that drags on long enough to have him scrambling for something appropriate to say to fill it. She saves him. "It was a little while later that I knew something wasn't right. I should have told someone, but… what exactly do you remember of that day?"

"You were crawling along the floor, groaning. I helped you get into bed and then I went and got the lady from next door."

"That's it?"

"Yeah. Look, I was only…"

"No blood?"

"What? No."

"Oh Kevin…"

"What?" he asks, failing to keep the exasperation from his voice.

"Kevin, there was blood everywhere."

"Blood?"

"I'd miscarried. There was so much of the stuff, we ended up having to replace the bedroom carpet and your dad even had to put a couple of coats of paint on the wall. Did something useful before he cleared off, I'll give him that."

"I don't remember any of that. Just a faint recollection of you crawling along the floor. I'd have remembered blood, surely."

"The mind has its own defences. Maybe it worked out what a five-year-old boy could cope with and reconfigured it into something more digestible."

"Why haven't you ever told me this before?"

"Maybe I needed my own defences." She breaks eye contact and rubs the insides of her wrists together. "Trouble is, I didn't just leave it at that."

"How do you mean?"

Another pause. More rubbing. A look away. "How about another pot of tea?"

"Sure, I'll get it, he says, biting down on his frustration. "Same again?"

When he returns, it's to find her resolved and ready.

"I need to say sorry, Kevin."

"For what?"

"For taking the cowardly way out. For blaming you."

"For what?"

"For everything. For you not being another girl. For the stretch marks. For the saggy stomach I couldn't shift and the weight I put on. For your father not finding me attractive anymore. For his affairs. For his leaving us. For my failure to make anything of my life. And even – God help me – for the miscarriage."

"*Me?*"

"I know, I know. It's inexcusable. But I guess that blaming you for everything was easier than asking myself questions I didn't want to answer. And no matter what I threw at you, you just soaked it up and kept smiling. And I went on doing it." The tears running freely now. "No mother should do that to her child. I know it was years later, but I can't help but feel…" Catches herself.

"What?"

"Stuff like that doesn't go away. It rots and festers and I still think it was part of what happened, you know, your little… er… *problem* later on at university."

"Breakdown, Mum. I had a breakdown. You can say it, you know."

"Sorry, but I can't even think about it without… about you going through all that. And I couldn't even bring myself to visit you. What a mother I turned out to be. Failed you again."

"I didn't want any visitors. I just needed space. To reset myself. But forget all that. What happened that day?"

"The miscarriage? As I said, I'd sensed something was wrong, wanted your father there and really resented having to keep you home from school that day. But you acted exactly like any five-year-old with a cold would. You did nothing whatsoever wrong. You were a poorly little boy and you just wanted a bit of attention; a cuddle now and then. I knew that, but I couldn't see past my own feelings. I stuck you on the sofa, wrapped you in a blanket and told you to watch the television. Some mother, eh? But you kept calling my name and I tried to ignore you but you kept on calling and I lost my patience and something snapped and I shouted down from upstairs for you to just be quiet and then I got this sharp pain and I knew it was all over. And there I was, dragging myself to the bathroom when I heard your voice behind me. I'd have told you to stay away had I known you'd come up. No child should have to see their mother like that. It wasn't fair, on either of us. I said I was fine but you wouldn't go. You were always so good like that. Such a caring little boy. Always wanting to help. And no matter what I said, you wouldn't leave me, so I said I just needed to get into bed and bless you, you did your best to help, and then I told you to go next door and get Mrs Edwards. And you did. As good as gold." She looks into his eyes but can't hold the gaze. Her lips quiver before she speaks again. "You deserved better for a mother. You really did."

"Hey. That's nonsense. You were..."

"Kevin, haven't you been listening? Why can't you just be angry? You have every right, so be angry. But please don't give me sympathy. I can't take your sympathy. I really can't."

"I don't know how I feel. It's a lot to take in. Who knows, I might get angry later, but right now it's more relief I'm feeling. It certainly explains a lot of things. Maybe I don't have to be like this anymore. I can move on."

"Unlike me, you mean."

Kevin answers with a silent shrug and for a moment fears she'll pull up the drawbridge, but she pleasantly surprises them both by offering him a smile, which he returns.

*

They find him round the back of the house tinkering with an upended lawnmower in the middle of a half-mown lawn.

"Nice looking lawn you've got dare, fella."

"Sorry, can I help you?"

"Mower problems, have we? Be a pity if yeh didn't get to finish up, the bit you've done looking so neat and tidy and all."

That makes him wary, as of course it should, but there would be many who wouldn't have twigged so quick, so respect where it's due.

"I don't know you, so why don't you just clear off."

"We just want to have a chat."

"We?"

"Behind you."

He looks over his shoulder and sees 'Mick' for the first time. Exhales audibly.

"Brave men. Hunting in pairs."

"What makes yeh think we're hunting?" No mug, this one. A different kettle of fish entirely to that snivelling little half-man.

"Aren't you?"

"Maybe we are, maybe not. Tell yeh what tow, yer sounding a touch guilty. Got something to be ashamed of have we, fella?"

"Look guys. I don't know what you think you know, but whatever it is, you've got it wrong. Do yourselves a favour and just clear off. My wife's probably on the phone to the police inside the house as we speak."

"Now that would be someting, seeing as she went off in dat snazzy little car of hers not twenty minutes ago. Pilates isn't it on Tuesdays, Mick?"

"Yep. Good for de core."

"So I hear. Very admirable. Women of her age so often let demselves go, particularly when dey've had nippers and dose old stomach muscles go. My dearest Maureen, God bless her soul, looks like a white chocolate walnut whip left out in de sun wid her kit off, but dare yeh go. What about yer Colleen, Mick?"

"Tits like balloons half full of water, fanny like a bucket and I haven't seen her belly button for ten years, not that I've been looking dat hard for a while now."

"Nicely put, Mick, and dat's some choice mental imagery you've given us to play with. Dat said, I doubt we're exactly oil paintings in our birtday suits. But fortunately, after so many years, a happy marriage is about so much more. And my good lady seems to find all de fulfilment she needs in her grandkids, her knitting and the ICA. But yer missus now, she clearly looks after herself. Why is dat, I wonder? She playing away, yer tink? Or scared yeh might be? Or maybe the pair of yeh are happy little bunnies going at it all de time. Dat right is it, fella?"

"None of your business."

"But she's not in yer house, and she's not ringing anyone. We both know dat."

"Can't blame a man for trying," he says with a shrug, steadfastly refusing to rise to the bait.

"Indeed not." He offers up a weak smile, then abruptly withdraws it. A tried and trusted technique. "But what *can* we blame yeh for?"

"Blame? Nothing I can think of."

"We'll see about dat. Take a seat over dare, my man," he says, motioning towards the patio.

"I'm all right."

"*Take a seat.* Please." That does the trick and they relocate. "Indulge me a while and I'll expand on my train of tought. I'm tinking dat we all like to take a peek when we can and sometimes maybe when we shouldn't. Yeh know what I'm talking about; some girl comes towards yeh and yer eyes go down to tose pert wee breasts or dat short skirt and all dat bare flesh and just when you've had yer dirty little tought and imagined what you'd like to do to her given half the chance, yeh look up to her face and realise she's a slip of a girl nowhere near sixteen like. And you feel a twinge of shame but it's no more dan an innocent mistake and dare's no denying she has certain, how should I put it… *charms* and it's a reasonable mistake and it's not like yer actually would or anything, so no harm done. Healthy desires and all dat. What makes de world go round. Now I can see yeh looking a bit confused dare, so let me change tack ever so slightly. What's it called Mick, when yeh sort of fancy a bloke like?"

"Man crush?"

"Yeah, man crush. Dat's it. Yeh know, when you look at a handsome chap, and for the briefest of moments have to admit he's got it all going on and when all's said and done, he's a fine-looking fella. Hey, Mick, can yeh tink of any examples for yer man here? Yeh know, if someone put a gun to yer head and said yeh like totally had to, or else, who would it be?"

"Well there's a question, Paddy." Pause for scratching of chin and wistful look. "If we're talking just spending some quality time then I'd be after a little twinkle in the eye and an air of mischief, so dat'd have to be yer man Colin Farrell. But I'm suspecting yeh have something a little bit more *participatory* in mind than a friendly chat over a beer, in which case I suppose it would depend on whedder I was giving or receiving, if you catch my drift. Now if I was giving, I'm tinking, mmm, maybe that Torres or what's his name, yer tennis player, Nadal, dat's it; some fine musculature to admire and run yer hands over and all dat long hair to play with, and if you're struggling to rise to the occasion den yeh could always pretend it was a bird like. But if I was receiving, den I wouldn't really care what deh looked like, would I, so basically anyone wid a needle dick."

Silence.

"I'm done," adds 'Mick'.

"Not sure what to say dare Mick. A little more detail dan I'd anticipated. Not so much take de ball and run with it, as take de ball, do a hundred keepy uppies and boot it in the back of de net."

"Dat good, eh?"

"To be honest, I'm tinking more of an own goal Mick, but no probs, we're amongst friends here and I for one won't be telling anyone. What about yeh, fella?"

"I have not got a *fucking* clue what you two gay boys are on about?"

'Paddy' gives the words some air. Strokes his chin contemplatively. Looks over at 'Mick'. Loving the performance of it all. The delicious anticipation.

"So diss school you work at…" He pauses to take in the look of surprise this engenders. Always an enjoyable moment, the first time a quarry feels outflanked and their mind starts chasing through its memory bank for any slip, any misdemeanour, anything that might validate this intrusion and the threat to self it implies. "All boys, is it?"

"What are you suggesting?" But the flinch tells him all he needs to know.

"Come on. I tink we both know what."

"Speak for yourself. I've been a respected teacher at that school for over twenty years. So if you think…"

"I'll tell yeh what I tink should I? I tink yeh like to look."

"What?"

"Dem boys of yours. Placed in yer care. Position of autority and all dat. Trust. Dat's the word. And what did yeh do with dat trust? Ever abuse it, fella?"

"Hang on…"

"Woah." Just the one word, and this guy isn't stupid; he knows where the power lies. Knows he's outgunned. Knows not to say anything more. "Be a good lad, now. I'm not necessarily saying you've been buggering dare little arses, but I am saying dare are plenty who you've humiliated and plenty who you've made to do some pretty sick and perverted things while yeh watched. Maybe played with yourself a bit. I'm tinking it's either a power or a sex ting. Maybe both. I reckon diss way yeh don't have to ask yourself a fundamental question yeh don't want to answer. Is dat it? No answer? Answer diss den: got any kids?"

"No."

"Figures. Nephews?"

"Two."

"How old?"

"I dunno, I'm a bloke. Why would I? They're both teenagers."

"And how do yeh think yer missus would feel if she walked in and yeh were standing dare with yer dick in your hand watching one of dem whimpering and doing feck knows what in the corner? Dat do it for yeh, does it big man? Would she be fine and dandy with dat, do yeh tink? Maybe we'll hang around and ask her, shall we?"

"She wouldn't believe you."

"I'm betting she would. And even if she didn't, the atmosphere is going to get a bit icy round here. In fact, I reckon she may have her suspicions already. She might even want to look into it a bit more. But we can find dat out for ourselves when she gets back."

"*No.*"

"Sorry?"

"No. Please don't." He scrunches his eyes shut and buries his head in his hands. "Who told you?"

"Nice try. And if I was yeh, I wouldn't even be trying to guess, cos dare lies a *whole* lot of bad stuff, if yeh catch my drift. I tink yeh need to take yer medicine and move on. Maybe tink about taking some early retirement. Spend more time with de missus. Enjoy dat firm, supple body of hers. Mind yeh, yeh may have no choice on the retirement front when we're done. Depends how the mood takes us. Guess yeh know what's coming?"

He nods, his stubborn defences crumbling.

"Oi, Sherlock. Got that old dear on the line for you again. She must be gagging for it, you sly fox." A self-congratulatory chortle is cut short by a familiar voice.

"Hello."

"Hello Mrs…"

"I've seen him again."

"Sorry. Who?"

"The man I told you about. The one who shouted at me. You know."

"You've seen him?"

"Yes. I just told you that."

"So you did."

"I followed him and I know where he works. Dreadful place."

"Could I possibly come over?"

"I'll put the kettle on."

*

Kevin could have done with company, for legitimacy and cover, if nothing else. But Carl had responded to the unlikeliest of invitations with a look of amused puzzlement and a disdainful declination.

"You're joking. Really not a good time. Sorry. Anyway, they've been badgering me to play against the First XI for ages and I made up some holiday. It wouldn't be right if I just turned up, would it?"

And that had been that.

So here he stands on his lonesome in a corner of the refectory, hiding behind a glass of white wine and a calm indifference for his surroundings that belies the inner turmoil engendered by wandering this far from his bunker; this far into his past.

He's sporting a laminated badge displaying his surname – Christian name checked in at reception, along with all vestiges of self-confidence; the school's way of re-establishing hierarchy – and year of leaving, gently perspiring in the first collar and tie combo he's donned in years. He's not sure what he wants more: someone to talk to, or for no one to recognise him and to last out this nightmare in a womb of invisible silence. He reminds himself why he's here, but even that does little to quell the impulse to turn and flee.

He's studying the shields on the walls for the umpteenth time when a slightly huskier version of a dimly familiar voice intrudes on his reverie.

"You on any of them?"

"Er, oh, hi. A couple."

"Ooo. An actual sporting hero. Which is the one for hop, skip and fart?"

"No, it was rugby actu… oh, right, that."

"Of course, I only ever saw your artistic side."

"Once was enough for me."

"Left you looking for a change in scenery?"

"No, er… oh, I see. Very good."

"As I recall, you had more than one string to your artistic bow. I remember you throwing some serious moves on the dance floor, robot boy."

"Christ. Thanks for dredging up that memory." Prays that's all she remembers.

"I almost didn't recognise you conscious and with your clothes on. Is that wine or aqua toilette?"

Kevin winces as scenes play quickfire in his mind's eye, none of them pleasant, and each a slash of pain that rips at whatever threads of willpower and self-assurance he's patched together for this reacquaintance with his past.

"I never said thank you for that."

"No," she replies, turning and walking away from him. "You didn't," she adds over her shoulder.

"Hang on," he shouts after her. She wheels around, but the intended belated expression of gratitude is lost in a rush of rationality. "What on earth are you doing here?"

"Charming. And so very Nethercottian." Something tells him the mispronunciation is wilful. "We will persist, however, and maybe one day we can drag this place screaming and kicking into the twenty-first century." Kevin is confused. "Co-ed?" Kevin is still confused. "Five years ago?" Kevin's brow is aching. "Blimey, you really are off the pace. The school merged sixth forms five years ago. Marlswood wasn't getting the numbers at eleven so they decided to open a prep school on site and grab the little princesses early. That meant something had to go and it turned out to be the sixth form. Nethercott initially said no to the idea of taking them on, but I guess money swayed it and here we are. They try their hardest to keep us away and Marlswood has its own events for us Old Girls, but there's something about Nethercott's male chauvinist pig-ocracy and their determination to alienate us that is like red rag to a bull, and enough to guarantee some of us traipse along each year and endure this turgid, ever-so-very-much-homoerotic piss-up just to stick it to *the man*."

"I didn't know."

"Clearly. What did you do to your eye?"

His hand instinctively moves to touch the bruising and winces from the self-inflicted pain. "Nothing much. Had an accident with a door... er... knob." Unsure why he's lying. Knows instantly that she knows he is.

"*Right*. See you later." And she's away, the sway of her body telling him she's not for turning again.

The only concessions to the occasion are the tablecloths on each of the long refectory tables. Kevin approaches his year's table and shrinks onto the bench before his name card.

There are those he would love to be here – well, two to be exact – some he wouldn't mind seeing again, and a few he hopes will not be in attendance. None is here tonight; Marsh's absence a source of some relief. Instead he has a table of the dimly familiar, many of whom he can't recall speaking to more than a handful of times in his entire four-and-a-bit-year spell at the school.

Those he did know a little better prove less than enthralling and wearyingly predictable. Hill regales Kevin with a succession of illnesses, breakages and unfortunate events; only to be trumped in the misery stakes by a gaunt Henderson who has battled testicular cancer and is in hopeful remission. Fulmington looks down his formidable nose at everyone, as he would a misplaced item of cutlery in a place setting at a formal dinner or an overfamiliar minion, enduring them until the port and cigars come out, at which point he readily relocates to a more upwardly mobile table of elitist brown-noses carousing like something out of *Brideshead Revisited*. Durbridge has at least broadened his skill set. Near enough every movement still generates a squelch, belch or parp. What maturity has added is a seemingly endless range of what he clearly believes to be hilarious euphemistic follow-ups: the vicar is repeatedly offered more tea, the actress regularly converses with the bishop, the big brown horn is blown, and so on.

Time, stress and gravity are already taking their toll. Chins sagging. Cheeks redder. Hairlines receding. Eyes that have seen more look tired and weary. Shoulders hunch forwards. And buttons and belts are under pressure.

Not that Kevin is in any position to feel superior. What he sees in the mirror on those rare occasions he braves a self-appraisal never indicates anything but a battle with life that is being slowly and inexorably lost.

A chorus of clinks and exaggerated throat clearances curtails conversations and turns heads towards the top table. Sir Reginald rises shakily to his feet and shamelessly milks a sustained round of warm applause. When hands eventually still, he welcomes and praises one and all. Kevin knows *he* isn't "the cream of England's elite", but there are plenty who think *they* are, judging from the general nodding of heads and self-congratulatory "hear hears" resonating around the hall. Then comes the bombshell: the following year will be his last as Headmaster. He pauses at this point for assorted "oohs" and "ahhs", a hint of the pantomimic to them, corroborating the feeling engendered by that overly effusive welcome that this particular cat has long since departed its metaphorical bag. The "oh my dear God" he hears is a step too far, and the repellent throwback who gets to his feet, reaches his arm out like some Nazi salute, though with his hand bent back at ninety degrees to his wrist, and gruffly proclaims, "Give that man a hand," deserves a slapping, and not the warm glow he will undoubtedly be experiencing as the other guests start to rise and mimic both the action and the exhortation. Kevin stages a silent, seated protest.

"Nethercott does Nuremberg. Or is it North Korea? Whichever, it's all *so* very quaintly charming." The voice laps at his ear in a warm wash of wine and perfume that is anything but unpleasant. He turns and is at once complicit with that sparkle in her eyes. "Fancy giving me the guided tour and leaving this bunch of fuckwits to their jaundiced sycophancy?"

They approach the doors at the back of the hall as bums hit seats and Sir Reginald headlines an announcement of "major import to the future of this venerable institution." Curiosity gets the better of them, so they pause and lean against the rear wall. But it's all anti-climax, as his successor is announced to be none other than Reggie Junior, or Gilbert, as the poor sod, with his thin and sloping shoulders, weak chin and general appearance of impending implosion, was christened. Not an obvious candidate, blatant nepotism aside, to fill Sir Reginald's brogues.

"Jesus," she says.

Much of the school is in effect off-limits, so the requested tour turns into little more than an Earl-of-Nethercott-themed treasure hunt, fuelled by a childish mischief born of a shared scorn for what they've left behind in the refectory; and the bottle of red wine she's smuggled out under her jacket.

By the time they squelchily sink, giggling, into the same leather sofa on which he'd perched that first nervous day at the age of fourteen, they've counted seventeen, including a number of satisfyingly ludicrous additions since Kevin's departure.

"That poor beagle on the last one had definitely received some *special attention* from his master, judging by the looks on both their faces," she says, lifting the bottle to her lips.

Kevin responds by shifting to see if he can still get a tune out of the sofa and succeeds in generating a sustained squeak that brings a smile of satisfaction to his face and a look of benign bemusement to that of his companion.

"Your first time at this esteemed gathering?" she asks.

"Yep. And last."

"Why's that?"

"Not my idea of good company."

"*Thanks.*"

"No, that's not wh—"

"Calm down. I know exactly what you mean," she says, her smile dousing the flicker of embarrassment.

"And you?"

"Third."

"Blimey. Must be something that keeps dragging you back."

"You could say that. Doubt I'll bother again though," she says, her eyes intent on his for the briefest of moments, before she lets her gaze float off over his shoulder.

A silence settles in as Kevin ponders yet another confusing riddle set by the opposing gender. If there's an appropriate reply to be made, it's lost on him.

"So why did *you* come?" she asks, after a while, rescuing him.

He instinctively fumbles for an evasive response.

"Try the truth," she follows up, throwing Kevin off kilter. "It's sometimes easier, and it's always better in the long run."

Finding himself disconcertingly at ease, he drops his guard.

"I came to confront my past." Pause for effect, but he's placed far too much emphasis on the 'came' for it to sound anything but corny. "God that sounded trite."

"No, it didn't. Well, maybe a little bit." That smile again.

"I left on bad terms with a few individuals. I came back to see if they were still here."

"And are they?"

"Not sure yet. Don't seem to be."

"And if they are?"

"I don't know. Maybe talk to them?"

"You sound almost evangelical."

"I wish. I could think of plenty of other things to do to them, but I made a promise to someone I know… knew."

"Who?" she asks, and Kevin feels his shoulders tighten. "I'm sorry. Too nosy. It's none of my business and I've made you uncomfortable."

"It's okay, that's not it," he falters.

"What then?"

He's confused. Not only does he feel able to tell her, but he desperately wants to. And that's a new and discomforting sensation for him. There's something about that look of patient, non-judgemental kindness that is reassuring and he has an overwhelming urge to let go.

To share.

And he does.

*

"What about you?" Kevin asks, guilty at having monopolised the last twenty minutes.

"Me? Not much to tell, really."

He fixes his interested face.

"You all right?"

"Fine," he replies a touch testily, shaking his facial features loose. "Go on."

"As I said. What's to tell? At sixteen I wanted to go to Cambridge or Oxford to study law, but I didn't get the grades and ended up at Leicester studying psychology. I aimed for a first and a handsome boyfriend and ended up with a two-two and a doomed relationship with an engineer from Bradford called Barry who made full use of that fourth year without me to go back into halls and indulge in whatever fresh meat he could persuade to let him screw them. For the first term of that year I turned up every fortnight on Friday evening and acted the exotic older woman to be fancied by boys and envied by girls. Then looked like an utter mug as I misinterpreted knowing glances as jealousy or admiration or whatever else I needed to think to avoid the blindingly obvious fact that he was a cheating waste of breath. Anyway my degree left me perfectly qualified to be a... er... teacher, which given my dislike of most children didn't appeal so I went to work for an insurance company. Met a bloke called Stephen who seemed nice enough and made me feel wanted again after Barry's random rootings. Unfortunately I rather over-reacted to a spot of kind attentiveness by marrying him. Full works as well. Vintage car, ridiculously expensive bridal dress with fifteen-foot train, stepdad in tears as he led me down the aisle, big reception, five-tier cake... the lot. Can't quite believe it looking back, but there you go. Seemed like a good idea at the time. Settled into a nice new-build two-up-two-down less than a mile from my mum and gave married life a go. A few years later we went all reckless and decided to get a conservatory added. Couple of strapping lads did the work. Must admit to the occasional extended stare and drool when the opportunity presented itself. Then one day I came home early and went round the side of the house rather than scrimmaging in my bag for my keys and found one of the builders in the half-built conservatory, doubled up over a Black and Decker work bench and groaning loudly. Before you give him too much sympathy, the cause of his noisiness was my dear husband's dick rammed up his arse. A tender and touching scene indeed. Took a bit of coming to terms with, I can tell you. The kind of mental picture that gets permanently burned onto your retinas and leaves you with a lot of questions."

Pause for much-needed breath and a messy slurp of wine.

"So now I live alone, different house of course, a flat in fact, and all I want to do when I get home is lock the door and lounge on my sofa in comfortable baggy clothes and a pair of fluffy slippers watching crap on the telly while swigging down mugs of tea and stuffing cake down my throat. So why can't I just do it? That's what makes me happy. But I can't, can I? Because everything I watch and read tells me that's a sad and pathetic thing to do and that I can't really be happy and that life is passing me by and I can't be anything worthwhile if I'm not getting admiring glances from men or applying the latest laboratory-my-arse-designed make-up or constantly dyeing my hair or injecting myself with botulism toxin or having hair extensions or faking a tan or have hundreds of *friends* on Facebook or meeting my ridiculously good-looking girlfriends in trendy cafés for energised and feisty conversations about men or fashion while we throw our un-split shiny hair around gaily and flirt with the world and have the right phone and the right car and the right handbag and the right hairdryer and the right shoes and of course all the right kitchen utensils because that's where us women need to spend most of our time if we're to be complete and my arse must be small and my breasts must be firm and displayed on a platter and my skin must be smooth and heaven forbid that I might have a wrinkle or cellulite or a spot or a stomach that sticks out. And there's a bit of me that knows it's all bollocks of course but a bigger bit of me is screaming that I need to get up and get out there or I'll never meet someone and even though I don't want to meet someone I also do but maybe don't want to admit that to myself. So there I sit throwing out answers to piss-simple patronising questions on TV quiz shows like that makes me a better or more intelligent person in some way and at least I can feel superior to the witless morons their selection processes filter in as they struggle to recall the capital of France or the name of the current US president and then there's the endless stream of voyeuristic patronising documentaries about really fat people or people with appalling disabilities so I can pretend I'm being compassionate and dig *real issues* when deep down I'm rejoicing that there are people out there who are fatter and uglier and having a shittier time than me and loving the chance to throw myself into a peer group in which I come out favourably. But then that voice starts up again and tells me to stop fooling myself and stop being so sad and useless so up I get and along I go to the next in an unending chain of pointless fucking socials and get-togethers in the same old characterless pubs and bars and restaurants with pretty much the same people I spend my working days with and the moment I sit down I cease to be me and lose everything individual to me and become something I'm not, just some tiny cog in a perpetual motion machine designed for other people's benefit and which just repeats the same charade that gets us all through another week deluding ourselves that we're popular and attractive and desirable and not glorified battery hens for five days a week and that life isn't passing us by while we do sod all with this one opportunity we've been given and the weeks turn to months and the months turn to years and the brown hair changes to grey or at least whatever colour we choose to hide the grey because heaven forbid we show any grey hair and every *smear* of lipstick, every *swipe* of mascara, every drop of *fake* tan, every bottle of hair colour, every *built-up* bra, every tummy-tightening pair of pants… they're all just lies and deceit and take you one step further away from who you really are and with each one there's a greater pretence that has to be maintained and whether it's some bloke or the girls you work with the distance from this pretence to what you really are gets bigger and bigger and the possibility of bridging it gets more and more daunting and you're stuck in this double bind and you have no choice but to cover and tighten and hide more because if you don't the world will damn you in a second and the thought of all those looks of contempt and disgust is too much to take so you keep playing the game. Their game. The game men came up with to keep themselves in charge and leave us dancing to their tune. So there I sit in the pub or whatever trying to feel aloof and apart from these people and reduce them and the evening to a nothing that can't impact me but at the same time it matters deeply and what they think of me matters and I hate it that it does. There's *Kate*, with those tiny prick-teasing skirts she wears that perfectly show off her pert little arse. There's *Paula*, who has these unfeasibly long lashes that she flutters up and down over her stunning green eyes. Then there's *Gabby*, and that coquettish thing she does with her hair, throwing her head over to one side and running her hands up and down that mane of hair like she's milking it while at the same time exposing that impossibly elegant neck of hers and flashing her cow eyes. And the blokes just lap it up, probably imagining it's their cock she's caressing with her fingers and bloody hell you're getting turned on just thinking about it."

"I'm not," Kevin flails.

"Mmm. So anyway I sit there aspiring to be in the haves whilst knowing deep down I'm with the have-nots. Just a hanger-on destined for cast-offs and waste matter. And round about eleven o'clock some bloke will come up to me and start chatting and I know immediately that he's running out of time and it's my potential to be that face-saving grope or shag that is my attraction not me as a person and that an hour or two earlier he'd been setting his sights far higher and he's been working his way down ever since. I know I'm not so much 'must have' as 'will do' but hell at least I've made it that high so the bit that wants to tell him to piss off is overridden by the bit of me that's grateful for the attention and for not being one of the 'wouldn't touch with a bargepole' brigade, at least allowing me to feel superior to someone and glad I'm a five-pint girl rather than a ten-pint one even if it's because of *what* I have to offer and not who I am. I'm a potential hole for them to fill and tell their mates about, or not. An extra X chromosome the only criteria I've needed to satisfy. A receptacle for their needs and hates and self-delusions. I know that yet there I am and however wise I am to what's going on when it comes down to it I want them to stare at my tits when I look away or at my arse when I head off to the loo but at the same time I hate them for doing it. I want to be more in their eyes than a piece of meat but in truth that's all I ever will be and I feel less if no-one's looking and I hate that in myself I really do."

Another partially successful swig from the bottle.

"Then I come along here for a change in scenery because I get to see people I haven't seen for years and who might provide something new and exciting in my life and persuade me that I'm more than I think I am and that I have more strings to my bow. And to begin with it feels good. We're not here because we have any desire to spend time with these arrogant self-obsessed relics. We're here just to piss them off. And that gives us a common cause that feels great and gives me a high at least for a while anyway cos after a few hours of them I realise I'm no more like them than I am the people I work with and I hate hearing about what great things they're doing and their high-paid jobs and their wonderful husbands and blissfully happy marriages and even if it is all bullshit it still sounds a whole lot better than my shitty life. Then of course I realise that anyone who decides to come to this kind of event has to be someone I don't want to know anyway and I just get even more depressed and the red wine just gets more and more attractive and just *what* are you laughing at?"

"Nothing."

"*What?*"

"I thought it was just me that's totally fucked up."

She snorts loudly and a bubble of wine-infused snot briefly inflates from a nostril before exploding messily and wetly on her upper lip. She dips to her left, fishes out a hanky and clears the crime scene, before fixing Kevin with a look of impressive innocence that denies everything, while at the same time threatening violence if challenged.

Silence.

Kevin can feel his lips compress.

Her eyes narrow.

"Did you see that?"

"What?"

"Nothing. Come on," she says, noisily extricating herself from the grope of the sofa. "Let's go and find out if those ghosts of terms past took the hint."

Kevin effortfully follows suit, rather pleased with himself at having bluffed his way through that awkward moment.

"You did, didn't you," the back of her head asks him.

"Yes."

"Shit. Knew it."

"It was very becoming."

"Sod off."

Their search ends at the notice boards, just as Kevin knew it would. Because he hasn't been entirely honest.

He knows they're still here.

After all, isn't that the only reason *he's* here? That casual browse of the normally spurned *Yearbook* a month or so ago. His apathetic gaze snagged by a familiar face floating in a crowd; a hand placed casually – proprietorially? – on a shoulder. And littered elsewhere the imprint of the other. Both potentially still dishing out their own particular brands of scholastic enlightenment.

And more importantly, he's pretty sure that they're not here tonight. Found that out hours ago.

*

Upon first arriving earlier that day, Kevin had set out on a series of furtive circumnavigations of the cricket pitch, starting several hundred yards beyond the boundary, behind a tree, and spiralling hesitantly inwards, utilising all available cover, until he found himself behind the pavilion. Entertaining fleeting *007* delusions of stealth, he had crept around the corner of the building, nimbly straddled the balustrade, sidled along the wooden balcony and peered in through the open doorway; quite the über-spy in the making. Nothing but framed photos of players past staring down on gently perspiring cellophane-wrapped food. The coast apparently clear. Even allowed himself a self-congratulatory smirk.

"What the fuck have you been doing for the last twenty minutes, you twat?"

He'd spun round and come face to face with a leering Hopkins in cricket whites. "What? Oh. You. Hi."

"We've been pissing ourselves watching you."

"What do you mean?" Hating those plurals.

"Yeah, right. Seriously mate, you should have been standing where we were. It was fucking funny. Your head poking out from behind a tree. That funny walk as you waddled over to the next one. Then your head poking out again. They even stopped the game for a few minutes at one point to watch. Their bloke couldn't bowl, he was laughing so much."

None of which was welcome news. All of which kicked the Bond fantasy into touch, along with what little self-esteem he'd arrived clutching.

"What were you playing at, you daft pillock?"

All defences by now in tatters, he had little choice but to come clean – at least as far as who he'd been avoiding, not why – and was informed there had been no sightings. A wave of relief slapped a smile onto Kevin's face and before he knew it, he'd acquiesced to Hopkins' request for some throw downs as he was due in next. A first for Kevin, who missed the point entirely, misreading it as a contest, not a partnership; zipping the ball at Hopkins' feet, then trying to get it kicking up at him.

Make him uncomfortable.

Gain some revenge for his self-inflicted humiliation.

Sending out a challenge.

A challenge accepted.

A reply dispatched…

…with interest.

*

So now he patiently waits until she spots the names, then fakes his response, briefly bowing his head each time a quarry is located – albeit in absentia, although who is he kidding; what would he, could he, really have done had they been here – relishing her hand on his elbow, the slightest of squeezes; basking a little in the gentle, warming heat of her compassion.

Her interest.

In him.

In his feelings.

378

In spite of his failings.
In him.

Back in the hall, the speeches, announcements and fawning have dissipated into a general milling about and decline into inebriation.

It's Hopkins who puts some meat on the bones for them. Kevin had been planning to extract more earlier that day, only for that cricket ball to intervene. To his credit, Hopkins takes it easy on him, to begin with at least, respecting the fact that Clarke has a bona fide female in tow. Asks him how he is with something approaching compassion, even paying him a non-compliment – "nice stop that; many would have ducked it" – that could sound genuine to anyone who hadn't been there to see Kevin scream like a six-year-old child, stagger backwards with hands clasped over his face and trip over the boundary rope, going down in extravagant stages that saw him career into the legs of a surprised fielder a good fifteen feet onto the pitch; halting the game for a second time.

"You dopey twat," Hopkins concludes, less generously, before fully restoring the school days dynamic by adding, "So where was your mate Evans then? We could have done with him at the top of the order today. Gave me some lame excuse, the big girl's blouse."

"Talking of absentees, surprised Luxley and Badger aren't here," says Kevin, sensing an opening.

"Me too. Luxers normally umpires, but apparently he had some sort of accident a week or so ago and is convalescing at home for the remainder of the term. That old poof Badger is away on compassionate leave, whatever the fuck that means. Pardon my language," he offers with a smirk and a flick of his fringe that isn't meant for Kevin, who at once feels like the gooseberry; how could anyone prefer him to the shock-haired, bronzed, sporting Adonis that is Hopkins. Kevin feels his stomach clench and his forehead prickle.

"Don't mind me. I couldn't give a shit," she says, adding to Kevin, "Coming then, big boy?"

Just as he turns to follow her, he catches the glimmer of a look on Hopkins' face that he has never engendered in another male before.

Feels a veil of vexing, teasing complexity descending on him.

And very much likes it.

Approaching ten thirty, the small group of ladies who have braved the early-onset-mid-life-crisis-testosterone-fest are required to board the coach and head back to their accommodation at Marlswood. A register is taken as they get on; old habits dying hard. Or more likely Nethercott ensuring that the contaminated site can now be given the all-clear. Kevin envies them their escape and that fresh air they will soon be breathing.

As he watches her walk away, he unclenches his fist and unravels the piece of paper he's had locked in its grip from the moment she passed it to him via an awkward and confusing handshake. He holds it up and twists it to catch what light there is. Makes out a couple of phone numbers and the word 'Wolsey'.

"Hey," he shouts, the force and volume of the word enough to turn every head within a ten-yard radius. She proclaims herself to be the recipient of his monosyllable with a few steps towards him.

"You summoned me, oh master?" she says as she approaches him, crossing her hands over her chest and bowing her head.

"Sorry. Wasn't thinking. What's your name?" The question sounding ridiculous.

"My name?"

"Christian name I mean. I've only ever known you as Wolsey."

"My name's Charlotte, Kevin."

"I'm sorry."

"It's not that bad. You could try Lottie, but I wouldn't recommend it. And Charlie will get you my knee in your testicles."

"Charlotte's fine."

"Why thank you. Then what are you sorry about?"

"Not knowing it."

"Why would you?"

"I dunno. I just feel bad. Why are you smiling?"

"I was just wondering what took you so long."

*

Kevin gets the news on his way home the following morning and heads straight for the shop. Or at least what's left of it.

He finds Ron sitting on a bench, impassively observing the clean-up operation.

"What happened?" he asks.

"You taking the piss, son?"

"Of course not. I meant *how* did it happen?"

"Now there's a question. You took your time getting here."

"I've been away. School reunion. Only just got back."

Ron removes the cigarette from his mouth and slowly steers his gaze away from the smouldering carcass of the betting shop and onto Kevin, into whose general direction he emits a cloud of smoke, maybe hoping to give Kevin an enhanced 4D experience of the chaos before them. Then raises an eyebrow.

"Yeah, I know," replies Kevin, wafting the smoke away with his hand.

"Thought you hated the place."

"I did. Still do. Bunch of tossers. But there was something I had to do."

Ron nods his head slowly and Kevin detects a hint of a smile, immediately withdrawn. Not someone he'd ever want to pay poker with.

Kevin folds first, turning away and properly assessing the considerable damage the fire has done. After a minute or two, Ron drops the butt and grinds it into the pavement with his heel.

"Dreadful habit," he mutters to himself, not for the first or last time. "Bit of a coincidence earlier on."

"What?"

"Your mate Peter just happened to be here. Cutting a rather unconvincing presence in the caff opposite. Looking so out of place Sharon might have had him down as a mystery shopper, if she had a sodding clue what one was. Funny though; never seen him there before. Not his cup of tea, pardon the pun. Yet there he was, sitting at the window, unable to keep the fucking smile off his lips. Having himself a right old gloat."

"No way."

"I admire your loyalty, but I know a gloat when I see one. And we both know that he's always had it in for me. That I'm his little *bête noire*." Savouring the words with audible relish.

"No way."

"So you said. Ne repetez pas s'il vous plait."

"Pardon?"

"Need to work on your accent there. Never too young for a spot of self-improvement, young Kevin. I've been taking French classes, tu vois. Keep the old brain agile. Vive le France and all that merde." And having feinted one way, he delivers the punch. "Don't suppose you ever mentioned the shop insurance to him." All casual like, as if he's just commented on the weather.

"No, why would I? Anyway, you're not that stupid. I do the books, don't forget. Just another one of those urban myths you don't mind being out there."

"But Pete doesn't know that."

"No… maybe… I don't know. Suppose he may have heard it in the shop. You know how the punters are. But what's that got to do…" Comes to a halt. Computing. Doubting. Opts for the firm ground of denial. "Surely you can't really think Pete did that," he says, as much to himself as Ron.

"Nah, he hasn't got the balls. But makes you think, doesn't it?"

Kevin would rather not. Hopes that the rhetorical question is the end of it.

"You still playing in that poker game Monday nights?"

"Yes."

"Who runs that?"

"Bloke called Andrew. Owns the snooker club in town."

"Andrew O'Riordan." Not a question. "And I think you'll find his association with the snooker club, as of this weekend, is a historical one." Can't help but smile at Kevin's mounting confusion. "Been on a sabbatical and got the call to return to the Emerald Isle is how I hear it, on the grapevine so to speak."

"But… how…"

"Never you worry. The thing with Andrew *is*, he's — how shall I put it — *connected*. I crossed paths a few times with his uncle Breandan a while ago. Bit of a legend was Breandan, on both sides of the Irish Sea. Had a nasty little double act going with a mate of his back in the day. They brought new meaning to the expression *tooled up*. Very imaginative they were. You didn't mess with them, or if you did, you lost. Andrew knows people who know people. People with niche skill sets, if you get my drift."

Kevin doesn't.

Then he does.

And starts to join the dots.

*

Monday morning.

He reads it through again. It can't have been easy for Uncle Malcolm to write, and he doesn't blame him for hiding behind an email, sparing them both the inevitable awkwardness of doing it face to face. Plus, there's due process to follow, and doubtless pressure from above, and probably below; he's struggling to think of a single ally in the whole building. Much easier this way. But despite the distance, the repeated use of the word 'regrettably' and plenty of beating around the bush – *budget cuts, staffing level targets, accountability, outside pressures, results-driven world, sign of the times* and so on – it is cold and clinical in its cut: two months' notice to deliver the impossible or his days playing at being a detective are over. And isn't this what he's been doing all along?

Well maybe it's time to show them all. The moment has arrived to deliver, to throw this ultimatum back in their faces. One last hurrah; or more likely a V-sign waved in misplaced triumphalism at turned backs as he exits the stage. But a gesture, nonetheless.

He knows what he needs to do next.

Because he's not ready to give up just yet.

The journey from glorified cubby hole to front door takes him round twenty-seven corners, through eight sets of doors, two of which require codes, up two flights of stairs and then oddly down one flight. His shoes protest squeakily at each change of direction, but for once his shoes lack the shine to match that of the polished floor. As if he knew that email was on its way.

He gets an "Oi Cagney, where's Lacey," a "Hang on lads, it's Dick of Dock Green" and a mock-respectful "Morning Mrs Marple." A low haul. An improvement? Apathy preferable to antipathy? Or maybe they all know. His cheeks colour at the possibility and he welcomes the car park and the cleansing daylight.

*

Even armed with the near certainty of his convictions, self-doubt taunts him. He fiddles with the knot in his tie and adjusts his cuffs. Style over content? Reaching into his jacket pocket, he extracts his ID card; could he hope to convince without it? He knocks on the door and prepares to swallow the usual debilitating cocktail of condescension, suspicion and distaste.

The door opens and he instinctively thrusts out the card to substantiate his presence before first impressions of him can undermine it.

"Hi. I'm with the police." Always the tremor in his voice and that slightest of hesitations as the subtle deceit catches in his throat and he awaits the recipient's challenge of this half-truth. "I'd like to have a quick word with you, please."

But the card is ignored and he is welcomed in without query or frown; just the mists of confusion, then a glimmer of recognition seeping through.

"Didn't we…?"

"Yes. In the final."

"Right. It's Kevin, by the way."

"David."

They shake hands awkwardly.

"Can I get you something?"

"No, thanks."

"Sure? Take a seat. Here about the fire, I suppose."

"Er, no," replies David, momentarily thrown.

"Where I work."

"The bookmakers."

"Yes."

And with this mundane exchange departs the fleeting sense of purpose that has brought him here for this intended denouement.

"What happened?" David asks, abandoning himself to the flow.

"No one knows yet. Looks like an accident but… probably an accident."

"You worked there long?"

"Twelve years."

"Wow." And having given himself away, David blunders on. "Odd choice of career. I mean… sorry. That came out wrong. I'm sure it's…"

"Don't apologise. It wasn't my first choice. Bit of a maths prodigy in my day. Always thought I'd do something with that."

"Why didn't you? You could have gone to university."

"I did."

"Oh. Where?"

"Oxford."

"Bloody hell," exclaims David, doing his own arithmetic and wondering how Kevin plus Oxford equates to working in a bookmakers.

Kevin gets there ahead of him. And feels like talking; realises he needs to; realises he can. "Full disclosure? I did maths, further maths and physics at A Level. Couldn't get enough of it. It all just clicked into place. I got three As. The school had started pushing me towards Oxford or Cambridge from Lower Sixth. I wasn't that bothered but I went along anyway for an interview and they must have liked what they saw. Never really sure what that was, but I got a place. Balliol. And there I am, like I'm in an episode of *Morse*. Did you ever watch that?" David nods. Every episode. "I loved it. Felt like I finally belonged somewhere. Used to spend hours sitting with my books on one of the benches in the gardens there, just soaking it all up. I'd been top dog at maths at school, but suddenly I was surrounded by people who were just as good, even better. And I thrived. Really brought me on." He stalls.

"But I still don't understand how a degree from Oxford gets you where you are now."

"What degree? I was absolutely fine in the autumn term; Michaelmas, they called it. Lapped up that kind of thing at the time, but sounds a bit naff now. Worked hard, joined some clubs, got to know a few people. There was this girl on my course. Her name was Claudia. I liked her. A lot. Thought she liked me as well. Spent more and more time with her and her circle of friends. Then at the end of the second term I got an invite to a big party they were all going to over the holiday. I hated parties. Still do. But I thought this might be the time when Claudia and I… you know. It took me over three hours to get there. Somewhere in Surrey. Had to get the tube into London and then the train out to the middle of nowhere. Decided to walk to the house. A lot further than I expected and it started to rain before I finally got there. It was bloody obvious as soon as I saw the house, but I was soaking by then so I rang the doorbell anyway. The girl whose party it was opened the door wearing her dressing gown. Me standing there dripping wet holding this bottle of cheap wine. I remember her first words. "Oh no, no one told you, did they?" Turns out there had been a death in her family and then she'd gone down with some bug, so she'd cancelled. And not one person had thought to tell me. My new friends. More specifically one friend. She was very nice about it. Made me a cup of tea. Let me down gently with the news that had the party gone ahead, Claudia would have been there with her boyfriend of two years. Some aspiring merchant banker a few years older than her. She could tell I was smitten, but let me escape with some dignity. Back into the rain and the long journey home."

He pauses, and David knows to wait.

"I started struggling then. Went down with her bug. Moped around. Got angry. Got depressed. Didn't do enough revision. I tried to play it cool and relaxed with Claudia when term started, but got it all wrong. Couldn't be in a room with any of her lot without thinking they were secretly laughing at me. Started to get behind with my work and one day, it was like… like I was drowning. Pulled under. And there was nothing I could do to get my head above water. Everything just felt so… bleak. Pointless. Nothing to live for. Turns out I was having a breakdown. Wiped me out completely and I ended up in an institution. Spent months there before they deemed me fit for normal life, whatever that means. I don't remember much about my time there. Spaced out of drugs for most of it, feeling totally lethargic, although I can remember the fixed smiles on the faces of the few who did visit; their pained embarrassment."

"Sounds like that Claudia has a lot to answer for."

"Not at all. She didn't do anything. It was always going to happen sooner or later. Just needed to hit the reset button, was how someone put it."

"Did you ever go back?"

"To Oxford? No. Rustication. That's what they call it there, when you have to leave because you can't hack it. Horrible word. I miss the place itself, but I wasn't made for everything else."

"What did you do?"

"Sat around at home while my mum and sisters handled me with kid gloves and tried to pretend they were happy to have me there. Then one day Ron turns up. No idea how he heard about me, but there he was: a breath of plain-speaking fresh air. Came with a plan and left with an employee. I wasn't sure what to expect, but I liked it from the first day and I've been there ever since."

"What are you going to do now?"

"Haven't a clue. See what Ron decides first. But that's not why you're here, is it?"

"No. Right," announces David firmly, as much a call to arms to himself; a statement of intent. This is it, after all, the crowning moment, the euphoric culmination of months of sustained super-sleuthing, the victorious climax when he reveals to the perpetrator just how preternaturally clever he's been and validates his much derided and demeaned existence; gives the finger to all those piss-taking colleagues and rams their taunts back down their throats.

But as he stands on the brink of fulfilment and vindication, he falters and the resolve built and fortified over the past few days crumbles in the blink of an eye. "Actually, I will have something, if that's okay. A tea?"

"Sure. No problem. How do you take it?"

"Not much milk. No sugar."

Kevin lopes off and David slumps back into his chair, sinking into a mire of self-loathing. It's a familiar place, not without a comforting charm. He feels safe here; unthreatened, unchallenged. He could drink his tea, talk about snooker, concoct some reason for this visit and then walk away. The appeal is considerable.

Or not.

When Kevin returns, it's a fleetingly emboldened David who grabs the mug of tea with purposefulness, takes a confident slurp, burns his lip, spills a dollop into his lap, curses himself, places the mug on the coffee table, flaps at his crotch and turns, red-faced, to his host.

"There's no easy way to say this," starts David, keen to divert attention. "But I believe that I have uncovered a series of acts of vigilant... ee... ness... er..."

"Vigilantism."

"Yes. Exactly. And despite the public's romantic attachment to vigilantes, the criminal justice system takes a very dim view of members of the public taking the law into their own hands and meting out their subjective, often emotionally-charged version of justice, particularly when we have the police and the courts in place to do just that." That's where the rehearsed rhetoric ends and David starts.

Or rather stalls.

"Go on," says Kevin, looking disconcertingly at ease, in illogical spite of David's presence, his own undoubted guilt and David's clear allusion to it.

David takes this apparent nonchalance for arrogance and, spurred on again, reaches down for his bag, from which he produces one of the London buses and the black shoe, placing both on the table, careful to avoid the smear of tea emanating from the base of his own mug.

Touché.

Kevin raises his eyebrows, drops them into a frown and waits.

"Recognise them?" asks David. Silence. "Well? Of course, I could always have brought a dog turd as well, just to jog your memory."

"Pardon?" The eyebrows climbing once more.

"A dog turd. I could have brought one." The words sound silly and he blushes.

"Is this going to be like Cinderella?"

"What?"

"The shoe?"

"Would it fit?"

"It might, but there are plenty of blokes wearing size eleven shoes out there."

"*Ha*. Size eleven?"

"Shit," says Kevin, then surprises David with a smile. "I'm not very good at this."

"That makes two of us," replies David, and can't help but mirror the smile. "I'm not sure you're taking this very seriously."

"If this were a film, you'd have a wire and there'd be a team of armed police crouching outside the door, ready to burst in the moment I incriminate myself, shouting 'armed police' or 'clear' or whatever it is they say."

"It isn't and I haven't. You can check if you want."

"No, I believe you," Kevin laughs. "But why *have* you come on your own?"

"I don't know. Probably because no one would believe me if I told them."

"And you brought all your evidence?"

"No. Just some of it. The rest and a detailed log are back at the station. I'm very thorough."

"I bet you are," says Kevin, doing his best to stifle his amusement at such earnestness. "A detailed log, you say," he adds, as much to hide the resulting half-smirk. "Colour coded?"

"Of course."

"Come on, then. What you got?"

David hesitates, wanting so very much to release the shackles and abandon himself to the intellectual pleasures of full disclosure and open debate, yet still feeling the tugging gravitational pull of professional obligation inherent in a position he has struggled so long and hard to establish and validate in the face of near constant ridicule and dismissiveness.

"Right," says Kevin, with barely disguised exasperation. "I'll give you one for nothing. You may already know about it of course, but I don't know that, do I?"

"Go on," says David, teetering, not in need of much persuasion.

"Okay, how about the vanishing conservatory?"

"Sounds like an Agatha Christie novel."

"So not on your list?"

"No." It is, but gift horses are so rare, and in any case, he can't bring himself to douse the flare of excitement that has lit up Kevin.

"Ha! Our crowning achievement. That one had the lot. Villains? The snootiest couple in the area doing everything in their well-connected powers to veto each and every planning application for miles around. Crime? Petty vindictiveness, compounded by gross hypocrisy, as they built themselves a conservatory that exceeded the legal limits without planning permission. Opportunity? The annual late autumn fortnight away at their *chateau* for some pre-winter sunshine and an opportunity to polish their claws and patronise the French. The heroes? The usual crew, plus a few useful contacts in the building industry. The *coup de grâce*? Demolish-it-yourself: our attempt to breathe fresh air into an overkilled acronym and, for my money, far more interesting than the usual predictable and saccharine fare. We should pitch it. Over the course of a few nights we systematically and lovingly dismantled and removed every brick and pane of glass. Left them with a very passable patio complete with now-superfluous under-floor heating system working overtime and an ornate dining room table and chairs struggling to masquerade as garden furniture."

David can't help but smile. "Don't you wish you could have been there to see their faces?"

"Always. That was the unfortunate, but necessary, downside. So come on then. Which ones did you get? Or do you have to caution me first?" Says it all casual and jokey, leaving David unsure of where he stands. This isn't going to plan.

"Probably. Possibly. We should really be doing this down the station."

"So why aren't we?"

David shrugs. "I don't know." Lets his head hang forward.

"Are you okay?"

There's the question. And it's one David has been avoiding. Then from nowhere emerges another question, the words escaping his lips before he's conscious of their existence, taking them both by surprise.

"Did you throw that frame?"

"What?"

"That frame. In the final. Did you let me win?" Sees Kevin's eyes tighten. "Be honest." Kevin scratches at the side of his chin and appears lost in an internal debate. "It's important to me to know."

"You played well."

"Please."

"You ask me that in this situation and expect an honest answer?"

"Yes."

"I guess I did and I didn't."

"What does that mean?"

"It means it wasn't that straightforward. It's not like I deliberately fouled or anything. I didn't chuck it away as such. Just gave you the best chance of winning."

"Thank you."

"No problem."

"Not for doing it; that's the last thing I'd want you to do. No, for being honest."

"Oh, okay."

"So now tell me why?"

Kevin thinks hard before he replies. "Because when I looked round the room, I had more in common with you than I did with the idiots in my team. And you looked like you needed to win more than I did. So I made my choice. I doubt either of us really fit in, so maybe I recognised a kindred spirit. I had a chance once before, many years ago, to do the right thing, go against the crowd, and I bottled it. It's just not that easy working out who really counts when there's so many telling you it's them who do. People like us spend all our time trying not to stand out and that can mean we sometimes fail to recognise the people who really matter, even when they're standing right in front of us. We're so busy defining ourselves in terms of how others see us that we lose sight of ourselves, struggling so hard to end up somewhere, then realising we don't actually want to be there."

"Sounds like you've given this some thought."

"You could say that. Recently anyway. Let's just say my eyes have been opened."

An awkward silence follows and pursues David, leaving him nowhere to hide from the dawning realisation that Kevin could just as easily be talking about his own emotional retardation.

"Are you okay?"

"I'm fine," replies David, and finds himself smiling.

"Am I under arrest, then?" asks Kevin.

"No."

"Because of the snooker?"

"No. It's like you said. I've spent years trying to prove myself to a bunch of people who think I'm some kind of super nerd and who couldn't care less about me. Trying desperately hard to win their affection and their respect, and they still think I'm a twat. And they always will. Doesn't matter what I do. They use me or abuse me when it suits them, but otherwise I might as well be invisible. And all the time I've been chasing you lot down, it's been in the stupid naïve hope that it'll make me one of them. That I'll be accepted. By that load of morons. Like that's some kind of achievement. As if their approval was all that mattered. And this…" he shakes a hand at the shoe and the bus, like a trainee magician waving a wand, determined to turn them into something more impressive, "…well it might not be much, but at least I did it. I was right. I don't need to give it all to them. It's enough for me to know." He takes a breath. "And I don't think you enjoyed some of it any more than I've enjoyed walking into the station five days a week just to be laughed at and belittled and hidden away in a glorified cupboard."

Kevin nods his agreement. "It's a relief to tell the truth."

"And it's not as if it ever got out of hand."

"No," replies Kevin, just a little too quickly, and for a moment appears to lose himself in self-reflection.

On another day, with another person and in a different mindset, David might wish to follow Kevin to whatever location he's fleetingly visited, but this isn't that place or that person, and he hasn't the inclination anymore, so he lets it go. "And if I'm honest," he says, "I kind of admire what you did. Having seen the police in action at first hand I can understand why you might take the law into your own hands. There's probably a bit of the vigilante in all of us."

Another silence, but this time one they're both content to inhabit.

It's David who breaks it, recognising the need to meet Kevin halfway if this uneasy, yet increasingly appealing, union of lost souls is to be prolonged.

He starts to relinquish his inventory of now-solved mysteries – their first public airing – feeling a pang of loss as each of his much-nurtured babies is released from the protective womb of his mind, no longer a source of nourishment for intellectual and fanciful pursuits.

Kevin nods through the first few, admitting defeat, then interrupts. "What gave it away? That they were all linked, I mean."

"Your little calling cards."

"What?"

"The playing cards. A bit clichéd really. Trying to be clever. Sooner or later, it always happens." Immediately regrets that last aside, implying as it does an empirical knowledge he doesn't possess.

But he needn't worry. Kevin's eyebrows experiment with a fresh configuration, knitting together. "I don't know what you're talking about."

"The perp wants to be given credit. Take ownership."

"No. What you said about the playing cards."

"Nice try. Your idea then, was it?"

"No, really. I haven't a clue."

"Is that your poker face?"

"It's my what-the-*hell*-are-you-on-about face."

David believes him. "You didn't know?"

"Know about *what*?"

David tells him. Shows him the stained card from Mrs Warburton's garden in its well-sealed plastic pouch. Follows it with the one that was attached to the bus. Lets Kevin know he has others back at the station, although he's light on detail.

Observes his reaction throughout.

And knows this is news to him.

"So, this was…"

"Stuck in one of the dog turds you and your… Black Panther mates considerately covered an old lady's lawn with." He's rather pleased with that reference, and is irritated when it appears to go unnoticed.

"Don't believe that little old lady bit. Lady Muck more like. She lives in the biggest house for miles and flaunts her *perfect* garden to the world. She probably has more lawn than the rest of the road put together. Even has an open day each summer, when the plebs get to tell her how great it looks, though they get barked at if they put a foot near it. Yet despite all that grass at her disposal, several times a day she walks her dog a hundred or so feet down the road, if that, and stands there watching it take a crap in whichever front garden takes its fancy. Then leaves the steaming pile where it lands and strolls back. Sod whoever lives there, like they're some kind of inferior beings. Snooty cow. I remember seeing one woman trying to bundle her young kids into the car one morning, only for her toddler to slip over in a piece of what was very likely *her* dog's shit and end up sitting there smearing it on his face."

"Hardly the crime of the century."

"We never said it was. That's the whole *point*. We've got you lot to deal with the crimes. But there's this whole layer of selfish, obnoxious, anti-social behaviour going on just beneath the law which the police couldn't care about, but which touches normal people's lives every single day. And people get away with it all the time and there's nothing anyone can do about it. We just thought we'd fight back a bit and teach some of them a lesson. Try and be a bit imaginative while we're doing it."

"Make the punishment fit the crime?"

"That sort of thing. Best way to send a message."

"Hence the dog poo."

"Seemed appropriate. I thought we were quite artistic. Took a load of preparation and a hell of a lot of freezer bags. We were collecting them for almost a year."

"But she said you shouted at her at least once about it and gave her a load of stares. Weren't you running the risk of her linking you with it?"

"Yep," he says with a slow shake of his head. "That was really thick of me. It was one of our golden rules. We had to be at least a couple of steps removed from the victim. But I didn't tell the full truth when I suggested it. Otherwise it would have got turned down by the others. But I couldn't stop walking past her house every day. Well obviously I could have; it was on my route to work, but I could easily have gone a longer way round. Maybe I wanted to keep stoking up the anger so I didn't start to feel bad about what we were planning. Stupid really. I guess that's how you got me."

"You could say. It's definitely why I'm here now, but it's the cards that really did it. Without them, I'd never have made links and kept looking. That was the big mistake."

"You keep talking about these cards, but I'm telling you again, there weren't any. It was just us teaching selfish people a lesson. No one got hurt or anything; that was the other rule."

"But people did get hurt."

"No, they didn't. Not really."

"What about the motorcyclist? Okay, it was just cuts, bruises and a couple of broken ribs, but he could have been badly hurt, even killed. I came very close to handing over everything I had at that point."

"Hang on. What motorcyclist?"

"The one you took out with that patch of oil in the bend."

"What *are* you on about? We never did anything like that. When was it?"

"Earlier this year."

"Then no chance. I'd have known."

"The facts say otherwise. The locals told me he used to rev his bike up the hill and round that bend in the early hours every morning making a right racket. Rattled windows. Got dogs barking. Woke up kids. Then he skids off on a freak patch of engine oil no one ever remembers seeing before and for which there was no logic. No one would ever stop on a bend long enough to leave that much. Then we find a playing card wedged into the kerb just where he came off."

Kevin is still looking puzzled, though clearly wavering. "Where was this?" he asks, and when David tells him, realisation dawns.

"What?" asks David.

"Tell me about any other cards you've got and where you found them."

David hesitates. "I'm not sure I want to give you everything." Regrets it immediately; a step back after taking so many forwards.

Kevin shakes his head. "I think we're past that now, don't you?"

"Sorry. Reluctant to let go, I guess."

"I get that, but look, I think I've just realised who that might have been and where these cards have been coming from. But I need more detail if I'm to be sure."

David runs through the others, some receiving a smirking, silent acknowledgement of ownership, others just a grim nod.

"That it?" asks Kevin. "I mean, are there any more?" he adds in a softened tone in response to the look of hurt that passes like a shadow across David's face.

"No. That's it," replies David, still deflating.

"Impressive. I'll give you that," offers Kevin, doing his best to apply a patch to the puncture. Follows it up with a tight-lipped smile that is part apology, part reassurance.

"Thank you," accepts David, balance restored. "Your turn."

"There was someone."

"Who?"

"Nice try. He was only there because he was a mate of… look, we didn't know, honest. We put up with him because we had to, simple as that. It wasn't a problem to begin with. In fact, we sort of looked up to him. There was this bloke who'd got off a driving ban on three occasions despite being done for speeding time after time, just because he had the money to hire one of those shyster lawyers who puts procedural irregularities over morality and kept getting him off. That really got to him. He'd rant away about it, even say he hoped one of the lawyer's kids would get injured by a speeding driver one day, just to serve him right. Anyway, he cased the driver's house for weeks and then one night broke in, nicked the keys, took the car out and drove it way over the speed limit past every speed camera he could find. Then calm as you like, he dropped the car off, popped the keys back where he'd found them and let himself out without leaving any sign of a break-in. Worked a treat and the bloke had his licence taken away for two years. He loved that, and it certainly got our respect."

"You're saying he's a burglar? Might already be known to us?"

"Doubt it."

"You mean you don't think he's ever been caught? You can't be sure of that."

"Whatever. We're not going there. Anyway, he said he was happy to play along with our rules, but there was always something a bit unhinged about him. Nasty. Constantly pushing us to go a little further and getting annoyed when we told him we couldn't because it was too risky, or not what the whole thing was meant to be about."

"And you think it's him."

"I'm sure of it. That Cayenne you mentioned. I think it might be one P… we saw swan into a car park at a gym and go straight into a disabled bay, just so the very-obviously-able-bodied woman could waddle ten yards less in her tracksuit. Once was irritating, but she made a habit of it, and then one day we watched some bloke who clearly was disabled have to park on the far side of the car park. Only problem was that it was one of us that gave her the evil eye and got the finger in return. That meant we weren't two steps removed, so we had to bin it. Led to a bit of an argument, but in the end, we agreed to let – you know who – use a couple of blokes he knew to remove the tyres one night and leave it on four piles of bricks. Could have been anyone doing it, so nice and anonymous. Not poetic, maybe, but it seemed like a decent compromise. Trouble was, they took it a little further than that. The bloke who'd first seen her using the disabled bay drove by the next morning to enjoy the moment and it wasn't just the tyres. They'd used acid to take off the paintwork and sprayed words all over it: 'selfish fucking cow' and so on. Vicious it was. And bloody stupid. We all said as much, and he swore he wouldn't do anything like it again. More fool us for believing him."

"Do you reckon the bike accident might have been him?"

"Most definitely. He'd have loved that. Hang on. You know that concrete one."

"The driveways?"

"Yes. Talk me through it."

"Why?"

"That was another one he wanted to seriously up the ante on."

"Three families woke up to find piles of concrete dumped across the entrances to their driveways, completely blocking them in. Impossible to drive over, not in the least – and this was what threw us – because someone had thrown rubbish and a load of bits of wood into the concrete before it set. Then they'd emptied the contents of neighbours' bins all over the rest of the garden."

"They were fence ornaments actually," interjects Kevin, clearly savouring David's confusion. "A gang of kids had been making a nuisance of themselves for weeks. Tipping bins over, vandalism, swearing at old people. Maybe doesn't sound like much now, but you try walking past a group like that, or if it's your mum or gran getting told to 'fuck off', too scared to go out of their house."

"That happen to you?"

"Not me. That would have been too close. But we knew someone who knew someone who was speaking for a lot of people living round there. All of them sick of it, but too scared to do anything. This friend of a friend tried. Found them bold as brass, pulling the wooden baubles off a fence in broad daylight. He told them to stop and they just laughed in his face, spat at him, tipped over the rubbish bins and then threw all the wooden balls down the hill, banging into cars, pedestrians, whatever. Then they threatened him and taunted him when he walked away. They were only thirteen or fourteen years old."

"We never worked any of that out. Nearest we got was that one of the fathers was known to us. Bit of a local crime lord, or the nearest you get to that round here. We ended up putting it down to some feud and left them all to it."

"Well, there you go. That's where we came in. Your lot weren't going to do anything, so it was down to us. Or rather people we knew who could pull off that kind of stunt. We just sourced the fence ornaments and got creative with the garbage. So I can't help you there. And it definitely wasn't our *friend* going off piste."

"But nothing else happened on that one?"

"No. That was it. Why?"

"It didn't stop there. One of the kids, a thirteen-year-old son of one of the families, was attacked a few days later. Some blokes in balaclavas cornered him and pelted him with more of those wooden balls. Cut his head. Bruises everywhere. Then they gave him a little speech, broke his finger and told him they'd be back to do much worse if he was ever a *bad boy*, their words, again. Scared the shit out of the boy. Refused to go out on his own after that. Had to be driven everywhere. Have to admit, I did feel sorry for him at the time."

"He was a cowardly little shit, but no one deserves that and it had nothing to do with us. The rest of us, anyway. Another cup of tea?"

"You're on."

Kevin stands and moves towards the kitchen; then comes to a halt.

"One thing."

"What?"

"Did you, or did you not, say *perp* back then?"

EPILOGUE

"Are you all right if we pop in here for a minute?" she says, immediately rendering the question mark redundant by darting off at a right angle and through a door before Kevin can offer an opinion.

Inside, he slips his mind into neutral and dutifully follows her through the aisles. It is only as she pauses to scan a rack of shelving that he realises he's unwittingly strayed into that lair of unnerving femininity, red in tooth and claw: the female hygiene section. Not a problem for New Kevin of course, a modern man no longer in denial about all matters menstrual.

"Stop wrinkling your nose and straighten out that sneer."

It says little for Renaissance Kevin that it is initially relief he feels upon observing her reaching instead for a pregnancy testing kit. Then the penny drops.

"I'm late," she announces, answering his thought. "That time in the maze," she adds, answering his next thought. "We got a bit carried away. Remember? Stop smirking." His face balances out and he feels her staring at him intently. "You okay?"

"Fine."

"Sure?"

"I'm sure."

"Not going to run a mile?"

"Why would I do that?"

"Others might."

"I'm not others."

"Come on. Let's see about that, shall we?"

*

Charlotte holds out the plastic indicator for Kevin to take, but he momentarily hesitates.

"Don't worry, I've dried it."

"It's not that." It is. "I was just…"

"What?"

"Nothing. What am I looking for?"

"Blue lines would mean I'm pregnant."

"I can't see anything."

"There you go."

Kevin is distracted from processing this information by her obvious elation.

"Relieved?" he asks, fleetingly unnerved by a twinge of disappointment that catches him unawares.

"I'm happy."

"Of course you are. It really wouldn't have…"

"Kevin…"

"I mean I can understand it," stumbles on Kevin, blundering through the metaphorical forest of the emotionally crippled; feeling safer indulging in a bout of self-deprecation than facing up to something more profound lurking in his peripheral vision. "It really doesn't bother me, you know. I doubt I'm good parent material. Not with my family experiences, believe me, and I just don't seem to get people. You can do a whole lot… why are you laughing at me?"

"I'm happy, you big clot, because it just hit me that I wouldn't have minded had it been positive. In fact, there's a big bit of me that wishes it had been."

Which is all too much for him as he summons up a smile that seems at odds with the tear that escapes an eye and trickles down his cheek. He feels an explanation is due.

"I guess I can't understand why anyone would possibly want to have a child with me."

"Well I'm not anyone, I'm me. And I think you'd make a bloody good dad. Get used to it. And who's to say that two fucked-up parents won't make a balanced, normal child. I reckon just knowing we're fucked-up gives us a head start on most others. Now come on. We need to get going."

*

"Hello, Mrs Morris."

"Hello, Kevin. And please call me Nancy. You used to be able to do that, I seem to recall. And this is?"

"Oh. This is… er… Charlotte. She's my… my… er…"

"Kevin is trying rather feebly to say I'm his girlfriend. I might take it personally if I didn't know him better. Hi."

"Hi." The smile is warm enough to relax Kevin, only for the follow-up to throw him off balance once more. "It's been a very long time, Kevin. A Christmas card once a year and that's all, then here you are out of the blue. Why the sudden wish to see Charlie?"

"I… er… I…"

"Oh for goodness sake, Kevin, just say it. She won't bite." Charlotte's admonishment is the hefty shove that sends the words tumbling from his mouth.

"I sort of ran away last time. I couldn't handle it. However much of an idiot he was to have that fight at school, I should still have been there for him, but I wasn't. I let him down, and then when I came here, I made him a promise and I couldn't even keep that. And I was so annoyed at myself that it was easier to find excuses not to get in touch and time just went by and the longer it went the harder seeing him became and the more reasons I could find to put it off and do nothing. But some things have happened recently that have got me thinking and I know it's selfish of me to turn up like this after so long just because it suits me when it might not suit you or Charlie but that's a chance I have to take because I really do need to tell him I was wrong and that I'm sorry because otherwise I'm just dumping all my crap on him rather than facing up to it and he needs to know that I get what happened and that I'm prepared to take my share of the weight." Kevin comes up for air. "That last bit was Charlotte. I don't normally say stuff like that."

"No, Kevin. It was you. I just helped you find the words. The thoughts were all yours."

A look passes between Charlotte and Mrs Morris that is beyond Kevin's stunted male comprehension, but he can sense an unspoken connection being made and sees the brittle defensiveness leave Mrs Morris's body with the slightest of drops of her shoulders and a flicker of a smile.

"How is Charlie?" he asks.

"Better, thank you. He's in an all right place right now. Has been for a while, but he's still very fragile. That accounts for my question just now. It's very hard not to feel protective after all we've been through. We converted the end room and the garage into a self-contained annexe for him. Give him a degree of independence, though I think that's as far away as he'll ever manage. But it works well enough. He's through the door along there. Just knock first."

Kevin pauses and looks helplessly at Charlotte.

"Go on. I can't come with you. This bit's down to you. I'll be right here when you've finished."

That's enough to nudge him along the corridor and knock on the door at the end.

It opens to reveal a Charlie little changed from the mental picture of Morris he's carried with him since their last meeting. He's minded of those old toys on *Antiques Roadshow* that have never been taken out of their boxes and played with. More valuable maybe, but ultimately a little sad and pointless. Like some ornate doll. Physically, he's ageing well, though Kevin knows that with Charlie, outward appearances are frequently deceptive.

There's a moment of shared panic when Kevin thinks they might embrace, but they both instinctively pull back from the threat of such physicality and take refuge in banal pleasantries that serenade their shuffle into a lounge area. Kevin takes in the room. It's more sterilely functional than homely; low budget show home. What few design features are discernible, most of them floral, are likely as not maternally imposed. There's little obvious of Charlie here: a couple of mounted certificates on the wall; a framed photo of mother and son; a cuddly toy sitting on a shelf; a pristine Formula One magazine on the coffee table. Though what does he really know about Charlie anyway? *Motor racing*?

The awkward opening exchanges exhausted, Kevin prepares to jump in. Then procrastinates by assuaging his curiosity.

"I didn't know you were into F1?"

Charlie frowns.

Kevin asks the question again by opening his eyes wider.

Charlie's frown deepens.

Kevin asks the question a third time by pointedly moving his head and staring at the magazine, before returning his head and gaze to its starting position.

Charlie finally twigs, much to their mutual relief.

"Oh that. Another one of Mummy's attempts to get me a hobby. She's desperate, bless her. She thought it was the kind of sport I might be suited to."

"She's got a point," offers Kevin.

Charlie contemplates the import of Kevin's clumsy intrusion and elects to save Kevin's blushes by ploughing on regardless. "I made the mistake of saying something while a race was on the telly and that was all it took. Now I get that magazine every month. I'm not really bothered, but I play along and watch the qualifying rounds and the races. Have them on in case she walks in."

"What *do* you like then?"

"I like computers. I write my own programs and stuff. I like the way they're logical and predictable and do what you tell them to." He laughs nervously. "Unlike people." A wave of panic washes over his face. "I don't mean you," he stammers.

Kevin lets it go and an uncomfortable silence descends.

"Where's your friend?"

"Her name's Charlotte and she's with your mum."

"You could have brought her in. I don't bite." Another fragile titter.

"I know that and she wants to meet you after…"

"After?"

"After I say what I want… what I need to say."

"You don't have…"

"I do, and I just wanted to say that I get it. I really do."

"Get what?"

"You know what. All those years ago at that fight. Why you picked it and why you needed me to step in. You were suffering really badly and I didn't see it, or didn't want to. You needed reassurance. Needed to know that your wingman – sorry, hate that word – was still right there at your side. You set me up to prove myself. Only I failed. I was embarrassed. Angry. I couldn't believe you were doing it. It was just so stupid. I didn't mind all the other times. Honest I didn't. You were worth the lot of them put together. But watching you flailing around that day, I think maybe I even hated you for a moment. Sorry."

"For what? Saying you hated me?"

"Yes."

"Was it the truth?"

"At that moment it was."

"Then you've got nothing to apologise for. I guess I was a pain in the backside a lot of the time."

"No. Well, not all the time. Sometimes you were. It was like you deliberately set out to wind everyone else up."

"It was just the way I was. The way I am. It's difficult to get others to like you if you hate yourself. Not that I cared what they thought, so long as *we* were okay. That was enough for me. I admit I had my nose put out of joint when Evans first came. Why wouldn't you want to spend time with him? He was always the cool kid, while I was just… you know. But it more or less worked most of the time. I was jealous as hell when you and he got put in the same room, but to get stuck with that thug Marsh was more than I could take."

"And I couldn't even keep my promise," says Kevin.

"What promise?"

"Not to say or do anything. That time I visited you here after you'd left. But I couldn't help myself. Probably because I felt so guilty for the way I'd abandoned you. I had to take it out on someone. Make myself feel better, even though you'd told me not to."

"I didn't mean it."

"What?"

"Deep down I wanted you to. Why wouldn't I?"

"But you s—"

"Another test. Sorry. What did you do to him?"

"Them. Started off with Marsh and thumped him a couple of times. Caught him by surprise as he opened the door of your room, if you want a mental picture to treasure. Hit him very hard, you'll be glad to hear. Then tracked down the two esteemed adults in positions of respected authority and dished out more of the same. Thought that ponce Badger was going to crap himself, he was shaking so much. I let them know I was on to them. That I knew what they were and that I'd be back for more and tell the school if they didn't leave. Said a load of pretty vicious stuff basically, most of it probably from movies I'd seen, but it made me feel better and seemed to do the trick at the time. Felt I'd got my message across."

"My hero," Charlie says, with a genuine smile. His first.

"I thought I'd sorted it out, but apparently not. The bastards are both still there doing – you know what – to other boys. Not anymore th—" He catches himself, but too late.

"How do you mean?"

"It's probably nothing, but…"

"But what?"

"I mentioned it to someone I know – knew – someone we played poker with. He owned the snooker club I play for. But it turned out he wasn't who we thought he was. It seems he knew some pretty serious people and we think they may have been settling some old scores for us without us knowing. Some kind of favour. But he's disappeared, so I can't ask him. And I went to the Nethercott reunion back in the early summer – yeah. I know – but I'd seen Luxley and Badger's names in the school magazine and I couldn't believe it, so I thought I'd go along and… I don't know what I thought really. What I thought I'd actually do. But I had to see for myself. Maybe that if they caught sight of me, it might scare them a bit. Act as a warning."

"And?"

"They weren't there. I asked around, and all I could find out was that Luxley had had some kind of *accident* and Badger was taking compassionate leave, whatever that means."

"Sounds promising."

"That's what I thought. I was going to try to find out more, but…"

"You didn't want to implicate yourself?"

"Something like that. I could try if you want?"

"Don't be silly. And anyway, I kind of like the idea of imagining the worst. The very worst."

There's nothing Kevin thinks he's qualified to add to that and they drift back into silence.

"But the point is, and what I really came here to say," resumes Kevin, "is that however much it might suit me to paint what I did on that final day at school as some kind of gallant revenge mission, what really lay behind it all was my guilt. I may not have recognised it at the time, but that was what made me do it, and it says loads that it was easier to thump two teachers and a 1st XV prop than it was to walk over, step in front of Marsh and pull you to your feet that day. Instead I got to watch Carl do it and although, if I'm honest, I was thankful at the time, it's eaten away at me ever since. I failed you and I am so sorry, Charlie. I really am."

Charlie sniffs. "You'll make me cry."

"I've made myself bloody cry," says Kevin, smearing a palm across his eyes.

"You of all people don't have to say sorry to me. But thank you anyway, and please now do me a favour and stop beating yourself up about it. You're – you always have been – the best of them."

This is all too raw and uncomfortable for them both, so they retreat once more.

Charlie takes a deep breath.

"You know, there's a book I read recently."

"Yes?" says Kevin, grateful to be returning to the calmer waters of the banal and everyday.

"Not my normal type of thing. I don't like horror as a rule, but I saw a good review somewhere so I thought I'd give it a go. It was Swedish, I think, but translated, obviously. Anyway, it was called *Let the Right One In*. I like that title."

Kevin senses something approaching.

Feels a tingle of apprehension.

"You asked me earlier why I didn't just say something to you, instead of having that silly fight?"

"Yes?"

"Tell me; is Charlotte the love of your life, do you think?"

"*Love of my life?*" Kevin repeats with a contemptuous snort.

"Yes." Deadly serious.

"I think she might be," replies Kevin, surprising himself by overriding the emotionally autistic default setting that would normally abort such a frank exchange at the first hint of debilitating sensitivity.

"Good. But have you told her that?"

"No. Not yet."

"Because it would make you feel vulnerable?"

"I suppose so." Knows so.

"I mean you'd be opening yourself right up, exposing yourself completely, trusting her with your feelings, not to throw them back in your face. That's a huge step to take. You'd be gambling a known present you can live with and risking losing the lot."

The words hit home with unerring accuracy and Kevin can only nod.

"Well if you're struggling to take that step now as an adult, with everything to gain, think what it would have been like for an immature seventeen-year-old boy with everything to lose."

The implication evades Kevin for a few moments; then strikes.

"I didn't know," is all he can manage.

"Maybe not consciously, but I think unconsciously you did. And I expect it scared the hell out of you. Why wouldn't it? That's probably why you hated me that day and couldn't bring yourself to intervene. You were answering an unconscious question from me with an unconscious response. I might not have liked the answer, but it was the truth, and I couldn't stay after that. I had to go."

"But…" Kevin starts. Settles for a resigned shrug.

"I'm not blaming you. But when you've opened yourself up that much and been turned away, the only safe option can appear to be to close yourself up. Build a wall. Create a sanctuary. Which I did." He looks deep into Kevin's eyes. Reads the hurt. Sees the self-loathing. "There's no fault here. It was what it was. Simple friendship for you. Everything to me. Shit happens."

Kevin can only smile at the blush this rare expletive elicits in its author.

"Indeed it does."

"I think the term is unrequited love."

"Been there. It's a bugger." Unfortunate choice of word, but if Charlie's experiencing the same mental imagery as him, he's hiding it well. Kevin shakes his head clear of unwanted thoughts.

"So, are we okay?" Charlie's voice wavering as he asks; so much riding on four little words.

"I think we might be," replies Kevin.

ABOUT THE AUTHOR

Marc Lindon lives near High Wycombe He spends his working days playing with numbers and, with what little energy remains, he writes. This is his first novel.

Matador

For exclusive discounts on Matador titles,
sign up to our occasional newsletter at
troubador.co.uk/bookshop